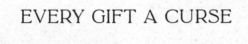

EVERY GIFT A CURSE

EVERY GIFT A CURSE

CAROLINE O'DONOGHUE

WALKER BOOKS

Text copyright © 2023 by Caroline O'Donoghue
Interior illustrations copyright © 2023 by Stefanie Caponi

First US edition 2023

Library of Congress Catalog Card Number 2022915229
ISBN 978-1-5362-2840-3

23 24 25 26 27 28 LBM 10 9 8 7 6 5 4 3 2 1

Printed in Melrose Park, IL, USA

This book was typeset in Warnock Pro.

Walker Books US
a division of
Candlewick Press
99 Dover Street
Somerville, Massachusetts 02144

www.walkerbooksus.com

TO THE
UNLIKEABLE
MAIN CHARACTERS

PART
ONE

1

HERE'S SOMETHING THAT THEY DON'T TELL
you about being cursed: The first thing you feel is fear. But the second
thing—the thing you really notice—is beauty. The world is so beautiful when you don't think you'll have long to look at it.

The colors shine brighter. Even now, in the December twilight,
when it's almost completely dark. The chilly mist from the river
melds with the light of the city, and all you can see is a gold-and-blue
blur. A box of jewels you need to squint your eyes just to look at. The
sense of a city dancing in your blood.

Thirty-six days have passed since I became responsible for the
deaths of two women. One who tried to kill me; the other who died
trying to save my life.

"There you are," Fiona says, flinging open the door to Nuala's house.
No matter how early I get to Nuala's house these days, she's always here
first. "Come on, the Apocalypse Society is already in session."

She takes me through to the kitchen, and everyone's here:
Manon, studying a bound stack of paper; Nuala, taking something
out of the oven; Roe, peeling an apple with a knife; Lily, sitting on the
kitchen counter.

The question: Were we directly responsible for the death of

Heather Banbury and Sister Assumpta, or was it all an accident? Does the Housekeeper even care about accidents, or does she swing the ax regardless of who's guilty?

"That's the problem," Nuala says midflow, gesturing with a wooden spoon. "The Housekeeper is revenge without judgment. She's not a thing who can make her mind up. She's a windup toy. Isn't that right, Maeve?"

I haven't even taken my coat off. "How come no one ever says hello to me anymore?" I say indignantly. "What am I? Dead?"

"Not yet," Manon muses, highlighting a line of text with a yellow marker. "But soon, perhaps."

"Well, joyeux Noël to you too."

We know of three Housekeeper summonings, spread out over the last thirty years. The first was when she was summoned by Nuala's sister, Heaven, who traded her own life to bring on the death of their abusive father.

The second was Aaron, when he called her to break out of his far-right Christian rehab center. She took his friend then. Matthew Madison. A death that Aaron spent three misguided years trying to atone for within the gnarled fingers of the Children of Brigid.

And the third: Lily. A botched tarot reading that ended in chaos, and that brought us all together.

Who knows what a fourth visit might bring about? Who might fall victim, and who might be spared? Aaron hasn't waited around to find out.

I bend down to kiss Roe on the cheek, the movement unraveling my thick scarf.

"Hello," he says, nuzzling me. "You're cold."

"Hey." Lily is drawing on the window with acrylic craft paint, her knees under the sill, feet trailing in the kitchen sink. She appears to be drawing a very complicated pig, its face filled with red and green swirls.

"What's this?"

"A boar. A yule boar."

"Of course."

Lily pushes a strand of blond hair back off her face. "I didn't want to do something boring like a Christmas tree. I thought we would do something pagan. For winter solstice."

"Hence the yule boar."

Lily starts to smile to herself and keeps painting. "Hence the yule boar, yes."

When Lily and I summoned the Housekeeper, it happened in days. And we hadn't even meant to call her. She was just a spirit who was accidentally woken by a combination of my sensitivity, the Well of magic below Kilbeg, and the throbbing hatred Lily and I had for each other. Dorey told me almost a month ago that she was planning on calling the Housekeeper—surely she would have done it by now.

Dorey's warning to me was clear. She spoke like the Queen of the Fairies, offering foul bargains through a glinting smile. The Children wanted total dominion over the Well in Kilbeg, and would do anything to get it. Anything, that is, except kill us. Murder in the magical world is more trouble than it's worth: everything comes back to you eventually. But if you have just cause for summoning something like the Housekeeper, you can let her do the dirty work for you.

So where is she?

"We must first understand," Manon says, "whether they truly do have just cause."

"We killed Heather Banbury," Roe says flatly.

"No, we didn't," Fiona responds, her voice unusually high-pitched. "She accidentally died."

"While she was magically bound to our will," Nuala corrects. "Although, if the Children hadn't come to the tennis courts, it wouldn't have happened at all. So they could be equally responsible."

"In the eyes of who?" Lily asks, still painting her boar.

"I don't know." Nuala throws her hands up. "The great cosmic abacus that doles out fairness?"

"Justice," Fiona says, holding up the tarot card. I might be the sensitive, but Fiona's eye for tarot is now every bit as good as mine. She shuffles the pack and straightens the cards, tapping the deck twice on the table so they're neatly aligned.

At that moment, as if in response, there is a tap on the glass panel of the kitchen door. An orange-tipped magpie flutters outside, waiting to be let in. Fiona reaches for the handle.

"We cannot let that thing in here," says Manon, wrinkling her nose.

"Don't talk about Paolo that way," Fiona says defensively. Paolo and Manon have very quickly become the two great obsessions of Fiona's life, and so of course they are permanently in opposition.

Manon shudders. "I hate birds."

Paolo the magpie hops in and balances himself on the long arm of the tap. Lily shuffles her feet over. Paolo starts noodling the spout with his beak, looking for drops of water.

"Can I fill a bowl, Nuala?" Fi asks.

"You can, love."

"Fionnuala!" Manon protests. Manon has an abandoned child's tendency to be overly formal with her own mother. "*Fin.*"

"Manny," Nuala replies soothingly. "He's no harm."

"I don't *like* him."

I'm nearest the cupboard, so I fill a bowl for Paolo. I even get him the filtered water, out of the fridge. I don't have any sense of what

4

Paolo thinks or feels, but I do think that he prefers filtered water. He's Fiona's familiar, after all, and Fiona does enjoy the finer things.

Fiona rests her gaze on him and, after a moment, he comes to perch on her shoulder.

"Well?" I ask, trying not to sound too expectant. "Does he have any news?"

Fi tilts her head for a moment, then closes her eyes. The magpie doesn't touch her, doesn't fuss with her hair, but it's obvious that they are communicating. Paolo has become our little drone, scouting the city from the air.

"No," she says at last, blinking her eyes open.

"Are you sure?" I press. "How can you know?"

"I know what Paolo knows. He hasn't seen him. Or the Children, for that matter."

"Are we still acting like they're two different things?" A long line of skin has fallen from the apple that Roe is peeling, almost touching the floor. "I mean, let's face it. He's gone back to them, hasn't he?"

"We don't know that," I reply. "We have no proof of that."

Aaron disappeared after the conversation with Dorey, on the day of Sister Assumpta's funeral. There are only two ways to interpret the disappearance: betrayal or cowardice. It's hard to know which with Aaron. He was, after all, a master manipulator working on behalf of a right-wing religious cult, which indicates weakness and betrayal. He also had the courage to leave them and to radically reassess his own worldview, which signals bravery, as well as character.

Where are you, Aaron?

The first time we met him, Aaron was mentally torturing teenagers in order to get them to join the Children. Roe and I had a fight then, on the bus home. *You guys are two sides of the same coin.*

5

I had flipped out. But it turned out that Roe was right. Aaron and I are both sensitives, both born to safeguard the magic of our respective hometowns, and had both failed at it. The longer I sit with that information, the more it disturbs me. The violence, the callousness, the predatory behavior I had witnessed in Aaron—is all of that in me, too? The only thing that separates us are the meager facts of our own lives: that I was born to a liberal, artsy family who let me traipse around the place with tarot cards, and that Aaron was born to a right-wing Christian family who locked him up as soon as his sensitivity—as well as his OCD—started to show.

I want him to come back, and not just because we need him if we're going to fight the Children. I want him to come back so he can remind me that we're different, and I want him to come back so he can reassure me that we're the same.

"Paolo says that there's new MISSING posters," Fiona suddenly says. "Some boy."

"Who?"

"He doesn't know. Paolo can't read."

The "duh" here is implicit.

"But he can read the word *missing*?"

"He can *intuit* it."

Nuala puts a cup of tea down in front of Fiona. "Where, Fi?"

Fi closes her eyes again. She is gathering a picture, in the same way I gather mine with my telepathy. Worming her way into a bird's memories, trying to see what he saw, pushing against the limitations of the fact that his brain is the size of a peanut.

"The writing is all blurry," she says, "but he's white. Brown hair. The poster is . . . it's not in the city, it's in some village in the countryside. I can see, like, farm stuff in the background."

Manon has put her book down. "Incroyable," she says, and means it. Manon is aloof about 80 percent of the time, but whenever she says something in French, she's being utterly sincere.

Fiona's concentration breaks at the compliment. I don't know whether she has told Manon how she feels yet. She hasn't even told *me* how she feels about Manon yet, but she knows I know. When you know someone's brain so well, you can't help occasionally stumbling into it and picking stuff up.

There's an awkward kind of intimacy to having a telepath for a best friend: we both pretend I don't know things, and in that pretending there's a kind of gratitude. *Thank you for not confronting me about my own secrets.*

Nuala takes out a notebook and writes down the information that Paolo has shared. "That's the third in a month," she says.

"How many missing kids is normal?" Roe asks. "And yes, I realize that is a weird and profoundly tragic question."

"In Kilbeg County?" Nuala muses. "Maybe a dozen a year."

Lily turns around. "That feels like a lot." And she is, of course, thinking of her own disappearance. It was hard for Lily to understand at first that what was a profoundly liberating experience for her was the source of huge trauma for everyone she's ever known. But she's grasping it now. Grasping life again, and the emotions that come with it.

"You were an unusual case, Lily," Nuala says, inspecting the yule boar. "Middle class, white, nice school. You got a lot of coverage. But you know, immigrant communities, Traveler communities, or just very poor kids—we hear less about those kinds of people. And Kilbeg County is big. You're city kids, so you don't think about it. But all the townships have their own little issues."

"So if one kid, on average, goes missing a month," Fiona says, "we've tripled our numbers in the last thirty days."

"And still no Housekeeper," Roe adds grimly.

"And still no Housekeeper," I repeat.

Then silently, to myself: *And still no Aaron.*

2

IT'S STILL TECHNICALLY A SCHOOL NIGHT, even though it's hard to take school seriously anymore. First, because it's only a few days until the Christmas holidays. Second, because there is no school to go to. The fire that killed Sister Assumpta and Heather Banbury also took down about two million euro of real estate, the pristine new refurb that was granted to St. Bernadette's under the condition it came under Children of Brigid's control.

The younger years have all been absorbed into different schools, and there's a general sense that St. Bernadette's, as a concept, is over. There is no St. Bernadette's without Sister Assumpta, after all. But at some point it was agreed that the Leaving Cert students, only months from their exams, shouldn't be exposed to any more trauma. So we all tune in on our laptops every day, cameras off, playing out the end of our schooldays alone in our bedrooms.

Roe drops me home at nine, giving me a long kiss from the driver's seat.

"Oh, Maeve. What*ever* will I do now?"

I smile, leaning in. "Well, gosh. I can't think."

"Drive around, I expect. Get into a switchblade fight in a car park." He raises an eyebrow, a pantomime James Dean.

"Getting yourself into all kinds of trouble."

"All *kinds* of trouble," Roe repeats, sliding a hand underneath my sweater, fingertips cooler than rain.

"I guess I'll see you . . . when I see you."

Roe smiles. "See you when I see you, Chambers."

We are smiling because we love each other, and we are smiling because we have a secret.

I go inside. I talk to my parents. They are frightened of me now. The fact that I was there when the fire happened, that Sister Assumpta inexplicably left the school building to me, and that several journalists have been in touch about doing a story around the Famous Witch of Kilbeg has alienated them to the point that they don't know how to speak to me. Can you blame them? I used to be the black sheep of the family. Now I'm the Black Death.

The siblings will be home in a few days, so we talk about that, and then I say that I'm tired. And then I go upstairs.

I go into the bathroom, the one that Aaron said was now a magical hot spot and might wreak havoc on the next people who live here, and I start my spellwork.

I came home one day, a week after Sister Assumpta's will reading, and all my magic books were gone. My crystals, my tarot collection. It would have been more upsetting if I hadn't known it was coming. My parents had been thinking about it for days, as the newspapers kept circling around the story of the lucky girl who inherited a fortune.

I siphoned off the valuable stuff well in advance—the good ingredients, the powerful crystals, my one really important tarot deck—and hid it all in a shoebox in the ceiling tiles of the bathroom. What my parents have confiscated are the spell books, some stuff on Wiccan theory and magical history, a random book about pagan myths. I don't need any of it. I can make up my own spells now, and I'm pretty good at it.

I pour chamomile blossoms and lavender sprigs into my palm. Weirdly, sometimes I find myself narrating my own process, like I'm one of the authors of the spell books. "Chamomile flowers," I say in a singsong voice. "Available cheaply in any health food store!"

My thumb is wet with rose oil. I crush the mixture into a pulp, grains and stems grinding under my nail, stabilizing my palm by pressing down on the knuckles. I feel like I'm about to drive a hole through my own hand. I turn the tap on. "Deep sleep," I say simply. "Deep sleep, deep sleep, deep sleep."

The oily flowers swirl around the drain, clogging briefly at the plughole. There's a burning at the back of my throat, the feeling of magic talking back. I gesture to it in my mind. *Hello, hello,* I say. *You're here again. I just want everyone to have a nice sleep.*

I'm better at magic since the fire. More intuitive, more confident, more capable of calling to something that I can feel but can't see. "Maybe she's born with it," I murmur to myself. "Maybe she's a magic teen!"

I can feel a tide of swirling energy, and I can feel it agree with me. It goes down the plughole and into the pipes, and soon the house will hum with cozy peace. My parents, who could not sleep for days after the fire, will rest soundly. An alarm might wake them up, but a front door closing won't.

An hour later, I leave the house, and I don't even bother to tiptoe. I go straight to St. Bernadette's, wrapping my big black overcoat around me. It's a man's coat, technically. I would have felt weird about wearing men's clothes a few years ago, before Roe made me see how weird it is to give fabric a gender. Now I love the drama of this big thing, leaving me snug against the December chill.

The whole building appears as though it's slouching on the thick ring of scaffolding that surrounds it. An old woman leaning on her crutches. It looks impossible and dangerous to penetrate, with its layers of police tape and boarded-up windows. But we are, it turns out, impossible and dangerous. I climb through, phone flashlight shining out from my breast pocket.

As soon as I'm inside, I hear the sound of an unplugged electric guitar being comfortably played by Ireland's next greatest rock star. I follow the sound and stumble into Sister Assumpta's old office, tripping over a pile of rubble that seems to have fallen out of the ceiling.

"Oh," I say in mock surprise. "Fancy meeting you here."

Roe looks up from the battered old couch, one of the few things you can still sit on and not come away covered in ash stains. We've bought blankets from charity shops to layer over it. Towels from home.

I watch him for a moment. Pale skin, red mouth, black hair.

Delicious delicious delicious.

His eyes follow me around the room, but he doesn't say anything. Just keeps playing the guitar, fingers picking out a blues scale.

"You know," I continue, "this *is* private property."

"What's private," Roe replies, "between two old friends?"

"You tell me," I say, and slowly start unbuttoning my shirt. Coat still on.

Would I be able to talk like this, act like this, if we were in the car or my bedroom? I don't know. But there's something about this building. Something about knowing that it's *mine*.

There's a click of a space heater, the room filling with stiff warm air. Another thing brought from Roe's house. I would be nervous of the electrics here if it weren't for Roe's gift for them.

There are no buttons left.

Roe speaks again. Throat stuck. Voice warm.

"I think we can go more private than that."

I let my coat fall to the floor.

·))●((·

There are so many things in my life that I am forced to feel strangely about, but sex, thank god, isn't one of them.

It can be difficult to find a time and a place. My family hardly leaves the house these days, and Roe is constantly doing something with the band. I imagine plenty of teenage relationships have this problem, and we're uniquely privileged in that I happen to be the sole benefactor of a giant, empty house. With a giant, empty sofa.

"Has there been any research into the possibility," Roe says, twirling a length of my hair as I lie on his chest, "that you are the hottest woman in the country?"

"Not nearly enough research," I reply, tracing a circle on his bare skin. "It's so hard to find funding for that kind of thing."

"A real shame."

"I know. Think of everything we could learn."

Roe kisses the top of my head.

"You love to accept a compliment, don't you, Maeve Chambers?"

"Well, I don't get *that* many." I used to be the kind of girl who couldn't accept a compliment. Now I am the kind of girl who could be dead in a week. I am going to feel as good as I can until then. "Do you think she's coming?"

"The Housekeeper?"

"Who else?"

"I don't know. It feels as though we've been waiting a long time for this threat to materialize. Maybe she's dead. Or maybe sealing the Well means that there's less magic for her to live off."

It's not the first time we've shared this theory, and now we've shared it so many times that it's become a bedtime story. Something to soothe us, ease us into sleep.

I look up. "You have eyeliner boogers," I say. "Black eye snot."

"Ew, get it out."

Tenderly, I swipe my pinkie finger under his eye, picking up traces of kohl as I go. I show Roe the accumulated grime. "Make a wish. A Christmas wish."

But instead of making a wish, Roe just pulls me closer. Or maybe that is the wish. It's hard to tell. I lay my head on his chest and try to listen to the quiet. Sometimes I convince myself she's still here, somewhere. Sister Assumpta, I mean. I don't always come to meet Roe. Sometimes I come alone, to feel her out.

I tried to explain this to Roe once, and he wasn't impressed.

"So according to you, we're boning under the watchful eye of a dead nun?"

"No!" I exploded. "Don't make it weird."

"You're the one who made it weird!"

But I like to think of her here, casually underestimated by everyone, straining hard to protect Kilbeg with the magical strands she managed to weave into a blanket. I close my eyes, focus my brain, and I almost feel like I can connect with her. The sensitivity thread that connects me and Aaron must have also existed between me and Assumpta. I try to access it. I cannot tell if I am experiencing supernatural phenomena or a strange form of delayed grief, but sometimes, I can feel her. A presence. A *something*.

There's a sound. A clatter. The sound of a foot going through a floorboard.

We both jump. I grab the blankets instinctively, painfully aware that I am nude except for my socks.

"What the *hell* was that?"

Roe gets up immediately, pulls on a sweater and underwear. He turns around, takes a look at me. "It's not the Housekeeper," he says soothingly. "Her thing isn't breaking and entering, is it?"

"No," I reason, still freaked out. "I suppose not."

Roe's sweater is emerald green, and so loose that it falls around his arms, exposing a shoulder.

"It's probably nothing. Come back to the couch," I say quickly.

"When, in any horror film, has 'it's probably nothing' turned out to be nothing?" Roe responds, pulling on jeans.

Another clatter. The sound is getting closer now, and I'm beginning to regret trying to communicate with Sister Assumpta's ghost.

"*Shit*, Roe."

"I'm going to check it out."

"Don't *leave* me!"

But Roe is already halfway out the door, so I throw on my own clothes as quickly as I can and follow. The space heater ticks and crackles, and I think: *If I lose the one nice thing left in my life, I might truly go insane.*

3

I REGRET NOT PUTTING MY SHOES ON. BY the time we're in the hallway, I can feel that my socks are caked in ash, dust, and general debris. Little splinters of wood, tiny bits of gravel that have somehow found their way inside.

"It's coming from upstairs," Roe says, putting one foot on the stair. He closes his eyes. "Hang on."

I can see him burrowing down into his gift, talking to the house. The pipes, the wiring. "Hold my hand."

I lace my fingers through his. He leads us up the rotting staircase, dodging each faulty step, taking his hand off the banister whenever he knows there's weakness.

"Your hand is shaking," Roe notes. "You're not *really* scared, are you?"

"No," I say. It is not convincing.

"It's probably squatters. Housing crisis, you know."

But Roe didn't talk to Dorey at the funeral. Roe didn't see the satisfaction in her eyes, the sense that the package would be all wrapped up just so. There was zero doubt in her voice that day. What if this is it? The end?

"Roe," I say. "I love you, OK?"

"Huh?"

"If anything happens, I don't want our last conversation to have been about eye goo."

"OK, Maeve, I love you, too."

But there's another sound, a sound of feet, a sound of furniture being dragged, a sound of movement. I feel Roe's hand tense. Feel him think: *Maybe it's not nothing, after all.*

Up the stairs again. We're on the third floor now. Memories of doing my geography homework on the landing, notebook propped up on my thigh, minutes before class. Fiona telling me to hurry. That was only seven months ago. Can really so much have changed?

We reach the door of 3A, and there's no doubt that whoever is in my house is behind that door.

"Hold on," Roe whispers, looking around. He crouches down next to a defunct radiator, one of the many radiators I used to spend the winter months sitting on, and runs his hand along the thin copper pipe fixing it to the wall.

"Come on, sweetheart," he whispers. And the pipe, swooning, comes away in Roe's hand. He examines it, focuses on it, and slowly it bends into the shape of a crowbar.

"Did you just make a weapon," I whisper back, "out of a *radiator* pipe?"

Roe shrugs like it's nothing. "Come on, then."

And, with his hand on the door, he opens up 3A.

We don't see anyone at first. But what we do see is this: a sleeping bag, a backpack, and a camera. The camera throws me. It's a Polaroid, but one of those updated Polaroids they started making a few years ago and that girls sometimes take to parties. It confuses me, but Roe's thought pattern is instant, clear: *Why has someone brought a camera to a place where I have sex with my girlfriend?*

A strange mix of terror, relief, and disgust washes over both of us. *Oh*, I think. *It's just a pervert! A run-of-the-mill pervert. Not a revenge demon. Well, that's something, isn't it?*

Then a voice. A familiar one.

"Roe?"

I whirl around, and Aaron is standing by the window, partially obscured by what's left of the curtains. I don't know why he says Roe's name first, or why he sounds so confused. But Aaron's here, and I feel a release, as though I've just found my passport.

"What the hell?!" I say. "Aaron?!"

Aaron is hanging out the window, smoking a cigarette. There's some scaffolding that he is half balancing on, a pole he is leaning his back against. His hair is buzzed short, his eyes tired. He's lost weight. He didn't have very much of it to begin with. I can see the frame of his face much more now, the bones of his cheeks jutting slightly.

"Dude," Roe says, already picking up the camera, "what the *hell*?"

"Put that down," Aaron says, far too fiercely.

"Why are you sneaking around St. Bernadette's? With a camera?"

It's the emphasis on the word *camera* that throws Aaron slightly, and he pauses to take us both in. Then he realizes that we've clearly dressed ourselves in a hurry.

"Wow," he says dryly. "I didn't realize I was interrupting the fall of Sodom and Gomorrah. Why are you carrying a copper pipe? Are you going to beat me to death with it?"

"Jury's out," answers Roe, still holding the pipe.

"Oh, for god's sake, what are you doing here?" I ask. "And where have you *been*?"

Aaron looks at me oddly then, cigarette hovering in front of his face. His eyes go between me and Roe, and back to me again.

"Around," he says at last. "I've been around."

Next to the sleeping bag is a black plastic sack of clothes and a small backpack with a zipper open. I can see a can of deodorant, some shower gel, a razor. "Aaron, have you been sleeping rough?"

"I've . . . not been sleeping soft."

"So, what, you've been around the world and now you're crashing here?"

He squints at me, as if trying to figure out my game. As if I'm the one talking in riddles. It's too frustrating. I can hear my voice taking on a high, manic tension, the tone of someone who might cry if she doesn't scream.

"You've had us all *sick* with worry, Aaron, and we're all terrified of this Housekeeper stuff as it is. The least you can do is tell us why you left."

"And why you're back," Roe adds. "With a camera."

Roe moves toward it again, brows furrowed. Aaron steps away from the window.

"Don't touch it, Roe."

His voice is low, with a hint of his old fundamentalist condescension. That tone of *I know better than you do, kid.*

"Why?" Roe snaps. "Why don't you want me to touch it?"

I'm struggling to understand why Roe is so interested in the camera. Even on his worst days, it's hard to imagine Aaron snooping around, spying on us. But then I realize that the new-old Polaroid camera is giving off a frequency that only Roe can read. In the same way I can see people's colors, Roe can see some kind of charge in the air, strange atoms that are sluicing off this tiny machine.

"Just don't, OK?" Aaron says, almost threateningly. "Just don't."

"Why are you *here*?" I stress, trying to get back to the matter at hand.

Roe is moving closer to the camera, and it's like watching two siblings in a turf war over a shared bedroom. Aaron is twitching, like he's about to spin out.

"Oh, for god's sake, Maeve, you know why I'm here. I'm here because you sent me the note."

"The note?" I'm deeply confused by this.

"The *note*?" Roe says, horrified. And finally, they forget about the stupid camera.

"What did it say?" I ask, carefully assessing my memories, checking for any note-sending. When Heather Banbury was draining my magic, my movements were so fuzzy and hard to remember. Could some of that sickness be hanging over still, without me realizing?

But no. I had no idea where Aaron even was. How on earth could I send a note to him?

"It doesn't matter," Aaron says.

"Was it to meet Maeve here?" Roe asks, sounding deeply suspicious. "Alone?"

"Something like that, yes."

"Which is why you were so surprised that I was here." Roe's parents wanted him very much to be a doctor, but in my opinion, he would be a much better lawyer.

"Jesus, Roe," Aaron says, sounding exhausted. He starts massaging his temples, like he has a migraine coming on. "Give it a rest, will you? Sorry I interrupted your . . . *rendezvous*. I would make sure your tetanus shots are up to date, by the way; this is not a safe space to take your clothes off."

Aaron leans out the window and taps his cigarette, and I can see a postcard sticking out of his jacket pocket. A postcard with writing on the back. Roe sees it, too.

"Is that it?" Roe asks. "The note?"

Roe reaches forward to grab it, and Aaron pushes him off. Only he pushes a little too hard. So Roe pushes back.

Aaron's knees buckle against the windowsill, and instinctively, he grabs at Roe to steady himself. But all he does is drag Roe out with him.

Suddenly, both of them have gone out the window.

I scream and rush to the sill, terrifyingly conscious that it's a three-story drop and Fiona is at home in bed. There's no one to mend broken legs, to stop heavy bleeding, to knit skin back together.

I shouldn't have worried, though, because as soon as I get to the window, I see that the scaffolding has caught them. They are both gingerly getting to their feet, the "ground" only two planks of wood wide.

"Well, thank *god* for that," I breathe, almost feeling like I should say a prayer to something. "Come on," I say, holding out my hand. "I'll help you both up."

But it's not over. Roe moves toward Aaron, furious.

"Why the *hell* did you do that? Why did you drag me out with you?"

The scaffolding rattles underneath them.

"Why did you push me out the window, you asshole?"

Aaron swipes at Roe, almost like a slap, except that he catches the heel of his hand off Roe's neck. Roe catches Aaron's arm and twists it. Roe's shorter than Aaron, but stronger.

"Stop!" I scream out the window. "Stop it, you *idiots*."

It's not about me, or the camera, or the note, or the fact that Aaron deserted us. It's about all those things, but it's also about this: that ten months ago Aaron showed up to Roe's gig, washed a kid's face clean of makeup, and incited a riot. Roe can understand on an intellectual level that Aaron is trying—or at least *was* trying—to atone, but at base, this is who they are to each other.

"Get in. *Stop*. You're acting *nuts*."

But they don't hear me. I burrow into their minds, and it's a thick knot of fury and contempt.

I try to quickly dive into their thoughts, access both minds at the same time. For some reason, I can only get Aaron's. That snap of sensitivity puts us in the same frequency, and I get a stream of his thoughts as the scaffolding rattles.

Galatians 5:19–21—Now the works of the sinful flesh are obvious: sexual immorality, impurity, complete lack of restraint—

The sudden stream of Bible verse blows me backward. I've never been able to access Aaron's mind quite like this before, and the magnitude of it, the fierceness of it, is terrifying.

—idolatry, sorcery, hatred, discord, jealousy, outbursts of anger . . . Then his thought pattern pauses briefly. *What's the rest of it? It doesn't matter, does it, because I don't believe that anymore. Do I. Do I? God, Roe, calm down, for god's sake, Roe.*

The thought breaks again, and he's back to Bible verse. *I warn you, just as I also warned you before, that those who continue to do such things will not inherit the kingdom of God.*

Then something else happens. Their gifts—Roe's for machinery, Aaron's for finding weakness—seem to twine around each other. This can happen. Together, Lily and Fiona can charge a phone back to 100 percent. Roe and I can switch the radio station. Our gifts work in combination, but nobody has ever combined with Aaron's before.

I can feel a tremor from underneath. The scaffolding is shaking all over.

Shit.

Impurity, sorcery, hatred, discord.

"Stop, *please*," I beg. "I think your gifts are . . ."

Usually when our gifts come together, it's in the spirit of

24

collaboration. But right now, they're coming together in combat. Aaron sees weakness; Roe talks to machinery, to buildings, to things that have been constructed. And so now the whole building is screaming with fragility.

Impurity, sorcery, hatred, discord.

I run downstairs, jumping over the faulty steps, desperate to catch at least one of them when they inevitably fall. Aaron's thoughts, still pounding in my head, are compulsive, confused, and unwelcome. *Impurity, sorcery, hatred, discord. You don't believe that. Or you do. It's all connected. Magic sex sin hatred sorcery hell. All connected. Or it isn't.*

I make it outside just in time for them to notice that the house is shaking. I think of Sister Assumpta, her solid armadillo body, her cold trembling hands. She feels alive for a moment, alive in the spirit of her cherished school.

"Your gifts are combining!" I yell from the ground. "You need to stop."

They stop fighting. There's a moment of stillness. And then:

Crack!

The wooden planks snap beneath them like a biscuit. They fall, the next level catching them. I wince when I see that Roe has landed awkwardly, on his side. He's wincing like a piece of metal has just pierced him. I remember the scar on his stomach, still angry red, from the knife back in March. Still delicate, in the tight way of new wounds.

But the school goes on trembling like a spooked horse.

"We *have* stopped!" Aaron yells back.

I wrestle with my own gifts, trying to regain a sense of control. What's *happening*?

They may have stopped punching, but their powers are still

scratching at each other like cats. They are witches, after all. And witches don't fight the way regular people do.

Crack!

Another layer down. Both their bodies crash, and Aaron howls in pain.

"You have to stop being so pissed with each other, I think," I yell. "Stop being pissy."

Impurity, sorcery, hatred, discord.

They jump from the first-floor scaffolding to the ground, cradling their wounds as they go.

"I am not being *pissy*," Roe retorts, but the building does not agree. He tries to focus his gift, to relax the house like he sweet-talked the radiator. But it's too late; he's too mixed up in Aaron's talent for weakness. The building is too enmeshed in the dynamic, confused by itself.

I hate this. I hate them for being stupid, and I hate them for jeopardizing my only responsibility in the world: to keep this place safe. This, the mouth of the Well, the place that Sister Assumpta gave to me. My own rage unfurls, a hot sense of justice flooding through me. They're being pigs. I wanted Aaron to carefully explain what happened after the funeral. I wanted to feel less alone in my sensitivity. I didn't want this childish swiping and stupid aggression. We've been through enough, haven't we?

They both look at the building. "Nice work, man," Roe says dryly.

"As *if* you're going to blame this on me."

A flood of white rage feels like it's about to burst me open, and then . . .

The feeling of something. Stars, moons, planets. The shattering of a thousand dinner plates. I'm momentarily certain I have had a stroke, an aneurysm, a heart attack. The sense of something stretching. A new frontier being reached in my brain. My hearing goes fuzzy and my face gets hot.

"What the hell?"

Aaron says it first, then Roe says something similar. I don't know. It's suddenly hard to focus.

I look to both of them, and their eyes have gone milky.

"I can't see," Roe says. "Maeve? Why can't I see anything?"

Their eyes are like opals, like white smoke, like saucers of cream. It's terrifying to look at, both of their faces so strange, so fundamentally wrong. I feel like I'm in a dream, a dream where life is the same as real life except for one horrible, jarring thing.

They feel around, and I take a step backward, fear trumping everything. Even love. Even friendship.

"I . . . I don't know."

I remember myself and try to recover. I slip my hand in Roe's. "Don't worry, babe, I'm here."

I feel his hands clutch me, grateful. I reach out for Aaron, grab his shoulder. "Dude?"

"I . . . I can't . . ."

The tremors have stopped. That, at least, is something. The scaffolding has broken but the house is thankfully intact. I try to sound authoritative, calm. "Listen," I say clearly. "I don't know what's going on, but we'll fix it, OK?"

A cloud passes in front of the moon, and rain starts to fall. Scattered drops, cold and slight.

"It's gone," Aaron suddenly says, blinking his eyes back to their ordinary blue.

Roe is the same. Liner smeared, sockets like big dark shadows. "OK, wow. That was . . . not good."

At least they've stopped fighting. They are now just partners in the inexplicable. They keep looking around, pupils refocusing, like kittens that have just opened their eyes for the first time.

Roe and Aaron were blind only for a minute, but I can tell it's not something either of them will forget in a hurry.

"Maybe she was protecting herself," I say, gazing up at the house. "Or maybe I was protecting her. A sensitivity thing, y'know?"

"The Kilbeg sensitive," Aaron agrees, still brushing himself off. "Protecting the Kilbeg Well. It tracks."

We stand together, looking at the old building. "Maybe," Roe says, sounding ashamed.

"Lots of people get struck blind in the Bible," Aaron murmurs. "Saul."

"What was the deal with him?" Roe asks tentatively.

"He persecuted Christ, and then he was blinded for three days, and then he saw the light."

"Then what?" I nudge. "What happened to Saul?"

"Then he became the apostle Paul."

"Name change," Roe remarks. "Love that for her."

Aaron raises an eyebrow. "You two should really know more about this stuff, you know. You went to *Catholic* school."

"I'm a Protestant, so it's really more about traybakes and church bingo," Roe says.

"And my parents are agnostic," I reply.

"Figures." Aaron sighs, with implicit disrespect for the term *agnostic*. "All right, shall we go somewhere and talk like grown-ups?"

So we go back into Sister Assumpta's office, and I wonder how long it took for the other apostles to accept that Saul wasn't up to something.

4

"FIRST OF ALL," I SAY, HANDING AARON A granola bar from my satchel, "why don't you try telling us where you've been?"

Roe and I sit on either end of the couch while Aaron sits on the floor, his back against the wall.

"And why you disappeared," Roe adds.

"I was scared," Aaron replies, and just lets it hang there. It's hard to believe. He doesn't sound scared. He sounds like himself.

"Well, we're *all* scared," I say irritably. "That's no excuse to abandon your friends."

Aaron starts turning over the granola bar in his hands, catching the foil packaging in the light. "It's different for you guys. You weren't there, that day on the bus. With Matthew. The last time you came up against the Housekeeper, you won. You've got a gambler's mentality. You don't think you need to leave the casino. You believe that you'll win again."

He looks up at us, the circles under his eyes deep as bruises.

"But when I hear the Housekeeper coming, all I know is that I'm going to be found dead next to someone I care about, or they're going to wake up dead next to me."

"So, what, you'd rather be alone?" I ask, perhaps a little too dryly.

"Than find another friend's corpse? Yes," he says. "Neither of you have seen a dead friend. What if it was Lily? Or Fiona? That's your last image of them forever, you know."

Neither Roe nor I know how to respond. Does Aaron really believe there's no chance of us winning? Particularly when things have been so quiet, for weeks?

"There's something else," he says, getting back on his feet. "My visa."

"Your *visa*?"

"I don't have one. I was here on a work visa, remember? Under the Children's sponsorship. Now I'm here illegally."

Roe snorts. "Oh, come *on*."

"What?" Aaron replies, immediately defensive.

"You're a white American," Roe says flatly. "No one in Irish immigration is going to throw the book at a white American. Get real."

"I *am* being real," Aaron snaps. "Why do you think there hasn't been a single mention of Heather Banbury in the newspapers? Dorey has everyone in her pocket. She's a puppet master. I've had to throw another phone away, because I keep getting calls about my *status*. And these were not friendly calls."

There's something about the way he says "puppet master" that makes me think it's more than a figure of speech.

"What do you mean?" I ask. "What do you mean by puppet master?"

"Dorey's a sensitive, like us. Didn't you feel it, when you met her? Her powers are all about seeing people, controlling them. You can read minds, I can see vulnerabilities, but Dorey . . . she can manipulate them on, like, a cosmic level."

"Cosmic how?" Roe asks, interested.

Aaron runs his hands through his hair. "Like, the day I met Dorey I was a grieving eighteen-year-old who was into tarot cards and felt pretty strongly that my church was wrong about gay people."

Roe nods. "And she made you into baby Hitler?"

"Right." Aaron grimaces, but doesn't correct him.

"Assumpta could see the future," I say, just realizing that all sensitives do have a kind of "seeing" power. I had never put it together before.

"How do you think Dorey got that insane contract to effectively take control of your school? She can make people do whatever she wants. She just needs to talk to them for a while, work her charm, get a string on them. Then she can pull that string forever."

"And you think . . . what? She could get you deported?" I press. "If she doesn't kill you first, I mean?"

"Deported, imprisoned for breaking the terms of my visa, you name it."

Roe keeps a steady eye on Aaron, still reluctant to believe him. "So what have you been doing, then?"

Aaron shrugs. "I've been around."

"Around *where*?"

"Places where you don't need a last name to stay."

"So, what, like? Shelters?" Roe suggests.

"*Motels?*" I say, and immediately feel stupid, like I'm someone playacting for an American movie. Ireland doesn't have motels.

"Shelters, hostels, bus stations. You know. Squats." He stops to look around at the still-intact ceiling of Sister Assumpta's office. "I'm surprised this place hasn't become one."

I'm conscious of how sheltered Roe and I are. How alien we are to this kind of nomadism, how much younger we must seem. We are, at the end of the day, just a couple of middle-class kids who have always—no matter how bad things have been—had a warm bed to sleep in.

"That's part of the reason I wanted to talk to you," Aaron continues. "I stumbled on some . . . some pretty messed-up stuff. Stuff about the Children."

"I thought you got a *note*," Roe stresses, and Aaron ignores it.

"I was in Limerick," Aaron continues, "and I met a kid. A runaway. A former Child. He used to come to my meetings at the old apartment. He sold me the camera. The one that Roe is so nuts about."

Roe's eyes flicker to the camera, currently resting on a dusty end table. There's some kind of energy pouring out of it, a mood only he can see.

"And he told me . . ." Aaron walks to the window, his hands in his jacket pockets. He's talking like he's still trying to figure out what he's going to say, or whether he believes it. "He told me about the Lodge."

"The Lodge?"

"A home for the Children's most devoted. Kids are running *away* to this place."

"Why?"

"This kid, Connor, he had a bad situation at home. Abuse, drinking, the works. He had been spending time at Children meetings just to feel . . . I don't know, like he had a community, I guess. Pretty soon he gets invited to live at this place: the Lodge. He figures it can't be any worse than what he's got, so he goes."

Maybe it's my imagination, or maybe it's our shared sensitivity, but a picture of this kid starts to form in my head. A picture of the whole situation: the camp beds he and Aaron are sitting on, the gentle bustle of volunteers handing out blankets. The way both of them are holding on to their bags of clothes, even as they talk to each other. Connor with tufts of red hair, a blaze of freckles across his face.

"He said that it was normal and fun, for a little while. Lots of games and trust exercises and sharing chores. Real commune vibes. But then it gradually started to . . . I don't know. He was confused about it."

"Confused how?"

"Like he didn't trust his own version of events. His memory was spotty. But he did say that they were sternly encouraged to make a lot of sacrifices. Like to not eat, or to . . . to punish themselves."

The squint comes back into Aaron's eye. A nervous twitch that looks a little like the pained blink of an old dog.

"So he escaped. Not left. Escaped. He had to wait until night, walk miles into the nearest village, hitchhike at dawn. He was really scared of being caught, even though he couldn't put into words why. I asked him if he thought they would hurt him, and he said no. Not physically. But he saw people changing around him, going nutty. He was afraid."

Silence. The world outside is starting to brighten, as though it's beginning to move through a paint swatch. Midnight blue to royal. It's almost four a.m. I think of Paolo, scouting the area out for Fiona, finding the MISSING posters all over the city. Did he see Connor, too?

"I just can't believe . . ." Aaron begins, and then stops. Tries again. "No, I *can* believe it, that's the problem. Did I always know that this is where it was going?"

"What do you mean?"

"If I hadn't . . . left. Because of you guys. Would I be there? Getting kids to starve themselves? And for *what*?"

I can feel that Roe wants to say "Probably, yes" but chooses to ignore the question entirely.

"Tell me about the camera," he says instead.

Aaron goes to the end table and hands the camera to Roe. They exchange a look—a *We're good now, yeah?*—and Roe starts turning it over. He pops the back, where the film should live.

"It's empty," Roe says, but he keeps running his hands over it.

"They take your phone away when you get to the Lodge," Aaron continues. "But they give you one of these instead."

"Pretty crappy trade," Roe says.

"I guess. But I think part of the allure of this place is, you know, we're all going to unplug, go off-grid, phones are ruining our brains, blah blah blah."

"I mean," I reason, "they probably are."

"So they give them these cameras instead. And it's very: We're going to make amazing memories! We're going to scrapbook! We're going to build a wall of photos as we make our new home beautiful!"

Aaron says all this in his most American voice, like he's a youth pastor for a megachurch. Which, I guess, at one point he was.

"And that *works*?"

"Oddly, yes."

"So you bought the camera off him."

"Yeah. I thought it might . . . I don't know, I thought we could do something with it."

"So . . . you were always planning on coming back, then?"

Aaron shrugs. "I don't know. After a few weeks of not dying, I thought I should probably make some kind of plan."

"A plan sounds like something we should all be making. So where is it, then? Where's the Lodge?"

"I don't know. The kid didn't know, either. His memories weren't working right. There must be a ton of charms on the place." Aaron gestures toward Roe. "I thought Thomas Edison over here might be able to work something out with the camera."

Roe looks up. "I don't know. It's not really saying anything.

There's no film in it, so there's no imprint, no shadows. It's just an empty camera with bad juju." He takes a long look at it again, holds it at arm's length. "Leave it with me."

"OK. But be careful. That thing cost me two packs of cigarettes."

Exhaustion starts to snap at me like a hungry animal. We were only supposed to be here for an hour, and it's almost dawn. I have school in the morning. I stand up, stretch out my arms and legs.

"Sleep here tonight, Aaron," I declare, half yawning. "There's a heater, and we'll leave some snacks. But go to Nuala in the morning. Ask her if you can stay with her and Manon."

"I'm not sure if Nuala will want . . ."

"She will," I say with finality. "Besides, we've been keeping track of these kids going missing. She'll want to hear what you have to say. We need to get on this. Who knows what the Children are planning?"

I start lacing up my boots, and Roe rubs his eyes. "I'll go warm up the car," he says, kissing the crown of my head. He turns toward Aaron. "Let's not wreck a building and go hysterically blind next time we meet, m'kay?"

Aaron nods. "Deal."

I'm still lacing my boots when I catch Aaron, leaning against the opposing wall, watching me with a worried look.

"*What?*"

"There's still . . . There's still the postcard."

"Right. My alleged note. What did it say?"

He passes it over to me wordlessly.

> *Aaron,*
> *I need you to meet me at the school tomorrow night. Just after midnight. We need to talk about us.*
> *Maeve*

I keep blinking at it, the words smearing together in my exhaustion.

"We need to talk about us?" I stumble. "What *us*?"

He plucks it out of my hands.

"Well, I don't know. That's why I thought it was weird. I didn't want to bring it up in front of Roe, though, in case he put two and two together and made five million. He already wanted to kill me the second he saw me."

"Who would send this?"

"Someone who wanted us all in the same place. Take us out, maybe."

"But no one's here. It's just the three of us."

"Well, then." He looks at me, then back at the note. "Someone who wants to cause friction, I guess. Mission accomplished."

The shaking building. The collapsing scaffolding. The terrifying minute when Roe and Aaron were struck blind.

"You think it was the Children?" I say, dumbfounded. "Doesn't passing notes seem, I don't know, a little below their pay grade?"

"Nothing is below their pay grade. We have to ask ourselves: What do they have to gain from seeing us fight? Clearly, they knew you and Roe were coming here. They wanted something to happen. Divide and conquer."

I suppose it makes sense. Now that the Housekeeper is a no-show, perhaps they're looking for more organic ways to fracture the group. It can't be comfortable for them to know that so many powerful witches are gathered together, and against them.

"OK. Let's tell the others," I say, and then pause. "But maybe let's leave out the 'we need to talk about us' bit."

Aaron cocks his head. "Are you and Roe really that unsure of each other? He knows there's no 'us.' There never was."

"I just . . ." I don't really know what I'm getting at, except that Aaron is back, and we have to be able to work together. If tonight's performance is anything to go on, Roe and Aaron need very few excuses to fight. "I just don't want to make things more difficult than they have to be."

Aaron nods, takes a lighter from his pocket, and sets the postcard alight. I watch it burn for a moment, and wonder if truly innocent people set fire to things.

I head out to the car, my head aching from tiredness, deep pressure forming at my temples.

"Is he all right?" Roe asks.

"I don't know," I say. And then a new fear unfurls in my chest. "They've been watching us."

5

I'M SO TIRED THE NEXT DAY THAT I CHALK
everything strange up to my own exhaustion, and almost miss something else. My laptop screen looks different. There should be a word
for digital feng shui, when your online layout is just slightly off and
it sort of trips you up all day. Like when they add a new button on
TikTok, or something.

I finally zero in on it after lunch: it's our class layout. It's different. It's usually a grid: six by six, thirty-six pupils in all. That's how
many people are left in our Leaving Cert class, after the fire. Today
the final row only has five windows in it.

Is someone missing today?

Lorna, Fi messages back. **Lorna McKeon.**

Right, of course

There's nothing "of course" about it, though, because I probably
wouldn't have remembered Lorna in a million years. She's a perfectly
nice, blend-into-the-background kind of girl. Smart enough to be
in all Fiona's classes. Brown swinging ponytail. She let me borrow a
pencil once.

If this were an ordinary day of school, I wouldn't have noticed,
because people are missing from school all the time. But since school

went online, there have always been the same number of us every day. Even when you're sick, you log on.

That's obviously not the only reason I'm suddenly distracted by her absence. I can still feel the chill of the Lodge in my bones, like a shadow, the fragments of a fading dream. We're all supposed to go to Nuala's again tonight, where we can talk about it properly. Nail it to the floor. Dress it up in logic and reason. I wonder if Aaron has made it to Nuala's yet, or whether he's deserted us again.

I follow Lorna on social media, but we've never interacted and so the algorithm keeps us apart. I look at her, observing for the first time the private life of a girl I've gone to school with since I was twelve. She hasn't posted anything in months, which isn't unusual. Most people rarely commit to the grid. Even I get performance anxiety about it: the last thing on my profile is a picture from the summer, of a box of onion rings. The caption just reads "ahnyun rings."

It was very funny at the time.

Lorna's pictures reveal someone who is well-behaved, modestly dressed, and smiley. The longer I look, the more I feel myself adding a narrative. Is she *too* modestly dressed? Sleeves to the wrists, collars to the neck. Is this the Children's influence? Is she in the Children? Is her smile real? Is the group photo of her family at a relative's birthday a shiny front for some kind of hidden abuse?

I put the phone down, realizing I have spun out for twenty minutes about a girl I don't know whose only crime is not logging on to class today.

There are two days until the Christmas holidays begin. I guess I can keep an eye on her until then.

Roe picks me up, and the fight with Aaron is already forgotten. He's spent the day with the band; they're strategizing their single release like dictators pushing flags around a map.

40

"I don't think 'Wolf Girl' is our *best* song, but it hits all four of the banger quadrants," Roe says, gripping the steering wheel a little too tightly.

"It's a banger, for sure," I say, patting his knee.

"Big chorus, check. Good lyrics—but not, y'know, *too* good, too good to go over people's heads, anyway—check. Musicianship, check. Dee sounds amazing on it. And vocals, you know. I think I sound pretty good."

That queasy feeling again, that Roe's own trajectory is leading him away from magic. Away from me. Who needs the occult when you have fame calling? Who needs a high school girlfriend when you have the world at your feet?

Even with his memories, Roe is straddling two worlds. The one with us, and the encroaching adult world that has already laid a claim on him. Neither of us will win, so we have to learn to share.

We talk about the single, allowing ourselves to bounce around the world of wardrobe choices and magazine features, until we pull up outside Nuala's house and fall silent. We sit still.

"Are we going to go in?" I say finally.

"Yeah," Roe says, rubbing at his temples. "I'm just savoring this moment, before we tell our friends that the Children are watching us."

"I think on some level," I say carefully, "we kind of knew they would be."

"Just the idea of us going into the school the last few weeks, our only time alone together, and that . . . they were keeping tabs on us the whole time. Like, how much did they *see*?"

"God. I don't want to think about it."

"There's also the whole thing of . . . y'know, telling the gang we've been using the school as a shag palace." Roe grimaces. "Lily and I are close but we're not 'siblings who talk about their sex lives' close."

I grimace, opening the passenger door.

"Come on. Ask not for whom the uncomfortable-conversation-bell tolls. It tolls for thee."

"Poetry!"

"You know it."

We get inside, and Aaron is already there. Fiona, Nuala, and Lily are at the kitchen table, Manon sitting on the countertop. Manon's wearing a big shirt, presumably her father's, and tapping the end of a pencil off the tip of her nose. Paolo is perched on top of the fridge.

Lily looks up as we come in.

"Hey," she says, appearing slightly disturbed. "Aaron just told us."

"It's not a crime," I reply, feeling a bit defensive. "It is *my* house after all."

"What?"

"I told them about *the Lodge*," Aaron stresses. "I thought I'd leave the other thing up to you."

"Oh."

"What did you think he told us about?" Fiona asks, confused.

"Uh, just, the Children are sort of . . . watching us, and they sent Aaron a forged note pretending to be from me. To bring us all together at St. Bernadette's last night. And cause, like, a fight."

"Why were you and Roe at St. Bernadette's last night?" Manon asks. And then, as if she has answered her own question, "Oh."

Nuala is unfazed. "I assumed they would be watching us. Now we need to be watching them. We need to find out about the Lodge. Aaron mentioned a camera. Roe?"

"Right." Roe digs out the old Polaroid from his bag and explains that there's no film. "I think I have an idea, though. Nuala, do you have a white sheet? Something that you don't mind destroying?"

"Ominous," Nuala says. "Let me look."

She leaves the room and comes back with a bedsheet, tossing it toward Roe. It seems we won't have to talk too much about either the sex or the weird postcard. Or, I realize, the fight. I train my mind on Aaron and Roe: they, it seems, aren't too keen on talking about it, either. Or the temporary, inexplicable blindness.

"Great. Thanks," Roe says, catching the sheet. "And a line of string. Or yarn, or something?"

Nuala grabs a roll of string from the top drawer and throws it to him.

"OK, everyone get up."

We're all mystified as we watch Roe fix the string between two cabinets on opposite walls. Then he drapes the white sheet over it, like a makeshift cinema screen. Roe turns off the lights and moves a desk lamp in from the living room, pointing it so only the white sheet is illuminated.

"Are you quite done ruining my house, Roe?" Nuala murmurs.

Roe stands on a stool in front of the sheet. "So. The guts of the camera has no memory, yeah? But the bulb itself does. It remembers everything it's flashed at."

He swivels, pointing the camera to the sheet and pressing the flash button. The room lights up white for a moment, dazzling us all.

Roe studies the sheet, then quickly goes to it, taking a Sharpie from his pocket. He removes the cap with his teeth and draws a big shape. We watch him, his mop of curly hair blocking out most of the drawing until he stands back from it.

"All that," Manon says finally, "for a rectangle."

It's actually a square, a rectangle, and a squiggly line.

"OK, look," Roe says, trying not to be dissuaded, "I know this doesn't look like . . . much, but the picture isn't clear in my head yet. All I can see are gray shapes, so I'm drawing where I can see the shapes."

Aaron steps toward the white sheet, tracing Roe's abstract drawing. "You're saying that this could be where the Lodge is?"

"It's a reasonable guess, right?" Roe says, excited that someone is finally grasping it, even if he's disappointed that it's Aaron. "If the Children-in-training are all at the Lodge, then it seems likely that the last photo taken is of the building."

Aaron nods. "The kid says he used up all the film before he left."

"Maeve." Roe beckons to me. "Come over here. Merge your gift with mine for a minute. You can read minds; maybe you can get the camera to jog its memory, get a clearer picture."

I go, bewildered by the request, but stranger things have happened. Our gifts once melded so that we could listen to phone calls through Roe's car radio, so anything is possible.

"Look through the viewfinder," Roe says, holding my hand. "Press the flash, and tell me what you can see."

"Hang on, hang on, hang on," I say, trying to find my bearings. "I can't just switch it on like that." I focus on Roe's grip, Roe's crystal-white light, his connection to the camera. The camera as an extension of Roe. "OK. I'm ready."

I press the flash and immediately understand why Roe needed the white sheet. Like a black-and-white photograph that is only just starting to develop in a darkroom, I can see lines and shapes, the suggestion of an external location. But nothing else. Just lines. Just shapes.

"It's no good," I say, still peering through the viewfinder. "I can only see what you see."

"Let me try," Aaron suddenly says.

44

"What? Why?"

"Maeve doesn't really do memories. She does what people are thinking, here and now. My gift is about delving into people's histories, bringing out the stuff they wish they could forget. It seems . . . pertinent."

"That's a good point," Nuala says. Manon nods silently, takes a notebook from her breast pocket, and writes this down.

"I would like us to talk about that," Manon says to Aaron, sounding like a therapist. "Later."

Roe eyes Aaron suspiciously. "All right," he says at last, reaching out his hand.

Aaron hesitates. "Just grab on to my wrist, or something."

Awkwardly, Roe grabs ahold of Aaron's wrist, his hand like a bracelet. Aaron takes a few silent moments, settling his gift. Then he looks through the viewfinder, and the room flashes white.

"OK," Aaron says. "Big building. No. Big . . . castle."

Roe throws the Sharpie to Lily. "Lily," he says quickly. "You're the artist."

Lily catches it. Goes to the sheet. "What kind of castle?"

"Like a . . . like a Victorian gothic castle. But you know, not real. Fake. It's made to look like that, but it's new, you know. There are solar panels on the roof."

Lily starts drawing. "Turrets?"

"Three."

"Where are they?"

"You can *see* all this?" I say, dumbfounded by this new aspect of Aaron's power. He seems a little taken aback, too. He's talking quickly, like this power is a runaway train he's struggling to keep ahold of.

Aaron nods, his eyes manic. He pushes the flash button again. "It's on an incline. Like a hill."

"And roads?" Nuala interjects. "Landmarks?"

"No. No roads," Aaron answers. "It's all overgrown. Long grass. Nettles. Those yellow flowers."

"Gorse?" Nuala suggests.

"Huh?"

She goes to the books lined up on the windowsill and pulls out *Ireland's Wild Plants*. "Long weedy-looking things, yellow petals," she says, flipping to a page and showing him.

Aaron nods. Lily takes a look at the page, too. "OK, where are they?"

Aaron snaps the flash again. "Bottom right. Actually, the whole bottom of the photo, scattered, except for the very left-hand corner."

"What's there?" Lily says, taking her art case out, trying to find yellow.

"A fence. Wire fencing. The kind you put around a building site."

We go on like that for an hour. Aaron snapping, Lily being the visual stenographer. Roe in steady concentration, too focused to speak. Nuala taking out reference books, aerial survey maps, travel guides from twenty years ago. What began as squiggles and shapes emerges as a real drawing. A recognizable landscape.

I keep expecting one of them to ask for a break. Fiona, Manon, and I try to offer snacks or cups of tea, but we end up just watching. Useless, but fascinated.

Finally, Aaron flops down into a chair. "There," he says. "That's it. That's as close as we're going to get, I think."

We each step back, surveying the bedsheet like it's a fresco.

"A fake castle," Fiona murmurs.

"It's hideous," Manon adds flatly.

Nuala starts nodding. "A Celtic folly. Maeve, get another round of teas in."

I start collecting mugs. "What's a Celtic folly? Is that another Irish mythology thing? Like the Housekeeper?"

Nuala actually spit-takes the last of her tea. "No," she laughs. "Nooo, not a mythological thing. Very much a 'humans are idiots' thing."

We all look at her, dumbfounded.

"Christ." She rolls her eyes. "Sometimes I forget that I hang around with teenagers. Right. So, you know the financial crash? 2008?"

Only Fiona and Aaron look fully confident. "I've heard *of* it," I say defensively.

"After the crash, there were all these luxury hotels that were partly completed and ran out of investor funding. So these big behemoths were left to rot, often in the middle of nowhere, because they were planning on tourism booms that never happened. This"—Nuala points to the sheet—"is a failed hotel. I'd bet my house on it."

Fiona nods. "My mum has told me about them. Spooky." She whistles sharply, and Paolo flies down from his fridge perch. "You OK, pal? Can you see that drawing?"

The bird observes the drawing, rotating his head to different angles, like his body is a lens trying to focus.

The two of them fall into a silent communication, and every few seconds Fiona murmurs something affectionate in Tagalog. She speaks to him very softly, like baby talk, like how she must have been spoken to when she was a small child. She opens the window, and Paolo flies off into the night.

"He gets it," she says, closing it again.

"You're teaching him your mother tongue?" Manon says, sounding impressed by Paolo's existence for the first time.

"I don't know, it just comes out naturally. I'm a bit like his mother, I guess."

"He's your familiar," Nuala says fondly. "It's a special thing."

"I wish I had a familiar," Lily and I both say at once, sounding like petulant children.

"I'm your familiar," Roe says, putting an arm around my shoulder.

"Oh, we're familiar all right."

Lily puts her hands over her ears. "Can we not? I thought we avoided that conversation pretty well, no?"

We managed not to say a thing about the fight, the white eyes, the rocking scaffolding. The tension between Roe and Aaron, which hinges at least partly on me and therefore would embarrass them both. It's only later that night, when I wake up after a dream about blindness, do I wonder whether we should have avoided it.

6

I FORGET TO CHECK FOR LORNA McKEON
the next day in class. The dream woke me up at three a.m., and then
I couldn't get back to sleep for an hour. I log on late and cranky, and
with the dream in fragments. The whole day gets away from me then:
I can't concentrate, can't remember what homework I've done or not
done, what test prep I said I'd do. It takes the whole afternoon to
piece the dream back together, but this is what I end up with:

I'm in a house. An old house. It is genuinely old, not fake old
like the Lodge, so I know it's not a vision about the Children. It's
dirty. Every surface has a drink on it. A wine goblet forgotten on a
mantelpiece, a teacup left to grow mold on an end table. Everything
is beautiful and weary, like it's the night after a party. There's a card
table in the center of the room, but with playing cards, not tarot.
Kings and Queens stuck to Twos and Fours, all grime, no order.

I hear a noise. I turn around. There are people, but I can't make
them out because my vision is blurring, and then my sight is gone. I
can still hear people, feel the edges of tables, the plushness of the rug
under my feet. It's a feeling of flailing.

Lily phones the minute I close my laptop. She doesn't really text.
Every so often in the group chat she'll smash a few weird emojis just
to show she's alive and agrees or disagrees, but usually she calls.

"Hey," she says. "Can I come over? Can I use your bathroom?"

"You want to come over to use my bathroom?"

"Is that a problem?"

"No, I guess not."

"Great, I'll invite Fiona, too."

I'm puzzled. "Does she need the toilet, too?"

"No, why would she?" And she hangs up.

Fi arrives before Lily does, and we eat toasted scotch pancakes with thick slabs of Kerrygold butter. She's just as confused by Lily's summit as I am. It's only when we're on our third pancake that I remember.

"Hey," I nudge. "You know that girl Lorna?"

Fi is licking melted butter off her hand. "Lorna McKeon?"

"What's she like?"

"Quiet? And, uh . . . organized?" She takes a bite. "Why?"

"I don't know. I have a feeling. She was missing yesterday."

She thinks. "She was missing today, too. There's only six of us in physics. She wasn't there." Fiona eyes me thoughtfully. "You don't think . . . ?"

"The Lodge? I don't know. We literally just learned about it, so maybe now I'm just, like, hyperaware of people not being where they should be."

"The Lodge is the hammer, and now everything looks like a nail, that kind of thing?"

"Yeah, I guess."

Lily arrives, marching through the front door with the smell of winter on her, a supermarket carrier bag swinging from her arm.

"Yo," she says, sounding furious. "So, I guess we *are* being watched."

She takes a copy of the *Kilbeg Evening Star* out of the bag and slams it on the kitchen table. The Christmas tree quivers slightly at the force of her.

The newspaper is already folded open to the relevant page. It's a feature on "The Witches of St. Bernie's": me, Fiona, and Lily.

There are quotes from anonymous classmates, and a rundown of the strange events of the last year. The events as they are known to the public, anyway. It begins with me, and the tarot. Then Lily's disappearance in February, followed by her strange reappearance a month later. The article refers to The Chokey throughout. Always in scare quotes, as if it's a place we went to choke people.

Then the fire, Sister Assumpta's death, the strange will she left behind bequeathing her property to the troublesome Maeve Chambers—the failing student who has been variously accused of witchcraft, bullying, and downright stupidity. And who, crucially, was there when Sister Assumpta died.

You have to admit, it's a pretty compelling story.

Worst of all, there are photos of us. Complete with little text boxes about our "traits." All our school photos have been used. My picture is horrible. My hair is huge and frizzy, an oily shine on my forehead and nose. Lily looks completely checked out, like she hasn't even seen the photographer, her eyes half-closed. Fiona, predictably, looks amazing. Huge glowing white smile. Bright brown laughing eyes.

LILY O'CALLAGHAN, 17
— **Talented artist**
— **"She had a crush on me!"**
— **Pisces!**
— **Disappeared last February for a month**

FIONA BUTTERSFIELD, 17

— Aspiring actress

— Taurus!

— "Was always nice to everyone . . . until she wasn't . . ."

— Irish father / Mother immigrated from the Philippines in 2003

MAEVE CHAMBERS, 17

— The ringleader

— Chambers began reading for classmates before Lily's disappearance

— "A real cow"

— Sagittarius!

"Who gave you this, Lil?"

"A girl in Youth Orchestra. They went crazy over it. They all wanted me to sign their copies."

"They all had a copy?"

"Yeah, it's a free paper. There was a big stack of them left in the hall we practice in."

"Oh, god, Lil, I'm sorry. That sounds shit."

"It *was* shit!" She slaps the paper for emphasis, rattling the table. "I'm trying really hard, you know? To be a person, be a body, be a thing that dies. Even though it feels, like, completely freakish and unfair. And when things like this happen it just feels so much *more* freakish."

Fiona and I each put a hand on her shoulder, making quick, concerned eye contact with each other. It's so hard when Lily gets upset like this. I wish Hallmark had cards that said "I'm Sorry You're No Longer a River."

"Hey," I say, trying to find humor in the whole thing, "I wonder who called me a cow."

"Might be a shorter list if you consider who *doesn't* have a reason to call you a cow," Fiona says, elbowing me.

"OK, bitch!"

"Hey, at least no one's citing your parents' immigration history," Fi says, examining the piece. "This is so screwed up."

"Absolutely FUBAR," I agree. "Sorry, Fi."

I turn to Lily. "Why did you want to use my bathroom? Are we doing a spell or something?"

Lily reaches into the carrier bag and takes out a bottle of bleach and a bottle of blue hair dye. "Sort of."

·) ❭ ● ❬ (·

"Right," Fi says, gathering Lily's fair hair to the nape of her neck, "are you sure?"

"Yes."

I'm sitting on the edge of the tub with Paolo, and Fiona looks more nervous than Lily does.

"Can you make it grow back if you mess it up, Fi?" I ask, before adding, "Not that you *would* mess it up."

"Uh, maybe?" Fi says.

"Just do it," Lily says to her reflection.

Fiona gathers the hair again and swipes through it with the scissors in one clean movement. Six inches of hair comes away clean in her hand, a ponytail without a pony. We all look at it in silence, remembering Heather, remembering the tea bags she saved from each cup to drain my magic, remembering Fiona's eyelash and handwriting in her journal. The evening in Nuala's bathroom, when Fiona rolled down her tights and told us through tears that her gift had begun to cease, but that her self-harm had not.

I told Fiona to go speak to Heather. We so badly needed therapy after the ritual. Miss Banbury. What a genius construction. The right thing at the right time. A sympathetic ear that was sucking us both dry.

We all say the same thing at once.

"Burn it."

We put Lily's hair in the plastic shopping bag that the dye came in, ready to be burned later, and Fiona starts layering on the bleach. I inspect the newspaper article again.

"This is them," I say. "This is the Children."

"You think they *wrote* it?" Fiona asks disbelievingly.

"I don't know. We already know they have connections everywhere, and that they're watching us. Maybe they didn't write it, but maybe they can influence the people who do. Or the owners of the paper, or something."

"What makes you so sure that we're not just . . . a very compelling human-interest story?"

"This is burning," Lily interrupts. "Is it supposed to burn?"

"A little, yes."

"It doesn't mention Heather Banbury, right? Because Dorey knows if people go poking around about Heather, they'll end up at her eventually."

"Right." Fiona nods. "So why would they plant this story about us, then?"

"To discredit us," Lily replies. "So if we come forward with anything, there's already a narrative of us being murderous weirdos."

"Jesus, I hadn't even *thought* of that," I say, so exhausted that I lie down in the empty tub. "This makes me want to sell the stupid school and move us all to Fiji."

"That's literally what the Children want you to do," Fiona says. "Pass over the showerhead. Lily, lean your head back over the sink."

I pass her the long metal snake of the showerhead. "I know that's what they want me to do, but I can still *dream*."

My phone buzzes. Roe.

You at home?

"Roe's coming over," I say while texting back. "Full house of O'Callaghans."

I sit up, watching Fiona rinse Lily's now yellow-white hair. "The other night," I say carefully. "Roe and Aaron went blind."

"What do you mean they *went blind*?"

"Like, they lost their sight."

"For how long?"

"Like, a minute."

The girls don't have a chance to respond because Roe crashes up the stairs hollering something about being a rock star. He bursts through the door, looking drunk already.

"Oh wow, bathroom orgy!" he proclaims. "What the shit?"

"We're dyeing Lily's hair," I reply. "Now that we're famous."

He looks confused. "Huh? Since when are you famous? I'm the famous one."

"What?"

Roe holds up an issue of *Hot Press*. "Single of the Week, baby!"

We all go nuts. Roe's got his own carrier bag, only this one is full of cava. He's got three bottles, and the first one gets utterly lost to drenching us all like Formula 1 drivers.

"Oh, my god, Fi, this won't mess with the bleach, will it?" Lily says, holding up a strand of soaked yellow hair.

"No." Fi laughs. "Sit back down, I'll paste some blue on."

"Single of the Week," I say, marveling at the tiny review that might just change Roe's life. "Roe, this is huge."

"Huge," he agrees, happily slugging from the bottle. "It can be seen from space. Wait, what were you guys talking about?"

We explain, while the blue hair dye sets, about the Witches of St. Bernadette's. Roe examines the newspaper wincingly.

"Wow," he says flatly. "Way to steal my thunder."

I don't dare tell him what I'm thinking, and what Fiona and Lily must be thinking also. If the Children were responsible for that piece in the *Kilbeg Evening Star*, could they be behind the piece in *Hot Press*, too? One is a local paper, and the other is a national magazine. One article is a deliberate attack on us; the other is a few sentences about an indie rock single. What would they have to gain from printing a rave of Small Private Ceremony?

Fracturing, I suppose. They've seen how our powers can merge, and we're getting better at it all the time. Roe and Aaron tracing their location, just by fusing their gifts together. We are undoubtedly stronger together. Why *wouldn't* they try to split us up?

The more attention SPC gets, the more gigs they do, the likelihood of us losing Roe increases. But Roe, having been almost lost, surely can't be mislaid again.

Can he?

We all marvel at Lily's new hair. Which, despite Fiona's reluctance to dye it, actually looks pretty great. Lily looks impish, full of pretty mischief, and can't seem to believe her luck.

"Can you believe it?" she says, admiring her reflection. "Don't I look incredible?"

"I agree," I say. "You look incredible."

"All right," Fiona says, admiring her handiwork, "I gotta get home. Mum's doing fajitas. Are we still going to this thing tomorrow night?"

This "thing" is Holly McShane's Christmas party, a supposedly annual event that Fiona has been to and that Lily and I had never heard of. We're invited this year, though. There's a sense that the remaining St. Bernadette's girls are bonded by trauma, or at least by our own rarity. We're the last dodos, the final graduating class. It's a sentiment that trumps cliques or vague ideas of popularity. Or at least it did before the article.

"I don't know," I say, glancing down at the newspaper again. "I mean, after this? I don't know if I want to party with people who are ratting us out to the press."

"Calm down, Lady Di," Fiona replies. "They were probably made-up quotes. Or if they weren't made up, taken out of context. Give them more credit than that." She looks at the time. "All right, it's fajita o'clock, I'm gone."

Lily ends up going with her, admitting that fajitas are one of the few things that being human can offer that being a river cannot. Then it's just me and Roe, drenched in cava and blue hair dye and sitting in the tub.

"Read it again," Roe says. "Read it out loud this time."

"OK." I grin, taking a long slug from the bottle. "'Small Private Ceremony is an eclectic punk-rock foursome from Kilbeg who first attracted attention touring with Honor Own earlier this year. Their first single, "Wolf Girl," is a full-throated, foot-stomping anthem that asserts itself as both a classic ode to young love and a breathless story of transformation.'"

I look up from the magazine, full of glee. "I *told* you they would love it."

"You did. Read on."

"'The single, paired with the mischievous yet defiant B-side, "Mind Your Business Glinner," firmly places Small Private Ceremony within the Irish queer music scene. Special mention should go to Roe O'Callaghan, whose voice rings out like a velvet buzz saw—a little Luke Kelly, a little Dolores O'Riordan. If "Wolf Girl" is anything to go by, they might just be the next great Irish vocalist.'"

I put the magazine on my chest. "Babe," I whisper, "they called you the *next great Irish vocalist!*"

"Maeve," Roe whispers back, with a smile so big I think it might be generating electricity, "they called me *they.*"

I pick it up again and scan the last line. "Oh yeah!"

There's a small silence, a happy silence, and I know it's my job to let Roe fill it.

"It feels really *good.*"

"What does it feel like?"

"It feels like . . . like graduation. Like I'm ready? Ready for . . . I don't know. Ready."

"To do the pronoun thing?"

I immediately want to hit myself on the head for referring to it as "the pronoun thing." Thankfully, Roe just nods.

"Yeah. To do the pronoun thing."

"Oh, my god," I say, and I rest my head on the cold enamel of the bathtub, looking at this person. The winter sunlight falls through the small circular window in the bathroom, shooting a prism of color across the tiles, and I can see them for all their vivid multiplicity.

"Congratulations," I say shyly. "Should we toast?"

"Yeah," they say, holding up the cava. "To, uh, self-acceptance and self-knowledge."

"And Spanish champagne."

"Yeah. To self-acceptance and self-knowledge and Spanish champagne."

We kiss, and it's the Roe I grew up with, and the Roe I almost died with, and the Roe the world gets to see onstage. All of them, all together. All at once.

7

IF ORDINARY SCHOOL WERE STILL ON, THE last day of winter term would be spent watching movies, exchanging stupid little gifts, and gossiping. There would be house parties, and shopping trips for glittery clothes, and hot chocolates in town. Instead, school ends the next day after yet another conspicuous absence from Lorna McKeon, and an email from Miss Harris.

Well done, girls, on finishing out this term under exceptional circumstances. Please enjoy the break, and I will see you all in the New Year.

I close my laptop, and school is done. All that is left of my academic career is the three months between January and April, and then study month, and then the Leaving Cert, and then nothing.

Our homework journals have a directory of class phone numbers printed at the back, all of them landlines. I find the McKeon number easily, but I dawdle for a long time before dialing it. We are, after all, not friends.

Eventually, I give in. The phone rings a long time before anyone picks up. Which doesn't mean anything, I remind myself. Sometimes I forget that we have a landline, and I have to go looking for it when it rings.

"Hello?"

It's a man's voice. A dad voice.

"Hello, is Lorna there?" I ask, as naturally as possible.

"Who is calling?"

"This is . . ." I stall, remembering the newspaper again. "Veronica Talbot."

I cannot believe that this is the fake name my brain reached for. It's so obviously, patently fake that I can feel Mr. McKeon's disbelief echoing down the line.

"It's Ronnie," I say, trying to recover. "From school."

Ronnie? From school?

"Lorna isn't here," Mr. McKeon says bluntly, fully convinced that I am trying to waste his time. I hear another voice then, a woman in the background. A dim "Who's that? Someone for Lorna?"

Mr. McKeon half covers the receiver. "Some silly girl asking for Lorna."

And then, "Well, she might *know* something?"

My blood chills. So Lorna's not sick, then. I hear the bash of plastic, the sound of hands. Then the woman's voice.

"Hello? Are you a friend of Lorna's?"

"Uh," I hesitate. "We just go to school together. We're working on a project and she hasn't been online the last few days, so I thought I would check on her."

Mrs. McKeon seems to realize that I don't know anything new and suddenly becomes strangely defensive. "She's staying with family," she says abruptly. "I'll tell her you called."

And she hangs up. It's all very jarring, and I sit for a minute feeling queasy and strange, unsure the conversation even happened.

I text Nuala.

Lorna McKeon. Girl from our school. I think you need to add her to the list.

Nuala takes a long time responding. Then:

She's the second person I've added today.

My skin prickles with an itchy tightness, an irritable dread. A sense that things are happening but not in an order I can understand. The Children are pulling strings so subtly that I'm having trouble differentiating between what is a string and what is just atmosphere. I remember Fiona's comment about when you have a hammer, everything looks like a nail.

Lorna could be doing anything. She could have run off with a boyfriend, for all I know. The newspaper article could just be a human-interest piece, if a somewhat tacky one. Roe's single review is probably just evidence of Roe being talented.

This, I realize, is in many ways worse than being drained and poisoned and bewitched. At least those things were obvious. This is just the slow unwinding of circumstance, of things that feel fairly close to ordinary.

I ask my dad to drive me to Fiona's so that we can all get ready together. He jumps at the chance to be needed and chatters to me happily in the car.

"Everyone's back tomorrow," he says. "Abbie's flying in at lunchtime, the boys are driving down in the evening. Jo says she'll come back tomorrow, too."

I bother my fingers with my teeth.

"You all right, Mae?"

I hesitate. Sometimes it's helpful to throw them a bone, something they can manage. Maybe Lorna is one of those things.

"There's a girl in my class," I begin, "who hasn't been around the last few days, and when I called her house to see where she is, her parents were really weird with me."

He nods. "Maybe she was too sick to come to the phone."

"No, she wasn't sick. She was not there. They tried to see if I knew anything, and when I didn't, they hung up."

"I see," he says, nodding again. "Well, maybe it's a delicate situation. A family thing. People are still very private about things. There's an Irish instinct for hushing things up, I think, that we're not quite over."

When we get to Fiona's house, he gives me a half hug around the shoulders. "You'll stay safe, won't you? No talking to anyone strange."

"Do you think that's how people go missing?" I ask. "Because they talk to someone who's strange?"

He looks briefly mystified, like I am challenging him. I can tell that even my dad, my lovely, funny dad, still believes that girls who disappear must have done something to deserve it. Or not deserve it, but explain it.

I glance back at him through drizzle, his face already a blur.

Fiona's house is always the best place to get ready because her mum has the best clothes. Marie also takes it as a compliment to her everlasting good taste if we want to borrow anything, so she's always flinging clothes at me. The spare bedroom is loaded with her touring outfits from her own musician days.

"Maeve, take this," Marie says, handing me a pink cowboy shirt with red piping. "I wore it in the eighties, but I see these in the shops now. They're everywhere."

She's right, they are everywhere, and it looks great on me.

"Keep it," she says.

"No," I reply, feigning protest. "I couldn't."

"Shhh, of course you could. You already have. Let me press it first."

I wrestle the shirt off and give it to her, then sit in my bra on Fiona's bed.

"What are you guys getting for Christmas?" Lily suddenly asks once Fi's mum leaves. "From your parents, I mean."

"Money," Fiona says.

"Money," I repeat.

"Money." Lily nods. "I think I'm going to buy a tattoo gun."

"What?" I ask, astounded. "Why?"

"Well, they're only, like, seventy euro on eBay. And they don't look difficult to use. I've watched tutorials."

"No, but, I mean, why tattoos?"

She suddenly goes shy. "I went into a shop the other day," she says, "a tattoo shop. Just, you know, to look at the sample tattoos on the walls. It's a bit like going to an art gallery."

She says this like tattoos have been a private part of her life for some time now and she has chosen today to share the information. It's best not to jump on Lily too much when she gets into sharing mode. It comes rarely enough, so you just need to wait for her to tell you more.

"One time, I was in there and the guy let me watch him tattoo someone. It was a big piece, a back tattoo, and he let me just pull up a stool and watch."

I try to prevent myself from asking "And when exactly did this happen?" so instead I just nod and say nothing.

"And you know, watching the ink flowing through the needle, and then it getting transferred onto the skin, and hearing the buzzing, I don't know, guys, I just . . . It made me feel so calm."

"How?" Fiona asks.

"It kind of reminds me that the good thing about being alive is that you can always change. Even if it's something small."

"That's so cool," Fiona and I both say, clearly relieved that Lily has found something to like about being a person.

"And . . . Uh, I gave myself a stick-and-poke."

"A *what*?"

"A stick-and-poke. Like a homemade tattoo. With one of my dad's clean insulin needles. And ink."

At this, she kneels down on the ground and rolls up her black pleather leggings, exposing her white calf. At first, I have no idea what I'm supposed to be looking at. Then I peer more closely and see a little black speck that I first mistake for a freckle.

:D

And suddenly Fiona and I are screaming laughing. There's something so unbelievably funny about Lily, the blue-haired Buddha that she is, tattooing herself with a little open-mouthed smile emoji. Lily, thank god, laughs, too.

"I know it's silly," she says, cheeks bright red. "But, you know, it's very hard for me to like things. And this is a little reminder. That things are . . . nice."

I sling my arm around her, my oldest friend, and kiss her head. "I know, love, I know."

"I want one," Fiona says. "In the same place."

"Me too."

We say this meaning we want one eventually, but Lily smiles mischievously and reaches for her bag. "Well, I've got the stuff with me. The needles and ink, I mean. I just need gloves and sanitizer."

Fiona's eyes widen. "Oh, my god. Wait there."

She disappears and comes back with the cowboy shirt, rubber gloves and sanitizer hidden underneath it. "Mum is on dinner now. She won't come up again."

We're buzzing with this new plot, which is dangerous without being the mortal danger we're used to and falls firmly under the umbrella of teenage rebellion. It always feels like we're playacting when we do stuff like this: the kind of stuff that other teenagers might do.

Lily washes her hands, snaps on the gloves, and starts scratching at our skin with ink-soaked needles. It doesn't hurt very much. It feels like a sharp fingernail scratching hard. Uncomfortable, but not necessarily painful.

We line up our ankles, our stupid :D tattoos all grinning away moronically at each other. We cannot, for the life of us, stop laughing.

"If we were real witches," I say to Fiona, "we'd all be getting pentagram tattoos."

"Or tarot symbols. Wands. Cups."

"But no," I reply. "Just these dumb little guys."

Fiona shrieks with joy, catching sight of her tattoo again in the full-length wardrobe mirror.

"I love these dumb little guys!"

And despite everything else that's going on, it's not a bad way to begin the school holidays.

8

THE CHRISTMAS PARTY IS BEING THROWN by Holly McShane, a very beautiful girl who lives approximately four minutes away from me, but whom I have nonetheless never really spoken to. Maybe she got her tarot read by me back in February. I don't remember. If she did, the reading was probably as sweet as she is, and hence not memorable. In fact, I bet I can guess what her reading was: lots of low-numbered Cups—Aces, Twos, Threes—maybe a Sun major arcana thrown in for good measure. Lots of unity and friendship, gentle romances and positive outlooks.

Holly answers the door, and it takes her a moment to recognize Lily. "Your hair!" she says, clapping her hands together. "I love it. Did your mum freak?"

"I haven't really asked her opinion," Lily says. It comes out in her usual docile voice, but in this context it sounds quite deadpan and off-the-cuff. And, well, cool.

"Wow," Holly says, genuinely impressed. "Well, come in. Fiona"—she grabs Fiona's arm—"how *are* you?"

Fiona slips easily into the role she played for so long, before we were all friends: Girl Who Everyone Likes. Which is different, I think, from being a Popular Girl. Popular is a caste. Being a girl who everyone likes is a thing you have to do every day. She asks questions, smiles a lot, says things that are on the safe side of funny. I'm in awe of her when she's like this. I wish I could do it, too.

"Hang on," Fi says, looking down at her phone. "I've been getting missed calls from a weird number all day."

"From who?" I ask.

Her phone starts ringing again.

"Hello?" she says, and then frowns. "Sorry, I can't hear you. I'm just going to . . ."

Fiona looks to Holly, who motions up the stairs to a room where she can take the phone call. Fi disappears, and I'm left with a vague sense of unease that the call is somehow Bad.

"Everyone's outside, or in the conversation pit," Holly says, gesturing to the couches in the floor.

"The conversation . . . pit," Lily repeats.

"You can leave your drinks on the table or in the fridge," she says, waving her hand toward the kitchen. There vodka bottles, cans of Bulmers, and a bottle of Southern Comfort stand like girls waiting to be asked to dance. There are a few alco-pops, although I'm surprised to see them, as I thought alco-pops were for fourteen-year-olds and hence beneath our dignity. The whole table looks like a shrine where Lily and I are expected to produce offerings.

I take a bottle of Malibu from out of my bag, which Jo agreed to buy for me because "it wouldn't get a flea drunk," and pour myself a glass with Coke and ice. Lily hasn't brought anything. I should have probably told her, but it's been so long since I've been to a house party that I've forgotten some of the rules. I wasn't very good at them, even when I used to go.

We're not left alone for very long. A call comes from the conversation pit.

"Maeve! Lily!"

Becky Fogarty, another girl too pretty for me to have ever really spoken to, is sitting with Holly, her boyfriend, and his friends. I recognize the boyfriend from Roe's year. He must be in college now. We go and sit down.

"This is Fionn," Holly says, stroking her boyfriend's back. "And Des and Mark and Fintan. This is Maeve and . . ."

"You're the fire starter, twisted fire starter," laughs Des, quoting the Prodigy. "I saw the paper."

"We *all* did," Holly says. "It was so stupid. No one was scared of any of that witchcraft stuff. Everyone knew it was a bit of fun. Obviously none of us talked to the papers."

"Oh yeah, no," says Becky. "I wouldn't talk to a *free* paper."

I'm not even sure if this is a joke.

"My dad is in property," Fionn says, "and he says that building could go for three, four million. Easily."

A few girls come in from the back garden, smelling of smoke and cold.

"Four million *what*?" someone calls out.

"Euro," Holly calls back. "What would you do with it?"

Becky has her answer immediately. "Island. In the Caribbean."

"I don't think four mil is island money," Mark says dryly. "It's not even archipelago money."

Mark was one of the more tolerable boys who used to hang around Niamh and Michelle when I was in their gang. The boys used to call him "Shrek"—pretty unfairly, I thought. He's very tall, and wide like a rugby player.

"Well, a nice *house* in the Caribbean, then," Becky says. "And obviously, I'd give some to charity."

"How much?"

She thinks. "Ten grand?"

"Ten grand is all you're giving? Out of four million?"

There's nothing technically wrong with this conversation, but it has the shared attributes of being both quite boring and lightly offensive. This isn't a lottery win, after all. This is an arbitrary sum of money devised from the fact that a woman—a woman that the girls, at least, have all known since we were thirteen—is now dead.

"Is Lorna here?" I ask, looking around. "Lorna McKeon?"

The girls who came in from their cigarette break are now all perched on the back of the sofas, their bodies framing the boys like angels in a Renaissance painting.

"I didn't invite the *whole* year," Holly says defensively.

"But you did invite *us*?" Lily says, mystified.

"Lorna's gone mad," Becky says dismissively.

"What do you mean?" I ask.

"Oh, she got deep into all that stuff last term," she says, waving her hand toward the kitchen like it's a stand-in for the past. "You know, when those weird virginity boys showed up?"

"The Chastity Brothers," Lily and I say together.

"Yeah, I mean, everyone knew pretty quick that they were, like, a Catholic culty thing, but she started dating one of them."

This is the first time that anyone outside of our group has brought up the Chastity Brothers. We assumed that everyone had forgotten about them, that the strange draining magic that the Children inflicted on us all had effectively bleached out their memories as well as their sense.

I can see Becky perking up from the attention. Not just from me and Lily, but the other girls, too. She had obviously assumed that any information about Lorna McKeon, an essentially boring person, would be useless. The surprise discovery that it has value has straightened her shoulders, added bass to her voice.

"We used to get the same bus," she says grandly. "And she had two SIM cards. I used to see her swapping them out on the bus and texting really furiously. So eventually I asked her what it was all about, and she said she had a boyfriend, and that her parents didn't approve because he was older. I said how much older? And she said four years. I was like, wow, Lorna, nice going, where did you meet him? And she said she met him at school."

There's a chorus of responses, of "Wow" and "No way" and "Which one?" and "Was it the hot one?" and "Which one did you think was the hot one?"

"It was probably like catnip to someone like her, because her parents were religious and strict anyway," Becky continues. "And I guess when your parents are religious but your boyfriend is *more* religious, it probably feels, like, fine to lie to them. She got a lot more Jesus-y when she was going out with him, though."

"So what now? She's missing?" Holly asks.

"I didn't say she was missing. Who said she was missing?"

"She wasn't at school this week," I reply. "And I rang her house, and her parents were cagey as hell."

Becky shrugs. "Maybe she ran off with him, then."

The conversation descends into gossip, spurious observations about Lorna McKeon's character, and pondering whether or not she and the Jesus-y boyfriend were having sex. "If you're going to run off with your older boyfriend and *not* shag him," Holly says, "it kind of defeats the purpose, no?"

I mull this all over, catching Lily's eye as we silently follow the same train of thought. It's clear to me now that Lorna is at the Lodge. Perhaps her parents even let her go, if relations between them had disintegrated so much.

Eventually conversation moves on. Someone asks us what we're planning to do after school, and Lily volunteers information for the first time that evening.

"Tattoos," she says. "I'm gonna learn how to do tattoos."

There's an immediately warm reception, a glowing sense of gratitude from the party, as if Lily has just put all their minds at ease.

Yes, of course, the blue hair, the weird clothes, I get it now, I see where you might fit in, "And you were always good at drawing weren't you?" *yes, I can see that for her, poor old Lily O'Callaghan, she might be all right, coming out of herself a bit more, god love her.*

We somehow become the center of the conversation pit, Lily rolling up her leggings to show everyone her stick-and-poke.

"That's stupid," Des says. "It's barely even a tattoo."

"Do you have a tattoo?" Lily asks mildly, but once again it comes out like she couldn't give a shit, and he looks stupid for challenging her. Everyone says, "Oooooh" and I can actually feel Lily's social capital increase.

"Did it hurt?" Holly asks.

"Yes," Lily responds. "But that's sort of the point."

Everyone looks unsure, and Lily explains herself.

"Like, lots of things hurt, but you're not prepared for them, and the surprise makes it worse. Having a painful thing for a few minutes, but then you get a cool drawing on your body at the end of it . . . I don't know, I just like it."

Everyone nods and looks at one another, and someone laughs and says, "Deep." But they actually *do* think it's quite deep. Or unusual, anyway. People are charmed by Lily. I wonder if everyone's reached a new level of maturity now that we're so close to graduating. No one wants to play silly games, no one has the energy for bullying. They're just interested in her.

"All right!" Holly puts her drink down with such force on the glass table that a splash of Coke spills and gathers around the glass. She doesn't wipe it, or notice. "I want one."

Everyone laughs, but Holly starts rubbing her hands together to indicate how game she is. "No, I'm serious! Lily. Let's do it."

I nudge Lily. "You don't have to do this, you know."

Lily just shrugs, but gives me a small, almost nervous smile. "No, I want to. The practice would be good. And . . . I like it."

"Giving tattoos?"

"Yeah. And, well, having a thing, I suppose."

A jolt of anxiety surges through me, like I've just sat on an electric fence. I know exactly how seductive having a thing can be. Having a thing was how I ended up being St. Bernadette's performing tarot monkey. Having a thing is how I ended up accidentally calling the Housekeeper.

But Lily looks happy, and like she's not taking all of this too seriously, so I just sit back and let my friend do her thing.

Holly wants it on her foot. "I want the number thirteen," she says. "It's my lucky number."

Becky doesn't let this go easily. "Thirteen is Taylor Swift's lucky number. That's Taylor Swift's thing."

"She doesn't own it," Holly says defiantly.

"She kind of *does*."

"Becky," Mark says sharply.

"Whatever," Holly says. "I want it."

Lily puts her gloves on and cleans Holly McShane's foot with a baby wipe and some antiseptic. It's weird, because I know this is part of the process, but effectively what's happening is that the former outcast of St. Bernadette's is washing the feet of the most popular girl in school. It feels like something from the Bible.

"Are you ready?" Lily says. "It will hurt a bit."

"I'm ready," Holly says, and all the girls hold their breath. Lily scratches at Holly's skin, and Holly yelps.

"Should I stop?" Lily asks.

"No," says Holly, steeling herself. "It's only small, and it won't take long, will it?"

There's a nervous, impressed rumbling in the room. People are halfway between horrified and desperately wanting to copy Holly. Fionn says he'll get a matching one, a 31 for her 13.

"Because I'm her opposite," he says, holding her around the waist, his head lolling on his girlfriend's shoulder.

"Do you mean her reverse?" I ask.

"Yeah, it's the same."

Fiona reappears as I'm observing Lily's handiwork. She looks different: shaken, excited, like she's taken some drug that has only just kicked in. Which, at this party, is not impossible.

"What's up?" I ask, holding her shoulder, looking steadily into her shining eyes.

"Can I talk to you?" she whispers, and as we leave the room she casually swipes a bottle of vodka and tucks it under her skirt.

All the bedrooms are taken so we end up sitting on the landing of the stairs.

"Who was that?" I ask. "On the phone?"

"It was, uh . . ."

I don't know what I'm expecting her to say. The police, telling her that her family is dead? The Irish lottery, to say she has won the rollover?

"It was a producer. A TV producer. They're casting for a Netflix show about witches and they saw my picture in the paper."

I blink. I can't take this all in. A *Netflix* show? "Like, a documentary?"

"No, like a fictional show. It's called *The Coven*."

"I'm sorry, *The Coven*?"

"It's about, like, a family of witches, and they're looking for someone to play the ward, Lita."

"I'm sorry, the *ward*?"

"Like a person who is not family but who lives with them. You know, a ward."

I am baffled by this. "They saw your picture in the paper about you being a witch," I say slowly, "and they want you to play a fake one."

Her face reddens. "Well, they looked me up online, after that. They read that I wanted to be an actor, and they saw some videos of me doing *Othello* on YouTube, and you know, they thought I seemed good, or whatever."

"I mean, you are good. You're great. So what now?"

"They want to meet," she says. "Tomorrow. At one."

"Tomorrow?"

"I said I'd meet them at the bubble-tea place. You need to come with me."

"Me? Why?"

"Because if this is an insane trap by the Children to suddenly whisk me off to the Lodge or something, it would be helpful to have a telepath in the meeting." She breaks off, pauses. "It's weird, I've spent my whole life dreaming about this kind of insane twist of fate, and now that it's here all I can think is this feels a little too convenient."

I feel an immense sense of relief that Fiona is already suspicious, because I know that if I had suggested this to her, she would have been mortally wounded.

"OK, I'll come," I reply. "I'll let you know if anything suspicious is going on."

"Great. Thanks."

"And Fi?"

"What?"

"Congratulations, you talented bitch!"

Fiona suddenly lights up. "This isn't really *happening*, is it?"

"It could be, dude. It could be." I pause. "*The Coven.*"

"*The Coven*!!!"

We let out long, screaming laughs, falling backward on the landing, our giggles rising to the ceiling. We pass the bottle of vodka back and forth, and we are suddenly crying with how funny this is: the fact that Fiona, a real witch, will be playing a fake witch on TV. We wonder if they will let her bring Paolo, and whether Paolo will have a separate bird-size trailer. And after a few minutes, the laughter dies away, and she's contemplative.

"There's just one thing, though," she says, taking another nip from the bottle.

"Go on, tell me."

"Oh, Maeve. Come on. You know. I know you know."

"Is it Manon?"

She nods solemnly. "It's Manon." Fiona is silent for a moment, and then makes a sound like she's just burst into flames. "She's just so *nice*! Aggghhghgh! What if I go off to do this TV show and she leaves while I'm gone? I mean, she can't stay in Ireland forever."

"Are you going to tell her? That you feel this way?"

"What good would it do? I don't know if she feels the same way. Or whether she likes girls, or boys, or whoever."

"I mean, you're both the hottest people I've ever met. I feel like gender shouldn't even matter. It's just hotness coming together," I reply. "And she's not that old. She's the same age as Aaron."

Fiona cocks her eyebrow. "All right," she says. "That came quickly."

"What do you mean?"

"You and Aaron."

"What do you mean, *me and Aaron*?"

"Just . . . I don't know. You're two sensitives. It's a vibe. If you wanted to say something about him, I wouldn't tell anyone. Even Roe. I would never bring it up again if you don't want me to."

I know she's a little drunk, because she keeps reconfirming the conditions of her own secrecy. I think about it while she talks, and ask myself how I really feel. Because she's right. It is a vibe. And even though I never wrote that note to Aaron, he clearly thought it was real. I think about the physical pull I feel toward Roe, the craving to be touched, the frustration of not being kissed.

I don't feel that way about Aaron. But what I do feel is a certain fascination. A fascination that edges, sometimes, between disgust and a weird sort of admiration. He's the only person I know who worries about their own goodness and badness as much as I worry about my own.

There's a deep *pop* from outside, breaking my concentration.

"Oh, my god," Fiona says, getting up. "Fireworks."

I stand up and immediately feel the urge to pee. "I'll meet you out there. I need the loo."

When I come out a few minutes later the living room is empty. Everyone is on the back patio, trying to capture the fireworks on their phone cameras. And then I hear a soft giggle, and I realize that Lily is still with someone in the conversation pit. I pin myself to the side of the bookcase, instinctively knowing not to interrupt.

Her head is bent deep in concentration, scratching her needle over Mark's shoulder. The whole scene vibrates with intimacy, the tattoo she's giving Mark already carrying a different energy from the tattoo she gave me or Holly. I try to find a way out to the patio without being spotted and ruining her moment completely.

"I'm so glad you knew what the Scorpio symbol was," Mark says to her.

"Oh yeah," she answers, dipping her needle in the ink again. "I know them all."

"Scorpio is good, because it's an M shape," he continues. "M for Scorpio, M for Mark. Do you think that's good?"

"I mean, yeah," she answers. "You're a Scorpio, and your name is Mark. So."

He turns his head slightly. "Are you making fun of me?" he says softly. She pauses before responding.

"Would you mind?" she says. "If I was?"

There's a silence then. But it is not the sound of nothing. It is the sound of something very big, but something without words.

It is the sound of Lily's first kiss.

9

IT'S IMPOSSIBLE TO LEAVE THE ROOM WITH-
out making noise, and I can't hang out behind the bookcase forever,
so I just stride out and pretend like I haven't seen a thing.

"Maeve!" Lily says, sounding mortified.

"I didn't see anything!" I say loudly, and book it out the porch
door.

The fireworks are still going, and Fiona is clutching her drink,
head angled right at the sky. An explosion of fuchsia sparks lights up
her face, and I see that tears are streaking her cheeks. I put my arms
around her.

"You OK, pal?"

"Yeah," she says, squeezing me back. "I'm just a bit scared, is the
thing."

I nod, because yes, it seems scary. Not scary like the end of the
world, which we're used to. But scary because she's entering a *new*
world, the one Roe is already half in. The adult world.

We watch the fireworks together, not talking much. The sky is
so much like my mind whenever I start the Process that my brain
immediately starts imitating it. My mind clears, and the colors in the
sky are joined by the colors of all the people around me. Reds and

yellows and navy blues and bottle greens. All their secrets and anxieties flow into me, their family problems, their pets' names. I try not to be burdened by it. I try not to pay too much attention.

It's hard to be telepathic at a party.

·)) ● ((·

"Hey."

Lily's voice comes from behind me, and I turn to grin at her.

"Having a nice party?" I ask.

"Don't say *anything*."

"Under the mistletoe, are we?"

"Shut *up*."

When Lily first returned from the river, I thought she would never get back to who she was. And I was right. She didn't. She isn't the old Lily, the one I grew up with, the shy kid with the fantasy books. She's someone else, an evolution on an evolution. She's original and kind and witty and beautiful, and I feel my chest bursting with pride at having been the one to know her first.

Midnight comes and goes, and the temperature drops to below freezing. About fifteen of us end up on the trampoline in Holly's back garden. Shoeless, phones stuffed in cups, Christmas songs playing. Even wrapped in coats and blankets, I can still feel the dampness of the trampoline soaking through to my bum.

It's worth it, though, for this little moment. The only light is the stars and the orange glow of cigarettes. Lily and Mark don't make a move toward each other again, and I think: this fits. They're both private. Or, from what I know of Mark, he has always seemed to be. He'll get her number at the end of the night, and soon enough Lily and I will be on double dates together.

There's a flutter in the air, and I look up to see Paolo flapping his wings overhead. I nudge Fiona. He could have news about the Lodge.

"I'm going to walk around," I say. "Get some air."

"I'll come, too," Fi and Lily both say at once.

"If you're going to vom," Holly calls, "avoid the roses, will you?"

There's a stone birdbath at the end of the garden, more decorative than functional, but Paolo perches on it and waits for us. Fiona holds out her arm, and he flies to it like a trained hawk. Fi closes her eyes, strokes his inky feathers.

"Nothing yet," she says, opening them again. "But on the plus side, he has ruled out a lot of places."

"How is it taking so long?" I ask. "Surely there aren't that many fake castles in Kilbeg?"

"Paolo is a *bird*," Fiona says testily. "He doesn't know what a *castle* is, the way you and I do. He just sees shapes. He takes snapshots in his brain and shows them to me, and I tell him how close he is. Then he gets closer to the answer the more he rules stuff out."

"What snapshots does he have today?"

"Well. He's shown me a big Aldi."

"An Aldi? Christ, we're going to be at this all year."

"Hey, be patient with him."

"I don't know if we *can* be patient," I say. "We found out tonight that Lorna was going out with one of those Chastity boys. She's definitely gone to the Lodge."

Fiona bites her lip. "He's doing his best."

"I'm sure he is," Lily says, trying to sound diplomatic. "But . . . he *is* a bird."

"He's not just a bird," Fiona says fiercely. "He's sort of, well . . . He's part of me, too."

Lily and I look at each other silently, and then at Fiona. It's odd because this is usually how Fiona and I are when Lily talks about the river: a mute sense of trying to understand but not remotely understanding.

"I know it's going to sound mad," Fiona says, all too aware of the dynamic shift, "but he's the reason I stopped . . . you know."

She makes a vague sawing action at her arms.

I try not to look too shocked. I had thought Fiona had given up on hurting herself over a month ago, when Heather Banbury was still alive. I had no idea it had continued.

"It's not that I was doing it a *lot*," Fiona says urgently. "It's just, you know, after the funeral, things were so dark, and so tense. I needed"—she squeezes her eyes shut—"a release, or something. But then I saw that it hurt Paolo, too. And I couldn't do that to him.

"Anyway," she says briskly. "He'll find the Lodge. I know he will."

We walk back to the trampoline and climb through the black netting. My eyes take a second to readjust, but I see that two people are lying down now, taking up the space that the three of us briefly left by leaving.

It's Mark. Lily's first kiss, with Becky less than an hour later.

"Just what in the *hell* do you think you're doing?"

I'm screaming, suddenly. Why am I screaming? This is shitty behavior, but is it a screaming offense?

Mark suddenly comes to his senses and either remembers his Lily kiss or regrets his current one.

"Shit." Mark turns to Lily. "Sorry . . ." he says limply, and maybe if I were sober I would give him the benefit of the doubt and believe he really was sorry.

But I'm not sober. And he's not sorry.

"Lily *O'Callaghan*?" Becky says with complete disgust. "Mark, do you even know what she's *like*?"

I can feel something cooking in her throat, some long litany of horrible things about Lily, sins both real and imagined. Anything to distance herself from the fact that she kissed the same guy as Lily O'Callaghan, the class freak.

"Becky Fogarty," I snap, before she can even begin. "Do *you* even know that Holly and Fionn call you Becky Foghorn?"

The shock hits Becky like a hailstorm. "What?"

"That's not all," I continue, casting my mind back to the fireworks moment, when all their secrets fell down on me. "Becky Fuckface. Becky Full-of-Shit."

"*Maeve.*" Holly says it in one sharp in-breath, like she's reminding me that this is *her* party.

"Your friends don't even like you, Becky, so I wouldn't worry too much about Lily's reputation."

"Dude," Fiona says. "Cool it, that's enough."

"Why would you say that?" Becky asks, winded by the pain of it. "Why on earth—"

"Because you lie all the time, and you're loud," I finish. "Come on, guys, let's get out of here."

Lily and Fiona are transfixed, too stunned by this attack to move. I can feel everyone's eyes on me, the girls I barely know, the boys whose names I don't remember, all staring at me from behind the orange cherries of their lit cigarettes. This would be the time to stop. But I see Mark's stupid face locking eyes with another boy across the trampoline, a look of *these girls are nutters*, and I whirl on him.

"You would be so lucky to go out with Lily," I say.

"Maeve," Lily says, yanking my shoulder. "Stop."

"Enough reindeer games, Maeve," Holly says, desperately trying to reestablish order at what had previously been a very successful party. "Just leave. I can't believe I even invited you."

"Yeah," I spit back. "I can't believe you didn't invite that guy you're cheating on Fionn with."

Then I turn to a horrified Fionn, who has done nothing to me at all. "Hope you like your tattoo."

"You bitch," Holly snarls. "You've always been a bitch."

And then I slap her, hard, across the face. The whole thing happens in slow motion, like I'm watching a movie of someone else.

"Jesus *Christ*!" one of the boys yells.

Holly goes to hit me back, but her feet are unsteady on the trampoline and she falls forward. Suddenly her whole weight is on top of me.

At the corner of my vision I can see Lily, lit up by the moonlight, her hair beginning to produce static. Oh, god. Lily is about to light up Holly's back garden, and all to protect me. Because I was trying to protect her.

"Get *off*!" I scream, trying to shove Holly off me. It's all so stupid, like a wrestling ring, but all the same it is enough like the fire at the tennis courts to make me panic. The protective rage over Lily starts to mutate into something else, something stronger and intent on devouring its host.

I get an arm free and bring the heel of my hand to Holly's forehead. It doesn't make much impact, but her expression begins to change. The color flows out of her eyes, and a lens of cloudy white falls. Just like Roe. Just like Aaron.

Her scream is so loud that it summons a curious Paolo, who lands in the middle of the trampoline. Holly rolls over and everyone sees it. The glowing white irises, like cat's eyes on a dark road.

A deathly, deadly silence. And then screams.

"*What did you do?*"

"Holly! Holly! Holly!"

"Fucking Maeve Chambers. I knew we shouldn't have invited her."

Then, Holly blinks. Her eyes have returned to normal, but the damage has already been done. Lily's hair is crackling with static, her body coursing with electricity. Paolo is freaking out, swooping and landing, swooping and landing, making the impression that he's getting ready to peck someone's eyes out.

"Paolo!" Fiona screams. "Stop! Stop it!"

Paolo calms down, like a dog suddenly reminded of obedience school. That he has clearly taken this order from Fiona is even more chilling. Nice, normal Fiona. The girl who everyone likes.

"What the fuuuuuuuuuuu . . ."

"Fiona? Did you?"

"You have a bird? You were controlling the bird?"

"What *are* you?"

"So it's true, then? Jesus Christ."

All three of us bolt back toward the house, still shoeless, not even trying to explain. Lily's bare feet spark off the dewy grass, the electricity pouring off her like a layer of sweat.

There's no two ways about it. We look like witches.

We have to walk, barefoot, back to my house along the river wall. Cold drizzle sweeps through our hair and underneath our clothing, freezing our bones. Our feet are cut from the gravel, and yet I would still take the pain over the wall of fury coming at me from Lily and Fiona.

"What *was* that, Maeve?" Fiona hisses. "Why on earth would you do that? It was just so . . . *cruel*. And unnecessary."

"I . . ." I trail off. "Becky Fogarty was going to say something just as horrible to Lily. And Mark . . . He kissed Lily and then he kissed someone else? What the hell is that?"

"Thank you for sharing," Lily says miserably. "An explicitly private moment with everyone. Really. Can't thank you enough."

"I was defending you," I stress. "I thought he had hurt you. It was awful behavior from him."

"Why are you acting like I'm made of glass?" Lily says, sounding genuinely confused. "I don't need you to protect me, Maeve. Not from . . . some random boy who kisses me and kisses someone else at a party. It's a party. I *know how they work.*"

Lily is making complete sense, but I can't shake the feeling that it actually *is* my job to protect her. It's an instinct, fierce and fatal, running through my veins like electricity runs through hers.

"So you're not mad?" I counter. "You're not mad that he kissed you then kissed Becky Foghorn?"

At this, a rage emerges from Lily that feels like it started at the pit of her stomach. She doesn't just raise her voice. She screams at me.

"I was the *river!*"

It's like the river itself hears her. It seems to shimmer a little more, glowing under the reflection of the streetlamps.

"I was the river, Maeve, how do you still not get that?" She puts her hands over her eyes. Like glimpsing the water is too painful.

"There are bones down there. Bones worn away to almost nothing, dust that is part of the riverbed, keys that fell out of pockets, strips of leather wallets that get eaten by fish. That was part of me. All of it was part of me. You think I really care that some random boy who kissed me at a party, and who is going to die one day, also kissed someone else?"

"Yes," I whisper. "Because you're a river, but you're also a girl."

She stares at me, hard. Fiona has already stormed ahead, her arms wrapped around herself, trying to keep warm.

"Fi," I call. "Fi, don't rush ahead."

We already agreed that everyone would sleep at my house tonight. It's closest, after all. But that was before I ruined the party. Fi keeps walking, her body wrapping tighter and tighter around itself.

I jog to meet her, each step agony on the cold ground.

"Fi," I say again. "Fi, come on."

"I just don't understand why you did that," she says tonelessly. "Why you came out with all that. All their secrets."

I struggle, trying to find the words to describe what I myself find indefinable. "Lily . . ."

"Don't give me *that*," she snaps. "You were enjoying yourself. You were enjoying being cruel."

I don't contradict her.

"Tonight's going to have repercussions, do you get that? Do you *ever* get that?" Paolo perches on the river wall, cocking his head at Fiona in an expression of *u ok hun*. "How's Becky gonna cope when she realizes her friends hate her? How are Holly and Fionn gonna cope?"

"I guess she'll get new friends who like her," I say, pretending like it's as easy as all that. "I guess Holly and Fionn will break up. Or, I don't know, they'll all get over it, the way popular kids do."

"How?" Fiona asks sharply. "There's no school, nowhere to patch things up. This is going to just stew, and then they'll all go their separate ways forever. You could have just changed the trajectory of their entire lives."

Guilt tightens my stomach, a black snake making a knot of itself.

"You're being dramatic. Besides, they don't have to deal with anything compared to us. And look at us."

"Yeah," she says, disgusted. "Look at us."

I thought the frostiness might thaw once we got back to my house, but I'm wrong. They borrow shoes, they call cabs, and they wait in silence. The atmosphere doesn't improve, even while they're sitting at my kitchen table, staring at their phones.

"Holly went blind," I say, trying to break the tension. "Are we going to talk about that at least?"

They put their phones down in that passive-aggressive way you put your phone down when your parents won't stop talking to you.

"I'm sure everyone will be talking about it for a long time," Lily says flatly. "I'm sure it'll be in the paper by tomorrow."

"No, but can we talk about *why*?" I press. "It happened the other night, with Roe and Aaron. Only for a minute, and only when I was really angry."

Fiona goes back to looking at her phone. "Maybe your gift is evolving," she says absently. "Maybe it gets stronger the more you act like a bitch."

"Fiona, I said I was sorry."

"Not to them."

"Oh, my god, Fi, will you give it a rest? I'll say sorry to them. Can't we talk about this blindness thing?"

"People in that room used to *like* me, Maeve," she says. "I used to be *liked*."

I bristle at this. "What's that supposed to mean?"

She narrows her eyes at me like I should know what it means.

"You're the mind reader," she snaps, and I don't need to read her mind. Her decision to be friends with me has cut a path off to her that was once open, and for the sake of a few moments, she would like me to feel guilty about that.

"Well, sorry you had to trade in being popular and basic," I snap back, "so you could be a freak and extraordinary."

It's harsh. Too harsh. But it's also true. Fiona is, after all, going to be on a TV show because ten months ago she made a decision to be friends with me. It's a sentiment that is too ridiculous to say out loud, but Fiona glares at me anyway, sure of the subtext.

Fiona gets up. "I'm out of here."

They both go, and I'm left alone, shivering in my wet clothes.

I have no good reason to go to the school. No Roe to meet me, no point to prove. But it's the loneliness that gets me in the end: the loneliness of paranoia, the loneliness of feeling as if nothing is real and that everything is a trap. I want to find one thing that's real, one thing that belongs to me, one thing that I have dominion over.

I am so lonely, in the end, that I would rather try to talk to a ghost then talk to no one at all.

10

I HAVE NEVER UNDERSTOOD GRAVEYARDS, or the point of visiting them. Even now, as someone whose whole life is so occult-adjacent, I'm still alarmed by my own blind spots. The way I don't care about star signs, for example, or the fact that cemeteries have no profound effect on me. I've gone with my mum before, to visit her mum, and always come away from the experience feeling cold. Not in an eerie way, but in a way where you feel nothing at all.

But now, sitting in what feels like a mausoleum to Sister Assumpta, I get it. I get how a graveyard can be a reflecting pool for your own self-pity. That might sound cruel, but it's how I feel: like I can soak the misery of my evening in a dead nun's memory.

I think of her, on the day Heaven arrived. A fresh sensitive, a scholarship kid, the girl who would bring the Housekeeper to Kilbeg. The relief that Assumpta must have felt that somebody was going to take over. The excitement that a new sensitive had been nominated by the Well. The joy that not only was Heaven a witch, she was also a good person, a bright girl, brimming with empathy and activism.

The longer I sit here, the more I find myself resenting Heaven's death. She would have been a great sensitive, an efficient warden of the Well, strong and smart like her sister Nuala, and in her late forties by the time the Children came sniffing about. Not tired, like Sister

Assumpta. Not too young and too stupid and too selfish, like me. Me, who could not even attend a Christmas party without it ending in tears and screamed confessions and fits of blindness.

I sit at the piano bench, touching the keys, despising my own misery but unable to remove myself from it. I was not supposed to be in this position. It was supposed to be Heaven. It's not my fault that I was given a job that I'm too young for.

It's a pit too steep to climb out of, clumps of muddy reasoning falling away in my hands every time I reach upward.

Until, of course, I smell smoke.

I raise my nose to the air like a gun dog. Not another fire. Not tonight. Too much has happened, surely, for something else to happen tonight. But it's cigarette smoke, and it's coming from upstairs.

I follow the smell up the stairs, and there's Aaron in an exact copy of the pose Roe and I found him in a few nights ago. Halfway out the window, the metal pipes of the scaffolding still in place, the boards having collapsed.

"You couldn't sleep either, then?" he says.

"I guess not."

"Is Roe downstairs?"

"No."

"Ah. I'm safe, then."

"Oh, come on, you two are over all that now, aren't you?"

Aaron shrugs. "Ask him."

It's strange, how *him* already feels foreign. "It's *them* now. Pronouns-wise, I mean."

Aaron pauses to consider this.

"Ask them, then," he replies.

"Hey, can I have one? Please?" I don't smoke, but I feel so miserable that I'll do anything to feel even slightly different.

He holds out the box and I lean against the window, lighting up uncertainly.

"Ugh, gross," I say, hating the taste but continuing anyway.

"What's eating you, then?"

"I went to a party tonight with the girls. And, well. It happened again. The eyes. A girl I got angry at went blind."

"What? Are you serious?" he replies urgently, and I'm grateful for his disbelief. Fiona and Lily were so casual about Holly that I was starting to wonder if I was going insane. Maybe they didn't see her eyes like I did. Maybe it wasn't clear, in the dark and in the confusion.

I nod. "I got into a fight with her, and her eyes just went white."

He looks at me then. His eyes, blue with the tiniest fleck of rust-brown near the pupil. I can feel his gaze move to each feature individually: my eyes, my nose, my mouth. He looks at me for so long that his cigarette starts to burn down to his fingers.

"What?" I say, and I am suddenly extremely aware of how alone we are, and how late it is. How anything that happens between us would be just that—between us. And I'm suddenly driven by the notion that something *could* happen. I could even instigate it.

It's exactly the kind of disaster you imagine just because it's possible. Like throwing your phone out the window, or jumping off a cliff. You look over the edge and think, *It would certainly be terrible if I had the sudden compulsion to jump*, and you wonder if the thought itself is the compulsion.

"*What*, Aaron?"

He keeps looking. There's a sudden warmth, a charge. A thing. A flicker of *I wonder what it might be like to kiss someone different. Someone not Roe.* In that split second, that's who Aaron is: just some older blond boy.

I'm suddenly horrified by myself, by the implicit betrayal of my own thoughts. For a moment I think he's going to move toward me, and I jump up from the window, jangling with nerves and leftover vodka.

"*Don't*," I snap, moving toward the center of the room.

"What?" he replies, genuinely confused. Then he realizes. "Oh, for god's sake, Maeve, grow up. I wasn't going to *touch* you."

He says the word *touch* like it's poison. Like it's a nasty, vulgar thing, synonymous with bodily fluids and squalor.

"Don't make out like I'm crazy just because I interpreted you acting creepy with you wanting to do a creepy thing," I snap. "That's . . ." Only I can't think of the word. The word for making someone think they're crazy. "That's fire lighting."

"You mean gaslighting?"

"Look, you're doing it again!"

"Maeve, shut *up*, will you?" He stubs his cigarette out. "I think . . . Look, I don't want to worry you."

"Well, *good job* on that one," I answer sarcastically. It's clear to me that this conversation would be going better if I wasn't still slightly drunk.

"I think you're changing," he says at last. "I think something is happening to you."

I step backward, the back of my knee hitting the table. "What do you mean?"

"I don't *know* what I mean. That's why I was looking at you just now. Maybe it's because I went away for a little while and came back, so I'm the only one who notices. The others have been too close. Or maybe it's because I'm the other sensitive. I don't know. But something has changed. Like, fundamentally. Something in your body."

I instinctively shield my torso with my arms, uncomfortable at the mention of my body. Aaron shakes his head. "No, not your body.

I mean . . . your *atoms*. You're the same, but you're, like, molecularly different."

"You're scaring me."

He's saying this all with such certainty that I can feel panic rising up through my stomach, cooking my insides.

"That's why I wasn't going to say anything."

"What, you were just going to stare at me *like a rapist*?"

"Holy *hell*, can you just—"

Then we both stop. There's a noise, almost animal, and it's coming from somewhere else in the building. From underneath us.

But unlike the other night, when Roe and I heard all that bashing around, this is more mournful. It's the sound of grief.

"Someone is crying," Aaron says.

We creep out onto the landing, ears cocked. "It's a woman," I whisper. It has a strange, heaving tenor, the sound of someone who has been crying for a long time and does not know how to stop.

We descend the stairs and find ourselves outside 2A, the cries leaking through the closed door, the brass handle visibly quivering with stress. I can hear the screws rattling in their setting, torment vibrating through them.

Aaron and I exchange a look, and I feel the odd jangle of our sensitivity. The sense that we are both intuiting the same thing. This is not a present-day cry. This is something that is echoing, something years old, a trapped memory in the walls of the old building.

"Do you have any experience," I say quietly, "with ghosts?"

"Ghosts?" he ponders in a whisper. "No, not ghosts. Demons, but not ghosts. You?"

"Sister Assumpta died in this building. She was a powerful sensitive. Maybe she's come back."

"I never met her. Will she be . . . you know, a friendly ghost?"

I think about this before answering. "Uh, probably? She wasn't all there, if you know what I mean. Kind, but not all there."

"Well, she's very here now," Aaron says, his gaze fixed on the vibrating door handle.

"Come on, then," I reply, and decide in one fluid motion to open the door and confront the trapped spirit of Sister Assumpta.

When you are expecting a ghost, anything that is *not* a ghost feels like an anticlimax. Perhaps that's why Aaron and I don't react when we enter the space that was once 2A. We just look and walk. Our feet are loud, the way your steps sound in a museum. And slowly, we realize that while we may not be confronting the ghost of a person, we are witnessing the ghost of a place.

The boxy room that was 2A is now a long, wide hallway. There are pictures on every side, no windows in sight. Maybe too much natural light harms the paint. Maybe this is a place where you put things you don't want anyone to see. My eyes scan each frame: all portraits, all people who are wigged, coiffed, and steeped in that strange alien look of the past.

"Where *are* we?" Aaron finally says.

"I think we're at St. Bernadette's. But, like, a long time ago."

"We specifically said ghosts," he says to the walls. "I did not sign up for time travel."

I stand in front of one of the portraits. A girl with black hair, a pink dress, and a parasol to match. Aaron is gazing at the picture opposite. It's a man with a musket and a dog at his side.

The only thing that remains from the real world is the sound of crying. The only door in the room is at the other end of the long corridor.

The only way out is forward.

We pass the paintings, the lacquered furniture. All of it is too small, too fussy. I notice the vague, itchy sound of fragile ticking, and follow it to a golden carriage clock, sitting smugly on the mantel.

Aaron picks it up. "This is real gold," he says. "We could take this back and sell it."

"In terms of Ideas That Sound Instantly Stupid, that one is right up there with building a house on an ancient burial ground."

He scowls, putting the clock back in its place. "I wasn't going to *actually* do it."

We reach the end of the corridor, where the crying is at its loudest. Next to the door is another portrait, and it's the only one we both recognize. White dress, dog at her side, the faraway, slightly inhuman expression. The Housekeeper, here to greet us.

"You can see her, too?" Aaron murmurs. I nod, and we are both lost in her for another silent appraisal.

"At last," I say finally. "We've been waiting for her all this time, and now here she is." I step forward. Touch the oil. "She's been around a long time, hasn't she?"

"Yep," Aaron says. "Maybe that's why she hasn't come for us yet. Maybe she's tired."

"Maybe she's dead."

"Don't get your hopes up, Chambers. Hope is dangerous."

I step away from the painting, and my vision blurs a little, the way it does when you pull a Magic Eye picture slowly away. She seems three-dimensional briefly, like she's popping out of the frame. I shake my head and turn my attention to the door at the end of the corridor.

"Are you ready?" I ask.

"Ready for what?"

"Ready for whatever's on the other side of this door."

"Something tells me that it doesn't matter whether I'm ready,"

I remind myself to take in roads, trees, defining aspects of the landscape, but it's too dark. I press my face to the glass, squinting, trying to make out anything: car license plates, streetlights, telephone poles.

"This one's empty, too," Aaron calls from across the hallway.

I keep looking out the window. I realize that it's not just that I can't see anything, it's that there really *isn't* anything. No lights from a nearby town, nothing on the grounds of the hotel itself, no upstairs bedroom twinkling from a house three miles away. I haven't stayed at very many hotels. When you're from a family of five kids, you don't tend to go on hotel holidays very much. But I know that hotels usually have gardens, and terraces, and swimming pools, and *things* attached to them. That's what's eerie, here. There are no things. Just this strange building, plonked in the middle of nowhere.

"Where *is* everyone?" I say to Aaron, who just shrugs.

We walk down the Lodge corridor, and it gradually becomes apparent that some of the rooms, at least, are in use. We pass about seven or eight where the resident didn't bother to even close the door properly. Maybe because they're comfortable showing everyone their room. Or maybe it's an act of defiance, a way of saying, "I know the locks don't work, so I'm not going to help you hold up the facade that they do."

These rooms have beds. And sinks. But the strangeness doesn't evaporate just because the rooms are occupied. There are things, quite ordinary things, that are odd just because of the fact that they are happening inside a hotel. The beds, most of all. Every hotel bed I've ever encountered has been a tight arrangement of sheets and quilts, stretched in layers like a fussy French pastry. These beds are covered with ordinary duvets, with ordinary duvet covers: flowers here, stripes there. A Sheffield Wednesday bedspread. Another one with pugs on it.

Aaron feels it, too. He touches the edge of a quilt covered in a pattern of blue hydrangea.

"Brought from *home*," he says. We don't have to discuss the wrongness of this place. It's everywhere. I don't want to breathe too much, in case it creeps inside me.

"Why aren't you guys downstairs?"

Aaron and I whirl around. There's a girl there, and it's hard to tell how old she is. My instinct is that she's a couple of years older than me, but the more I take in, the more I doubt myself. She's extremely skinny, her frame oddly shrunken, swamped in big comfortable clothes. She looks like a child in pajamas.

Aaron and I say nothing.

"Oh, no," she says, looking to the bed. "They're not moving me *again*, are they?"

"No," Aaron suddenly interjects. "This is just room inspection."

"Oh," she says, looking relieved but not altogether happy. She sits down carefully, easing her frame into an armchair. "OK, then."

Aaron gives me a hard look of *just go with it*, and I pull the duvet off the bed and begin patting it down. Looking, I hope, like someone who has a methodical system for room checks in place.

And to my immense surprise, I find tarot cards under the pillow. A simple Rider-Waite-Smith deck, the cards still waxy with newness.

"Why aren't you downstairs?" Aaron asks, sounding authoritative for someone who is bluffing his way through this interaction. "No one is supposed to be up here when we do our checks."

The girl starts picking at her nails, her head bent. "They told me to come up here," she says moodily, "and think about my choices."

"Did you not behave in a God-honoring way?"

Aaron's voice is sterner now. Clearly the muscle memory of the Children is still present in him. I examine the cards. Two are already turned over: the Seven of Swords and the Hierophant. Strange, to just do a two-card spread for yourself. Usually people do three, minimum.

"Yeah," she says. For a moment, I feel like she's not going to tell us, and then I see Aaron's strange magic working on her like a sedative. Her body starts to ease slightly.

"I used the kitchen phone," she says, her eyes darting to me. I meet her gaze and am distracted for a minute by how rich and brown her eyes are. She looks like a squirrel: big eyes, small mouth, her features all the more expressive because of how little flesh there is left on her face. "To call my sister."

Over her shoulder, I silently show the cards to Aaron. He narrows his eyes but doesn't comment on them.

"And do you understand," Aaron says coolly, "why we can't let you do that?"

"I know." Squirrel Girl brings her hands to her mouth and I hear the hard click of tooth hitting nail. "I know I have to concentrate on devotion, and I can't do that if I'm distracted."

"And calling your sister is . . ." Aaron says, leading the witness.

"A distraction. I know. I just get a bit sick of living like this, you know? And it doesn't help that they move us around so much. You can't even settle your stuff in one place."

A pause.

"Sorry," she says nervously. "*You* move us around. I don't mean to complain."

"It's fine," says Aaron tenderly. Bread-crumbing his empathy, just like the old days. Giving them just enough love to keep them hooked. "It's OK to vent sometimes."

The wardrobe is filled with sweatpants and hoodies. There are no jeans, no outdoor jackets. At the same time, the sweatpants aren't a uniform, either. They're Abercrombie, Penneys, H&M. Like they were given instructions before leaving home: *bring soft clothes.*

I start to look for the girl's light, but it's hard to access. I don't have a good enough sense of her yet. I can't hook into anything. Instead, I look for the other lights in the building and try to count how many people are actually here.

"And you understand why we have to move you, don't you?"

There are dozens of lights, clustering all together, and not very far from here. There are bigger and smaller lights, and I know instinctively that the bigger lights are leaders and the smaller lights are the diminished personalities of the people imprisoned here.

"Yes," Squirrel Girl says, sounding sulky. "I know attachment is bad. Especially to silly things like bedrooms."

She lets out a long sigh. "And if I'm attached to material things, how can I have a spiritual connection? And if my spiritual connection is off, how can I, you know, do good stuff? Save others? I want to be as close to Him as possible."

The tarot cards seem stranger than ever now. Surely, someone this interested in Him and His approval wouldn't have a deck stashed under their pillow?

"Yes," Aaron says, sounding like he understands this concept perfectly. "That's what we all want. Eventually."

"I'm so bad, though. I basically fail the weather reports every week."

Weather reports?

"Angela," Aaron says. "Are the wardrobes clean?"

"Yep," I reply, wondering why he chose the alias "Angela." "All good. Um . . ."

I try to mimic Aaron's trick of sounding authoritative. I turn to the girl. "Have you spoken much to Lorna lately?"

"Lorna," she repeats, a little confused. "Uh . . ."

Something happens then. Something inside her brain. Her thought process plunges briefly, like a foot through a missing step. She looks queasy and vacant, and then her expression clears. It only lasted a few seconds, but it was so uncanny that I feel like I was watching something very slow and protracted.

"Lorna," she says again. "Lorna left."

"She left?"

Squirrel Girl looks at me with suspicion, like this is information I should already know. "Well, *yes*?"

A bell rings then, a handbell, like the kind they rang for lunch in primary school. There's a dim shuffle, the sounds of a few dozen people getting to their feet.

"Well, great." Aaron stands up. Puts a hand on the girl's shoulder. "I hope this talk has helped."

"Yeah," she says, nibbling her hands again. "Oh, don't tell anyone, will you? That I've been, you know? Complaining? You said it was OK to vent."

"It is OK," Aaron says. "Maybe, just don't vent to anyone else, all right?"

"All right."

We need to leave. But I can't let the question of the tarot cards go unanswered.

"You have a deck of tarot cards under your pillow," I say bluntly. "You know how we feel about that kind of thing."

Her eyes shift nervously from me to Aaron.

"Dorey gave them to me," she says. "She said they weren't sinful. Only paper. She said that they might help me with . . ."

The bell gets louder, and we can hear people making their way up the stairs. We leave the room.

"Run," Aaron says once we're in the hallway. "Fast."

And luckily, the door to the Corridor is open.

THE HIEROPHANT

12

"ON THE *PLUS* SIDE," HE SAYS, SOUNDING LIKE
he's about to vomit, "Lorna isn't there anymore."

"No," I agree. We are sitting on the stone steps outside St. Bernadette's, shivering and holding on to our knees, sharply inhaling the
night air like we are recovering from motion sickness. Both of us are
trying to metabolize what we've just seen, our bodies rejecting the
hollow eyes of Squirrel Girl, the empty rooms. "No, which is good,
because . . . it means you *can* leave."

"Yes," he says, his face white. He needs the comfort of this information, and badly. "Yes, you can leave. I mean, that boy left. The one
with the camera."

"You made it sound like he escaped."

"Yes. Well. Who knows? Maybe he was being dramatic. Maybe
he could have left through the front door, like Lorna."

"Well, she didn't say that, either." I hesitate again, trying to separate the facts of what we've seen from what might be convenient to
believe. "And if she *has* left, why hasn't she gone home?"

"How long has she been missing from your school?"

"A few days." Then I pause. "Although. I only have one class with
her, so . . . it could be longer. It's hard to keep track with these online
classes."

The light begins to change, dawn gradually diluting the sky. A milk truck trundles past. It's chilling to think that morning will break over us the same way it breaks over the Lodge, only their day will be very, very different from ours.

"What did she mean when she said 'weather reports'?" I ask.

"It's a game," he says, squinting slightly, the memory clearly painful. "You remember those games we used to play, like Two Truths and a Lie? That weird confession game? We had lots of little things like that. And I always thought . . . you know, lots of these kids are kind of awkward, find it hard to make friends, let's play a game. Y'know. To connect everyone."

"Connect everyone to *you*," I correct him, "so they would become completely addicted to your approval."

Aaron waves his hand. "Yeah. All that. But after Dorey came, when the Children were big enough in Kilbeg for her to actually care . . . the games got weirder."

"Like what?"

Aaron describes Weather Report. It's like that memory game you play as a kid, where the first person says, "Today I went to the market and I bought an apple." Then the next person says, "I bought an apple and a can of beans." The chain keeps getting longer, and you have to remember everything the other players have said. Except with Weather Report, you're not just saying random items. You're saying everything you noticed that day, starting with the weather.

"That doesn't sound so terrible."

"It doesn't, no," Aaron says. "But it's like 'Today it rained before breakfast, and I ate an orange, and swore when I stubbed my toe, and Laura showed unhealthy attachment to material things, and Charlotte didn't respect her body.' You see, it's a way of constantly policing each other. A way of saying: I noticed you were bad today.

While also appearing to own up to your *own* badness. It's a perfect combination of confession and snitching."

I feel a shiver at the base of my neck, wanting to believe I would never fall for this but remembering how I behaved in the animal kingdom of St. Bernadette's. How quickly a clique of girls who were slightly cooler than me were able to morph my behavior completely, and without even really meaning to.

"When that girl said she was always failing the weather reports, what did that mean?"

"It could mean she had a hard time remembering stuff," he says. "But . . . I don't know. I feel like everything has gotten darker, even in a couple of months."

He looks like there's something else, something he's not saying. He chews on it awhile, then spits it out.

"She hadn't eaten. Not for over a day."

"For over *a day*?"

"Yeah, I don't know about you, but it was hard for me to get a read on her. All I could make out was that she was really, really hungry."

"When I asked her about Lorna," I say slowly, "she had a reaction. Like . . . I don't know, like it was a trick step in her brain or something."

"I didn't cop that," he says.

"Wow."

"Wow what?"

"You 'copping' things. You're getting more Irish."

He gets to his feet, gives a weak smile. "Yeah, well, I have to do something to stop them deporting me. Let's get out of here."

We walk to the end of the hill, the gleaming river before us. We don't hug when we part ways, the way I would hug Fiona or Lily. It's not in our lexicon. We just look at each other, hands in our pockets.

"The tarot cards," I say. "What do you think that was about?"

"Maybe Dorey is trying to ferret out more sensitives, just like we thought. Or at least kids with magical abilities. That's how you realized, right? When you found a deck."

I nod. It makes sense. "But surely she would know as soon as she meets someone, right?"

He shrugs. "People change when you put pressure on them. Show their gifts. As you well know."

I laugh, because it's almost a joke.

"When you said I was changing," I say, "I still don't know what you mean."

He looks at me sideways. "Maybe I don't know what I mean, either."

·) ☽ ● ☾ (·

I wake up at midday, fuzzy and haunted. Last night sits in my memory like a crushed car, something that was once vast and technical and now has been condensed to cube size.

The party. The fight. St. Bernadette's. The Lodge. Aaron's words ringing in my ears.

Something has changed.

Like, fundamentally.

Something in your body.

I close my eyes, searching myself for the kind of change that he was only able to see by leaving and coming back. I can feel shame lodged in my gut, sticky and purple, the suspicion that he's right, the suspicion that I'm wrong. Not wrong as in incorrect, but wrong as in *bad*. Bad as in *made badly*.

There's a tickle of forgotten dreams, pushing at the edge of my consciousness. More dreams about playing cards. Eight of Hearts,

110

Eight of Spades, Nine of Clubs. Stuck together with filth and dried rum. I don't know much about poker, but I know there's nothing you can do with that hand.

I sit up, take out my tarot deck. Nuala once taught me how to tell tarot with ordinary playing cards, as a party trick. Of course, it only works with the minor arcana. Hearts are Cups. Spades are Swords. Diamonds are Pentacles. Clubs are Wands.

Eight of Hearts. Eight of Spades. Nine of Clubs.

Eight of Cups. Eight of Swords. Nine of Wands.

Abandonment. Imprisonment. Defensiveness.

Any of these cards might be fine if they came up in a happier spread, but together, it's hard to find anything positive about them. The Eight of Swords chills me the most: a woman with a blindfold on, swords surrounding her body. The blindfold is meant to represent insularity, like she's so in her own head that she can't see the threats around her. But I just see Holly's blank white eyes, glowing as I put my hands on her. The girl at the Lodge, so panicked about her weather reports that she didn't even realize that Aaron and I were complete strangers. She immediately assumed we were staff.

I look at the card again, the Eight of Swords, and wonder if there's anything I'm missing. Some threat that's right under my nose, like Heather Banbury. Something I'm missing because I'm focused on the wrong things.

Fiona!

I jump out of bed and pull clothes on, realizing that twenty minutes have passed since I started dithering around with tarot cards, and Fiona is meeting her TV people at one.

I'm halfway down the street when I remember that Fiona is mad at me, so I slow my steps a little. Last night's conversation did not end well, after all. Fi heavily implied that she might be better off never being friends with me, and I—rather shamefully—implied that our friendship was the only reason she was getting this TV opportunity.

I flag down a bus, wincing at the memory. A bubble of fury rises through me. A bubble that says *Screw you, Fiona. Screw you for making me feel like your loser friend who has destroyed your credibility, even if it's true.*

Then the bubble bursts. She is my best friend, and I did behave like a lunatic, after all. Besides, what if they really *are* the Children, waiting to lure Fiona into some kind of trap?

I reach the bubble-tea place only ten minutes late, with the meeting already in progress. Fiona is sitting with two vaguely stressed-looking people in their thirties, a man and a woman.

"Fiona!" I say brightly, as if we're fond acquaintances rather than fighting friends. "Fancy seeing you here!"

"Oh, hi," Fiona says, equally as fake. "Hi, Maeve."

I stand in front of the three of them, trying to latch on to their energy. There's an awkward pause, and Fiona quickly tries to recover the situation. "This is Paula and Nick," she says grandly. "We're having a meeting."

"Hello," Paula says politely. "Are you an actor, too?"

"Um . . ." I'm still trying to find their colors, so Fiona has to talk for me.

"No, Maeve doesn't act."

"You were in the newspaper, too, weren't you?" Nick says. "One of the Kilbeg witches."

I latch on to their energy, sea-glass green and light blue.

"No," I say bluntly. "Fiona, I'm just going to sit over there, OK?"

"OK." Fi nods. And I *think* she looks grateful. I think she does.

Fiona talks to the producers for an hour, and for the most part, there isn't much difference between what they think and what they say. They talk about authenticity and ask Fiona if she really does know Wicca and tarot. But they ask the way you ask someone if they can do the splits. They don't think she can actually do magic. They just want something that looks good and natural on-screen.

For the most part, though, they think she's talented and charismatic, and notice that she seems very grounded. Older than her years. They want her to do a taped audition, but they are fairly sure it is a formality. They've struck gold: a real witch, a talent, a beauty, and through a local newspaper. The PR opportunities are endless.

They both think about Fiona's race. The woman is excited by Fiona being Filipino, because of how it will improve the show's diversity. The man isn't so sure. He thinks Fiona is great, but he wonders whether the moneymen will need convincing. The writers will have to change the character's storyline, after all, to factor in how Fiona looks. The writers might not like that.

In this world that is wholly dependent on visual storytelling, it doesn't matter if they're thinking positively about her race or negatively about it. They are thinking about it. And Fiona must know that on some level.

I might worry that everyone thinks I'm an arsehole, but at least they're judging me on the stuff I do and say, and not so much on what I look like.

Eventually they leave. Fiona races over to my table. "Well?"

I smile at her. "I think they're probably, like . . . fine. Not outwardly evil."

"Where's the doubt?" She looks worried.

"I mean. They're TV people. They think about how you look and stuff."

"But they like how I look?"

"I think so."

"And they didn't think anything Children-y?"

"Not Children-y, no."

"OK, good." Then she looks addled. "So I can actually take this *seriously*, then? As a *real* opportunity?"

I nod solemnly. "It is one hundred percent a real opportunity."

We look at each other and, for a second, weigh up whether we have the energy to still be angry. Fiona suddenly breaks. She starts laughing uncontrollably.

"What the *shit*, Maeve?" She giggles, covering her mouth. "How the *hell* is this happening?"

"You're going to be a TV actor, Fi." I smile at her. "This is it. It's happening."

"No," she says, not quite able to believe it. "I still have to do an official audition."

I shake my head. "It's a formality," I say. "I heard their thoughts. They want you, Fi."

The tears come then. Crying and laughing, laughing and crying, hiccuping from one extreme to the other. "I hate that we fought last night," she says eventually. "I'm sorry I said that stuff."

"Same," I reply. "I acted crazy. I'm so sorry for humiliating everyone. Most of all myself."

"You were drunk, and you were trying to protect Lily," she says. "I shouldn't have gone off on you like that."

I tell her I will apologize to Holly and Becky. I'm so grateful for her explanation that I was drunk and protective, even if I can still feel Aaron's words echoing through me.

Something has changed.

Like, fundamentally.

Something in your body.

We drink our bubble teas, and I counsel Fiona through a range of emotions about being on television. "What if I'm trolled?" she asks. "What if I'm canceled?"

"Canceled for what?"

"I don't know, maybe I've done something."

"You haven't," I say, shaking my head. "You're beloved."

"What if I'm secretly problematique?" she says, French-ly.

"That's a question for Manon."

She bites her lip, remembering our conversation from last night. "Manon," she says.

"She'll be here when you get back."

"Will she?"

"Maybe if you go away for a while, she'll realize that she likes you, too."

"That feels like . . . not a thing."

"You never know. Sometimes people go away and they . . . they notice new things about you."

Fiona goes home soon after that, hugging me tightly before she does. "Now I need to explain this to Mum," she says, rolling her eyes. "I feel like it might be an easier sell, seeing as I can do school remotely now, anyway?"

"You never know," I repeat, which seems to be my catchphrase now. It's fitting. At base, I truly do not know anything.

13

WHEN I TELL THE GANG ABOUT THE COR-
ridor, they all look at me as if the information is incomplete. Like
there's a middle chapter missing, linking Holly's party to the Lodge.

"I don't understand" is the first thing anyone says after Aaron
and I finish the story. It's Roe, looking puzzled. "Why were you at
St. Bernadette's in the first place?"

"What do you mean?"

We're gathered in Nuala's kitchen again, the room rich with
cooking smells.

"OK, so," Roe continues slowly. "You went to the party . . ."

"Yes."

"And you had some kind of . . . fistfight?"

I twitch a little. "Becky Foghorn was being mean to Lily."

The truth is, I still don't have an explanation for why I flipped
the way I did. Defending Lily is one thing, and pummeling Holly
quite another. It's a level of violence I didn't even know I possessed.
Wild, reactionary, thoughtless. Not slow and plotting, like they tell
you female rage should be.

Roe turns to Lily.

"That's right. She was," Lily says, sounding profoundly untrauma-
tized by the experience. "So Maeve, uh, went nuts on her."

"Why did you go nuts on her?"

"She was a bit drunk," Fiona interjects, trying to make up for our fight last night by over-defending me today.

"But you don't *fight* when you're drunk," Roe goes on, still looking confused. "You get, like, sleepy. And silly."

"Why are you so fixated on this?"

"It just doesn't sound *like* you." Roe pauses again. "And so what, it's the middle of the night, and you head to the school? Why? We didn't have a plan to meet. Did we?"

Tension envelops the room, a sense that this is about Roe and me, and not about the gang as a whole. Manon and Nuala start to look uncomfortable, like this is really none of their business.

"The important thing," Aaron reminds us, "is we have a path into the Lodge now. Some kind of . . . I don't know, vortex has opened up at the school. Maeve and I were there. We talked to that girl. We know how they're living."

"And," I add worriedly, "Dorey gave her those tarot cards. She must be looking for a new sensitive. One to replace me after she's killed me, probably."

"But why would she even need a sensitive?" Fiona asks. "She can't drain the Well through one. Not since the ritual sealed it. So what is she *doing*? What's her game?"

"Sensitives are rare," Manon muses. "One in a generation. Sometimes less than that. Their powers are not limited to a Well. A young person with a gift for magic, but who doesn't know it yet? They are like diamonds." She thinks quietly for a moment. "And like diamonds, they often form under pressure. Which explains the starving, the mind games."

"This girl," Nuala says. "The one from your school. The Lorna girl. What do you know about her?"

Lily, Fiona, and I look at one another, each of us expecting the other to have something solid to say. I picture Lorna, her smooth features and dark, thin eyebrows. She isn't stupid—she couldn't be, she's in all the top classes—but whenever I picture her, she has the mild expression and slight dopey blankness of a cow.

"Fi," I nudge. "You had more classes with her than anyone."

"I'm thinking," Fiona says, furrowing her brow. "Uh, I don't know. Quiet, I guess. Not, like, absurdly shy or anything, but just kept herself to herself."

"Who are her friends?"

Silence among the three of us again.

"I don't know," Fiona finally answers.

I realize that Lorna occupied a similar place in the social strata to me last year: floating between cliques based on class schedules and little else. I wonder why it never occurred to me to be friends with her. Probably because she seemed a bit boring.

Manon is interested now, forming a theory. "Is there anything to suggest that she may have sensitive leanings?"

"I don't think so," I answer. "But there was nothing to suggest that I had leanings, either."

"What are *leanings*?" Lily asks. "We can't just decide that there are leanings all of a sudden."

"She's right, we are talking out of our arses here."

Manon stands up. "Lily is right. No more talking out of assholes," she says, and it is, for some reason, far more explicit in her accent. "Let's go to the school. We need to see what is going on with this Corridor business."

We take two cars. I sit in the passenger seat next to Roe, with Lily and Fiona in the back. A hard rain has started, pelting thick against the window.

Roe is strangely quiet, concentrating on the road in a way that I know they don't really need to. The rest of us chat, batting our theories around, discussing whether or not we think Lorna McKeon is a sensitive, too. Roe says nothing.

"Any more chat on the single, then, Roe?" I say, trying to draw them in.

"We got on a playlist," Roe says after a brief pause. "The Alternative Éire playlist on Spotify. It's got, like, a quarter million subscribers. And they used our picture for the cover image. So. That's something."

"That's brilliant!" I reply.

"It's OK. I mean, if this were the nineties, we'd be talking about, you know, radio and CD singles. Instead it's digital streams and a penny for every hundred thousand plays. Hard to get excited."

A pause follows as we all consider how to comfort them about the utter madness of a life in music. Fiona looks embarrassed. I haven't asked her how much she'll get paid for this TV show, but I know it won't be pennies.

"I *also* hate when things are not the nineties," Lily says, and it's so perfectly piss-takey that Roe breaks into a cackle.

"Sorry," they say. "I'm just feeling a bit under pressure, you know? College, the band, this tour in April. We've spent so much on this single and I just want it to *work*."

We arrive after Nuala's car does. Our phone flashlights out, we all stumble into the building, Fiona's hand in mine, mine in Lily's. I'm usually here in the middle of the night, and it doesn't feel the same in the evening. I can still hear traffic outside, and the quality of darkness isn't quite the same. There are cool shadows, beams of streetlight illuminating scraps of rubbish and Milky Way wrappers. Dilapidation, but not mystery. No magic. Just ruin.

We pour into the old office, and I notice someone is missing.

"Manon," I say. "Where's Nuala?"

"She's . . . Uh, she's taking a moment."

"I'm fine," Nuala calls from the hallway. "I'm just, you know."

Manon casts a worried glance out the door. "This is where they told her about my aunt, Heaven."

Nuala stumbles in, her eyes shining. Manon puts her arms around her mother's shoulders. "I'm grand, Manny, I'm grand. It's just, I said I'd never come in this room again."

"It's not really here anymore," says Lily sympathetically. "Or it's not the place it was. You won, Nuala. It died and you're alive."

Sometimes Lily says things and I'm reminded why, at six years old, I picked her to be my best friend.

We wait. We look in 2A, we creep up each workable stair and peek in abandoned classrooms. We tell tarot to pass the time. Roe wanders. Touches the guts of the building, and we start to hear the pipes gurgle slightly with the last remains of water. The banker's lamp on Sister Assumpta's desk flickers on when Lily touches it. An hour passes. And no crying.

Aaron, who had been silently and compulsively reciting the Book of Job to himself, looks up.

"Maeve," he says. "Do you hear that?"

It is only nine p.m., but the crying has begun again.

The cry we heard last night was bereft, solemn. Tonight's cry is edged with a scream. With fear, with hysterics, with the sudden discovery of something brutal.

And of course, no one but me and Aaron can hear it. The screech vibrates within me, drawing my bones together. I put my hands over my ears.

"Jesus Christ, can none of you hear that?"

The rest of the room looks mystified.

"All right, Chambers," Aaron says solemnly, brushing the dust from the mantelpiece off his hands. "Off we go. Let's follow the screams to our certain death."

Roe stands up. "Uh, no? We're obviously all going up."

We all trail upstairs, following the terrible sound. Lily has her hands in her pockets so she doesn't accidentally spark the fragile building and send it tumbling down.

The shrieks, still rolling through the building, become louder and settle into a pattern. A spike of high-pitched wailing, then an undulating cry.

"What's it like?" Lily whispers.

"Like a banshee," I say, pressing my fingers down more firmly on my ears. "Like everything you associate with a banshee."

There's a snap from behind me, the sound of tired timber finally giving in.

"Merde!" Manon's foot has gone through the staircase, her body crashing into the building. She screams, grabbing out in front of her, catching Fiona's jacket. Fiona falls, too, and a cloud of dust explodes into the air in a creamy wave.

"Christ!" I scream, momentarily drowning out the banshee moans. "Are you guys OK?"

The dust has cloaked everything, and all I can see are limbs and wood.

"Putain d'escalier de merde!"

"Manon is hurt," Fiona calls.

Nuala and Lily each take one of Manon's arms over their shoulders, lifting her out of the stairs.

"My ankle," Manon cries. "My ankle is shit."

"I'll fix it," Fiona says. "Come on, let's get you to the couch downstairs."

"Splinters, Fiona," Nuala says worriedly. "We'll need to get out the splinters. Can you do that?"

"Probably?"

The roaring in my ears is getting louder, and I can tell it's getting louder for Aaron, too. I can barely hear them, the din is getting so loud. I can feel my eardrums rupturing, the sound so piercing that I'm convinced it will carry on ringing deep in my brain forever.

"Come on," Aaron says, both hands on his head. "I can't stand it."

Fiona, Nuala, and Manon are already downstairs, Manon's cries joining the haunted din. Lily and Roe are still with us.

"Stay together," Nuala calls up the stairs. "Don't separate."

The four of us are huddled outside 2A, my fingers on the door handle. "All right, guys," I say. "Are you ready to go to the Lodge?"

Only, when I'm on the other side of the door, it's just me and Aaron again.

14

THE DOOR AT THE END OF THE PAINTED
corridor opens not into another hallway, but into a small room. Dark,
rich, and quiet. But strange. Everything just a little bit off.

The art on the walls does not quite go together, for one thing. A
landscape, an oil painting of some ducks, a big modern canvas. It is
art that has been bought in bulk and arranged to suit a color scheme.
Which, in this room, is gray, green, and chocolate brown. There is
a little memo pad on the desk, like something you keep next to the
phone, and a bottle of water with a spring latch on it.

It is a tasteful room, but it is not a nice one.

She does not see us at first. Her head is bent and she's looking
into some kind of filing cabinet, peach-painted nails running over
folders. She's too in her own world to see us. She must spend so
much time with teenagers looming in doorways, waiting for her next
order, that she barely registers movement around her at all.

And then, she looks up. Eyes wide and pale blue, sharp as a husky's.
There's a moment of surprise, but not shock. Not joy, but not dis-
pleasure, either. Like she has just realized that there will be more
people coming to her garden party than she expected, and she will
have to wash extra glasses.

"Maeve," she says softly. "Aaron. Welcome to the Lodge. Or

welcome back, I should probably say. Are you coming in?"

Everyone here knows the rules of magic. How we are stuck in a strange cosmic war of diplomacy: she can't hurt us or she'll lose her upper hand with the Housekeeper. We'll be even for Heather, and she doesn't want us to be even. She wants us to be in her debt. She wants leverage.

So in a way, there is really very little risk to stepping into the Lodge. We won't be killed. But there are other things besides being killed to be afraid of.

I look to Aaron. He knows her better, after all. He gives me a very slight nod. We step in.

The door doesn't close and lock behind us. Bars don't come down. We are not stricken by magical paralysis. Dorey simply points at two leather chairs and goes to sit behind a large desk.

"My two sensitives," Dorey says, sitting back into her chair. "Little divining rods."

"What are you doing, Dorey?" Aaron says. "What's going on?"

She turns her body slightly, looks to the window. It's dark, with only the faint outline of trees.

"You'll have to be more specific."

It's hard to know whether she's playing dumb or she's genuinely confused. We leave a silence, waiting for her to remember, and I start to speak.

"Kids are disappearing," I clarify. "And you're going after St. Bernadette's girls now? What good does it do? Starving teenagers?"

She gives me a deeply wounded look, as if she is too frequently misunderstood by people she tries to respect.

"I am shocked that you think I would starve anyone. We have plenty of food here. Go to the pantry and help yourselves, I beg of you."

"Why aren't people eating, then?"

"They're choosing not to eat. They're fasting. You've heard of Lent, haven't you, Maeve? You must have grown up with it, going to school in Ireland."

Lent: the glum frigid period between Ash Wednesday and Easter. We all used to pretend to give up chocolate and make feeble attempts to raise money for the poor.

"It's not Lent," I say carefully. "You're just trying to make people weak. Dependent on your approval."

"Common misconception," she says swiftly. "We don't take people who are feeble, Maeve, we take people who are malleable."

A slight panic rings through me, mainly because the word *feeble* had just occurred to me when thinking about Lent, and now it's coming out of her mouth. It's an uncommon enough word that it makes me think she's reading my mind, subtly looking for a place to tie a string.

"What you have to understand, Maeve, is that bringing an individual into the Children takes time and resources. If they're just going to buckle and break after six months, it's like throwing money out the window."

She turns toward Aaron, her nose slightly wrinkling. "Speaking of throwing money out the window . . ."

Aaron tenses. "You got me for three years, Dorey. You got a servant and a Well. I think you did OK."

He says it all between his teeth, like showing his tongue might be dangerous. Dorey smiles, her gums pink.

"I think *you* did OK, Aaron. Lovely home, unimaginable power, a little bevy of followers. A purpose. My word, what must it *be like* in that brain of yours now, eh?"

Her grin is like a tiger. She keeps talking, poking, prodding.

"Sinners, witches, whores. Do you picture yourself as some

kind of Christ figure? Trying to save them, not passing judgment, loving them all? Hoping love will be your salvation? Or have you just accepted you're all going to Hell, made your peace with the flames, all that?"

Sinners. Witches. Whores. Is that what this woman thinks of us?

And did Dorey just call me a whore?

"You don't even believe in any of that, Dorey, so I don't know what you're trying to pull," Aaron spits back.

"Yes, but *you* do, darling, don't you?" She knits her fingers together, her thumbs resting on top of each other, her sled-dog eyes resting on Aaron. "And you know, they've done studies on this. It's easy to make someone believe something new."

Isadora Manford suddenly, slowly, begins to lift her arm. It's like she's stretching, yawning. She starts circling her wrist. Rotating it, her fingers spread, thin diamond bracelet jangling slightly.

"You know, to bolt a new detail onto an existing conviction," she continues. "God hates witches; he must hate whores, too. But it's very difficult to un-write a belief altogether, so naturally I'm very interested in your predicament, Aaron. Psychologically speaking."

As she's saying that, she keeps curling her wrist around in a circle, like she's conducting a symphony. She starts to smile in delight, and I'm confused until I see what is happening to Aaron sitting next to me. He is doing the same thing, except he's not doing it willingly. His arm is being dragged up into the air completely without his consent. He's trying to fight against it, his teeth clenched. This is Dorey's power, I realize: the Puppeteer.

But not me, though. My hands stay in my lap.

It's starting to make sense to me. Dorey can control people, but only people she's got her hooks in. And her hooks are still in Aaron. Magically, psychologically, emotionally. She's in there.

"You're one of those people," she says, still focusing on him, "who really *looks* like their name, you know?"

Aaron is silently trying to pull his arm from the sky. It remains fixed, firm, as if tied by an invisible rope attached to the ceiling.

"Aaron was Moses's silver-tongued brother, wasn't he? He could make anything sound good. The Bible's first spin doctor." She turns to me then. "I imagine you're still at it, spinning silver with your little gang. What's the line? That he was led astray by big bad Aunt Dorey?"

My fingers twitch involuntarily, and I can't tell if it's nerves or her power quietly slipping threads around my hands.

"Traumatized?" she volunteers. "Waking up on the bus next to that poor Matthew boy, that old song and dance?"

I hear Aaron's jaw click, like his back teeth are grinding together. But he doesn't speak. I'm not sure if he can.

"Has he made you all feel *sorry* for him?" She smiles widely, deeply amused by this. "The boy who went on national television to say . . . what was it?"

She gets up, and for some reason, we are stuck to our chairs. Mute, like two children in the principal's office. I lean slightly, though, and see the papers on her desk. There are a few forms, handwritten and obviously by teenagers. I can read a few of the printed questions upside down.

When do you feel most unhappy?
When are you loneliest?
Do you think your life would be different if you were different?

But under the white paper, there's the slight glow of red, blue, and yellow. The determination of primary colors. I peer at it. Cards. There are tarot cards under there.

Dorey extracts a folder from her filing cabinet and opens it on her desk. Clears her throat.

"Now, what was it you said, Aaron? Ah, here it is. 'I just think we need to be conscious of how young children are being sexualized.'"

She pauses. Looks at me. Continues quoting.

"'Why should a twelve-year-old have to think about their gender? Or their sexuality? Is it naive to think that childhood should last a few more years?'"

Dorey puts the file down, rests her eyes on me. "I know I agree, dear, but do you? Given your . . . you know? Romantic history?"

I remember the note then, the one that was designed to cause friction between Roe and me, between Aaron and Roe. This is what Dorey fears most, I realize. Not just me, not just Aaron, but our combined power. The six of us working together. Dorey may not be behind Fiona's TV show, but she nudged enough of Fiona into the public consciousness so that *someone* would notice her and take her away. She wants fractures. She needs it, clearly, to carry on with whatever comes next in her plan.

A plan that must have been hastily cooked up. Because the original plan, the Housekeeper, has not worked.

This realization that Dorey is resorting to Plan Bs makes her suddenly seem weak to me. It's enough to wrench the invisible string she has wrapped around my fingers.

"I don't see how you're in a position of authority, Dorey," I say. The words come out hard and crisp. "You can't even summon the Housekeeper. It's been weeks. Where is she, eh?"

Aaron's arm finally collapses back into his lap. I have broken Dorey's spell, if only temporarily.

There's a box of tissues on the desk, and I pick it up. "Is she in here?" I say, and Aaron actually laughs.

But Dorey's smile just grows wider.

"I have to thank you, Maeve," she says. "Really. You know, when Aaron and Heather both failed at capturing this Well, it forced me to spend more time here. Ireland, I mean. Oh, I hated it at first, of course. Months in a provincial backwater, where farmers are still killing each other with shovels?"

It's shocking, somehow, to hear her talk like this. I've heard her dismiss all kinds of people, but never the country generally.

"But you know," she continues, "the country air is good for me, I think. And the history is just fascinating. I'm learning so much. All the time."

My insides turn cold. What are you learning, Dorey? What does she know?

I keep my gaze steady, my mouth shut.

"The thing about you, Maeve," she says, turning her head to the side, "is that you've forced me to innovate." She pauses. "How are you feeling, by the way? Any changes?"

It's such a shift in tone from how she spoke to Aaron, the surprise almost slaps me on the side of the head. Her voice is gentle, maternal. The word *changes* startles me. She has also noticed the thing, the ineffable alteration in me that Aaron saw.

She moves her papers then, revealing the tarot cards underneath. The same simple Rider-Waite-Smith we saw in Squirrel Girl's room.

"They are fun, aren't they?" she says, holding up two. "Two of Wands. Page of Pentacles. What do you think that means, Maeve?"

I automatically decipher their meanings without saying them. Forward planning. The quest for knowledge.

"I'd be great if I knew where Lorna is," I reply, ignoring the cards in her hands. "I know she left your freaky cult, so where did she go?"

She looks quite bored now. "I haven't the faintest clue," she says, waving her hand. The door starts to move, and at first I think there's someone behind it. But no, it's moving on its own.

"I think that means it's time for you to go," Dorey says. "Much as I would love to keep you both in here and dig the marrow out of your bones, I have a meeting."

I stand up. "What's the point, Dorey? Of trapping all these kids here?"

"How many times do I have to tell you that we are not trapping anyone?"

I remember Squirrel Girl and her strange, wasted expression. "You're vampires, then. Draining their magic, their life."

"Well, you could call an employer a vampire, couldn't you?" she says, waving a hand. "You work, and at the end of the day, you're tired. That's simple enough, isn't it?"

Aaron finally speaks, as if he's only now capable. "But people work in exchange for money."

"And they work in exchange for other things. Now, I really must go. Do stay safe, you two."

The door opens behind us, and we're looking into the Corridor.

15

"GIVE ME A MINUTE," AARON SAYS WHEN we're back in the Corridor. He sits down on one of the tiny chairs, the sides thin as the bones on a wrist.

What little color Aaron had in his face, whatever health he had regained from a few days of Nuala's cooking, has vanished.

"What a bitch," I say, and it's such a ridiculous understatement that he can't help laughing. A dry, exhausted laugh, but a laugh all the same.

There's a silence between us as the carriage clock ticks rapidly, like a mosquito.

He raises his head to look at me. "You didn't . . . You don't think I'm just manipulating you or something, do you? Saying whatever to get you on my side?"

I think about this as seriously as I can. "I don't know. I have my doubts sometimes, if I'm honest."

Aaron flinches. "That's fair." He twists at his fingers. "Remember when I told you about when I was really young and everyone thought I was this God prodigy, and I was always paranoid that maybe I didn't mean it? That I was lying to myself, and to everyone else?"

"You said, 'What if God knows I'm faking?'"

"Right. What if God knows I'm faking?" He breathes in. "And now I'm like, what if I'm faking again? What if my thoughts aren't my thoughts, but just, like, the thoughts of the group I happen to be part of?"

Dorey's words come back to me. *What must it be like in that brain of yours?*

"I'll level with you, Aar," I say, and then stop, because I have never instinctively shortened Aaron's name before. Like I would with Fi, or Lil. He is surprised, too, but doesn't say anything. "I'll level with you. Sometimes I think you're full of shit, too. Sometimes I think that we're crazy to hang out with you, given everything you've done to us. Especially Roe. I mean, *Jesus.*"

I trail off briefly, and realize that I am not helping.

"But I also think," I continue inelegantly, "you know, you believed terrible things, and you benefited from believing terrible things, and you gave up those benefits. I mean, you don't have a phone or any money or a place to live. You might get deported. So you must be serious. Why else would you be here if you weren't serious? It's not as if the Children kicked you out and you had no place to go. You left, right?"

He nods tightly, his mouth a thin line.

"And then I think . . . I have some pretty awful thoughts, too, y'know? Like . . ." I suddenly remember the other night, the why-don't-I-throw-my-phone-out-the-window moment. I shake my head, trying to banish it. "Like sometimes I think if people knew my inner monologue, they would *hate* me. But I guess it doesn't matter what you think, in the end. It's what you do."

Aaron nods slowly, his gaze focused on me, his body language gradually shifting. His hands clasp on the arms of the chair. He is coming back to himself.

"It is terrifying," he says finally. "It is *genuinely* frightening how good you would have been in the Children."

"I'll bet." I sigh. "Come on, let's get out of here."

·) ● ((·

The five of them are waiting outside the door, Fiona on the stairs, supporting Manon and her damaged ankle. We come out of the Corridor to a barrage of questions.

"Where did you guys go?"

"You disappeared!"

"It was like you *evaporated*."

"Did you go to the Lodge? Did you see the same girl again?"

"Are you OK? Are you safe? Do you feel OK?"

"We're fine," I say. "It was . . . We talked to Dorey. We're fine, though."

I feel slightly guilty, given that they have all clearly been so worried and we didn't exactly rush in getting back. We were both so spooked, though. Particularly Aaron. The old adage about putting on your own oxygen mask first comes back to me, that we needed that five-minute pause before rejoining the gang.

"Maeve," Nuala says sternly. "You must tell me exactly what she said."

"It was typical Dorey," Aaron says. "Vague and very confident that she's doing the right thing. According to her, no one is starving themselves. It's all like . . . Lent, or something, just normal spiritual fasting."

"Her main thing with us, I think, is that she wants us to fight and separate. She knows we're most powerful as a group. She was trying to turn me against Aaron, even in the room. And she was trying to turn Roe and Aaron against each other."

134

"And what about the Housekeeper?" Manon asks. "Did she talk about her conjure not working?"

"No," I say. "She had tarot cards, though. And she talked about, I don't know, learning things."

"Which cards?"

"Two of Wands. Page of Pentacles. Kind of boring." I think again. "That's another two-card spread. Most people do three minimum, right? Do you, Fi?"

"Yeah, mostly," Fiona says, shrugging. "Did you see anything else? Anything we can feed back to Paolo?"

I suddenly notice Paolo perched on the banister. Listening, or at least looking like he is.

"No. Just the inside of her office."

"I noticed something," Aaron suddenly says. "I looked out the window. There were trees. Quite distinctive trees."

I was dimly aware of the trees, but hadn't noticed anything distinctive about them.

"Go on," Nuala urges.

"They were odd, no leaves of course, but blown sideways. Like a claw."

Lily opens her bag and takes out a sketch pad, and Aaron draws a tree. It does look like a claw, the bark bent to the right, the branches like talons.

"Hawthorn," Nuala says. "They're hardy and they can grow anywhere, but they grow to the right where there's a lot of wind." She pauses. "Meaning it's probably coastal."

"*Coastal?*" Roe clarifies. Kilbeg city is at least forty minutes from the coast, and even then, the county's coastline is ragged and vast.

I notice a shimmer of raindrops on Roe's shoulders. "Did you go outside?"

"I was going out of my mind with worry," they respond, "so I walked around outside for a bit. I told myself that by the time I came back, you'd be home safe."

I reach my hand out and touch their damp hair, curling frantically as it dries.

"It wasn't raining," I suddenly say. "At the Lodge. There was no rain on the windowpane."

"The rain sometimes skips the coast. It's a microclimate out there," Nuala says, then turns to Fiona. "If Paolo sets out tonight, could he find somewhere coastal with the driest soil? With the bent hawthorn trees, like Aaron's drawing?"

Fiona motions to the magpie, who flies to her shoulder. She strokes his feathers with her thumb and murmurs something, her eyes unfocused. Then she goes to the window, pulls it up, and allows Paolo to swoop out. We all watch him as he disappears into the darkness. Each of us with our own gift, each of us a little jealous of Fiona's.

We head back to Nuala's house, all of us too wired to go home, and all too aware of the Christmas holidays to want to. We stop to get fish and chips on the way, our arms heavy with greasy paper bundles as we walk up Nuala's drive.

Something is obstructing Nuala's driveway. Something lumpy and difficult to make out in the darkness. For a brief, horrifying second, I am sure it is a dead body. But whose? Lorna McKeon? Squirrel Girl? I do a quick head count. We're all here, so no one in the core gang. A family member. No—not Jo, or my parents? Not Tutu?

As I get closer, I see that they are separate packages, and my first thought is: *So they decapitated the body, then?*

And then I am closer, and I see they are gifts. Christmas gifts, wrapped up in paper. Food hampers covered in cellophane. A box that looks like it's filled with wine bottles. Before I can even vocalize that I think it's a trap, I hear Nuala groan.

"Oh, for god's sake," she says. "Manon!"

"What!" Manon says. "What have I done?"

"You *know*."

Everyone who is not Nuala and Manon immediately feels awkward, knowing we are about to witness a family spat whether we want to or not. Our paper packages of chips burning our hands, our faces going numb in the cold.

"Can we go inside, or . . . ?" Lily volunteers.

"There's cheese!" Fiona says. "French cheese. You shouldn't leave it out here, Nuala, the foxes will take it."

"Manny," Nuala says sharply. "Did you tell him where I live?"

"Yes, of course. I had to," Manon says, not sounding remotely sorry. "He's my father, he wants to send Christmas presents. It will be my first Christmas without him, and he's lonely."

"Lonely!" Nuala exclaims, with a sourness that feels incredibly uncharacteristic. "*Lonely!* I have had sixteen Christmases alone in this house, Manny. And not by choice."

"Yes, by choice," Manny snaps. "Yes, *very much* by choice."

"I have a key," Aaron whispers. And we all carefully walk around mother and daughter, avoiding the hampers like they're land mines.

PAGE OF PENTACLES

16

"RESPECTFULLY," ROE SAYS AS SOON AS THE five of us are in the kitchen, "what the *hell* was that?"

"Don't get me started." Aaron sighs. "They do that all the time, you know. Last time I was living here, too."

"What's the deal, then?" I ask. "Do you know?"

"I try not to pry, but, like, they'll be absolutely fine and then Manon's dad, René, will come up and they'll just go nuclear on each other. What I can gather is that Nuala walked out on Manon as a kid, and there seems to be some dispute over whether or not that was Nuala's choice."

We have all put some version of this together ourselves, and still remain puzzled by the missing pieces.

"Nuala would never willingly walk out on her kid," Lily says defensively. "It must be Manon who has it wrong."

"Divorce is hard on people. My mum had a first husband," Fi says. "They had my brother together, and they're still in his life, but not in each other's. So."

Fiona is not particularly close with her brother in Boston, so I'm inclined to think she's only mentioning him so she can spring to Manon's defense.

Manon and Nuala enter the kitchen, still tense, still unwilling to talk about it.

"Everyone," Nuala says grandly. "How do we feel about a little Christmas party on Monday night? I suddenly have rather a lot of food to get through."

Manon starts taking the hampers in from the porch, her back to her mother.

"She's only saying that so she doesn't have to eat any of it," she calls back, and Fiona goes to help her.

"Well observed, Manny," Nuala says airily.

Roe gets a phone call and takes it in the kitchen. Manon, Fiona, Lily, and I unpack all the hampers in Nuala's living room, a shabby and rarely used space that is a temporary bedroom for Aaron. I notice his backpack and rolled-up sleeping bag propped next to the couch.

There's packing straw everywhere, and seemingly endless jars, tins, and bottles of things. Cured meat, soft cheeses, a big jar of cassoulet. Cherry tomatoes that look like they've been polished by tiny elves. Chocolates. Bunches of dried lavender.

"Your dad is very . . . generous," I say, trying not to betray Nuala by saying anything too positive about the mysterious René.

"It's Christmas, and he's rich," Manon says, carefully unwrapping everything and noting it dispassionately, as if adding it to a household inventory. "She's only doing this so that when he phones to ask if Fin enjoyed the food, I have to say 'She didn't eat any.'" Manon sighs. "She is such a baby."

"I'm going for a drive," Nuala says flatly. "Aaron, can I please have your cigarettes?"

Aaron throws his packet over without questioning her, and Nuala catches them midair.

"Thank you," she says shortly. "And will you go check on the chickens? I saw some hungry-looking foxes on the road earlier, and I don't want to lose the new batch."

"Right-o," Aaron says, pulling on some women's Wellington boots and leaving the room. "And here was me thinking I had escaped farm life."

Nuala silently heads out the door and to her car. We watch her from the window, smoking in the passenger seat, with clearly no intention of driving anywhere.

"Come on," Manon says. "Help me with this stuff. Don't pay attention to her. Try anything you want, it's all the best stuff. It's all delicious. Look, this preserve is from Céret, where I was born."

It occurs to us then that while Nuala is our dear friend, so is Manon. And for the first time ever, she wants to share something with us. She talks, quite animatedly, about the town where she was born, the Pyrenees mountains, the way she and her parents used to drive to Spain for the afternoon when they still lived in the hills. "I could speak Catalan, too," Manon says shyly. "I still remember some of it, even though I was only five."

"When did Nu . . ." I start to ask, then wonder if Manon and I are at that level of closeness. I don't know if I can ask her when her mother left. I break off, but I can feel Manon's eyes on me.

"Has he talked to you," Manon asks me, "about his power?"

"Who? Aaron?" I ask, realizing he is the only "he" left in our circle. She nods, looking at me steadily. "Not really. Why?"

She sits back, legs crossed, and stares absently at the mantelpiece. She looks like a little god. "Sometimes I feel like he is a foster brother, or something like that," she says. "Like I have to teach him things he did not learn from his first family."

"What do you mean?"

Manon shakes her head. "I suppose it's probably private," she says. "Here, smell this." She passes me a bundle of dried lavender. It's richer, cleaner than I remember lavender smelling. Not like old ladies at all. More like peppermint.

We sit on the floor, tasting and trying things. It is all delicious. At some point, I realize that Roe has been gone for a long time, and I drift into the kitchen to find them.

"Hey," I say. Roe is leaning against the counter, typing on their phone. "You OK out here?"

"Yeah. Just, you know, band stuff."

"What kind of band stuff?"

"Um . . ." Roe gazes out the kitchen window for a moment, clearly wrestling with some competing emotions. "So, earlier. In the car."

"Right."

"I told you about the playlist thing."

"Yes."

"Turns out it's a bigger deal than I initially thought."

"OK . . . ?"

"So we were always supposed to be starting the tour with Honor in April, right? But now, well, some people have reached out to us. It might make sense for us to do more solo shows before the tour starts. With us headlining, I mean. Like a mini tour."

"Wow," I say, leaning back against the counter. "That's great."

"It would start in January, and probably go until the end of Feb. With some UK dates and everything."

I blink. "So you'd have March at home," I say slowly. "And then you're out on tour again in April."

They nod. "Well, March we're supposed to be recording the album."

"Right."

There's a silence, and then I remember myself.

"Well . . . uh, congratulations?"

But neither of us can muster up much enthusiasm. This is at least four months of Roe away from Kilbeg. They look at me, eyes streaked in black, their expression unreadable.

"Yeah," they say. "Congratulations to me, I guess."

Another tense silence. "Listen, let's just say it." I finally start speaking, trying to adopt as positive a tone as possible. "We're not going to see much of each other for a few months, which, given that I'm supposed to be studying for exams, might be a good thing. Give me time to focus, y'know?"

I refuse to indulge the insecure part of myself that is always just a little bit frightened of being left behind. I remember Fiona at the party, quaking with nerves about leaving Kilbeg, wondering if it's all a bit too soon. I can't think about myself too much. Fiona and Roe are, after all, doing the scary thing. Not me.

Roe nods, trying to be reassured by this. "But . . . Dorey. The Children."

I shake my head. "Listen, if there's one thing I've learned about the Children, it's that their concerns are bigger than us. From that horrible conversation tonight, we know we're not exactly Dorey's top priority now. We should relish that."

I almost say, "Starving and emotionally torturing other people is her top priority right now!" but I don't want Roe to feel guilty about leaving, so I stop talking about Dorey. "We have to live our lives, Roe. Fiona too. This was always in both of your plans. You've always known you want to be artists. Upending your life plan is . . . letting them win, in a way."

Roe laughs softly. "You sound like one of those 'If we don't go on holidays, we're letting the terrorists win' people."

"Well, maybe they have a point," I say, and I wrap my arms around them. "This is *amazing* news," I stress. "Let's just have a fun Christmas, and a good New Year, and we'll worry about long-distance stuff when we have to."

Roe finally manages a smile, a real one. "God, look at you. Miss Emotional Maturity. What happened to that bitchy little schoolgirl?"

"I'm still a bitchy little schoolgirl."

We kiss, the terror of losing each other so huge that suddenly my back is pressed against the fridge, and we have lost ourselves to making out in Nuala's kitchen.

"Jesus," Fiona interrupts. "Get a room, you two."

"*Don't* get a room," Manon calls. "Go outside. Animals."

I laugh. "I should go," I say, looking at my watch. "My parents are going to be livid that I wasn't home earlier. All my siblings are back today."

"I'll drop you," Roe says. "Fi, Lil, I'm heading out soon."

Lily gets up, still eating a chocolate Père Noël. "Bon."

"I might stick around for a bit," Fiona says quietly, then checks to see if Manon reacts. Manon is busy collecting the paper and cardboard for recycling.

"Yes, stay," Manon says, sounding distracted. "So my mother can't go crazy again."

We leave soon after, Nuala and Aaron both smoking in the car, Fiona and Manon sitting on the living room floor. I make desperate eyes with Fiona as I put on my coat, trying to signal a *please text me the instant anything happens.*

As usual, Roe drops Lily off first and then me. We sit in the car and watch the windows of my house like it's a theater.

"I better go in. Mum will be so annoyed I didn't come home sooner."

"Wait a second," Roe says, pulling me back, tucking me under their shoulder. "You freaked me out today. You just disappeared into thin air."

"I know, that must have been so freaky. I'm sorry."

"It wasn't just that. It was that you disappeared together."

"Oh."

"It was, like, I finally understood why you would get so weirdly jealous about me and Fiona, or me and the band, or whatever. I thought you were just being immature. But . . . seeing someone you love have a connection with someone who isn't you, even if it's, I don't know, platonic. It's hard."

A pause.

"I *do* trust you," Roe says unconvincingly.

"OK," I say slowly. "The way you're saying it doesn't sound like you trust me very much at all."

I remember the moment at the school, when I thought Aaron might want to kiss me. The hint of excitement at what might happen. Shame burbles through me, but then I remember my own advice: it's your actions that are important, not your thoughts. I had jumped up, ending the tension as soon as I realized it was there.

Suddenly, I'm annoyed. Why does everyone feel so comfortable reprimanding me all the time? If it's not Fiona, it's Roe; if it's not my parents, it's my teachers. If it's not my classmates accusing me of making Lily disappear, it's Lily herself, furious for bringing her back. I'm just a person. A person who didn't ask for any of this—not for the magic, not for the responsibility of keeping the Well safe. Yet everyone else seems to cope just fine, and I have somehow become the lightning rod for every minor complaint.

"It's just," Roe continues, "you have this connection, the two of

146

you, and I know you can't help being sensitives. But the way you were at the school together, just by coincidence. And that note . . ."

"This is why you're nervous about leaving, isn't it?" I snap, suddenly very bored of this. "That whole business about being nervous about Dorey. You just think I'm going to cheat on you if you leave."

"No," Roe says quickly. "I don't think that."

I gaze out the window. "I have to go," I say.

"Don't go, Maeve."

"I have to."

"Why?"

"Because I'm afraid that if I stay a second longer, I'll read your mind and find out how you really feel."

I don't slam the door. Slamming the door is something an immature person would do, after all. I kiss Roe on the cheek and leave the car quietly. I say hello to my brothers and sisters and act normal for an hour. Then I go upstairs to cry in bed. Maturely.

17

FIONA CALLS ME IN THE MORNING.

"I want to die," she says.

"All right. Do you want me to come over?"

"No, god no. Let's meet in town."

"OK. An hour at Bridey's?"

"You're a good friend."

"I know."

Presumably things did not go well with Manon, then. I shower and get dressed quickly, making a mental note to do the rest of my Christmas shopping after I see Fiona. There are a couple of messages from Roe: nothing with an apology, just lots of positive, smoothing texts about how we should get lots of date nights in before they go on tour.

I'm in such a rush to meet Fiona that I run past a telephone pole and almost miss the familiar face staring right back at me.

MISSING PERSON

LORNA MCKEON

18 years old, white, medium build. Last seen on the 14th of December wearing blue jeans, white sweater, and yellow puffer jacket. If you have seen her or know of her whereabouts, please contact Kilbeg Valley Police.

I stare at the poster for a long time. Tomorrow, Lorna will have been missing for ten days. How was the alarm not raised sooner?

It occurs to me then that online classes might even be beneficial to the Children. People always talk about boys being radicalized while alone in their bedrooms. But what about girls? Who could be more vulnerable than a friendless girl alone in her bedroom all day?

When Lily went missing, the police came to school. The whole city was engaged. The teachers talked to us. But now there is no school, and our remaining teachers are desperately trying to bring us over the finish line, probably while simultaneously looking for new jobs. But even so, Lily was on the news. There were search parties. I take a photo of the MISSING poster and send it to our WhatsApp group.

Why isn't there a fuss about this, I text. **The way there was a fuss about Lily?**

Because she's 18, Nuala messages back. **She has a boyfriend. Her parents probably thought that she had run off with him and were waiting for her to come back.**

She has a point. Plus, Lily went missing in the middle of the night. There was a sense of mystery that involved the entire community. I keep an eye out for more Lorna posters on the way into town. I see three. Lily's had blanketed the entire area. There was no one who wasn't talking about it. Girls weren't allowed out at night. One shouldered me into a locker because of it.

Fiona looks like she hasn't slept. She's sitting in Bridey's, clutching a mug with both hands. I hug her, my hair falling into her tea slightly. She barely notices.

"All right," I say gently, sitting down. "Tell me everything."

"So, we hung out all evening. And I stayed the night."

"Where?" I ask immediately. "There's only one bed."

Fiona's eyes bulge slightly. A silent cry of *I know*.

"Oh shit," I say, dropping my voice to a whisper. "There's *only one bed*."

"Yeahhh."

"So what happened?"

Fiona tells me what happened between her and Manon. I know Fiona's brain so well that the scene appears perfectly in my mind without even trying to read her, although every angle is colored with residual embarrassment.

"We were hanging out for ages, just the two of us," Fi says. "Just me and Manon, sitting on the living room floor, drinking her dad's wine."

I see it, Manon's already striking beauty embroidered with the love and dedication of Fi's memory. I notice the things that only Fiona has noticed: the round rusty freckles on the bridge of Manon's nose, her curls, her pupils that seem to be constantly expanding and contracting regardless of the light.

They talked about their lives, and the things they wanted for themselves. Manon spoke, more than she has ever spoken before, about her family. None of us have ever fully understood Manon's god lineage; we simply marvel at her trickster talents when she deigns to show them to us. After Nuala left, Manon and her father lived with her grandparents in a big country house an hour outside Paris.

"She didn't go into detail," Fiona says, "but I got the impression of, you know, horses and tennis courts. Like, her and her dad lived in their own *wing*."

"What's their deal, then? Where does the money come from?" I ask, momentarily forgetting Fiona's romantic failures, my curiosity taking over.

"As far as I can make out," Fi says slowly, "they're this extraordinarily old family and their whole deal is messing shit up for people."

"Why?"

"Because"—Fiona furrows her brow, clearly still confused by this—"when human beings think they're infallible, when they think they're in control, when they think they're so rich and so powerful that they are gods, things . . . get bad."

"OK, I get that."

"And so trickster gods—or, specifically, Manon's family—their whole thing is restoring humility and shattering delusions. Undermining politicians, making them look stupid. Screwing people over a little, making them realize they're not in control."

"That's mad," I say, wondering if Manon's family was secretly responsible for that British prime minister who got stuck on a zip line.

"I know. They take it very seriously, considering it's so obviously mad."

"I sort of get it, though. I get how it's important." I pause to consider it all. "So Manon just *told* you all this?"

"Yeah." Fiona sighs heavily. "It was awesome."

It was Aaron, in the end, who moved things along. He has to wait until everyone goes to bed so he can sleep on the couch, so he started yawning loudly until Fiona eventually took the hint. She began to order a taxi, but it being the weekend before Christmas, the app kept canceling on her.

Just stay the night, Manon had said simply.

"So I'm freaking out," Fiona explains, jittery and wild-eyed. "Like, on the one hand, this is literally amazing, and on the other hand, like, she's older? And she's *French*? What if she actually does

152

like me back, and she does want to do stuff, and I'm clueless because I've never done anything with a girl before?"

I rub her arm gently, trying to calm her. Hoping for the best, even though I know this evening has clearly not gone well.

"So she gives me some pajamas and I get changed in the bathroom or whatever," she says, eyes darting around wildly. "And we get into bed."

"And then what?"

"And it's awkward! Like, you know how when you and I share a bed, it's just very stupid and funny and we get all giddy and can't stop laughing?"

"I know it well."

"We were *deadly* silent," she says morosely. "Like, pin-drop type stuff."

"Shit."

"I know. It was so uncomfortable. But I can tell she's uncomfortable, too? Which is kind of telling, in its own way. Like, if she thought we're just friends, she wouldn't be uncomfortable, would she?"

"I guess not."

"So we're, like, we're pretending to be asleep. I can tell neither one of us is actually sleeping."

"I am dying. I am dying of how awkward this story is."

"So then she suddenly says, 'I can't sleep.' And I say, 'I can't either.' And we turn to face each other, Maeve, and our faces are so close, and we're just looking. I can literally *feel* her breath. Total silence. Then she very gently moves a bit of hair out of my face, and her thumb brushes against my cheek."

"*Oh, my god.* Oh, my god?"

"And then Paolo shows up."

"And then Paolo shows up?!"

My hands are clasped in front of my mouth, and I can't stop whispering "No no no!" as if I can undo everything just by saying it. Fiona is shaking her head, like she still can't believe it, either.

"Paolo taps on the window, and so I get up and let him in. And Manon hates Paolo, right, so I'm super self-conscious and I just want him to go away. But he won't go away. He keeps futzing around the room, hopping from one bit of furniture to the other, just not getting the hint at all."

"Oh, god. Fiona. No."

"So I'm just running around the room trying to get *my friggin' bird to leave* so I can kiss her, and Manon is like, 'What does he have to say, Fiona, listen to him.'"

She squeezes her eyes shut as if she's trying to erase the visual from her mind. I don't blame her.

"So I listen to him, and he knows where the Lodge is. He's found it."

"What?!"

I say it so loud that everyone in Bridey's seems to stop speaking to look at me.

"Fiona," I say sharply. "That's the kind of information you *lead* with."

Fiona has already put her forehead on the table, too depressed to go on. "I'm sorry, but I knew if I led with it, we would have to leap into action stations, and I wouldn't have gotten to talk about this. And I *need* to talk about this."

"OK," I say, trying not to jump all over her. "OK, tell me. What happened next?"

"So we decide to wait until morning to tell Nuala about the Lodge's location. I can't figure out exactly where it is anyway, but we know she will because he has a completely clear picture now. We go back to bed. But the spell is broken, and it's awkward as hell again. So I'm like, OK, Fiona, you only live once, and I . . . I sort of lean in and try to kiss her."

I hold my breath.

"And she . . . didn't kiss me back."

"Why not? Did she say?"

"It was confusing," she says, shaking her head. "She said I was too young, and too . . ." She winces. "Damaged."

"She said that?"

"Not in so many words. But I could tell that was what she meant." Fiona takes a deep breath. "So I waited until it was light and then left first thing in the morning."

I'm reeling at this story. "Oh, man," I reply, trying to focus on being sympathetic before I dash to the buried lead, the location of the Lodge. "I'm so sorry, Fi."

"It's good, in a way," Fiona says, her eyes brimming slightly. "Because now I can go off and make a TV show and not worry about it. Did I tell you they want to see me again before they go? They want to put an audition on tape."

She tries to brighten up at this, but her tone is artificial. Spun from nothing. "My dreams are coming true, after all."

"Yeah," I say, nodding ferociously. "You'll be doing that for a few months, and you can take some time to forget about the crush."

"It's not just a *crush*," Fiona suddenly snaps.

"Isn't it?"

She looks nauseous. "I don't know. If this is what a crush is, then I'm scared of it. I think about her constantly. Everything I do I'm like: Wouldn't it be better if Manon was here?" Fiona is making desperate, nervous eye contact with me, as if trying to communicate *Is it OK to be this vulnerable?* "Like even the show. I keep fantasizing about asking her to come with me. Which I know is stupid. I mean, what would she even do in Belfast?"

"They're shooting it in *Belfast*?"

"Yeah, didn't I say?"

"You did *not* say." The old panic rises up through me, the thing I have to so diligently squash. "That's so far away," I say weakly. "You have to *fly* there."

"It's only five hours in the car."

"That's so far."

"Not by American standards."

"But by *Irish* standards . . ." I twitch, changing gear. "So Paolo knows where the Lodge is, then."

She nods slowly. "Yeah. I guess this means we have to have another team meeting?"

"I'm afraid so."

We send the texts around and decide to meet tonight to discuss Paolo's discoveries. Nuala and Manon need to finish the day at Divination, Roe is with the band, and we three girls need to put in some appearances with our families. Every so often we have to pop in and remind them that we're not dead. Yet.

Fiona and I trail the streets, doing our Christmas shopping, Fi vacillating between profound misery at the Manon situation to manic excitement about the TV show. It's clearly unsettling her. She's so used to being in control of her emotions.

"I'm starting to think," she says while we stand in the Marks & Spencer's queue, our arms weighed down with gray knitwear for our dads, "that maybe I never even *really* liked anyone before this."

"Do you think you might be? You know? A lesbian, or bi, or what? Sorry, I know we're supposed to be beyond labels now, blah blah blah."

"I don't even know. Like am I bi or gay or pan or whatever? I've always just sort of fancied everybody, in a low-level kind of way. But I haven't been attracted to any guy since . . . well, that thing happened. They just feel a bit gross to me. Like, lesser."

I hug her arm. The boyfriend she had when she first came to have her tarot read, the one who forced her to do stuff and who the cards advised her to dump. I only wish I had started reading tarot a few weeks earlier. "Sorry your first big crush isn't going to plan."

"You know who else has a big crush that isn't going to plan?"

"Who?"

"Aaron."

"What do you mean?"

She narrows her eyes at me. "Come on now, Maeve."

"What *do* you mean, though?"

"I mean, he always seems to find a way to be wherever you are."

"That's the sensitivity thing, I think."

"Hmm." She pauses, redistributes her shopping in her arms. The queue moves forward slightly. "I mean, no offense, I know you're the more powerful witch, but he's the more powerful sensitive, isn't he? Not in a misogynist way, just, like, he's been doing this for longer. When we met him, he was controlling rooms full of people. Do you think there's a chance he's manipulating these situations, too?"

I look at her, horrified. *"No."*

"You trust him that much?" she asks, as if I could really be that naive. "He was asking all these questions about you last night."

"What? What questions?"

"Weird stuff. Just drilling for information. Asking if you seemed different lately."

This unnerves me. This theory of his is starting to bother me, particularly because he has nothing to back it up. I shake my head.

"Don't pay any attention to him," I say quickly. "He doesn't know what he's talking about."

"Manon says they've been talking a lot. In the evenings."

"Oh yeah? About what?"

"I don't know. Stuff about his power. About it not being as straightforward as he thought."

For some reason I don't tell her about Aaron's insistence that I am different. If we're going to deal with this Lodge threat, I don't have time for weird existential questions from the mind of a crazy person.

18

I SPEND THE EVENING WITH PAT AND CILLIAN, who have gotten their old game console down from the attic, and we smash through a few rounds of *Crash Bandicoot*. The dog's body is pressed firm against my thigh. Tutu is getting old now, and the noise of a full house is a little much for him, I think. It's fun, being with my brothers, even if I can't help but feel that I am wearing a sort of costume for every moment we are together. I laugh a little too hard, talk about the things they want me to talk about: school, TV shows, Fiona and Roe's new shared destiny of becoming extremely famous.

My entire family is thrilled about this when I bring it up at dinner, delighted that something has come along to distract from witchcraft, to dilute the closeness between us. Their desires are strangely aligned with Dorey's in that way: Separate them. Untie the pretzel of teen group dynamics. Make them independent.

"And you'll have your *own* thing soon enough," Jo says condescendingly. "Don't worry, it's not unusual to not have your shit together. You just come from an unusually ambitious friend group."

I remember those silver coins that the Children put on our skin to mute our power. Sometimes I wish I'd kept one, to muffle myself at moments like this. Moments when I have to be normal.

"Yeah, Mae," Patrick pipes in. "You know, you could always borrow my bass and start your own band."

"Uh-huh," I say, thinking: I'm currently trying to liberate a cult from a maniac, forgive me if I'm not that stressed about not having a passion for the humanities.

The one good thing about all of this is that my parents don't give me any hassle about heading over to Nuala's again. They seem to understand that my time left with Fi and Roe is dwindling and are trying to be sensitive to it. Jo drops me off on her way back to her own flat, babbling on about how I shouldn't worry about finding my "place" in the world.

And for once, I'm not actually worried. I have a place in the world. My family just doesn't understand what that place is.

There's a tension in Nuala's kitchen, subtle but unmistakable. I'm the only one who knows about what happened between Fiona and Manon, but because they're both such strong personalities, it's noticeable when they're feeling a little off. They're at opposing ends of the kitchen, both with arms folded, neither speaking very much.

Roe and I aren't much better. We don't acknowledge our fight last night, silently agreeing to smooth over it in light of Paolo's discovery. The air between us is still off, though, our body language stiff. You can tell that Lily, Aaron, and Nuala are slightly confused by the energy in the room, and it puts them in a weird mood, too.

"OK, Fiona," Nuala says, "what does Paolo have for us?"

The bedsheet is up again, the one with Lily's Sharpie drawing. Lily is poised with the marker, waiting to add more details. Nuala has even set up another sheet, in case Lily is tempted to doodle off into the walls.

"I've got some aerial shots, basically," Fi says, closing her eyes and absently stroking Paolo's monochrome feathers. "I've got a craggy bit of the coastline, shaped a little bit like . . . a horse?"

"A horse?" Nuala says, poised over an ordinance survey map of the county. "What do you mean?"

"Like, the bay is the shape of a horse's head. Long and curves around, with a pointed jaggy bit that's like an ear."

"Wynne Bay," Nuala says excitedly, circling it with a red pen. "Is this it?"

Fi opens her eyes. "That's it!"

She hurriedly closes them again. "OK, we're talking two miles east of the coastline, on a hill or a slope of some kind. Surrounded by fields."

"Hills, hills, hills," Nuala says, running her pen along each grid. "I've got three definite hills it could be."

Fi scrunches her face up, concentrating hard. "There's no road," she says. "The only road anywhere near is by a deer park about a mile south. I don't know how you'd get there."

"I imagine that's intentional," Aaron says dryly.

Nuala nods, still scanning with her pen. "Lots of those places are unconnected to roads. They ran out of money before they were given a chance to connect them to civilization." She looks up triumphantly. "I have it. Fiona, come over here and have a look."

We all gaze at the spot on Nuala's map: a patchy raised circle amid fields, with one side of it facing onto water.

"That's it," Fiona says slowly. "That has to be it."

"A fairy fort," Nuala murmurs. "If anyone had 'fairy fort' on their bingo cards, please mark it off."

"That's not *real*, though, is it?" Aaron says hesitantly. He can't tell whether this is in the realm of folksy Irish myth or something he has to actually worry about.

"Depends on who you ask," Nuala says. "I keep an open mind. I wouldn't touch one myself, but these people built a hotel on it."

"And then they ran out of money," Lily says, as if this proves something.

"And now Dorey is on it," I add. "So clearly she doesn't think it's an issue."

"Dorey wants to be near power of any kind," Aaron says. "Good or bad, real or imagined."

Nuala writes the map coordinates on the bedsheet, and I feel a tremble of excitement.

"Well, shit!" I yelp. "I can't believe we did it. We found the Lodge. They're finished, guys. They're done."

Nuala looks up at me. "Hold on, Maeve. Don't get trigger-happy."

I look at her, confused. "What do you mean?"

"We can't just barge over there."

"Well, why not?"

"Don't you think a plan of some kind would be wise?" Manon says. "They will have all kinds of precautions for us coming. We must pick our moment and know exactly what we're going to do."

"Manny is right," Nuala says. "We're too vulnerable."

For some reason, this really irritates me. "How on earth are we vulnerable? In this room alone, we have two sensitives, one healer, someone who can literally talk to machines, a shapeshifter, a witch, and a human Pikachu," I say breathlessly. "Plus Paolo. And what do they have?"

"Money, power, location, numbers," Roe says, listing the reasons on their fingers. "Manon and Nuala are right, Maeve. We're powerful but we have to remember what happened last time we got cocky."

"Yeah," Fiona says bluntly. "They ambushed us and burned the school down."

"And two people died," Lily says. "Although I do appreciate the Pikachu reference."

I know that they have good points, but I also can't shake the visual of Lorna's face on the telephone pole, or Squirrel Girl sitting hungrily on her bed. How can they just carry on with their lives when people are wasting away under Dorey's control?

"There's also the matter that we won't be able to find a way in," Nuala continues. "No roads for miles. So we'll have to come by foot, which will make it harder to escape if things turn nasty. This needs to be done very, very carefully."

"Aaron and I could go in through the Corridor," I say, trying to keep a level head. "And we could find a safe way for you guys to get in. There has to be some kind of secret road. I saw cars there."

Roe puts a hand on my shoulder. "It's too dangerous. You can't risk getting trapped there. You and Aaron don't have any hard power, like electricity. No defenses. She could eat you alive."

I notice Aaron's expression darkening when Roe says "hard power."

"It's a soft power I have, then? Manipulating people into thinking they hate themselves?"

"Yeah, it's mind stuff. It's not physical," Roe argues.

Manon ignores them. "And as much as Dorey does not want to use her own magic against you, if she is using it in self-defense it will not warrant the same kind of karma."

"Self-defense?"

"She will be defending her property. If you do anything destructive, she could seek revenge quite easily without repercussion."

"Then when do we go?" I ask. "Tomorrow?"

"Tomorrow is Christmas Eve," Fiona says.

"And we're hardly going to go on Christmas Day," Lily adds.

"I've got band stuff on the twenty-seventh and twenty-eighth," Roe says, looking at the calendar app on their phone.

"I'm doing my tape on the twenty-eighth, too," Fiona adds absently. "For the show."

I want to scream. I know that everyone is being reasonable. I know that strategy is important. But I also can't help but feel a furious resentment toward my friends, their lives and dreams so promisingly laid out before them, while the sole birthright of protecting Kilbeg sits on my shoulders. Perhaps if this was a different kind of night, I wouldn't feel so angry. If Roe and I hadn't fought, if Manon hadn't rejected Fiona. If my family hadn't been patronizing. If the vibe in Nuala's kitchen was easier. I don't know. All I know is that I can't take it anymore, how casual everyone is being.

"Kids are suffering," I say tightly. "Squirrel Girl might have keeled over by the time we get to her, never mind what's happening with Lorna. Wherever she is. Aaron, come on, you must have a feeling about this? You're being freakishly quiet."

Aaron is clearly undecided. "I . . . I don't know," he says. "I'm like you, Maeve, I saw Squirrel Girl, I had the conversation with Dorey, too, so it feels like we need to do something, like . . . yesterday."

"Right!" I can't help but feel grateful that someone is treating this with a little urgency.

"But. They have the advantage. They're on home turf. We've only seen a hallway and two rooms in the Lodge, Maeve. We don't know how big it is. If it takes us a little while to come up with an airtight plan, I think maybe that's . . . OK?"

That intense, bleaching rage comes over me again. The same

rage I felt when Aaron and Roe fought on the scaffolding. It feels hot enough to bake pottery. My hearing muffles and a surge of power comes through me, filling the veins in my arms. I know what's about to happen, because it's happened twice already.

"I mean," Aaron continues, watching my expression change, "we could always do another recon mission."

Don't blind them, I whisper to myself. *Control yourself, please. I really don't want to blind them, I promise.*

"Maeve?" Roe says. "Are you OK?"

Roe puts a hand on the small of my back and I immediately snap at them, moving sharply away. "Don't *touch* me," I shriek. It's building up in my wrists. The terrible anger that requires a direction, a force, a subject. My vision is blurred by tears, so I can't see Roe's hurt expression.

I can just about see the shape of the back door, and I push past Fiona as I move toward it.

"Where are you *going*?" she says.

But I'm already outside in the cold, clean December air, running up Nuala's garden, trying to put as much space between me and the house as possible. I finally hit the chicken house, where the new wire stands proudly around the pen. They are still wandering around, clucking and picking at the earth. They never seem to sleep, these chickens.

I slump to my knees, my fingers wrapped around the holes in the fence. The feeling of wire digging into my skin a strange relief from the pain of power. We boiled down Nuala's old chickens for fat, and made them into candles, candles we used in a ritual to seal the Well. We didn't feel good about it, but we did it anyway. Is this how Dorey feels about us? About all of Kilbeg?

My mind darkens, deadens. Something deeper than sleep.

Cards, cards, cards. Ace of Spades. Two of Hearts. Queen of Diamonds.

Visions of dirty rooms and sticky playing cards. My own sight leaving me. My weight falling, hard, onto the carpeted floor.

Then a new vision, emerging from somewhere else, from an older place. The feeling of walking through a field with high crops in a loose dress. The feeling of an animal pressing its weight against my leg. A companion. A wet nose.

My eyes open in sudden relief, like something poisonous has been drained out of me. My knees slide deeper into the dirt, my jeans ruined, my fingers limp against the chicken wire. I look up, and five chickens are looking back at me, their eyes white.

"Maeve," comes a voice from behind me.

I feel too far away from the earth to even identify who it is. All I can do is stare at the chickens, which are remarkably calm about their pale, glowing eyes. Perhaps they don't need their sight very much. Perhaps they can't see very well in the dark, anyway.

"Maeve."

I don't know how to respond. My tongue has forgotten how. But I can feel someone unpicking my fingers from the chicken wire, and a sudden wetness in my hands. I'm bleeding, I realize. The wire has left deep grooves in my skin, just under the knuckles.

I come back to my body. My legs and torso, flat in the mud. My hands in the fence, looking like someone who died trying to escape.

"It's Aaron, Maeve."

There's a strange sense of a long time having passed. Not just minutes, but hours. I slowly come onto my knees, my whole body cold.

"Where did you go?"

"What do you mean? I've been here."

He crouches down on the ground next to me, his expression like a worried doctor's.

"Maeve, we all came back here looking for you. You were gone. Everyone left, thinking you walked home."

I blink. "What time is it?"

"Midnight. You've been gone for almost two hours. I was just coming out to check the fence again, before I went to sleep."

"Jesus."

"Come inside."

"I can't." My body feels frozen solid, too cold to possibly move.

"You have to," he says, linking his arm into mine, trying to get me to my feet. "I need to talk to you. Privately. Come on, there still might be a pub open or something."

I'm too exhausted, too cold, and too crazy for this shit.

"No," I say. "I'm tired of being your Best Special Gal Pal. I only ever get in trouble for it. It's a bad idea."

"We need to talk," he repeats. "It's serious."

"I'm not going to fuck you, OK?" I suddenly snap. "I don't fancy you, and I'm in a relationship. So, sorry. Thanks, but no thanks."

A pause, not so much of hurt feelings, but of allowing me to take stock of the horrible thing I just said.

"Do you feel better now, for having said that?"

"No."

"How do you feel?"

"Like I'm losing my mind."

He sits down next to me, the chicken fence wilting slightly against our weight, and sparks up a cigarette.

"Are you ready to hear it yet?"

I hold on to my knees. He gives me a few seconds to respond, taking a long drag, the slight fizzle of burning paper just barely audible in the quiet night air.

"It's you, Maeve," he says.

For a very real and terrifying second, I think he means something else.

It's you, like: I've finally found what I'm looking for.

It's you, like: I'm in love with you.

It's you, like: it's you and me, kid.

"It's you, Maeve," he says again. "You're the Housekeeper."

19

"OH, GOOD ONE," I SAY. "HA, HA."

"It's not a joke," he says grimly. "And you know it's not a joke."

"You think I'm the Housekeeper," I repeat, forcing big, empty laughs up from my stomach. "That's just stupid."

"All this stuff that's been happening with you lately," he says. "You can't hide it from me, Maeve. There's something dark in you, and it's growing. The blindness, the weird fits of rage, the *thing* with me and Roe on the scaffolding. That was her, trying to protect the Well. I'm starting to understand now. You're her."

I shake my head. "That makes no sense."

The party, the secrets, the cruelty. The kiss I ruined for Lily. The explosion of Becky Foghorn's world. Why do I do these things? Why can't I stop doing them?

"It does. In a weird way, it does. And I keep . . . I keep seeing things, Maeve, and I know you're seeing them, too. The playing cards. The weird dirty room. It all goes back to her, I think."

I try to get to my feet, finally able to move my legs again. But the world begins to tilt slightly, and even though I'm crouching in the grass at the top of Nuala's garden, I feel like I'm about to roll off the edge of the world.

My knees tremble, and I grab on to Aaron to stay steady. I must be gripping hard, because he yelps. The world tips again, this time in the other direction, but I must be the only one who's feeling it.

"Come on," he says, getting to his feet and pulling me up with him. "I'm getting you out of here."

"Ha, ha," I say again, still stuck on my own bad, fake laughter. "Ha, ha."

"Are you able to walk by yourself?" he asks as I feel my legs moving toward the garden wall. "Can you jump the wall? I don't want to go back through the house and wake up Nuala and Manon."

"I *will* be able to walk by myself," I say fiercely. "Once the world stops moving."

Why would he say that? Why would he think it? The fact that I've acted like a bitch doesn't mean that I'm the Housekeeper. I'm frequently a bitch. I'm *famously* a bitch. The blindness doesn't prove anything, either. The Housekeeper has nothing to do with blindness. That's not her thing. Not at all.

Aaron helps me over the wall, and suddenly we are on the street. We walk for a bit, Aaron tugging at me to move along, clearly growing impatient with my limp, muddy form.

"You're insane, Aaron, do you know that? You're crazy. Everyone knows."

"With all due respect, you're the one covered in mud with blood all over her hands."

He hails a cab and bundles me into the back seat, clipping the seat belt over me like I'm a toddler. It feels like a straitjacket, like a rope being bound around my chest.

"Get it off," I screech, fumbling for the release button.

The cab driver visibly jumps in his seat. "Buddy," he says to

Aaron sharply, and in a Dublin accent. "I'm in no mood for trouble today. Tell your missus to keep it down."

My body feels like it is turning to black tar, and I dive quickly into the cab driver's thoughts, my power still high and tingling.

"Your wife left you," I snap. "So don't go throwing the word *missus* around."

Does it even make sense as an insult? I don't know. But my gift has stretched its wings. It is a bird that hunts from above.

"Right, get out," the driver says. "Get out. Now."

"Please," Aaron says desperately. "She's just . . . gotten some bad news. She's upset."

"I haven't!" I protest shrilly. "I have *not* gotten bad news. I have gotten a crazy theory from an unstable person."

"Please, dude," Aaron begs. "Can you just take us up the hill? Drop us at the end of Newman Street?"

"Newman Street?" I say. "You want to go to the school?"

"I'm not driving her anywhere," says the driver.

"I'll give you . . ." Aaron starts looking in his wallet. "Twenty-six euro. For a ten-minute drive. Pretty good, right?"

The driver can't resist, and he drives us. As the black tar starts to simmer down, I can't believe I said that about his wife. Why? When he hadn't done a thing to me?

The world stops teetering, and instead a dull, numb nausea sets in. I don't look at Aaron. I stare out the window, watching people as they stumble out of clubs. Girls in tiny dresses, too drunk to feel the cold.

"Come on," he says. "We're here."

The driver drops us at the school, and I mumble a "Sorry" to him. It's not his fault his wife left him, after all, she just fell in love with someone else.

The building is starting to smell different. The smell of St. Bernadette's has, for the last month, been almost comforting: old wood and ash, the slight liveliness of mold. Now there's a new element, warm and animal, that is curling my nostrils.

"Why are we here?" I ask, my eyes searching along the wall, trying to find the source of the smell. It's red and wet, like a barn after something is born. Did something die in the walls?

The crying begins, our signal to go to 2A, as normal now as a microwave's ding. "Come on," Aaron says. "I just have a feeling."

"I don't want to hear about your feelings," I snap. "Your weird fan theories about my life."

He pulls me up the stairs, hopping over the Manon-shaped hole, and puts his hand on the handle of 2A.

"Are you ready?"

He doesn't wait for an answer. He just pulls me in.

The smell is worse in the Corridor, and I gag slightly as we walk in. The odor is older, thicker, like copper coins and used period pads. Aaron pulls his T-shirt up over his nose.

The silence in the room shifts and becomes loaded. It's hard to describe. Like an invisible darkness, if there could be such a thing, or a cloak over the air.

"I don't want to," I suddenly blurt, my eyes filling with tears.

"You have to," he says sternly. He puts his hand on my shoulder and frog-marches me down the corridor. We get to the Housekeeper's portrait, and I turn my body toward the other door, fixing my gaze on the dark wood. The only surface with no paintings.

As the atmosphere becomes heavier, something primal and self-interested bubbles up in me, something that says, *Don't look, Maeve. Don't turn around.*

"Maeve," Aaron says softly. Because he knows. The metal thread of sensitivity yanks at us both, and we know. "You have to look."

Time moves differently in the Corridor, and it's hard to know whether I turn around ten seconds or ten minutes later. But I do turn around. And I do look at the wall.

She's the Housekeeper, but not as I've known her. The demon whose face looked more like a mask, whose eyes and lips are unlined, who was more phantom than woman. She's there, in her long white dress, the dog at her side—but she's a person. She's a young woman. Her hair is dark, somewhere between curly and frizzy, and falls over her shoulders naturally. The Housekeeper has always looked like she's been dragged by the collar out of the Beg River, but this woman is perfectly dry. Rumpled, maybe.

I step closer. She has blue-gray eyes, coin-shaped, somewhat sallow skin, and dark, thick eyebrows. The dog, too, is different. I've always seen him as a whippet or a greyhound, but this one is smaller, fluffier.

It's easier, I realize, to take in the picture one detail at a time than to step back and understand what it is.

Which is a picture of myself.

Which is a picture of the Housekeeper.

Which is a picture of myself.

The world tips again. Suddenly I'm on my knees, and every organ in my body feels like it is jammed inside my chest. The room fills with a dry, heaving wail, and for a moment I think the crying has come back: the crying that has become so normal for me and Aaron to hear, the crying that shudders from the bones of the house when it wants something from us.

The crying, I realize, that has always belonged to me. A wail and a sorrow so strong that it has become stuck in the mouth of the Kilbeg Well like a filling in a tooth. Maybe it belongs to other women, other Housekeepers, other creatures who found out, the way I am finding out, that they are doomed. Doomed to be an instrument of revenge, doomed to live forever, doomed to never really live again.

Then, from the bottom of all that murkiness, comes up something clean and crisp. A message from the Well, for the sensitive who was born to protect it.

You wanted to know who the Housekeeper was, Maeve?

Ask yourself: Who keeps the house?

PART
TWO

20

I WAKE UP ON SISTER ASSUMPTA'S OLD couch. Aaron is cross-legged on the floor, hands knitted together, his nose resting on his knuckles. He must have moved me here. I don't remember collapsing, but there's a stiff ache in my joints, something that tells me I hit the floor all at once. I stare at the ceiling for a few moments, the plaster in the corners of the room molded to look like roses. The fire damage has started to crumble away at the petals, chunks missing from the facade.

"So," I say, without breaking my gaze with the ceiling, "how long have you known?"

He looks past me for a moment, and I can't tell if he's thinking or avoiding the question. "Something's been happening to you," he says. "Like a disease, or an infection. But something has been happening to me, too."

"What?"

"You know what my gift is, right?"

"Yes," I answer, my throat still hoarse from screams. "Finding the worst in people. What makes them the most vulnerable."

"Right. That's what I thought it was, too. But what makes people vulnerable? Their memories. The little hidden shameful moments that they don't want to think about. That's what I did with the

Children, really. Excavating all this shame from people, then using it to control them."

I don't know what any of this has to do with me being the Housekeeper, but my throat is too sore to interrupt.

"But then I hang out with you guys and, you know, everyone's gift seems much simpler than that. Lily and the electricity, Fiona and the healing, you and your telepathy, Roe and the machines. My gift feels very . . . muddy by comparison. But then I started to realize, I specialize in shame because I always *feel* ashamed. My gift has been sort of warped by my years with the Children, I think. But I can feel my brain . . . calming down a little, for the first time ever, and I think I can feel the real gift coming through."

"Your brain is *calm* right now?" I ask, thinking about the insane snatches of thought I've caught from his inner monologue.

"Manon has been helping me figure it out. My gift is memories," he says, as if it's a relief to finally say it out loud. "My gift is the past. I'm getting all these traces of memory from you, but I don't think they're your memories. I think they're hers. I think that's what the Corridor is, too. I think she was in that room."

I bring my hands to my face, my palms still stained with dried blood. "I don't understand. You think you're creating the Corridor out of the Housekeeper's memories?"

"I think you *are* the Housekeeper, a new incarnation of her at least, and I think we're creating it together. That's why we're the only two people who can get in there. I think this curse is happening to you, taking over your body, and I'm, like, drawing out all these old memories. From her life. From before."

"From what? Two hundred years ago?" I shake my head. "None of this makes any sense, Aaron."

"It does, if you think about it in the right way. The Children wanted to call the Housekeeper on you, right? So they do it, only nothing happens. That's because you *are* the Housekeeper. I don't know why. Maybe she needs a new host body. Maybe it's destiny. But the Children summoning her has rushed along the process or something. Either way, you're becoming her. All this rage you feel, all this disproportionate anger, it only happens when people are vulnerable or under attack. That's her whole deal, isn't it, protecting the vulnerable? Right, Maeve?"

A coldness comes over me as I try to puzzle it out logically. There's no doubt that my new strange power, my rage and fury that suddenly strikes people blind, arrived as the Corridor did, and when Aaron came back. The Housekeeper portrait is in the Corridor. When I first met Nuala, she said that the Housekeeper was a myth from the Big House days, when Irish servants were so abused by English lords that they called on black magic to help them.

The tiny furniture, the gold filigree, the carriage clock on the mantel. Was it a shadow of the original house that Aaron's power was hauling up from the past? A memory, belonging to a ghost?

A ghost that I was slowly becoming. A ghost that I would make flesh again.

The pieces fit together in my head so naturally, flowing like a story that I've known forever. The Housekeeper must replenish, regenerate, find new hosts to dwell within.

"Cards, right?" he says. "You always have dreams about playing cards after you see me, don't you? In a dirty, grand house. This house, I think."

"I didn't tell you that," I say coldly.

"I know. But I can feel it. I just thought they were stupid dreams, but then these fragments keep adding to the scene. Something bad happening. Something to her, or to you, or both of you."

The portrait in the Corridor. It was inarguably a portrait of me.

"So why do we keep going to the Lodge through the Corridor?"

"I don't know."

We look at each other, empty of ideas, until finally it dawns on me.

"Oh, my god. The cards. Aaron, the fucking cards. Squirrel Girl had them. Dorey had them on her desk. They had tarot."

Aaron blinks rapidly, as if trying to let air into his brain to prevent it from overheating.

"You don't think she's . . . calling you, is she?"

"Maybe. Maybe she's calling the Housekeeper, and she's getting me."

My blood runs cold. She knows. She's known this whole time. Dorey has been watching this transformation since long before I knew something was happening.

How? How could she have found out before I did? Was she watching me closely, observing my rages and freak-outs, noticing the shifts in my behavior? Did she have her own Paolo, and did he watch me turn Aaron and Roe blind?

"We'll find a way," Aaron says, and I hate his voice this way, I hate that he is trying to be soothing. I hate him. "We'll go tell the others, and we'll find a way out. Nuala will know."

"No," I suddenly snap. "No, we're not telling the others."

"What?"

"We're not telling them. Not yet."

"Why on earth wouldn't we tell them?"

"Roe and Fi have . . . they have so much, Aaron. The gigs, the TV show. Do you think any of that would happen if they knew about any of this?"

His mouth moves silently, too stunned to form a response. "That stuff doesn't matter," he says eventually. "Not compared to, you know, you becoming . . ."

"I don't want to screw up their lives and careers over a hunch," I say definitively. "We've got to make sure first. That I'm really her."

"How do we do that?" he asks uncertainly.

"Exactly what you said. If I'm really becoming a revenge demon, then . . . let's get some revenge."

"No."

"Why?"

"Because I could be wrong. And we could be killed. What you have to remember, Maeve, is that even with the best intentions in the world, I'm still a fucking nutcase. My whole life has been paranoid delusion after paranoid delusion. I keep seeing all these visions with you, and I don't know what's true."

"Like what?"

"Like stuff with a field. And a dog. You in a field with a dog."

I wince, remembering my vision from the chicken house. The feeling of a wet nose, the good solid weight of a dog against my leg.

"What else?"

"A girl," he says after a moment. "A girl who has been kidnapped."

I perk up. "Lorna?"

"No, it's in the past. It's history, you know. It's this thing of, like, everything repeating itself. But it's the Housekeeper, or it's you *as* the Housekeeper, and you're trying to get a girl out of a house. And then something bad happens."

"What exactly?"

"I don't know. It's like a dream, where you get the sense of something happening, but not the details."

"And when do you get these visions?"

"When I'm around you, when I've recently spent a lot of time with you. I just ignored them. My brain does weird stuff, it always has. Compulsive stuff, crazy images. But then you kept changing. You're a different person than who you were a few months ago. Like all the cells in your body have been replaced or something."

I shiver and hold on to my arms. "I don't *want* to change."

"We can fix it," Aaron says, suddenly fierce. "We fix everything else."

"We break everything else, too," I say, gesturing to our ashy surroundings.

We leave the school. We walk in silence through the city, even busier now, the clubs spilling clumps of drunk people onto the street. Girls with their arms around one another, screaming "*Do they know it's Christmastime at all?*" and it feels oddly appropriate. It is the early hours of Christmas Eve, and I am walking through a tipsy city with a death sentence on my head.

Aaron walks me all the way home in the end. I don't know what we talk about, or if we talk at all. It seems as though we drift into filler conversation, aimless small talk, a lorem ipsum for depleted souls. Too frightened to talk about what we're frightened of.

"All right, Chambers," he says at my driveway. "Sorry I ruined your life."

I meet his gaze. He does look very sorry.

"I used to think you did ruin my life, you know," I say. "Now I kinda feel like I wouldn't get by without you."

We hug then, our bodies stiff. Touching is still strange to him, I think. My arms around his waist, my forehead flush with his sternum. We stand in the hug for a moment, and it feels more like exhaustion than intimacy. We break apart and give each other a gruff goodbye.

184

"Take care of yourself, kid," he says as I put my key in the door.

"You say that like you're never going to see me again."

Something passes over his eyes, perhaps another vision, or just an obscure piece of Bible verse. "Yeah," he says. "Yeah, sometimes I'm afraid of that, too."

21

WHEN I GET INSIDE, THE DOG IS FRANTIC. It's past two a.m., but he's yelping at me and scratching at my legs.

"Hey, Tutes," I say, holding his face in my hands. "What's your deal, buddy?"

He moans anxiously, smelling every part of me, unsatisfied with whatever he finds. Like he knows that I've changed, too. Like finding out tonight was the last piece of the puzzle. I take him into the darkened living room at the back of the house, where hopefully he won't wake anyone up.

I hold him on the sofa as he cries, his little doggy voice high and confused.

"It's OK, baby," I say, burying my face in his fur. "It's OK, I'm still me. I'm still me."

I start to cry with him, rocking his blond body back and forth like he is a baby, the weight of this new information crushing at my shoulders. What happens next? I don't know how I become the Housekeeper, but I can't imagine it without the death of myself as I am now. These fierce jabs of cruelty and violence will increase, presumably. My humanity will rot, developing blue and green furry spots, like old bread.

And my parents will lose me.

And my friends will lose me.

And I will lose me.

The heaviness, the panic, the doom, it wraps itself around my chest and squeezes me like a snake. The cries shudder through me, and after a while I have to push my face into the armrest of the couch. The smell of mildew pushing up my nostrils, the fabric getting wetter with each new bout of tears.

Tutu wiggles out of my arms, bored now, and I stand up in the darkened living room. Except it is no longer the living room, and I am no longer me.

I am in a field where some high crop is growing. Wheat, I think. When I turn back around, there's no room left, and no suggestion of how I'm supposed to get back.

I feel the snag and drag of green things, leaves and branches sticking to me, no clear path to follow. It tugs on the dress, which is when I notice it. I am wearing the white dress.

There's a building in the distance, about two miles away, and there's nothing to do but move toward it. It's in the center of a town, looming over one- and two-story buildings like a predator. It's Kilbeg, but a small Kilbeg. A Kilbeg that isn't much bigger than a village. I'm exactly where I was, I realize. I'm exactly where my house was, only back then it was just fields.

I walk with my hands out in front of me, pushing the thick stalks away, navigating while half-blind from the darkness and the leaves. It takes me a few minutes of fighting plants to realize that I'm not alone. There's a low rustling, the sound of a creature. Something on four legs. I step forward again. The creature is following me, and moving faster than me, the wheat trembling as it weaves through stalks.

I'm about to break into a run when a head pokes out from the green. A long, loping head, the shape of a greyhound, the size of a

Shetland pony. Its nose grazes my elbow, and if it were to stand up on its back legs, it could see clean over my head. But it is friendly, whatever it is. It pants softly, wet nose against my waist, its eyes a glinting silver, its coat a shimmer of gray so delicate it is almost lavender. It is here as a companion, rather than a stalker.

It presses its face into my waist, desperate for warmth, hungry for home, and I finally realize: if I am the Housekeeper, then this is the Housekeeper's dog. But *dog* feels too generic a word. Wolf? Hound? Hell-beast?

"Tutu?" I whisper. "Tutes?"

Tutu lets out a low whine of excitement, a "Hmmmnnn!," and beats his tail against the leaves.

"Oh, my god," I say, wrapping my arms around his neck. "This is happening to you, too?"

His big, almost horse-size head is warm on my shoulder, his breath huffing down my back. I am so sorry that this is happening to him, but so deeply relieved that I don't have to go through it alone. I may not be able to tell Fiona, Lily, and Roe. But I can tell Tutu. He's here.

"What are we going to do now?" I ask him, and he walks ahead of me, his big body clearing a path, trampling down wheat as we go. I follow, half leaning on his back, stroking him like he's an emotional support animal, which, I suppose, he is.

The moon is full and low, and it's another way of knowing that I'm not in present-day Kilbeg, where it is currently in its third quarter. The white light shines off the dog's back, Tutu's fur a reflective plate. I cannot stop touching my face. I need to know if it has changed, but there's nothing different that I can feel: same coin-shaped eyes, same bump in the bridge of my nose, same wild eyebrows.

I am so confident in Tutu's leadership skills that it takes me a while to realize that we are walking away from the house. We are walking instead toward a gathering of trees, where it looks like a wood might begin.

"Tutu," I whisper sharply. "Is this . . . ?"

But he keeps on going, veering toward the shadows, his strides long, rabbits scuttling out of the way as he passes. I wonder if he remembers being a cockapoo.

I think he's going to lead me straight into the woods, but there is a space at the edge of the wheat field, a circle where the crop has been cleared. It looks new, and unnatural, and like something you might get in trouble for making. The stalks have been pulled out and laid flat, a makeshift carpet woven under the moon's full beam.

And standing in the middle of it waits a pregnant woman. Mid-twenties. She is holding two dead hares, their long ears filling each fist.

I realize, for the first time, that there is a reason witchcraft happens under the full moon, and it is because of light. It's so obvious. There's nothing to do with gods and goddesses here, nothing particularly enchanted. Just a light to weave a clearing. A light to skin a rabbit. A light to call a witch.

"Thank you for coming," says the woman. She stops, gratitude and fear bubbling within her at once. "I heard hares were the thing."

The curse, which had been curled up in my feet, suddenly jumps to the base of my throat.

"Hares are the thing," I say softly. "For him."

I cock my head, motion to Tutu. He collects the hares, carefully, from the woman's hands. She jumps backward, letting them go too quickly, and then feels embarrassed. She so badly wanted to hold her nerve.

"And for me?"

She nods and reaches into her pocket. I don't know when her clothes are from. It's a simple dress, a dark blue color, made out of a kind of sacking material. At first, I think she has pulled out a coin: something big, gold, something a pirate bites his black tooth on. But it's not a coin. It's a brooch. She hands it to me.

"Thank you," she says again. "You're so . . ."

"No compliments," I interrupt her. "And never give me anything that you wouldn't miss dearly."

She looks at the brooch, and at me.

"It was my grandmother's," she says simply.

"Fine," I say, and pocket the brooch.

It's hard to know where this is coming from. It feels as though I'm acting out a scene I have performed thousands of times before, in the middle of an interaction where instinct comes before anything else.

"Sit down," I say. Although I don't myself sit down. I walk the perimeter of the circle, touching my thumb to my ring finger, to my middle, to my index, to my pinkie. As I do this, faster and faster, I feel salt start to run through my fingertips. I am not making the salt but calling it from elsewhere. I have a home. I know that for certain. My dress is long and white and it has no pockets, and I carry no bags, and this is a flex. I don't need to carry anything. When I own something, I can summon it.

"This isn't your first," I say. And she is about to correct me and say that it is, it's the first time she has spoken to a witch of any kind, but then I interrupt. "Baby, I mean."

"No," she says. "There's Una."

"And Una is why you're here."

She nods. "Una is why I'm here."

My cards appear in my hand. I tell her to take three. The Fool, reversed. Six of Swords. The Wheel of Fortune.

"When does she leave?" I ask.

She looks like . . . what does she look like? Like Squirrel Girl, I realize. Big eyes, small mouth. Nervous, and trying to be brave. Maybe there are no new people. Only new clothes.

"Tomorrow," she says, her voice bitten with worry. "Canada. John's cousin says he can get things set up for her. But it's such a long way. And the crossing . . ."

"Pray to St. Christopher," I snap, "if you're worried about the crossing."

She considers giving up. She is afraid of my anger, but then she remembers the brooch and decides she has already given too much to walk away. Just making the clearing was a risk.

"She's very pretty," she says, and her voice is desolate. "She doesn't know how things can be out there. With men, I mean."

A pause. The circle fills with violence, and our shared knowledge of it.

"And there's no saint for that, is there?" I reply, and my voice is not unkind.

"No," she replies. "There's no saint for that."

"Tell her not to go."

"I can't. There's nothing here for her. Only the Big House, or England, and it's no good for Irish girls there. She needs a new place. A starting-again sort of place."

I think about this. It's bad, out there. If her daughter lives, if disease or bad food doesn't wipe her out, then it will be through the good graces of bad men. Rape is a likelihood. A bad marriage if she's lucky. There will be no one to arrange things for her, no one who really cares, and this cousin will be useless. She needs something larger. Tougher.

"I will keep her," I say.

The woman is silent, as if waiting for something else, some finger snap, some guarantee of my power, of my protection, of my watch.

"I said, I will keep her," I repeat, annoyed.

"Thank you."

Tutu reappears, his mouth covered in the hares' blood.

"He will bring you home," I say. "It's not safe to go alone."

She nods and follows Tutu through the woods. I gather the hares, or what remains of them.

"It almost never is," I tell the moon.

22

I WAKE UP HUNGRY.

Tutu is curled at my side, down to his normal proportions now, and snoring loudly. I need to eat.

In the kitchen, Abbie is making breakfast. She's whisking a bowl of eggs together, and is using the leftover vegetables from yesterday to make a frittata. A frittata is a very Abbie thing to make: lightly sophisticated, and has lots of ingredients that she can list the benefits of.

"Happy Christmas Eve, baby," Abbie says. Abbie always calls me this. Apparently when I was born she used to tell people that I was "hers."

I start eating handfuls of cornflakes from the box.

"Stop," she says. "We're eating in a minute."

"I'll eat that, too."

And I do. I have the frittata, three slices of toast, a banana, half a scone, a handful of chocolates, and two cups of coffee.

"My god," Mum says, sounding happy with me for the first time in ages. "You're like a horse."

"I'm so hungry," I answer. "Like I've just been swimming."

That's really how it feels. That full-body hungriness you feel after you've done a swimming class, hungry in not just your stomach but in your arms and legs, too. It appears to be the only real proof that last night actually did happen, that I really did walk through those fields with Tutu, that I really did conjure salt from my fingertips, that I really did agree to use my magic to help a girl called Una find a new life safely.

I've watched enough movies to know an origin story when I see one. We're not in folktales anymore. We're in hard truths, and here's another one: it felt good.

Better than good. It felt like power and direction and focus. It felt like responsibility and action and reaction. It felt like purpose. After the woman left, I did something with what was left of the hares. I did something with the brooch. I did something that called to the Well underneath my feet, and a seed of magic rose to meet me, like a bubble being slowly sucked through a straw.

The girl, Una, is fine now. She's protected. No one will touch her, think about her, consider her vulnerability, because my circle is around her and will follow her all the way to Canada. She is happy, and she died over a hundred years ago probably, but she is fine.

It's a difficult needle to thread. I'm terrified of becoming the Housekeeper. But that brief experience of being her, before being a demon rinsed her of humanity completely, was exhilarating.

"You're in a good mood," Dad says cautiously. "You seem different today."

I nod. "I feel different today."

When I charge my phone I find a handful of messages from Fiona, Lily, and Roe. They're all worried, but, touchingly, they're more worried that I stormed off in a huff over their lack of urgency at attacking the Lodge.

Hey, says Fiona, at 10 p.m. **I feel like an asshole. I can't believe I said that thing about being busy with the show. I'm sorry. You're right. This is serious. Xxx**

Roe, 10:05 p.m. **Hey. I'm sorry about tonight. Should I come over later? X**

Lily, 10:45 p.m. **I don't mind storming the lodge. I'll waste those assholes**

Roe, 12:38 a.m. **Hey, can't sleep. Driving over. X**

"He seems very low-energy this morning," Dad says, scratching the dog's ear for him.

"He's getting on," Mum replies. "Look, I can even see some gray hairs on him."

And she's right: there are a few silver hairs that have sprouted up overnight, souvenirs from when Tutu was Wolf Tutu.

I try to phone Roe, but their phone is off, so I decide to go round to the O'Callaghans' house. I stop at a convenience store and pick up a box of chocolates for the O'Callaghans. Mum always says you should never go anywhere in December with your arms swinging, and it feels rude to pop up at the O'Callaghans with nothing.

"Maeve." Mrs. O'Callaghan blinks. She looks older every time I see her. Maybe all our parents do. "Happy Christmas."

I hug her, because it's polite to hug people you've known your whole life at Christmas, even if it is awkward. "Here you go," I say, giving her the box of Cadbury Roses. "Compliments of the season." Which is a thing I once heard Fiona say and thought was hilarious.

She nods, then opens her mouth like she wants to say something. Closes it again. I pretend, for a second, that I am still the powerful, dignified, ancient witch that I was last night.

"Is everything OK, Mrs. O'Callaghan?" I ask, as softly as I can.

She looks stunned, almost insulted, that a seventeen-year-old would talk to her like a social worker. But she relents.

"Maeve," she says hesitantly. "Will you follow me for a moment? Roe is in the shed, but . . ."

"I can follow you," I reply, and I follow her upstairs and into her bedroom.

I haven't been in Mrs. O'Callaghan's bedroom since I was about seven, but nothing has changed. Same vague green wallpaper, same heather-sprigged duvet cover, same heavy oak bedside tables. There's heaviness to everything, really. She is heavy, her heart a sinking brick.

She opens her chest of drawers—which match the bedside tables, which match the skirting boards, which supposedly complement the green wallpaper—and pulls out a small wrapped gift.

"For you," she says. I open it. It's a black wool scarf, with silver and gold half-moons and stars embroidered at each end. It's lovely. "Happy Christmas."

"Wow," I say, wrapping it around my neck. "Thank you."

I'm a bit embarrassed. It's too nice. I wasn't expecting it. I feel silly about the chocolates now.

"I actually made it for your birthday originally," she says. "But then everything, you know. At the school . . ." She trails off.

"Thank you," I say again. "It's so lovely. And thoughtful."

I wrap the scarf around my neck, and there's nothing else to say, so I say thank you again and turn to go.

"I don't suppose you know what's happening with him?" she suddenly says in one panicked burst.

"Who?" I ask. "You mean Roe?"

She nods and sits down at the edge of the bed. "It's the *them* stuff."

"Well," I say, joining her, "if you didn't know the gender of someone who you hadn't met yet, you'd say 'they,' wouldn't you? You'd say 'What time are they getting here?'"

She waves her hand at me vaguely, like Roe has explained this to her already, and like it doesn't satisfy her one bit. "But I *do* know his gender," she says. "I gave birth to him. I was there, in the room, when the doctor said, 'It's a boy.'"

"Right," I say. This conversation is way above my pay grade. I'm bad at explaining gender stuff even to myself; how am I supposed to explain it to a fifty-something-year-old woman? Who has already had her child explain it as best they can?

"I just think he's making life difficult for himself. People won't accept it. Not in a genuine way. And he's doing it for no reason." She shakes her head. "I don't understand the sense in it."

"I think you, actually, are the one who is making life difficult for Roe."

She looks at me, stunned. I can't believe I've said this to her, either. Our main thing is that we don't talk.

"Roe is actually trying to make life *easier* for themself, and lots of people get that. I mean, the band gets it, and I get it, and our friends get it. People get that everyone has a right to define their own experience. So when you say that 'people won't accept it,' you're actually part of the problem. *You* are the people you're talking about."

I expect her to tell me off, or to say I don't understand what it's like to be a mother, but she just keeps sitting there. Not really nodding, not really shaking her head, but doing some movement between the two.

"I suppose it's just difficult to understand," she says eventually. "The feeling itself. Being both genders, or no genders, or whatever it is."

I am about to say "Gender is a spectrum, not a binary," but I have the feeling that it won't really work here.

"Haven't you ever felt," I say, stepping very carefully, "that there's something inside you that keeps growing and getting stronger and harder to ignore? And the more you ignore it, the more it comes out in, like . . . destructive ways?"

"How is Roe being destructive?" she asks, shocked. "Is he on drugs?"

"I'm not talking about Roe," I say. "I'm talking about . . ." *Me.* "You. Haven't you ever felt . . . an emotion, or an instinct or whatever, that's impossible to describe, but it's an intrinsic part of you? Something that makes you who you are?"

She pauses. "Yes. Motherhood."

"Imagine if no one let you call yourself a mother, then."

"But I really am a mother," she replies.

"And Roe really is nonbinary," I say. I want to add: *And I really am the Housekeeper*. I almost say it, just to have someone hear it.

I get up from the bed, and wonder whether something of the Housekeeper's confidence has lingered after last night.

"Did you say they were in the shed?" I ask.

"Yes," she says, still sitting on the bed, and pauses before her next comment. "*They* are."

She says it like she feels silly for saying it, like she's playing a child's imaginary game. But she still says it.

·)) ● ((·

Roe has set up a makeshift recording studio in the shed outside the O'Callaghans' house. They record rough demos and then send them off to Honor to give her an idea of what they want for the final version. As insensitive and old-fashioned as Roe's parents can be, you have to give them credit for allowing this: there's a long power cord trailing from the house like a jungle snake, and the electric bills must be huge. I knock on the door, timidly at first. There's no response, so I knock harder. And harder again.

"Come in," I finally hear.

The shed is small and dark, and every corner has been soundproofed: either with blankets, tea towels, or egg cartons that have been lined with insulation and then superglued to the walls. It's dark and it smells of sweat, coffee, and the slight hum of wood varnish. Roe is playing guitar, headphones on, wearing a huge AGAINST ME! T-shirt with holes in the side. When they're crouched over like this, I can just about see the dark line of hair above their stomach. I feel the hair on my arms rise upward, wanting so badly to rush in for a kiss but unsure of how much Roe would welcome it.

"Hey," I say.

Roe lays the guitar flat on their lap but doesn't get up. "Hey."

"Your mum let me in."

"She finally gave you the scarf, I see."

I touch the black wool at my throat. "I know. What took her so long?"

"Hoping we'd break up, I suppose."

I flinch at the comment, lean my weight against the wall. "Ouch."

Roe just shrugs, fiddles with the knobs on the guitar. I realize that they are angry with me, and I assume it's about how I pushed them away last night, screamed "Don't touch me" before fleeing into the garden.

"I'm sorry about last night," I say slowly. "I just . . . I got so angry. It was like a panic attack. I couldn't control myself, so I had to get out of there."

"Where did you go?"

"Huh?"

"I said"—Roe's tone is sharp—"where did you *go*?"

I pause. Think about it. "Home."

Roe turns to face me fully. "You went home," they say flatly.

I sit down on an upturned milk crate, looking around the room. The guitar, the cheap mixing desk, the cable leading from the house. The song lyrics pinned to the corkboard above the wall. Printed-out statements from Small Private Ceremony's shared bank account. A whiteboard with numbers written on it, then crossed out—*50k, 65k, 80k, 100k!*—charting the number of streams they've had.

Eighteen years of dreaming that I could shatter in one sentence.

I'm the Housekeeper, Roe. There's a demon within me that is slowly taking over, and the moment I tell you is the moment you put life on hold while we look for a solution. No gigs. No pre-tour. No tour, maybe.

How can I tell them this, ask them to drop everything to fix this problem, when I'm not even sure if it *is* a problem? I remember how strong and whole I felt last night, after I left Aaron. The strongest I've felt in months.

"Yes," I say. "I needed to calm down, get some sleep. I turned off my phone and just went to bed."

"And you slept all right?"

"Yeah, fine."

"So you were sleepwalking when you got up to hug Aaron at the end of your driveway?"

It's like the air pressure changes in the room. Like we have suddenly entered zero gravity and my feet may leave the earth at any moment. There is a silence. A silence that seems to last a thousand years while every tiny detail of the room makes itself known to me: the dust motes swirling under the yellow light of the banker's lamp, the glowing red lights coming from the equipment, tiny dog-ears in Roe's open notebook.

"I couldn't sleep," Roe continues, not breaking eye contact with me. "So I drove over. You weren't answering your phone so I was getting ready to leave, and then Miel called me. So I was parked outside, talking to them, and I saw you come home." A pause. "I saw you both come home."

I stand utterly still. Determined not to lie, but not ready to share the truth. "Roe," I say. "I'm not cheating on you."

"Respectfully, Maeve, how on earth do you expect me to believe that?"

I don't know how to respond. I try to imagine a way of telling the truth that doesn't destroy everything for Small Private Ceremony. *I'm infected with a curse that might eventually turn me completely evil, but no big deal, please carry on with your plans.*

"We were at the school," I say, still upholding the letter of honesty, if not the spirit. "I wanted to break into the Lodge. That way we wouldn't endanger the rest of you, and could just get in and out. We still need more information on what's happening there. I thought it could be, like, a fact-finding mission."

And I was curious to see if I could enact Housekeeper revenge.

Roe nods slowly, and I can feel their brain scanning each sentence, examining its logic. "So you left, and then you called Aaron."

"Yes," I say, knowing that this is a lie, and although better than admitting to the Housekeeper, still not at all good.

"Why?"

"I mean, I just said. He's the only one who . . ."

"I mean, why did it have to be a secret? Why couldn't you have involved all of us in that plan?"

"It was late."

"You could have waited."

"I couldn't."

"So how was it?"

"What?"

"The Lodge."

"Oh. We didn't go, in the end."

At this, Roe throws their electric guitar across the room, where it hits the back wall and the whiteboard of streaming numbers falls to the floor. I jump off the milk crate in shock.

"Jesus Christ, Roe, don't *do* that!"

"Sorry, you're telling *me* not to do something?"

"It's scary. It's scary when someone throws something."

"Don't tell me what's scary, Maeve. Scary is seeing the person you're in love with run off with someone who once tried to destroy you. He tried to ruin my life; do you remember that? He tried to ruin all of our lives."

"Of course I remember that. I'm never not thinking about that."

"Is this it now? You've had your little dabble in queer-adjacent romance, now you're running off with Mr. Westboro Baptist Church? It's quite a turnaround."

We're screaming now. We never scream. We argue, but we never scream.

"I'm not running off with anyone, Roe! I'm trying to fix a problem that you're too selfish to give a shit about." *Oh, no. Oh, no. I can't stop saying things. God, if you exist, please make me stop saying things.* "There are kids our age getting lured away and starving themselves in some ramshackle building somewhere, and all you can say is 'Ooh, I've got band practice that day.' I mean, are you serious? You used to be all about protecting other people, finding safe spaces. Or is that on the condition that they worship you and your band?"

I have never seen Roe angry like this. I have never *been* angry like this. This isn't even about me and Aaron anymore. This is about everything: every unsaid resentment, every annoyance that we thought we were too mature to care about—but it turns out we were just burying under the surface.

"Maeve Chambers is calling *me* selfish," they say, tugging at their hair in frustration. "That's one for the books."

"Oh, my god, I know Lily is the voltage of the group, but I'm the lightning rod, aren't I? You and Fiona spend your lives on high horses, thinking you're so *evolved*, taking every little opportunity to call me a bitch. When I'm just trying to *do* something."

"By what—attacking random girls at house parties? Sneaking off with Aaron? It's not Nobel Peace Prize stuff, Maeve. Fiona told me what you did at that party. I couldn't believe it. You might think we're on high horses, but I assure you, they are regular-size horses."

Suddenly, we're silent. As if we can't believe the things we have just said to each other. The things we can't unsay.

I'm about to break the silence—with what, I'm not sure—when they suddenly pick up a big gray toolbox nestled next to the amp. It's got all the usual guitar-fixing bits in it, and Roe slides a compartment away to reveal a small tray full of silver.

Roe picks a coin out of the box. Stares at it in the flat of their hand.

"Lily gave me two of these," Roe says, "and said that if she ever got out of control, or flew off the handle with her electricity, I was to put one on her neck, the same way the Children did. So no one would get hurt."

I sit down on the edge of the amp and put my hand out, and Roe lets the coin fall into it. I forgot how the coins felt. Like a thousand little lizard's feet, clinging to a wall.

"If we're going to have a real conversation," Roe continues, "I need you to wear this."

I look up, shocked. "You can't be serious, Roe?"

Not long ago, I wished that I had kept one of these coins for moments when I wanted to mute my power. Now, however, the idea is horrifying to me.

"I think I am. To my own fecking amazement, I think I am.

Something . . . Something is happening with you, Maeve, and I don't know what it is, but I do know that I don't completely trust you not to read my mind while we talk about it."

"Why?" I reply, tears rolling down my cheeks now. "Why not?"

"I don't want to feel like you're coming to my conclusions before I do."

"I won't read your mind. I won't, Roe, I swear. I haven't been, the whole time I've been here."

Roe just looks at the silver coin in my palm.

"If you won't, then what's the harm of putting it on?"

And with that, I throw the coin across the room.

We look at each other in silence as it hits against a bass guitar—Pat's bass, borrowed for demos—and emits a loud *twang* followed by a *clunk* as the bass falls over.

"I can't believe you just asked me to do that," I say, quaking in whispered rage. "What *they* do to *us*."

"Why can't you understand," Roe says slowly, their own anger rattling through each syllable, "that you having secrets with Aaron is basically the same as you fucking him?"

I can't stand this. Roe's bereft expression, the confused hurt, the sense that I am loved but not trusted.

"If this is how you feel, Roe," I say suddenly, "just break up with me."

"*What?*"

"Break up with me," I say. "If you don't trust me, you shouldn't be with me."

I realize, with a gradual, creeping horror, that this might be the thing that saves Roe. That frees Roe, in a way. Having your ex-girlfriend become a demon is nowhere near as traumatic as having your *current* girlfriend become a demon.

I listen to the voice of the witch who has begun to live inside me.

You will lose Roe anyway, she says. *Lose them the most painless way you can.*

"Maeve," Roe says, crouching down to the floor. "Mae. This is you and me. We've been through worse than this."

Soon, my behavior will get uglier. The Housekeeper will devour me from the inside out, and I'll be a strange eternal creature. Unlovable. Unloved.

"Things will get worse," I say. And I mean it. "They already have."

"Then we'll get through that, too," Roe replies desperately.

I love you, I think. *I love you. I love you. I love you.*

"No, we won't," I say, standing up. "Not like this."

I'm not sure how long we stay there, talking and crying, but I know it gets dark outside, and I start to shiver. Eventually it becomes too much, and I go.

In the years I've spent visiting the O'Callaghan house, I've been here as Lily's best friend, as Nora's daughter, as Roe's girlfriend. As trouble, as a bad influence, as *that strange girl*. But as I pass through the kitchen and nod to Mrs. O'Callaghan drinking a cup of tea, I am leaving as something brand-new. As the girl who used to be Roe O'Callaghan's girlfriend.

23

AS AWFUL AS THE SHED WAS, THE WALK home is worse.

Every step increases the distance between me and Roe, and the more that distance grows, the more I feel like an astronaut cut loose from a ship. Because, yes, I did say it. I did ask to be cut loose. But the more we talked, and the more exhausted Roe became by me, I could tell that there was a part of Roe that saw the tragic sense in us breaking up. A part of them that thought: *She's going through whatever she's going through, the Housekeeper threat was clearly false, and I don't even know how much I'm going to be around, anyway. I'm recording an album. I'm going on a real tour. What can I give her? How can I even help?*

And no, I didn't read their mind. When you know someone, really know them, you don't need to.

Is there any way to describe heartbreak that doesn't sound like a bad song? The feeling of no air in my lungs, no bones in my legs, a deep black cavern forming like a sinkhole in my chest. My hands are so cold that I wedge them under my armpits, and eventually my face is so streaked with tears that I just tilt my head forward so I can cry directly onto the footpath.

People slow down their cars to look at me. A few people even beep. I'm like one of those pigeons you see hopping around, their wings too injured for flight, destined to be a fox's dinner and everyone knows it. A thing you consider putting out of its misery. Why won't someone come and put me out of my misery?

I think about Roe, writing songs about this. Roe, a single, nonbinary rock star touring the world. Roe with a bevy of partners. And me, rotting as I disappear into a demon's skin.

I wait outside my own house for so long that I'm almost blue.

It's hard to understand how time passes then. At some point, my sister finds me, and I'm shuffled inside. Someone puts me to bed and, strangely enough, I sleep. I suspect that it's my body, sleep-deprived from days and days of midnight trips to St. Bernadette's, sensing a weakening in my resolve.

The sleep feels deep and druggy, with nightmares of past and present colliding together. Skinning the hare, separating fur from sinew, the layer coming off like the fine membrane on a boiled egg. Then my own skin peeling off, removed carefully by Roe with the fine edge of a stone.

I stay in bed all through Christmas Day. I stare at my phone during the brief moments that I'm awake and see the messages from Fiona and Lily pour in. **Are you OK?** and **we heard.**

My mother brings me a roast dinner in bed. My sisters try to tempt me out with presents. I can hear my family playing Articulate! downstairs.

"OK, OK, a word for when a judge can't ethically preside over a case?"

"OH! Oh. He recluses himself. No. RECUSE!"

I have recused myself, and I have reclused myself. I no longer feel part of the living world. As the time passes, the sleep becomes deeper. I feel as if I'm finding new layers, something beneath sleep but above death, like I have accessed an underworld where the Housekeeper can find me. The feeling of salt in my fingers, summoned from nowhere. The feeling of being filled up with one thing while being drained of another.

I've given you long enough, she says. *It's time.*

Was it always supposed to be like this? I ask.

No answer.

At some point on the next day, Stephen's Day, I get up. "Maeve," Mum says brightly. In my awake moments, I have been dimly aware of my family discussing my heartbreak hibernation. They have all decided to not speak to me about Roe unless I speak to them first. "Orange juice?"

"Yes, please."

I drain my glass, the juice too tangy, and I wonder how much longer I have to sit here with everyone looking at me.

How long? I wonder. How long until this thing takes me over?

"How long what, Maeve?" Mum asks.

Everyone looks at me. I realize, a second later, that I said this out loud.

"How long," I continue slowly, "can someone live with a bad disease?"

My family looks at one another, startled.

"Viral or bacterial?" Cillian says right away.

"Who has a disease, darling?" Dad asks.

"No one," I say. "I was just wondering."

Another pause while my family briefly considers not just who but what I am. Jo speaks up. "Well, it depends. Things change all the time. Like, twenty years ago, HIV was a death sentence. But my supervisor lives with it, and he's fine. I think he takes, like, two pills a day."

"And he's fine?"

"Yeah, he's fine. He's had it so long that it's untransmittable."

"That's good," I say, and I know that I sound deranged. "That's good," I say again.

"Some emotional states," Dad says, clearly convinced I'm talking about the breakup, "feel a bit like a disease. But they pass."

People live with diseases. Can they live with curses, too? Are there ways of managing? Potions you can drink, rituals you can enact, sacrifices you can make?

I go back to bed for the day, alternating between crying and staring at the ceiling. Heartbreak and revenge strategies make strangely good bedfellows: your brain is sharp and ready to see the worst in people.

Perhaps if I concentrate, meditate even, I can locate the part of me where the Housekeeper curse lives, the organ where she has taken root. How long has this been going on? And who decided it?

I pull the blanket closer to me. It smells of sleep, and of toast. Dorey knows. She talked about learning, about researching things. About history. About Ireland. Has she known this whole time? And what is she planning to do about it?

I don't go downstairs again until it's dark. Pat and Jo are at the kitchen table, drinking.

"Mae," Pat says. "Mayday, mayday."

"We're going out," Jo says, eyes sparkling. "Do you want to come?"

"Where?" I say bleakly.

"Few people are meeting at the Silver Crane in town," Pat says, reaching for his coat. "It'll be packed out. Always is, on Stephen's Day."

Pat is glowing with excitement. So many of his friends left

210

Kilbeg, including him, and while lots of them are in Dublin, a ton are also in Canada, England, and Australia. But people are home for the holidays and Stephen's night is the one night a year where you're guaranteed to run into friends. Everyone goes out.

The idea of a pub crammed with people feels hideous. But another night by myself, in my bedroom, looking at tarot cards, feels even worse.

"How will I get in?" I dither. "I've no ID or anything."

Fiona, Lily, and I have a checkered history with getting into pubs at night. We can just about manage when we're on the guest list for one of Roe's gigs, but the rest of the time we have basically a twenty percent chance.

The tears rise up again at the thought of Roe's gigs, going unattended by me. Of the different path, the hideous one, that has been carved out for me instead.

As if he could read my thoughts, Tutu waddles up to me and rests his head on my lap.

"They won't look twice at you if you're there with us," Jo says. "We'll slip past."

Pat nods. "Yes, don't dress like a teenager who's out for the night. Be sophisticated."

"Don't dress like you're trying to look nineteen," Jo says. "Dress like you're already twenty-four."

I end up in a black velvet blazer belonging to Mum, black jeans, Jo's pointy boots, and a silky silver top underneath. The silky silver top is technically pajamas, but Jo says it's fine.

It only feels like minutes since I was upstairs crying for the loss of Roe, and now I'm in the back of a taxi with my half-drunk siblings, on the way to a pub I've never been to before because it's for, well, old people.

The Silver Crane is famous for two things: the stage and the smoking area. The smoking area is long and covered in fairy lights, the roof dripping with hanging plants and ivy that spills to the ground. There are so many outdoor heaters that there's a perpetual red glow cast over everyone's faces, slightly ghoulish, slightly red-light district, but very cozy. There's Guinness memorabilia everywhere, and long wooden tables that look like they were once used for Viking summits. Roe has always wanted to play a gig at the Silver Crane. Lots of big people have played here.

Pat gets me a Guinness. His friends are nice to me, and ask me a lot of questions, mostly about what music seventeen-year-olds listen to. My drink is too thick and every swallow feels like choking. Why did I come out? Why did I think that the hole in my chest would be filled by talking to people in their twenties, who mostly think of me as a novelty anyway?

I want Roe. I want Roe. What have I done? I want Roe.

The cigarette smoke is stinging my eyes, or at least that's what I tell Jo when she asks about my red-rimmed eyelids and the fact that I keep swiping my hands at my face. It's ten o'clock, and the pub is getting busier, and someone says that Fighting Crickets are on at ten thirty. I know Fighting Crickets, a little. They played with Small Private Ceremony a few times, and the lead singer, Lynn, once borrowed my eyeliner, and the thought of seeing her again and her asking me about Roe is enough to make me want to eat my own hair.

"I'm gonna take off," I say abruptly, almost climbing over the seat to get out. Jo and Pat look upset.

"Don't leave!" Pat says. "I thought you liked Crickets."

"I feel a bit sick," I say. And we both know it's code for: I'm so sad and I cannot stay here a minute longer without bursting into tears.

He makes a face and then nods. He reaches into his wallet and takes out a twenty. "All right, then. Get a cab home, though, will you?"

"I will." I nod. "There's a stand across the road."

"Do you want me to walk you out?"

"No, it's fine. Really."

At the stand, I open my wallet, where one of the silver coins still sits. Roe let me keep one. As a parting gift, or as some kind of apology, I'm not sure. It's important for me to look at it, nestled in my wallet, in the place where a boy might keep a spare condom. I have to remind myself how ugly things with Roe and me were beginning to get. The trust that was being quickly eroded, like the ocean eating the beach.

If Roe was comfortable asking you to wear this, I remind myself, *then things were getting bad.*

Just as I'm about to grab a taxi, I hear my name. I turn around, and it's Michelle Breen. She runs up, skirt flying all around her, and wraps her arms around me. I don't know what to do. I just stand there, rigid.

"Hey," I say.

"Hi!" She beams. Michelle left St. Bernadette's, so I haven't seen her since we broke up for summer. Not that I spoke to her much after Lily went missing. I feel slightly sick around her, not so much because of any quality she has, but because she reminds me of how I used to behave to get her approval.

"Where are you off to?"

"Uh, home."

Her face falls. "Maeve! No! Come out with us. We're going to a club."

She loops her arm through mine and turns me around, pointing at a group of four other girls who are lighting up cigarettes and cack-ling at something.

"Um . . ."

"Oh, come on, we haven't chatted in ages."

I look at her, wincing slightly. A look that says, *I think we both know why we don't chat very much.* She steps back from me, a cloud of cold breath escaping from her mouth.

"Listen . . ." she begins. "I feel like shit about you."

"Thanks."

"No, I mean, all the Bernie's stuff. I honestly . . . I hated that school, y'know? I was so miserable there. And I didn't treat peo-ple . . . great."

I'm genuinely curious about this. "You were miserable?"

"Yeah, mostly? I mean, all those girls on top of each other, all the mind games, and, like . . . we didn't even have PE, Maeve!"

I actually laugh at this. It's the first time I've laughed all day.

"I never thought about how weird it is," I say, "that we didn't have PE."

"Everyone else has PE!" Michelle almost shouts it. "Like, don't you think at least some of us would have benefited from, I don't know, basketball or something?"

"Yeah." I nod, laughing softly. "Maybe we wouldn't have been such little bitches to each other."

And it's amazing, being able to talk to her like this. School already becoming a distant memory, a new glow of adulthood lightly touching off our shoulders. We both feel it, I think. It makes us brave.

"I always wanted to say sorry to you and Lily," she says, steel-ing herself. "That's all. And you know, if you come out with us, we'll have a dance or something, and leave all that spooky, bitchy bullshit behind."

214

Maybe it's her genuine remorse, or the fact that she thinks that my spooky, bitchy bullshit could ever possibly be left behind, but suddenly I want to stay out.

"OK," I say.

"OK?!"

"OK," I repeat.

And we're off. The club, Scarlet, is at the end of the road. I don't have an ID, but one of Michelle's friends just turned eighteen and has her sister's old learner's permit with her, and she very generously gives it to me. For tonight, I'm not Maeve Chambers, witch, ex-girlfriend, and cursed teenager. I'm Sophia Mulready, older sister to Dani Mulready, and I can drive.

24

I'VE NEVER BEEN TO A PROPER CLUB BEFORE. Just gigs, usually, or pubs with sticky little dance floors. The bigness of Scarlet is immediately daunting, as is the darkness. All the walls are black, and a thin fog is coming from behind the DJ booth, so it's difficult to tell what is space and what is boundary.

Waves of colored light pass over my face, blinding me a little, sending my brain into process mode. I remember those epilepsy warnings you sometimes get before films or concerts: *This contains flashing lights, which may affect people prone to seizures.* I never thought they could ever apply to me. Now, I realize, they do. The fireworks did it first. Color and light set my mind off, give it a job to do. It immediately starts looking for heads to enter. Like an under-worked police dog, my gift is seeking a scent.

Michelle and her friends pull me toward the dance floor, and then Danielle, the girl who is supposed to be my little sister, hands me a shot of something that tastes like licorice. "Sambuca," she yells at me, and then everyone starts dancing.

They're a nice bunch, Michelle's new girls. I'm not sure what happened to her friendship with Niamh. Maybe that was one of the many decisions she made about herself after she changed schools. The new girls are loud and sweet, and none of them recognize me from the newspaper. They think I'm kind of cool, actually. They wish, privately, that they had the confidence to wear boots and jeans to the club.

I get a little drunker. My dancing gets bigger, the silly expressive way that Fiona and I like to do when we're out together, when we try to be Kate Bush. The girls laugh, but in a nice way, and slowly start to abandon the sexy bum shuffles that they began dancing with. We're throwing our arms all around the place, and one girl breaks into an Irish dance out of nowhere, and we all laugh and make a circle around her.

Then another girl, from another group, makes a funny show out of "challenging" her to a *Riverdance*-off. The DJ notices and puts on a sort of electronic Irish trad mix, and we go wild, believing ourselves to be the controlling stakeholders of the club, and wonderful dancers besides.

And it's all just girls, girls being stupid together. There's a touch of mourning to every movement, the grief of being without Roe, the loss of Fiona to Belfast. But there's hope. A tiny dash of it. Life isn't school, I realize. I don't need to live and die by Fiona's approval. I don't need to be afraid of other people. Some pal of Michelle's puts her arm around my shoulders. The collective noun for a group of girls is not "a threat." It can be anything. A gaggle of girls. A choir. A parliament. A galaxy.

The Caroline Polachek cover of "Breathless" by the Corrs comes on, the DJ attempting to gracefully transition us out of the trad mix back into proper dance music. A wash of colored light kicks me back into sadness like a hoof to the chest. Roe used to cover this song, played it the first time I ever saw Small Private Ceremony live. I still made Roe play it all the time, the two of us in their bedroom with an acoustic guitar.

And now I'm crying, of course, because I will never coax Roe into a shirtless rendition of a twenty-year-old pop song ever again. I have lost that right entirely.

"Oh, god, Maeve," Michelle says, rushing to me. "What's wrong?"

I cling on to her, this girl I never confided in even when we were friends, and bury my face in her shoulder. Gently, she whispers into my ear, "Is it Roe?" and I nod. "Let's go to the bathroom," she says, and shuffles me toward it.

In the restroom, Michelle mops me up, and even though I tell her very few details about Roe, the magnitude of my sadness attracts a circle of girls around me. "Fuck men," someone says, and I don't have the energy to correct her because I am crying too much.

"We're just," I hiccup. "We're becoming two different people."

Which is, in its purest sense, the truth. Roe is becoming a rock star, and I am becoming the Housekeeper. Funny how casually that fact comes to me, now. A dim, grinding realization, like knowing you have to take over an unprofitable family business, one day, but not quite now.

The tears finally dry up, and Michelle gently suggests returning to the dance floor. I nod, and she buys me another shot at the bar, and I swallow without bothering to taste it.

I'm not sure how long we were in the bathroom, but in that short time, the mood of the dance floor has shifted. The jolly silliness has morphed into something sexier, a crowd of boys having attached itself to our group. Girls are being spun out and back into the arms of their partners, half making fun of old-school Fred Astaire moves and half sick with longing for it.

I'm happy for them, but it's like looking directly at the sun after eye surgery. I can't bear the idea of it. Of someone touching me. Of being danced with like that by someone who isn't Roe. Of not being danced with at all. Michelle tugs my arm. "You wanna dance?" she asks.

"Nah," I say. "You go. I need a breather."

I lean against the bar, attempting to disguise my misery as mystery, and that's when I notice someone else leaning, too. It's a girl. My age. Slick blond hair, wobbly limbs. Her eyes half-closed, trying to bob along with the music, yet strangely unable to support the weight of her own chin. It keeps sinking down, her forehead falling forward, and then she wakes herself up. Her brain is a fog. A dim purple light, weak and distressed. There's a haze on top of her, and I assume she is just drunk, but underneath the sleepy distance is a hard nut of panic. *Why can't I think?* she thinks. *What's going on?*

She's clasping a glass, Coke mixed with something, both hands around it.

"Hey," I ask. "Are you OK?"

"Hmm?"

"I said, are you OK?"

She opens her eyes, too widely, her forehead creasing with the strain. "Did Ellie go home?"

"I don't know who Ellie is," I say slowly. I remember the twenty in my purse that Pat gave me. "Where do you live? Do you want me to get you a cab?"

I ask her a few more times, and she dithers, asks about Ellie again, but eventually I get her address out of her. It turns out she lives not far from Roe and Lily. Just one street behind.

"I live really near there," I say. "I'm going now, anyway. Do you want to share a cab with me?"

She twists her mouth, tempted but confused. "I shouldn't leave without Ellie," she says.

"I think Ellie might have left without you," I counter.

"Still, I can't leave without her."

I dig into her brain and get a vague picture of Ellie, curly short hair and a black dress, and glance around the club for her.

"If I take a look around for Ellie," I say, "and can't find her in five minutes, then can we go?"

"Yes." She nods. "Then we can go."

"And you'll stay here?"

But she has already zoned out, her chin falling again. I do a quick circuit around the club, looking for Ellie, mostly just to say I did. Danielle tugs me back onto the floor, and I fish into my wallet to hand her back her sister's ID. "Thanks," I say. "I'm going now."

"You've been a great sister," she laughs, hugging me. "Better than my real one. You can keep it if you want. I don't need it anymore."

"Won't she want it back?"

She shrugs. "I don't see her." Danielle gives me a sad half smile, a these-things-happen smile.

"I'm sorry."

"It's fine," she says, shrugging again. "She's a Jesus freak now."

I want to ask her more about this, but my eyes flicker to the blond girl at the bar. A boy is talking to her now, and I feel relieved because maybe she's found a friend and I won't have to look after her. But the more I look, the less easy I feel. The boy is close to her, whispering, and she continues to just bob her heavy head to her chest.

I move closer. Notice the hand on her back, a slow patting motion, as if he were soothing a spooked horse. Pushing past the crowd on the dance floor, I see that he is not really a boy but a man. Older, about Pat's age. Which is odd in itself because Scarlet is kind of a young crowd. I mean, there's a reason Michelle's gang chose here. It's notoriously a little easier to get in, if you're under eighteen, than most clubs.

I'm already tapped into the blond girl's mind, and it comes back into focus as I move closer to her. I hear his words landing in her ear, vibrating with the heavy bass. "You promise you won't be sick," he says, "if I get us a cab?"

Her reply is mumbling, but her thought is clear. *But I'm already getting a cab*, she thinks. *With that girl in the blazer.*

When she speaks, it comes out slightly muddled. She makes a few efforts. "The cab is coming," she eventually says. "I'm leaving with her."

"I think it's better if you got a cab with me."

I'm next to her now. "There you are!" I say, grabbing her wrist. "We're going, come on."

"Hello," the man says, and I look at him. He is very fair, with invisible eyebrows and a long, strange haircut like a medieval knight. A big white shirt, maybe a size too big, and with creases still molded into the front from the cardboard it came wrapped around. For a second, I think he might be her brother, just because they're both blond.

"Chantelle," he says, "I haven't met your friend."

He waits for Chantelle to introduce us, but she's miles away.

"Ready for bed, I'd say," he says to her, stroking her back. "Shall we head off?"

Chantelle wrinkles her nose. "Where?"

I look from Chantelle to him and back again. "Do you know her?" I ask.

He starts to look annoyed. "Well, of course I know her. Hasn't she ever mentioned me to you?"

He doesn't know her at all, clearly. If he did, he would know that I don't know her at all. I stare at him, worming my way into his brain, trying to find a quick route in. My expression must look doubtful, because he tugs at Chantelle again. "I'm one of her regulars," he says. "At the bakery. We chat every morning. Every morning she's working, anyway."

A fuzzy image from Chantelle slams into my head, of awkward chatter while she serves this man coffee and plucks croissants from a tray with long silver tongs. He asks her about weekend plans, he asks her about clubs, he asks her what "students get up to these days." He annoys her on good days, freaks her out on bad ones. Her manager makes sure she's never alone in the shop with him. He is overfamiliar, but never oversteps enough to be barred completely.

"We need to go," I say, and I practically yank her arm out of its socket getting her away from him. He looks at me, furious, and in that rage his brain unlocks and lets me in. I'm back in the takeaway bakery. He hates his own awkwardness, despises how frequently he messes up conversations with Chantelle. He knows he would get along great with her if only she wasn't so judgmental. He reads about a thing online that makes women easier to talk to. It's actually a natural herbal remedy. It's not Rohypnol, crucially. That's for rapists. This is more of a helping hand for people who find modern life a little fast, women a little distant. It's a leveler.

The word *spiked* hits me like a truck. I've heard about it, obviously. But it seems so impossible, so scary, a thing that happens in Dublin or London or New York, not in provincial clubs.

"You've *spiked* her?" It comes out like a question, when I know it's a statement.

"Don't be insane," he says, but panic cuts across his features. "Fucking crazy bitch."

"How fucking dare you?" I scream, and Chantelle wakes up a bit, looks around. "You're a rapist."

The bouncer starts to walk over and I signal to him, ready to explain everything. The guy, the rapist, starts to move back from me. Eyes on the exit. Chantelle lurches forward, her face stricken, and I think she is about to cry until she suddenly gets sick on herself. It's white, gluey, and trails down the front of her top.

People back away from her with shrieks and the man weaves through the crowd. The bouncer is furious. "All right, girls," he says. "Out. Get her out."

"This girl has been spiked." I'm the one shrieking now. "You need to catch the guy. Call the police."

He doesn't hear me, and just tries to shove Chantelle toward the door without getting vomit on his suit. "Fucking hell," someone says as she passes. "What a waster."

My brain starts to burn. Another wave of colored light passes over my eyes, and suddenly I am with the woman in the wheat field, two hares in Tutu's mouth, as we both discuss the fate of her teenage daughter. I will keep her, I said. I will keep her.

That's who she was. Just a woman who kept other women safe from men. It was that way a hundred years ago, and it's that way now. A demon is a cursed person who has no humanity left in them. But, good god, her humanity was huge.

There's a sharp burst of something in my head. A kind of falling shock, not dissimilar to the blast of adrenaline that you sometimes get moments before falling asleep. The music cuts. The lights cut, too. There's a moment of confusion, of "Awwww, what?!," of irritated glares at the DJ. It doesn't last long, though, because what comes next is a scream so loud it's like the room is being ripped in half.

The man, the spiker, the rapist, has crashed to the floor. He's inches away from the fire exit, was already finding an alternate escape route in case I really did manage to call the police.

The sound of no music in a club, of just voices, of just one man's scream, is a strange thing to take in. He becomes the de facto DJ by virtue of being the loudest thing in the room.

There has been, perhaps, a disproportionate amount of screaming in my life in the past year. The panicked crush of the gig at the Cypress. The shrill, frantic pitch of the fire at the tennis courts. These were the screams of young people as danger slowly enveloped them; the spiker's screams are different. They are contorted, malfunctioning, an animal with its leg caught in a trap. He writhes, and as I move closer, I start to see pink spots of blood emerging on his white shirt.

Another bouncer has appeared, and they try to pull him up, but he keeps tearing at his skin. I try to see, but there are too many people in front of me. But I can see gray streaks on his neck, on his hands, his collar and cuffs streaked in watery pink bloodstains.

"What's that?" someone asks. "Ash?"

"No," says someone else. "Fur."

25

THE BLOOD ON THE SPIKER'S SHIRT ISN'T the deep red of horror movies, or the stale black of a congealed clot. It's pink. It's light with fluid and is emerging in pinpricks as each new patch of fur pushes itself through the skin.

There's the sound of smashed glass. Someone has dropped a big bottle of something behind the bar. Another scream. A symphony of "What the fuck?," of "What the hell?," of "Someone help me!" ricochets around the room.

I scan the club and see that gray streaks are emerging everywhere. On arms, necks, shoulder blades. Not very much, and not very consistently. Someone has a patch on their hand, someone has it all the way down their forearm. All the fur is different, but it all has two things in common.

All of it is gray, and all of it is on the boys.

The girls are seeing it on their boyfriends, and the girls are screaming. Strangers who had been kissing have stopped, the girls clutching themselves, horrified. The girls keep looking at themselves, turning their wrists over, lifting their shirts to look for gray, for blood, for this strange new disease that is bristling through the club from nowhere.

"Is this real?" I hear someone say. "Is this happening?"

I back away, toward the DJ booth, trying to distance myself from the commotion. You did this, Maeve. You and the Housekeeper.

You *as* the Housekeeper.

The bar manager is talking into a walkie-talkie. "We need to get everyone out," he says tersely, fur on his knuckles. "Now."

He doesn't want anyone blaming the club for this. But who on earth could blame the club for this? This is inexplicable: a biblical plague, a freak occurrence, a collective hallucination.

Through the mayhem, I notice that Ellie, the girl who I was convinced had gone home, has found Chantelle. The shock of the situation seems to have woken Chantelle up a little, and she's taken to the restroom for a cleanup.

I suppose we always thought of the Housekeeper as a straightforward killing machine. Maybe the more human she is, the more creative and flexible her punishments become. *What else can I do?* I wonder.

A voice booms out over the speakers. "The club is now closed," the DJ says. "Please make your way to the exits."

Some of the boys are scratching at their skin, worried, but basically unharmed. Some are rolling on the ground, the combination of physical shock and too much alcohol having burst something within them. I have to literally step over men on my way to the exit.

"If you are too . . . unwell to leave," the DJ says, stuttering slightly, "an ambulance has been called, and will be here shortly."

Girls won't leave their boyfriends. They are screaming at the bouncers, who are trying to get them out while tracking their own fur growth.

Animals, I hear her say, somewhere deep within my inner ear—the place where water gets trapped after swimming. *They're all animals, no matter who they are.*

"Stop it," I whisper.

It's hard to get down the stairs to the exit. The club just wants everyone out, quick. The bouncers form a wall at the top of the stairs as they usher everyone down. People get halfway down before realizing that their keys are in their coats and their coats are in the cloakroom. They turn back, but the club is too spooked to let anyone back in, for any reason. People push up the stairs as others are coming down, and a knot of violence forms on the landing between the club and the exit.

An explosion of swearing, of punches, of people being knocked over as boys fall backward on top of girls and girls fall down.

"TO THE EXITS, PLEASE," someone screams. "EXITS, PEOPLE, EXITS."

There's a crunching feeling as the world becomes chaotic, and a bottle is thrown down the stairs, clunking me on the head. I lose my footing and fall forward, face-planting into the steps.

Someone, some boy, sees me go down and pulls me up by the hand. The fur is on his face. I put it there. "Are you OK?" he says. "Do you need an ambulance?"

Suddenly the knot unspools itself and a rush of people move forward and onto the street. The boy is still holding my hand. He steadies me, guides me into the cold night air. I touch my face and feel an opening above my eyebrow, blood flowering on my forehead.

"Are you all right?" he says again. "What's your name? How many fingers am I holding up?"

"Four," I say.

"And your name?"

I blink, not totally sure whether I want to tell him. Not now that Maeve Chambers is a name that means something. "Sophia," I say. "Sophia Mulready."

He runs into a fast-food restaurant and takes a stack of paper napkins, then sits me on the footpath. I hold the napkins to my forehead, watching the club crowd through a blur of cheap tissue and the thick red stain of my own palm. It has rained since I went inside the club. The pavement is slick and glowing from the streetlamp, the moon covered by clouds. I watch the boys, who watch their bodies. The long gray streaks are gone. The fur has disappeared under the night's irritable sky.

"What *was* that?" says the boy next to me, the boy who has been helping me. Has he told me his name? I don't even know.

I shrug. Everyone around us seems to be asking the same question. People on the phone, people talking uncertainly to ambulances, ambulances that seemed absolutely essential five minutes ago but now seem strange to have ever been called. "You saw it, didn't you?" I hear one boy say to another. "Man," the other says, his body still trembling with adrenaline, "I felt it."

The girls, weirdly, have already started laughing about it. It didn't happen to them, after all.

"It's not funny," I hear a boy snap.

"It kind of is."

The boy next to me is shaking his head. "I guess it's true, what they say about Kilbeg, then."

"What?"

"That weird shit happens here."

"Yeah." I nod. "Weird shit happens here."

26

THE NIGHT OF THE FUR FRIGHTENS ME SO
much that I retreat back into my bedroom, the many tentacles of
sadness wrapped around me and fixing me to the bed. The enormity
of my own power doesn't thrill me for long. All that I can think about
is how uncontrollable it was. How dangerous. And ultimately, how
lonely.

My retreat lasts seventy-two hours.

I've been ignoring everyone's messages, until finally Aaron—
who must have gotten a cheap phone from somewhere, possibly off
Nuala, possibly for Christmas—calls me.

"I saw the news," he says. "Strange disturbances at a nightclub.
Blood and fur."

I don't respond.

"It was you, wasn't it?"

Silence.

"Maeve . . ." he says. "I know about the breakup."

"How?" I finally say.

"Christmas Eve," he responds. Then, quickly, "Roe didn't show
up to the dinner either, by the way, but Lily and Fiona knew. We're all
worried about you both."

Again, it's hard to know what I can say. I feel like the inside of my throat has been hollowed out, my vocal cords gone, a big shad-owed space in its place.

"I'm sorry," Aaron says, and I think he's just saying sorry about the breakup, until he takes a deep breath and launches into his next sentence. "But if you won't tell them, then I will."

"What?" I snap. "What do you mean?"

"It's getting too dangerous. You're causing genetic mutations at nightclubs, by the sound of things. Sorry, Maeve. I'm pulling rank."

"Rank? What *rank*?" I say, outraged. "You're not my boss. You're not in the Children anymore. There's no hierarchy."

"Found your voice, I see."

I fall silent again, seething.

"Eight o'clock tonight," he says sharply. "Be at Nuala's."

"Or what?"

"Or I'll tell everyone without you."

"Aaron, no. It's not your business. It's mine."

"It's all our business, Chambers. Be there or not. I don't care."

He hangs up, and I stare at my phone in disgrace. Aaron, my one ally in all of this, is going to rat me out to everyone else. The gigs, the TV show, all the carefully laid plans upended because Maeve is out of control. And Roe. Roe will be there. Or will they? I can't decide what is worse: me going and Roe is there; me going and Roe is not there; me not going at all.

Eventually I get up, stand under the hot shower for as long as I possibly can, and drag myself to Nuala's.

I leave the house in plenty of time to get there for eight p.m., but find myself slowing down anyway. My hope is that I can arrive after Aaron has already begun explaining, so I don't have to see their initial shock when they realize that I'm about to take the shape of a deadly spirit.

I slow down at the river, gazing at Lily's lost home. And then what? I live for two hundred years in a body that slowly forgets itself. Will I begin the process as completely Maeve, or will the crossover to Housekeeper be instant? She was a real person, kind of. The witch I become in my visions is not a demon, but a woman. A woman with power. How long did she stay that way?

Aaron, annoyingly, has decided to wait until I arrive. I come through the back kitchen door, and I see everyone through the window. They look worried and confused, but not slack-jawed with disbelief or terror. They don't know yet. They can't.

Roe sees me first. They are leaning against the fridge, the very spot where they held me and kissed my neck just a few days ago. I stand in the garden for the moment, feeling the pain of their gaze too keenly to go in.

I love you. I think it hard, trying to make sure they can feel it. Can they feel it? Already it feels like something fundamental has been severed, that the pane of glass between us is spiritual as well as physical. Roe blinks, taps Fiona. She turns around, finds my eyes. Smiles. Weakly.

I go in. "Hey, everyone."

A chorus of "heys" goes up, and then an awkward pause.

"Sorry I've been ignoring everyone's messages," I say as I look around the room and realize that I have been off-grid for days among people I usually speak to every hour. And in fact, the last time they saw me, I was running out of the house in the midst of a panic attack. "I'm sorry that I . . ."

"Maeve," Nuala says. "It's OK."

She means "It's OK" as in "It's OK, we know about the breakup, and in fact your behavior makes all the more sense now."

This seems to be what everyone else is feeling, too: the tantrums, the panic attacks, the disappearances. It all makes more sense to them now, in light of the breakup. Roe and I were having problems, they just didn't know. Aaron grimaces a little. He clears his throat.

"So, I called everyone here," he says, "because there's something that Maeve has been keeping a secret. Something we both have, I guess, but it's new, and we wanted to see what it meant."

The mood of the room immediately shifts to alarm.

"I don't think that's any of our business, Aaron," Nuala says quickly.

"No," I interrupt. "That's not what he means." I look desperately to Roe, who is staring at their shoes. "That is *not* what he means."

"Well, what the hell does he mean?" Roe snaps. "Can we get it over with?"

I sit down at the table, my friends peering at me, and bury my face in my hands.

"You know how we're all so curious about why Dorey would threaten to summon the Housekeeper, but then she never came?"

"Yes," Nuala says.

"Well, that's because I am the Housekeeper. I'm her. She is me. I'm the new host body for her."

The air stands still. Then the silence breaks, and the questions come.

Fiona: "No. No way. Sorry, but no."

Manon: "Do you have any proof of this? Is this just an idea you have?"

Nuala: "How on earth could that be possible? No. Surely not."

Lily and Roe are quiet, but for different reasons. Roe is clearly realizing that this was why I lied about where I was, which became a huge fight, which became the reason we broke up. Lily is harder to read. She is strangely expressionless, spacey even.

"It's true," Aaron says, taking out the newspaper. "Here."

He shows everyone a headline: SCARLET NIGHTCLUB RED IN THE FACE.

"I saw that," Nuala said. "Something about finding animal remains in the club."

"Fur," I say bluntly. "They grew fur. Because I . . . basically lost my temper."

"You were at a nightclub?" Roe says, and it's the first thing they have said to me since I arrived. They clearly can't believe that I could muster the energy, in the midst of our mutual grief.

"Show us," Manon says, with an appraising look of suspicion. "Show us now."

"What?"

"How you are her. If you are her."

"I can't. It's only when, like, some injustice happens. Something bad has to happen to someone vulnerable. That's what wakes her up."

I've been dreading sharing this information for days, but I never pictured having to prove it. I realize, then, that there's a two-birds-with-one-stone approach here.

"Listen," I say desperately. "Dorey knows. That's why every time the Lodge opens up to me, Dorey has tarot cards. She's been calling me. Because that's where injustice is literally *happening*, and she knows it. She's been testing my strength."

Everyone looks at one another agog, trying to decide if I've lost my mind.

"Let's go," I say. "To the Lodge. Now. Tonight. Aaron and I will take the Corridor, and you guys drive."

Manon, to my surprise, nods. "OK," she says.

"OK?!" Everyone else looks just as surprised as I am.

She gets up and goes to the kitchen bread bin, which is filled with stacks of printed paper. She takes them back to the table.

"I haven't been sitting on my ass, you know," she says. "Dorey, the Lodge, the starvation. I have a theory."

We all turn to Manon. "I could not sleep the other night," she says, and I catch Fiona wincing, because she remembers exactly which night it was when Manon couldn't sleep. "And, well, I got up and started reading. Just books from around the house, you know, nothing serious. Something to send me back to sleep. And I found this."

She gets up and takes one of the books propped up on the kitchen windowsill. At first I think it must be a cookbook, so I'm surprised at what she sets down. It's a small, heavy leather book with gold embossed lettering. *A Child's Guide to Catholic Saints*.

Nuala actually laughs. "I got that as a present for my First Holy Communion," she scoffs. "What are you doing reading that?"

"I thought it might give me a laugh," Manon replies, deadpan. "But as I read on, I started to think: There are all these stories about young saints, martyring themselves. Always the same. The girls starve themselves and the boys punish themselves. Self-whipping. What is the word for it, in religion?"

"Self-flagellation," Fiona says. "That's when you, like, punish yourself to show you love God."

"Which I guess is what the kids in the Lodge are doing," I say. "But why?"

"These child saints, they had no doubt that their vision and their powers were real. They did heal people, it seems. Miracles *did* happen around them."

I start to find Manon's thread. "You think Dorey is trying to manufacture little saints?"

"Think of it logically. If every small act of choice—even if it is whistling a song—is an act of magic, think about what an extreme choice would do. A choice against your body's interests, like starving. It would, in theory, summon more magic up from the Well. And all of them living together like that—they are like an oil rig, pumping away."

Nuala looks terrified by this. "And it wouldn't technically be unnatural draining, like they tried to do with Maeve, and which the Well is protected against."

"No," Manon says. "Perfectly natural, the Well doing what it is supposed to do, releasing magic to the people of the town. Just an extreme version."

"But they're *miles* away," Fiona says, aghast.

"Yes," Manon answers steadily. "But the Well is large, you know. She may be on the outskirts, but she is still in Kilbeg. The edges of the Well are still beneath her."

"Since I left," Aaron says slowly, puzzling it out, "I've always wondered—why do they bother with all the religious stuff if they don't really care about any of it? I mean, I *kind of* got it as a way to manipulate all the right-wing money people, to give their organization some structure. But why keep up the pretense, even in their most private circles?"

"Because," Manon replies almost triumphantly, "religiosity is the best and oldest cover for magical manipulation."

"Jesus Christ," I murmur, still in shock.

"Yes, him," she replies. Manon clears her throat, brings her shoulders back. "Which is why I think, given everything we now know, we must go. Tonight."

"What?" Fiona says. "Surely it's still too dangerous?"

"This is how I see it," Manon says, drawing herself up to her full height. "We have two unproved theories. The first: that Maeve is inflicted with the curse of the Housekeeper. If this is true, we need to find a way to remove the curse, but first we must see if the curse is real."

She claps her hands on the words *curse*, *is*, and *real*. The authority of her. The power.

"Second theory," she continues. "That the Children are engaging in some kind of False Saint Method to hoard magic from the Kilbeg Well."

"The False Saint Method," Lily says in wonder. "She already has a name for it."

"That's academics for you," Aaron says, but he's clearly also impressed.

"We go to the Lodge tonight," Manon says. "The sensitives through the Corridor, the rest of us by car. We will investigate whether the False Saint Method is true. If it is, and if the Housekeeper is as obsessed with injustice as Maeve thinks she is, then she will activate, and we all observe. Two theories proved or disproved in one night."

"One very, very dangerous night," Nuala says. "No."

"Fin, you cannot assume leadership just because you are older," Manon snaps.

"I am not doing that," Nuala says. "I'm assuming leadership because it's my house."

"I'm not so sure, either," Fiona says. "It's way, way too risky. What if they spot us and beat the shit out of us? Or worse? If they really are false saints or whatever, what if they have crazy power now?"

"If that is true," Manon says, clearly surprised that Fiona is questioning her, "then Maeve's Housekeeper power will activate."

"But we don't know if she *is* the Housekeeper," Fiona stresses.

"And even if she is, what does that mean exactly? That she's a killer? What do we do then, if we literally have to watch her kill someone?"

"It's a gradual thing," I say. "I can control it still. Like the other night: bad stuff happened, but I was still in my body. Maybe she'll take over fully one day and become a cold-blooded killer, but I'm Maeve still. For however long I have left."

"Look," Nuala says. "Manon is right. It's not a dictatorship here. We'll put it to a vote. There are seven of us. Majority wins. If you think we should go to the Lodge tonight, raise your hand."

I put my hand up. So does Manon. So does Lily. I expect Aaron to put his hand up, too, but he looks unsure. "I don't know," he says. "I mean, it's getting stronger all the time. What if each time you become her, you lose a little more control. I . . ."

"If you don't think we should go to the Lodge tonight," Nuala interrupts, clearly tired of what-ifs, "raise your hand."

Aaron, Nuala, and Fiona raise their hands. I look for Roe's hand and realize that they are no longer in the room.

27

ROE IS IN THE LIVING ROOM, STARING AT what remains of René's feast. The food is starting to smell. The slightly acidic smell of fresh fruit left to breathe on the air, of cream cakes curdling, of wine turning to vinegar.

We stand there, not speaking to each other. Sorrow has sharpened Roe's features somehow. I feel like they've become older in the past week, or maybe a face just becomes more defined when you're not allowed to kiss it.

"It's weird," I say. "Not hugging you."

"We can hug," they say softly. And we do. It's a long, beautiful, horrible hug. A hug that neither one of us wants to end.

"This room stinks," they say.

"I know."

Another pause. "We should let go now, Maeve."

"But I don't want to," I squeak. The smell of Roe, the feel of their body, the easy place where my head rests on their shoulder. Crying about Roe alone in my bedroom was hard, but this is worse. This feeling of a familiar thing slowly becoming alien, like your home burning down in front of you.

"Come on," Roe says, peeling me off. Slightly irritated. "We can't do this."

Tears start to trickle down my face. *It's good to lose them now,* I remind myself. *Rather than losing them later, when you're full Housekeeper.*

"So," Roe says eventually. "You're cursed."

"I believe so."

"Do you really believe it?"

I pause. "Yes," I say, nodding slowly. "I do. I've seen her life. I've felt her inside me. She's in me now, like an infection, or a chronic illness."

Roe nods, their face pained, like they're trying to swallow something with too much texture. "And that's what you've been so secretive about. With Aaron, and all that. The hug."

"Yeah. He figured it out first. He was giving me a sorry-you're-cursed hug." Then, for no reason at all other than leftover spite, I add: "Rather than a thanks-for-the-shag hug, which is what you so kindly interpreted it as."

Roe flinches. "You didn't give me a lot of other options."

"I did."

"Like what?"

"The option of believing me. The option of trusting me."

There's a very real part of me that thought this breakup wouldn't take. You see those around a lot. Girls at school always had these on-again, off-again love affairs. Part of me assumed that, now that the Housekeeper secret is out, Roe and I would ping back into place like an elastic band. But that doesn't feel like what's going to happen. It feels like we've crossed the Rubicon, said things we can't unsay. It feels like a combination of too many things—secrets, curses, jealousies, increasingly different lives—have ganged up on us together and left us for dead.

Maybe it's been breaking for a long time, but animal attraction plus our general ability to have a laugh together fended it off. Did we talk enough? Was I supportive enough? Did Roe leave enough space for me, or was I just trailing around after them, playing the schoolgirl girlfriend of a burgeoning rock star? Everything has a new context now, and I feel like I can't trust my own memories.

"You wanted this, Maeve. You're the one who said we should break up. You said the trust was gone. *You*."

I bite down on my lip, trying not to crumble.

"You must be relieved," I say. "On some level. Now you can just go on tour. Do your thing. Be a rock star. Not have to worry about your schoolgirl girlfriend."

I meant it to sound comforting, but it comes out of my mouth covered in hard, resentful scales.

"Don't do that," Roe says. "Don't try to act like I'm the one who gave up just because I'm the one who has ambition."

It's like a knife. "You're right," I snap. "I was always destined to be the footnote in your biography, wasn't I? I'll be the one they interview about you after you're famous. The girl you left behind."

"I want you to know that you're the one bringing this 'left behind' narrative into the equation. I just wanted confirmation that you weren't banging Aaron. There is no 'left behind' story. You're inventing it."

"It's easy to say that when you're not the one being left behind," I say, and once again, it doesn't come out how I want it to. It's supposed to sound fierce, matching Roe's fury. Instead I just start to cry. Deep, thick, hyperventilating tears.

"I'm the one who is going to rot here, Roe."

And I mean it. I will quite literally rot inside my own body. I will become a powerful spirit of vengeance, justice herself. But I will die, in a way. The old Maeve will decay like the molding wood of St. Bernadette's.

The cries come out in hot, choking gasps, my whole neck a chimney for sadness. It winds me. I have to sit down on the footstool. I let the tears strangle me, and Roe gets on their knees.

"Oh, god," they say, grabbing a paper napkin from a stack on the table. "I'm sorry, Maeve. I'm sorry."

Roe mops at my face, and I disagree, and I say no, *I'm* sorry. Eventually we fall silent again. The crying stops. The next room is suspiciously quiet. I suspect they're all holding their breath, hoping that whatever comes from this conversation, it will make life slightly less awkward for them.

"Look," I say. "I love you, OK? I'm always going to love you. And this is . . . this is fucking hard."

"Cosigned," Roe says gruffly. "Cosign on all of that."

"But . . . Roe. We're going to know each other forever. Not just because we have all the same friends. But because . . . hardly anyone outside this house knows who we are and what we are. No one understands us like we do. We can't afford to lose that. Life's hard enough as it is."

They sigh. "It certainly is," Roe says. "It certainly is."

Roe's eyes glow while they scan my face appraisingly, revealing the roots of their dark, curling lashes as they finally settle their gaze on my chin. "I had to leave," they say, gesturing to the kitchen. "It was all getting too much. Like, earlier today I was still getting my head around the fact that I had no girlfriend. Now I'm supposed to accept that soon you won't be Maeve at all? That you'll be some demon?"

"Manon thinks we can get rid of it," I say uncertainly. "We're doing a vote."

"A vote on what?"

"On whether we should visit the Lodge tonight. We're a hung jury. Me, Manon, and Lily are for it. Aaron, Nuala, and Fi are against. You're the final vote."

Roe considers this. "And what do you think?"

I sit up and make my spine flush with the wall. I run a finger under both eyes and try to clear the dripping mascara. "I think Manon knows what she's talking about," I say. "And I think we need to act fast. Things are changing. Quickly. We don't have time to waste."

Roe just nods. "I haven't really been involved enough in any of this, have I?"

"You have. Just in a different way."

They shake their head. "I guess I've never thought the Children and their recruits were really worth worrying about. I mean, they've made their choice, haven't they?" Roe lets out a long breath, an exasperated, irritated sigh. "I'm not sure that's good enough, though. To just care about my people, my audience, my community. You sort of have to care about everyone, don't you?"

"I'm sorry about what I said," I whisper. "I didn't mean it. The thing about you only wanting safe spaces for people who were your fans, I mean. I was just angry."

Roe shakes their head. "No. I mean . . . it was horrible, but, like, you had a point. I'm getting so much more attention lately, particularly for, like, identity stuff, and so just being an out nonbinary musician feels like activism in itself. But that's a bit easy, isn't it?" Roe smiles. "Oh wow, the thing that could potentially make me rich and famous is also social justice work, how convenient for me."

"You're being too hard on yourself. You can't care about everybody. And it is activism, too. You're singing about being trans on the friggin' radio. How often does that happen?"

Roe smiles. "Almost never?"

"Almost never!"

"You're wrong, though. You can care about everybody. You do. Sometimes I think that's the most amazing thing about you. You genuinely care about everybody. You can forgive everybody. You just accept their humanity, whereas I go around acting like a tweet."

"Like a tweet?"

"You know, sort of self-righteous, I guess."

I manage a smile. "That's the nicest thing anyone has said to me in a while."

"Well, enjoy it. It's the last compliment you'll get out of me for a while. I'm serious. I need to actively forget everything I love about you if we're going to survive."

I frown. It's too sad.

"But," Roe adds, "I'll remember everything I like about you."

I lean forward, our foreheads pressed together. We stay like that for a second. Thinking about kissing. Wondering what we would risk by doing it. We decide, silently, not to.

We head into the kitchen and Nuala asks us to vote again. It's four against three. We are going to the Lodge.

20

IT'S COLD OUTSIDE. THE TEMPERATURE HAS dropped overnight, from a cozy kind of cold to truly Baltic. There are a few flecks of snow swirling in the air like dust motes. Roe and I watch it suspiciously, and then lock eyes. Remembering the deep enchanted snow, the month Lily went missing. Remembering how we held hands and ran through the street after escaping Aaron's terrible COB meeting.

"It's not that kind of snow," they say. "It's the normal kind."

"Right," I say, nodding. "You guys better go."

It will take them forty minutes to drive to the Lodge. We're supposed to wait until they text us to say they've found a safe way in. Aaron and I head to the school to wait in Sister Assumpta's office.

"So," Aaron says once we're settled and he's sitting on the couch. He flicks a piece of dirt off the edge of his trainer. "How's Una?"

I look at him squarely. I'm on the floor, my back against the wall. "You saw all that, then."

He nods. "I watched you accept the hares. I woke up with this long vision, like a movie."

"What did you make of it, then?"

"Strange. It was like you were . . . you, but the most evolved you. The finished version."

"Charmander has become Charizard."

"What?"

"Pokémon?"

"I grew up in the church, Maeve, I don't know what Pokémon is."

"No video games? No cartoons?"

"No video games. No cartoons."

"What else?"

"What do you mean?"

"What else couldn't you have?"

"Female friends."

"Are you serious?"

"Yes."

He keeps picking at the edge of his trainer, where the rubber has started to come away in one long, stringy piece.

"Riri was my first female friend. At Twin Pines. I mean, I knew girls, from being a youth counselor and everything, but this was the first time we talked about, like, normal stuff. The stuff friends talk about."

There's a tension then, a slight flush that crawls into Aaron's cheeks.

"Did you guys . . . ?" I ask.

"What? No," he says quickly. "As if."

"What do you mean, as if?"

"Maeve, you know what the inside of my brain looks like. Do you really think I could stop thinking about eternal damnation for long enough to have sex with anyone? Especially back then?"

I'm stunned that he would say it so directly. It's so different from the him I used to know, the him that used to go on the radio. The one full of euphemisms and veiled references to sin.

"After Matthew," he goes on, "I was so fucked up from guilt

and my brain was so crazy—so, like, terminally unhinged—that the Children's whole chastity thing became very . . . I don't know. Comforting, I suppose. Like a very clean and wholesome way to view my own garbage mind."

He breaks off then, and I assume this is the most he wants to talk about it. He keeps picking at his shoe still.

"And I know this is going to sound egotistical," he suddenly says after a long silence. "But I know what I look like. I know girls want to sleep with me, or whatever."

I can't help it. I actually laugh. I was so ready to feel sorry for him, and now I can't stop laughing.

"Shut *up*," he says, clearly annoyed. "Let me *finish*."

"Sorry, I was so overcome with lust, I couldn't hear what you said."

"OK, ha, ha. Hilarious."

"I'm consumed with desire," I say, still laughing my head off.

"Let me finish, you *asshole*," he says, but he can't help breaking into a smile.

"Please finish. I'm sorry."

I have to beg to get him talking again, and I feel bad for making him feel silly, if only because it's getting in the way of the story.

"So the Children, they tell you to use that. If you're good-looking or naturally funny or naturally athletic, they want you to use what God gave you, as they put it, because he gave you those gifts to help win over more people to his side. So they want you to flirt. They wanted me to sell chastity and also, I don't know, gently brushing back the hair off a girl's face while maintaining steady eye contact. That kind of thing."

I remember all this. I remember the Chastity Brothers doing it when they came to our school, and I remember Aaron doing it in the apartment. Big, lingering bear hugs with girls he was trying to shame about their sex lives.

"So I feel like, now that I'm out of the Children, and out of religion, I guess . . . sex is another one of those things that I can't figure out how I feel about. Because I've always associated it with either Hell or with manipulating people. I don't know how to think about it in a normal sort of way."

I don't know what to say. It's a level of trauma that I've never had to think about before. I've had a lot of things happen to me, but none of them have ever stopped me from being horny. I don't want to sympathize too much, or tell him that things will get better. Our relationship isn't like that. I just stick to the facts.

"Lorna was going out with one of them," I say. "Is that normal?"

He twists his mouth. "It wasn't at first. But I think it became normal. It's probably how he got her to the Lodge."

"Speaking of," I say, looking at my phone. "They should be there."

"What's protocol if we don't hear from them?"

"That we go through anyway, because they might have lost their phone signal."

When we step through the Corridor, the Housekeeper portrait is more me than ever. Her bare feet are covered in scratches, her forehead slightly scarred from the nightclub. And she's angry. Lips pursed, eyes like steel. I look around quickly at the other paintings, to see if everyone else is all right. Everyone, on the whole, looks a little sadder than they did last time. Or perhaps I just feel that way, because I know how sad we all are. Various stages of heartbreak, rejection, fear.

"It's open," Aaron says quietly.

The door opens into a field, and I hesitate before stepping through. I can't tell where the field is. Or when. Is it the Housekeeper's field under the moonlight, or somewhere else? And if this is the Housekeeper's world, who would Aaron be in it?

"Come on," he says.

It's cold, so bitterly, terribly cold. I briefly think it's another season, another time, an ice age maybe, but then I remember: it's the countryside. However cold it is in the city, it's always colder in the country. There are no buildings to shelter me from the sharp, icy wind, running its fingers through my hair, slithering under my collar. We cross our arms and lower our foreheads.

"There's the house," he says. "There's the Lodge."

I can see it now. We're about a quarter of a mile away from it, but it stands there like a palace after a war. It is only at this vantage point that I can appreciate just how unfinished the Lodge is. There is an adjoining guest cottage that has no roof. Rooms with a taped X over the windows, as if they have just been fitted. A dug-out pit where a swimming pool should probably have been.

"It's so ugly," he says. "Imagine thinking you were coming to some kind of spiritual retreat and finding this."

"I have no service," I say, looking at my phone. "Do you?"

"Coming and going," he says, then points to the house. "Look. They're outside."

I squint into the distance. Between us and the house there's a short, sloping hill, and on top of it, a wavering pool of light. A golden glow. My vision blurs as I try to focus on it.

"Smoke," Aaron says, swiping at his eyes with his sleeve. "What's on fire?"

It's hard to know how to advance closer. The land is so open and empty that there's really no place to hide, and no way we won't be seen as we come nearer. Our only hope is to approach slowly up the grassy hill, and to be quiet.

248

"It seems like a bonfire situation," I say. There's a crackling, autumn smell, and I can feel my body drawing naturally toward the warmth it knows is there, the sharp wind pushing me closer. We crouch and move quietly, hoping that the dark night sky and the charisma of the fire will keep us safe.

"Put your phone away," he whispers sharply. "They'll see the light."

As we crawl higher up the slope, I start to see the lights of the city. We can't be that far from Nuala, Manon, Roe, Fiona, and Lily. Can we?

The hope is to blend into the crowd around the bonfire. But the closer we get, the harder that is to achieve. First of all, the arrangement of people around the bonfire is structured. There are concentric circles, rings around rings, like the inside of a tree. There are about eighty people spread out over four rings. And as the flickering orange light bounces off their skin, I realize something else.

They are not wearing nearly enough clothing.

The girls are wearing camis and shorts. The boys are shirtless.

"What the fuck?" I whisper to Aaron. "It's below freezing."

We keep low, and somehow nobody sees us. They are too focused on something else, and that something is Dorey—in the center of all the circles.

It takes me a moment to realize it's her. She is dressed completely in white, something heavy and shapeless, like what the pope might wear. I feel uneasy, looking at her. I've only seen corporate Dorey, proper Dorey, suits and helmet-hair Dorey. I suddenly remember the night with the chicken-grease candles in the tennis courts, the feeling of being visibly satanic, despite our best intentions. It's the same here. They are so Christian that they've circled all the way around to witchcraft again.

The fire is tickling the sky, crackling and bursting through its layers of kindling like a great big body with its organs all working at once. The smoke is thin and gray, obscuring my vision. And yet, Dorey manages to speak the way she always appears: elegant, rested, concerned. Hypnotic.

"This seminar tonight," she begins, "is concerning a subject that is so alien to us, in the modern world, that it may . . . stretch your skulls a little. I don't know."

She smiles like they are sharing a private joke, and the audience is captivated. The nearly naked devotees of Dorey are standing barefoot on the frosted grass, clenching their back teeth firmly to stop from chattering. My stomach starts to churn. Once she gets a string on you.

"People often ask me," she continues, "where faith comes from. And it's a good question. Because you can read scripture, and you can pray and perform any number of devotional tasks, and still . . ." She places her hand flat against her chest, bows her head. "And still not feel it here."

There is a slight murmuring of the crowd. Or not even a murmur, but a shift. Some feeling of danger, of hesitancy, of recognition. My eyes flicker to Aaron, who's looking queasily around him. Not "feeling" faith, after all, was what started him on the road to Dorey to begin with. The fear that God might think he was lukewarm and a fake.

"In order for real faith to happen, something has to happen of itself," she goes on. "Something that is outside of you, because it is bigger than you. It has to be a surprise. And the thing with surprises is . . . well, you can't surprise yourself, can you?"

She waits for a response while her audience tries to understand whether this is a rhetorical question or a real one. It is a real one.

"You can't surprise yourself, can you? If you have hiccups and need to be surprised out of them, simply telling a friend to say 'Boo' won't work." She stops, smiles, takes in a titter of nervous laughter.

"Sometimes I think we are all just people with hiccups. Struggling to breathe, gasping for real life, caught between the worlds of the humdrum and the higher power."

Someone in front of me, an almost naked boy, rubs his right leg with his left foot as subtly as he possibly can.

"And we're not talking about ordinary surprises. We're talking about transcendence. We're talking about divinity. But how can we experience that when there's so much to distract us? How can we strip back our consciousness to being babies again, who are surprised by the newness, the divinity of everything? The answer is simple: we have to take everything away. Start again."

Aaron's eyes start to widen in horror. He is more used to the doublespeak of faith healers than I am, and he is becoming visibly unnerved by this speech.

"Spiritual blankness. Ideological purity. The notion of no prejudices, no bias. No negative self-talk. No sense of animal competition. Just open hearts, full of wonder. Only when you are capable of wonder are you capable of surprise. Grand, spiritual surprise."

I'm starting to notice that Dorey doesn't talk very much about God, or scripture, or any of that. It's all this vague spiritual language that you might see from an influencer trying to sell yoga mats.

"Which is why we choose to stand back from the fire," she says, smiling warmly to the near-naked Children in the back circle. "Why we choose to expose our flesh to the elements. Why we choose to abstain from food, from drink. It is not an easy thing. Not an easy choice. It is not meant to be easy. But with difficulty, we draw power. Power from the earth. Power we offer to the heavens."

Another pause. The fire crackles, whispering to itself. Choosing and choice. What is she getting at?

"And not everyone . . ." She stops then, and everyone looks up at her intently. Her voice seems to crack. Like there is real sorrow in her throat that she is trying to push past in order to maintain gravitas. And I know that sorrow is a lie. "Not everyone is built for that mission."

Silence. The moon bounces off bare skin, and I get my brain to burrow into the group as a whole. Not because my telepath skills are so advanced, but because they are all thinking the same thing at once.

It is one name, four letters, and all together at the same time.

Soph.

"As we all know," Dorey continues gravely, "Sophia had a very troubled life. She also had some preexisting physical health conditions that she did not declare upon entering the Lodge."

The group starts to pull away at this, and you can feel their reasoning depart from Dorey's firm voice.

"If she had let us know about those conditions," she says, "I would have advised against the course of divinity—this marvelous act of self-surprise—that she pursued. But she wanted clarity. She wanted transcendence. Isn't that what we all want?"

Again, the group's hive mind starts to pull away. They all remember Sophia. She had seemed very healthy.

Dorey gazes over her audience, and there's a harsh snap from the inside of my brain, the feeling of a rubber band bouncing back. Suddenly, everyone is aligned again. Sophia was a very unhealthy girl.

"I was extremely fond of Sophia," she goes on. "Which is why we stand here in her honor today. Grief is one of the most ancient tools of human bonding, and we are privileged to experience it together."

It finally hits me. Dorey's ornate, strange language has finally fallen away to reveal the truth to me. A girl has died. A girl has died while trying to achieve some mysterious spiritual awakening, and Dorey is quietly, gracefully, respectfully shirking the responsibility.

Someone approaches Dorey and whispers something to her. A few people move at once, and I can't see anything for a moment. My mind keeps reaching for Dorey, trying to push past the crowd and into her, but she's like a remote island.

"After tonight," she says, breaking away from the people who interrupted her, "I would like you all to keep Sophia in your thoughts, and to have a moment for her in your practice every day. Grief is cleansing. Try not to speak her name out loud, but use it as an interior tool."

One more string is attached to the community. An instruction to be metabolized so quickly that it appears in your subconscious as if it was meant to be there. *Do not speak about Sophia ever again.*

"Maeve Chambers," Dorey suddenly announces. "You are interrupting the grief of our community. And I hope it's for a good reason."

The crowd parts, exposing me to the full chill of the December wind. The Children wait for me to speak, in the dull, listless way that a cow waits for you to pass her field.

"Who did you kill, Dorey?" I say, because it's the only thing I can think of. "Who did you kill now?"

The wind whips at my face, and I can feel the Children close in around me.

"The question, Housekeeper," she replies, "is who will you kill next?"

29

DOREY'S HAND EMERGES FROM THE LONG
sleeve of her robe, and I see a deck of cards clasped within her fingers. She pulls one card and holds it up, the light of the fire bouncing off the bright ink.

"Three of Pentacles," she says. "Tell me, what does that mean, Maeve?"

I plant my feet and try to summon the witch who lives within me.

"Teamwork," I say coolly. "Collaboration."

Dorey nods, then flicks the card into the fire. There's a sudden burst, as though the card had been coated in petrol. I see half-naked Children wavering toward the heat of the flames.

She picks another, and even at a distance, I recognize it immediately. It's the card I once dealt for Roe.

"The Hanged Man," she says.

"Struggle," I answer. "The struggle before victory."

She smiles. "Apt. Very apt." Then a pause. "Bring her forward. My third card."

Of course. They were never two-card spreads. They were always three. Past, present, future. With the Housekeeper always in the third place: a call to me, to come through the Corridor.

"Any black magic, Dorey"—the words, I'm sure, are being stolen by the wind, and there's no way she can hear—"comes back to you times three."

But there's no black magic here. Just brute strength. I'm taken by both arms and dragged forward, my toes tripping off the icy, hard ground.

Suddenly I am close to the fire, my frozen skin thawing out rapidly and almost burning in the process. Dorey is in front of me, a wall of her acolytes behind me. They are all older, midtwenties to thirties. Her inner circle. Her trusted few. Children forever.

Dorey examines me freely, as though she were buying a horse. I remember the Chokey, months ago, when Heather did the same thing. Perhaps this is part of it. Perhaps when you feel strong enough from stolen power, you start thinking of everyone else as animals, as livestock. Free to slaughter or sell or sap as you see fit.

Silver coins are placed casually on the blue web of veins on the insides of my wrists. The horrifying feeling of muting, of my power being muffled. Like my brain is pacing the beach on a desert island while my body is deep underwater. She slides a finger down my nose and down to my top lip, the soft pads of her hand tickling my skin.

"You know, Maeve," she says at last, "you were born too late."

The rage burns within me. I call to the witch inside me, the original Housekeeper, like I'm trying to wake her up from sleep. I will not say a word until she's ready to join me and I can unleash her fury on Dorey.

She continues lightly tracing her fingers on my face. It's as if she's trying to map what parts of me are still human, and what parts are rotting under demon influence. "The thing about Ireland—and I've been learning this, you know, while I've been living here—is that it was pagan for thousands of years. Ungovernable. Unmanageable. Impossible. The Romans didn't even bother. Who could survive in a place so wild? So uncivilized?"

She's not wrong. It's a history that stays alive with bedtime stories: stories of warrior queens and legendary heroes, Queen Meadhbh and Cú Chulainn.

"And then, around the fifth century or so," Dorey continues, pushing down more firmly on my bottom lip, "suddenly the whole country turns Catholic. And why? Why, Maeve?"

The question is not rhetorical. Dorey is looking for an answer. I feel a pull in my brain, and I know she's got me. I have become interested in what she has to say. She has begun to flex her hold on my brain.

"St. Patrick," I blurt, like a child. St. Patrick, the former enslaved boy who converted wild old Ireland to a God-fearing new nation. The saint most synonymous with Ireland, but there are more. Tons. St. Brigid, who we used to weave crosses for in primary school. St. Christopher, who my dad still wears a medal for, even though he doesn't believe in it. And St. Bernadette, of course, the little French girl who the Virgin Mary supposedly appeared to.

"Saints," Dorey says triumphantly, finally stepping back from me. "Patrick being the most famous, of course. Young saints. Child saints. People who suffered. And the more they suffered, the more they chose to suffer, the more the magic of old Ireland would build up and burst. Creating Wells. Creating miracles."

Miracles. You need at least a couple to become a saint. I remember that from school. Sometimes the pope will make a decision about whether someone is a saint or not after reviewing if their miracle was truly real. It's a crazy religion, really. Crazier than anything Wicca can come up with.

"You want to make miracles," I say at last. "You want them to make miracles for *you*."

I gesture at the "them," the Children themselves, gladly suffering in her name.

Dorey smiles again. "As I said before," she says, "you've really forced me to innovate. The Well is sealed, but there are certain things it can't help but respond to powerfully. Suffering is one of them. Martyrdom, in extreme cases."

I can feel the Housekeeper's storm brewing now. It's stronger than any silver coin. It's just about waiting for the right moment to let her unleash.

Martyrdom. Is that what that poor dead girl was, the one they're all mourning? A martyr?

"When I say you were born in the wrong time," Dorey continues, with an air of *Thank you for coming to my TED Talk*, "what I mean is, the Well was created through a combination of pagan energy and religious rigor. Pagans created this vast enchanted wildness; Christians helped concentrate it to specific spots. The saints conjured so much magic through their sacrifice that the Wells formed in response. But the time for wildness is over, Maeve. And even demons like the Housekeeper can be controlled."

And it's on this word, *controlled*, that I feel the Housekeeper kick back. Furious at the implication, and ready to prove herself. The silver coins fall from my wrists, and my hands begin to fill with petals and stalks. *Foxglove, hemlock, laburnum,* the Housekeeper whispers, trying to teach me quickly. *Take it, throw it, burn it. Make poison on the air.*

I wait until my palms are full. The elder Child has relaxed his grip on my shoulders, although he hasn't released me yet. My fingers snap outward, as though I were suddenly performing jazz hands. The petals touch the fire, and the air roars hungrily. The smoke, once thin and gray, turns thick, white. The kind of white smoke they use to declare a new pope.

The Child coughs, and I tear myself away, circling the fire like it's a maypole.

The more I throw, the more appears in my hands. I'm not getting it from thin air; I'm borrowing it, from the lovely layer cake of the past.

I hear her, whispering to me. Tugging at me from her place in the past. Talking fast, like someone explaining a plan.

The smoke gets higher, and the hemlock heavier, and it's like I have the Children's hearts in my hands. Their breathing becomes heavy, their pulses feeble. They start to back away. One falls to her knees.

Only Dorey remains unchanged. Her hands together, underneath her robes.

"Very impressive, Maeve," she says. "Very primal. Very rustic."

I start running, throwing more and more flowers, bodies obscured by flame and smoke.

"You know, Maeve, it's only a matter of time before you're a contract killer. You might be able to balance your old self and your new one now, but trust me, darling—it's only a matter of time."

The world blurs, the faster I run.

"You'll be gone soon, you know. Under the waves. You're strong, but she's stronger. Her personality, her tastes, her urges. Her memories. No more Maeve Chambers. Someone is going to call the Housekeeper, and with each calling, the less you will know yourself. You won't be acting out your own little . . . quest. You'll be murdering someone, at the bidding of someone else. That's the job, after all. It's a mercenary's life, at the end of the day."

The smoke doesn't touch me but hovers away from my skin, as if the air has formed a protective cloak around me. Dorey seems to have a kind of invisible cloak, too. The Children are not so lucky. I hear their coughs, their splutters, and I suddenly realize that I have no idea where Aaron is. I stop running.

"I could free you from this, you know," Dorey says.

"Where's Aaron?" This newborn panic pushes the Housekeeper away, and Dorey's thin smile seems to gleam in the darkness.

"I've harvested enough power here that I could take it from you, Maeve. I could drain the curse out of you."

"And then what?" I spit back, insulted she would take me for such an idiot. "Add it to your pile of magic? Why, Dorey? For what?"

Dorey draws herself up to her full height, and the fire begins to cower. I can feel her controlling it, manipulating it. The summoned petals start to rise in the air, as if they had never been burned. The power she's taken through these kids. Her little saints.

"The world is in disarray," Dorey says, and she raises her voice, like she wants everyone to hear her. "Wild, like the old days. But even then, nature was still a governing principle. Sowing, tilling, harvest. Now we live in a world where nobody plants, nobody sows, nobody harvests. No one has a role they understand. School shootings, suicides, sex abuse. More hideous clothes made under slave labor thrown in landfills every week because girls your age have nothing to aspire to other than a beautiful body, made new again with every trend. Do you think this is good, Maeve? Do you think this is healthy? Do you think this is how people are supposed to be?"

I am reminded of Heather Banbury, who told me that working for the Children was simply a matter of taking the ideology you agreed with and dismissing what you didn't. She compared it to any big company, like Amazon or Apple. I remember Aaron, who used to begin every radio appearance with something bad that everyone could agree on, like children being addicted to porn, and would spin that out to sex outside marriage being sinful.

This is what the Children are good at. It's why they're so seductive. They find crazy, simplistic solutions to the most frightening problems.

Aaron. Where is he?

Dorey is on a roll now, though, enjoying the sound of her own voice.

"The Church in Ireland is no longer fit for purpose. That much is clear. But that doesn't mean that the role the Church fulfilled isn't still a necessary one. The world needs governance, community, steering."

She leaves a pause then, to indicate that the Children are the natural candidates to begin such steering. Her silence, however, is interrupted.

Somewhere—not very far away—there is the sound of a car horn, a skid, and then a crunch of metal. And I remember that Aaron isn't the only person I need to worry about. That the others followed us in their cars. I look around wildly, my hands filling with petals again.

But when I look up, Dorey is gone. Only her Children remain.

30

I NEED TO GET OUT OF HERE, BUT I NEED Aaron first.

"Aaron," I scream into the darkness. "Where are you? We have to go."

"We know who you are," comes a voice from the crowd. A boy. I follow the voice, my gift sharp from the Housekeeper's influence. I tunnel into his mind, trying to figure out what he knows, or what he thinks he knows. He is not worried about the car horn. He thinks it's the dead girl's family, coming to cause trouble. What was her name again? Sophie?

"You're a murderer," the same voice says. "That poor woman. Heather. She just wanted to get through to you, make you understand. And you burned her alive. Well, do you know that you're going to burn, too?"

I can't tell if the threat is real or spiritual. Do they mean burn in Hell, or burn on their bonfire?

"There's a place for people like you," he screams, his voice becoming shrill in the rising wind. "And you'll be there, forever."

So they do mean Hell. They are all illuminated by the bonfire, their cheeks gaunt, their eye sockets hollowed.

"*This* is Hell!" I scream back. "You're in it, guys. You're starving out here. You're dying. One of you is gone already."

Sophie Mulrooney. No. Mulready. Sophia Mulready. Did they say her last name? If they didn't, why am I so sure that I already know it?

Oh, my god.

I slide my hand into my pocket, my fingers so cold that it takes me a moment to find my wallet. I open it, under the light of the Children's torch, while they yell about hellfire, and discipline, and faith.

I slide the learner's permit out, the one Michelle Breen's friend gave to me. *She's a Jesus freak now.*

Where was Sophia Mulready while I was assuming her identity to get into a club? Standing six circles back from the fire, wearing a cami and underwear? Chewing on her fingernails for sustenance? Convincing herself that she was engaged in—what was it?—"grand, spiritual surprise"?

A few have visions. Soph. Sophia. All elbows and big hair. Committed. Sunny. Weather reports. *Today the sun was shining and Sophia said she missed her family.*

Suddenly my voice pushes out of my chest, loud and black, a wolf's howl. "This house won't keep you!" I scream. "You've chosen the wrong place."

And I say it again and again, feeling more powerful every time. They really do seem like children, the Children. Babies who have wound up in a bully's thrall.

I scream and scatter my herbs in the fire, and it's like an invisible shield forms, pushing the Children away. They walk backward. They retreat to the house. Their insides are lightly bruised from the poison air, but they will recover. It won't take a day. It will probably take three. These are kids who are attracted to power, after all, and maybe thinking about mine will turn their heads from Dorey.

"Aaron!" I start shouting again. "Aaron! Where are you?" Silence.

I remember my gift. How I can use my talent for seeing a person's light as a sort of radar. I stand there in the freezing wind. I try to remember what Aaron's light looks like. His is a mind I consciously stay out of—too dark, too self-punishing, too curiously filled with Bible verse. But I know what it looks like. Gray. Gray with a yellow edge.

I find it. It isn't far. But it's subdued, grainy, coming in and out of focus. *Don't be dying. Don't be dead.*

"Where the hell *are* you?" I scream out loud, and yet no scream comes back.

Holes. Holes. Aaron sees holes. Gaps. Flaws. Weakness. That's his gift.

"I'm a screwed-up person," I begin, hoping that admitting to weakness might somehow align our gifts together. "I'm a mean girl. And I'm suspicious, and jealous. I'm self-absorbed. I have awful thoughts about people. And sometimes I'm afraid that all the horrible stuff I've done isn't because there's a curse on my head, but because I'm just horrible."

Silence.

"And I'm afraid that if I didn't have someone else around, someone who really knows what it's like to be horrible, I'd feel so lonely that I would drown."

A murmur. A trickle of sound. Something like an animal with its leg trapped under a brick.

"Is that you?" I call. "I can't—"

Slightly louder now.

"What?" I ask the air.

"I said, don't drown."

I spin around, looking for the voice. "Where *are* you?"

"The hole. Be careful."

The hole where the swimming pool should have been opens like a bite a giant has taken out of the earth. There he is. Thrown down there, face covered in blood, arms at a strange angle.

"You need to get Fiona here," he calls.

I remember the others and feel a rush of panic. The car horn. The crunch of metal in the distance. "Aaron, I need you to come with me. The others might be in even deeper shit than you are. Come on. I'll drag you out."

I lie down, belly in the dirt, and stretch out my hand. I manage to grab on to his icy fingers. I feel like my arm is being wrenched out of its socket, but, somehow, we manage to get him out of the hole. Blood is caked in his nostril, and his eye is starting to swell. There's a thick black wound on his cheek that is already starting to crust over.

"Jesus, Aaron."

"I know. They beat the crap out of me. It's nothing compared to the ankle, though."

He pulls up the cuff of his jeans and reveals that his ankle has curved inward, so he has to walk on the side of his foot. It's horrifying, like something small but important has snapped under the skin.

"All right," he says miserably, "now what do we do?"

"The road," I say. "We walk toward the road. That's where they'll be."

"I can't do it."

"You can. Just lean on my shoulder."

He leans, and it's difficult trying to walk him along because he's so much taller than me. I feel like Dorothy trying to keep the Scarecrow upright. He hops along, and every few steps he has to stop, yowling like a cat whenever he unexpectedly puts weight on the bad foot.

"What happened?" he asks.

"I went Housekeeper," I say. "Full vengeance demon. Poison smoke. The whole transformation."

I explain about Dorey, and the dead girl—one of many dead girls, it seems.

"She offered me a deal," I say at last.

"Oh, god, of course. Dorey and her deals."

"She said she could get rid of the curse," I say, and I can hear my voice trembling. "Of course, I mean, I would never. I'm not that stupid, to trust someone like her. But . . . Eventually, someone's going to call the Housekeeper. For vengeance purposes, I mean. Maybe not for a long time because not many people really know about her. But it will happen. And I'll have to kill someone. That's how it works, right?"

He's silent for a few more labored steps. "Maybe you won't know you're doing it," is all he can say. "Maybe it will be like a dream."

"I'm still not happy about it."

"Name one thing," he says as we glimpse the road and the light of two sets of headlights, "that any of us are happy about."

31

THERE'S A GRASSY SLOPE THAT LEADS
down into the road, where I can just about see Nuala's car parked on
the hard shoulder. But where is Roe's?

Oh, god, no.

I should wait for Aaron. I should try to get him down the hill
safely.

I immediately start running down the slope, my breath heavy.
Not a crash. Not a crash. Not Roe.

I almost start bargaining with myself, trying to strike grand
pacts with the universe: Take Nuala, but not Manon. Or take Manon,
but not Lily. Take anyone, but not Roe. But I realize there is no bargain, no fair way to parcel sorrow. I can't lose a single one. They're all
too important, too central to the last remaining shards of my sanity.

I run closer, miraculously keeping my balance, until I see Lily's
blue head shining under a streetlamp. Manon's tight, honey-brown
curls. Both of them shimmering and safe under the orange glow of
nocturnal lighting.

But where's Nuala? Where's Fiona? Where's Roe?

I reach the road and finally see Roe's car. Its hood has been
crushed into the metal barrier, as if it spun out of control very suddenly. Lily and Manon jump, like they've seen a ghost. I look at them

more closely. The gash on Lily's neck, the wound on her head, the glass in her hair.

"Is everyone OK?"

It comes out in a wheeze. I breathe in the icy air, so sharp it feels like it's nailing my lungs to my skeleton.

Manon and Lily just look at me, covered in earth and Aaron's blood, smelling of poison smoke. Their eyes not quite believing it. I spot Fiona and Nuala sitting in Nuala's car, but it's too dark to read their expressions. Paolo is perched nearby, his head cocked in concern.

"Where are they?" I scream. "Where's Roe? Where the fuck is Roe?"

Roe's jacket, the red one with the leopard collar, is in a bundle on the ground. Streaked with liquid. Dark. Heavy. Shiny.

Blood.

And I know—I am certain—that Roe is gone.

A wail falls out of my mouth, and suddenly my forehead is on the ground. Long, weeping gulps. Roe. Not Roe. Roe, the best one. Roe, my favorite person. Roe, the only person I've ever been in love with. Roe, who I am in love with. Roe, who was supposed to be famous. Roe, the rock star. Roe in bed, their finger in front of their lips, telling me to be quiet. Roe in the underpass. No. No. Roe.

As I cry, I can feel the Housekeeper cry with me—my partner in grief. I feel her rise up, her vengeance meeting my sorrow. I feel the world open up, like I'm kicking my feet in a black abyss, hitting nothing, seeing nothing. Only rage.

Then I look up. And, almost in slow motion, I see Roe emerging from underneath the smashed car, reaching for the scarlet bomber jacket with their foot. Their hands are stained black. It wasn't blood on the jacket. It was oil.

Roe was under the car. Fixing it. Talking to it. I sink my head onto the road, wanting to vomit in relief.

"Roe," I whimper, getting to my feet, throwing my arms around them, breathing in their smell, their hair. "Roe, Roe. Roe."

Roe's hands hover above my waist, not quite touching me. I draw back and look at them. There's glass in Roe's hair, too, but no visible damage.

They all look at me as though a rabid creature has just tried to attack them.

"What happened?" I ask, trying to regulate my breath. "Thank god for Fi. Aaron and I got messed up, too. Him especially. Tell me what happened."

Aaron suddenly stumbles into view. He hobbles to Roe's crushed car and keeps himself upright, placing his hands on the passenger door.

"You're the Housekeeper, all right," Lily finally says. "Seems like there's no debate about that now."

I look around, and I see that there is glass everywhere. All the way down the road. And a smell. A smell of electrics and smoke.

"You screamed," Fiona says. "And it all went dark."

"Not just the lamps," Manon says. "But everything. The whole . . . the whole countryside."

"The whole world," Lily says softly. "The moon went away."

I realize that they never fully believed me when I said I was the Housekeeper. Never thought it could be possible. Even Manon, whose idea this all was. Even if academically she understood that it might be possible, she hadn't grasped the enormity of what being the Housekeeper is. What it can do.

"I'm cursed," I say quietly. Then I correct myself. "I am a curse."

Roe observes the ruined car while Fiona mends Aaron's ankle, his foot in her lap. I feel strangely awkward, oddly at a loss. A girl is dead. A girl whose ID still sits in my wallet. Sure, I was able to summon this power to cause a scene at the Lodge, but what could I actually do? Was it time to go to the police now? Was this too big for spells, for hemlock and foxglove?

Roe's hood is smashed, the paint scratched, the windshield wipers hanging on by a thread.

"Someone ran out into the road," Lily explains. "Roe swerved, and the car went out of control."

"I almost killed them," Roe says. "Whoever it was. It was lucky I saw them when I did. But yeah, we smashed into the roadside."

"Someone?" I ask. "A person?"

"Yep. They disappeared, though. I literally couldn't even tell you what they looked like. Skinny, I guess."

Dorey can make people run into traffic for her. What hope do we have?

"Poor dear," Roe says affectionately to the car. "Looks like a pug, doesn't she?"

And she does, sort of, look like a pug. Irritated little face. A "What on *earth*?" expression.

Roe turns the key in the ignition, switching the headlights on, then walks slowly around to the front of the car. Keeping one hand on her, saying something gentle. "Come on, sweetheart," they say. "Come on, now. Enough drama. Let's fix you."

And it sounds silly, but I close my eyes and pretend they're talking to me.

When I open them again, it's just in time to see the wrinkles in the metal straighten themselves out, the car morphing underneath Roe's hands.

"Oh, my *god*," I gasp. Then I look over at Aaron, who is now walking on both feet, thanks to Fiona. "When did you two get so powerful?"

"When you weren't looking," Roe replies.

My heart breaks into pieces again.

Maybe it is supposed to.

32

AARON RIDES BACK WITH MANON AND
Nuala, and the rest of us are in Roe's car. I don't know how it worked
out that way; maybe we all felt a silent urge to return to our original
gang. The core four.

When we eventually get to Nuala's, I expect the air to be filled
with questions, theories, statements. The False Saint Method, and its
deadly implications for the Sophia Mulreadys of this world.

Instead, it's just Manon and Nuala, screaming at each other in
the kitchen while Aaron sits on the stairs like a child of divorce.

The five of us peer through the glass door from the hallway
while they speak in a mixture of French, English, and, surprisingly
enough, something that sounds vaguely like Russian.

"What the . . . ?"

Roe puts a finger to their lips, the old ciúnas motion, and my
cheeks automatically flush. We cock an ear, and I get traces of the
English.

"Manny, you're getting a bit old for this Masters of the Universe
schtick. He's just a man, not some wizard with all the answers."

Then Nuala says something in French that sounds like a question.

"Oh, Maman"—that's new—"the idea of someone knowing
more than you is too painful, isn't it?"

"Don't be silly. I called you, didn't I? I just think we can—"

"It's the only reason you called me, isn't it? Why you wanted me to come here, to your home? To help with your *real* kids."

A moment of stunned, hurt silence from the kitchen, and the five of us look at one another, wondering if we're the real kids. We hear the back door slam, and the sound of Nuala swearing in a language I've never heard.

Suddenly, the kitchen door swings open and Manon stands in the doorway, both hands on the frame. She looks at all five of us—not with anger, but not with affection, either. Just coolly measuring us, making eye contact with each one.

"My dad is coming," she says.

After a few minutes of deep breathing in the garden, Nuala comes back inside.

"Her father should come," she says, addressing all of us and none of us. "He's probably the only one who can sort this out."

I pour her a cup of tea. "Why, exactly?"

"Well, Maeve." She looks at me levelly. "You know how I lost Manon, don't you?"

Manon lights a cigarette, not even bothering to go outside. Nuala sighs and faces the room.

"To make a *very* long story short, I had a choice: join the tricksters, which means becoming a sort of, you know, demigod, and stay with Manon and René." She takes a breath, the grief of it still winding her. "Or take a payout from her grandparents and leave. I picked the demigod option, naturally, but I had to perform a kind of ritual. Only, I failed the ritual. I didn't want to, but I did. And I lost Manon. I couldn't talk to her again until she was eighteen. She was five at the time."

The room is collectively devastated at this. Manon merely ashes her cigarette on the floor.

"You blame them," Manon says snappily. "But it wasn't as harsh as that. She was allowed to visit, after a while. And I visited. Twice."

Nuala shakes her head. "Your grandparents love you, Manon," she says. "But I'm always going to be this silly mortal to them. I was welcome, but I was not *welcome*."

"That's awful, Nuala. And Manon. I'm so sorry," Roe says, delicately as possible. "But . . . how does that help Maeve?"

Manon takes a long drag of her cigarette, her eyes firmly on her feet. "It was a changing ritual that my mother failed. Le grand passage. And really, she should have passed. She had carried me. My blood was her blood. She should have been able to cross over."

Manon flicks her cigarette again, a pile of ash growing by her bare toes. Clearly Manon thinks that Nuala failed this test because she wanted to.

"Alors. That has nothing to do with you, Maeve. What I mean is that it's the same principle. You have the Housekeeper within you. You're halfway between crossing over. Now you must simply cross back. It's the reverse of the same ritual. My father will come here to conduct it."

I blink, not quite believing it. "I can un-become the Housekeeper?"

"It won't be easy," Nuala says quickly. "You'll have to go deep into your visions. It's . . . quite intense. And your sense of purpose has to be resolute, Maeve, do you understand?"

"Resolute?"

"There will be things in there that will tempt you," she says extremely carefully. "But they will just be visions."

"Visions," I repeat, trying to muster confidence. "I'm getting used to visions."

But it doesn't feel right.

"The thing is," I say hesitantly, "is that the Housekeeper is all about vengeance, right, and protecting the vulnerable. I mean, originally, anyway."

"Correct," Manon says.

"Well, who's more vulnerable than the Children? A girl has died up there. Maybe we *need* the Housekeeper. Maybe she's the only one who can fix this."

I pull out my wallet. I pass Sophia Mulready's learner's permit around. "This is her."

Everyone looks at the license silently before giving it to the next person.

"Nineteen," Fiona says. "And a Virgo."

"A Virgo who *can* drive," Lily says, quipping from *Clueless*, which is a movie I'm surprised she remembers watching. "Sorry, that's not funny. She's dead."

"She's dead," Roe repeats. "Christ."

"Manon, your false saint theory has turned out to be bang on. Dorey basically told me everything. How Ireland was converted to Christianity, originally, using the power of saints. That's what made the Wells. There was all this wild pagan magic running through the country and then sainthood and sacrifice draws it all together. Concentrates it."

I can see Manon's brain working overtime, puzzling this out, cross-referencing it with everything she has ever read. She taps on her lips with her fingers. "There *has* always been a correlation," she says slowly, "between historically very religious places and Well places."

"Dorey feels . . ." I puzzle hard on this, pause. It feels spiritually damaging to imagine what Dorey feels. "Dorey feels that the world has gone mad, nobody has a place, communities are over, everyone's sick and struggling."

"Hear, hear," Lily says tonelessly.

"And that the role of the Catholic Church, in the old days, was, like, order, union, guidance . . ."

"Incarceration," Nuala adds. "Punishment, corruption."

"Yeah, all that. She feels like the Church is dead, but the job the Church did was a necessary one, and it should be her job now. I think she genuinely thinks that what she's doing is, like, very noble."

"Trust me," Aaron says. "She thinks of herself as *extremely* noble."

"Right. So a few dead bodies, a few Heather Banburys, a few Sophia Mulreadys—it's all worth it to her. For the greater good. What she thinks of as the greater good."

Nuala's expression twists. Nuala, who was born in an Ireland with no divorce, with laws against homosexuality, where condoms could only be bought with a doctor's note. Is this something Dorey wants to return to? Or could it be even worse? Every few weeks there's a story about how American laws are going backward. Could that happen here, too?

"Roe," she says suddenly. "Can you take Fiona and Lily home? I need a word with Maeve. I'll drive her home."

Roe nods, and we exchange a look. I don't know what Nuala wants to talk to me about, but maybe it's good that Roe isn't the one dropping me at home. After tonight, my urge to hold them, to be held, is stronger than ever.

Then it's just me and Nuala, and the empty roads. I assume that she wants to talk to me about this old Ireland that Dorey wants to return to, but she doesn't speak about that. For the first time ever, she wants to discuss René.

"Tomorrow," she says, "René will be here to conduct the ritual. The grand passage."

"That seems awfully quick. Doesn't he have to book flights?"

She grimaces slightly. "You'll find that admin is not the kind of thing that ever troubles René."

"I guess we'll both have to work with our exes then."

She smiles, for the first time all evening. "I guess we will."

"Are you OK? With him coming?"

She glances over at me, worried. "Maeve, I should be asking if you're OK."

"What do you mean?"

"Well, you're taking this curse surprisingly well."

"Ah," I say. "Yeah, I don't know. Enough weird things happen to you and, eventually, you get used to them."

She looks at me, baffled, waiting for something bigger than this.

"I guess . . ." It's hard to formulate what I mean, hard to find the words. "I guess everyone in my life has a kind of destiny, and it felt normal for me to have one, too."

"Destiny to play music or to act, Maeve," Nuala replies, horrified. "Not to murder people as a revenge demon."

"I don't know, Nuala." I shrug. "She wasn't always just this demon. I go back, and I'm the original her. And she's, you know, a protector."

Nuala suddenly pulls over and parks the car on the shoulder.

"Maeve," she says. "I'm going to tell you something that I've never told anyone."

Nuala covers her eyes with her hands, massaging her own face. For a second, she looks about seventeen. "When I did the changing-over ritual—le grand passage—I saw something. Someone. I saw Heaven."

She leans forward, her forehead lightly kissing the steering wheel. "I was supposed to follow this path, you see? The whole thing happened in a vision. I was supposed to follow a path and never, ever stray from it. And I was doing a really good job, even though it was hard, and painful, and then Heaven showed up. And she spoke to me."

"What did she say?"

Nuala pauses for a long time before answering. She straightens up in her seat. Steels herself.

"I'm not going to tell you that, but only because it wouldn't make sense to you. It was about our parents, and our childhood, and what she felt she was saving me from by calling the Housekeeper. You have to understand: Heaven's death was still largely a mystery to me. But anyway, I just stayed there, listening and listening, and the path fell away, and I couldn't find it again."

"And then what happened?"

"And then nothing. I woke up from the trance feeling groggy, but nothing had happened. I failed. I was too committed to an earthly relationship to become a demigod. And I never lived with my daughter again."

"Oh, Nuala. I'm so sorry." I wrap my arms around her, trying to get over the strangeness of comforting someone who is usually there to comfort me. "You're living with her now, though."

She doesn't speak for a long time, and when she finally does, it's a surprise. "Do you remember when I wouldn't sell you the herbs for that ritual? The one that brought Lily back?"

"Yes," I say, straightening up, embarrassed for her that my sweater is wet from her tears.

"I had no faith in rituals before I met you," she says softly. "The first ritual I had ever heard of killed Heaven; the second ritual was one I had failed myself, and lost everything." She breaks off, and I'm about to rush in to tell her I'm sorry, but she speaks again. "You and

I have very different relationships to the word *ritual*, Maeve. I think you see them as game shows. I see them as funerals."

I pause. Chew on my lip. How on earth do you reply to this much sorrow? "Thank you for telling me this, Nuala," I say eventually. "But why are you telling me?"

The windshield has misted over, a combination of muggy tears and the car's active little heater. Nuala pulls her sleeve over her hand and starts wiping the fog away.

"Because," she says, pushing her hand across the glass, "I don't want you to lose everything."

33

MANON'S FATHER ARRIVES THE NEXT DAY, on New Year's Eve. There's no good way to describe him except to say that he is like Manon, but more. Whatever indefinable *thing* that Manon has, that dappling of gold leaf that seems to surf through her bloodstream, René has more of it.

He is sitting at Nuala's kitchen table when I come through the back door, and dressed completely in tailored gray. The gray feels like a private joke. A parody of what a boring man might wear. It is clear from the elegant brightness that surrounds him that he could never be a boring man.

To describe him exactly, it's just a handful of nothing words: bald, dark-skinned, a neat black beard, smiling eyes, a vest that looks as though it's made of expensive wool. But it's the feeling of him, I suppose, that changes the room. The feeling of everything being a little silly. Not a big deal. Fun.

When I see him, he is sitting alone at the kitchen table, eating from a china plate.

"Hello," I say awkwardly. "You must be Manon's dad."

"René," he says, standing up to take my hand. "You're Maeve, aren't you?"

"Hello," I say again, and it trips out in a weird, nervous squeak.

"Sorry, I feel like I'm meeting a celebrity. Manon always talks about you."

"*Does* she?" he says, sounding mystified. "Well, I can assure you, you're the celebrity in this equation. What an exciting life you've had so far. Manon is just upstairs; she has a book she wants to show me."

His accent, which I was expecting to be French, is hard to place. It's clear and friendly English, but opaque in its origin. My guesses range from South African to Canadian to faintly Dutch.

The front door slams, and I hear Nuala and Aaron in the hall. My eyes dart worriedly to the doorway, wondering how she is going to react.

"Don't fret," he says to me softly.

Nuala looks shocked to see him, but not so shocked, I realize, to have forgotten to put mascara on. "You're early," she says. "I thought you were arriving after dinner." No hello. No hug.

"Fin," he says, getting up. He goes to kiss her on the cheek, but she turns quickly and he ends up getting her skull. "It's been a while."

"Eight years," Nuala says, with as little emotion as she can muster.

"Eight years, four months, sixteen days. Ten hours. Thirteen minutes."

Nuala raises an eyebrow. "You've been counting?"

"No, sorry. I made a guess."

René smiles, and it's unclear whether he is lying about the counting or lying about the guess. Then: "I helped myself to the leftovers."

He points to the china plate that is stacked with cheese, chocolate, some bread, a few grapes.

"René," Nuala says. "Did you take this plate off the wall?"

I turn around and notice that one of Nuala's decorative plates is missing.

"I just thought it was so exquisite," he says, examining the gold rim. "You have always had such perfect taste, Fin."

He really means it, too. His voice is deep, and rich with love for her. *No, Maeve,* I remind myself. *On top of everything else, you cannot have a crush on Manon's dad.*

Manon enters the kitchen with the *Child's Guide to Catholic Saints*, looking elated. "Papa, have you said hello to Fin?"

"I have," he says. "She hasn't taken me back yet, if that's what you're asking. But by this evening, she might have changed her mind?"

"Oh, for god's sake, René, don't waste my time."

And Nuala's house, which is so stuffed with awkward interpersonal dynamics, somehow manages to fit another.

An hour later there's eight of us crammed into the kitchen. I don't know why we never hang out in the sitting room, which technically has more space. Fiona, Paolo on her shoulder, Lily, and I are perched on the counter. My ass is fully in the sink. Everyone else is at the table.

"The issue is," René begins, stirring his tea in another exquisite piece of crockery that I have never seen before, "that it is not so much a changeover as a change-back. We want to remove the Housekeeper from Maeve. As with a lobotomy."

"A lobotomy?" I echo, horrified.

"Excuse me. Poor choice of words. Not a lobotomy—those are not terribly useful. This is more, ah, a parasite we're removing from you. Or rather, you're removing from yourself. Does that sound more appealing?"

"Slightly," I reply, although *parasite* isn't a much more cheerful word than *lobotomy*.

"To do this, we'll have to re-create the situation where the

Housekeeper entered you. Which is a hard thing to pinpoint." He pauses thoughtfully. "But my guess is that it took place when the four of you—Roe, Lily, Fiona, that's right, isn't it?—gathered to perform the ritual, and you survived it. That is when she decided you were her next host."

"It was three of us," Fiona says. "Me, Maeve, and Roe. We were doing it to bring Lily back."

"But she was there," René replies. "She was the river, wasn't she?"

I realize that René already knows everything about us, and questions none of it. Lily smiles, always relieved to meet anyone who believes her about the river the first time.

"You'll need to go into the river," he says. Just like that. Like it's simple.

"Uh," I say. "The river is kind of Lily's thing?"

"And it's, you know, not safe?" Roe interjects. "Like it's dirty."

"It's not dirty," Lily says, sounding offended. "It's very clean."

"You will need to go in," René says, as if we haven't interrupted him. "And after that, the passage should be very simple. You'll feel like you're drowning at first, but you won't be. We will be holding you. Then whatever you see next is between you and the great beyond. You just need to keep to the path."

The word *path* does something to Nuala. She clatters her cup down, rattling the saucer.

"René," she says sharply. "You can't do this. Not again."

René puts his hands up, like he's facing the police. "What am I doing? That's how it is, isn't it? Fin?"

"You're acting like it's easy," she says, and I can see her hands vibrating from where I'm sitting in the sink. "It's not. You always *do* this, René. Act like things are easy when they're not."

If Nuala sounds like a teenager, then Manon looks like a little girl. Her eyes are suddenly enormous as they flit between her mother and father.

"It actually *is* simple, Fin," René says, "when you don't hold the burden of trauma."

He says this softly, so softly that I think Nuala is going to cry.

"Excuse me," I say. "But I actually do hold the burden of trauma."

"Yeah," says Fiona. "I think we all do."

"Well, then I suggest you take some time to yourself," René says to me, "to think about all the things that may come to you, within your visions. The things that may tempt you from the path." Nuala looks at him sharply. "The things that may *affect* you," he says, correcting himself. "And, excuse me for saying this, I think there should be as few of us there as possible."

"What do you mean by that?" Roe asks.

"I mean, Maeve's subconscious will be in a very flexible state. She might sense one of you there and it may distract her."

"Or it might give me strength."

René considers this. "It could," he says eventually. "But I don't know if we want to risk that."

"Sorry," Roe interjects, "but she's my girlfriend, and I'm not letting you do some mad shit to her while I'm not there."

The room goes weird then, obviously. Roe doesn't seem to realize what they've said for a second or two, and then goes red in the face.

"Fine," René says crisply. "You may be present while I do—how did you put it?—'mad shit' to your girlfriend."

"I'm going to be there, too," Lily says fiercely. "The river is my place. What if I'm helpful?"

"Lily is always helpful," I add, looking to René.

"And I'm not letting you go through it without me," Fiona adds.

"Very well," René says. "All of us, then."

I see Fiona and Roe exchange a look, and I know exactly what they are thinking. I know that Fiona has more meetings with the TV producers; I know Roe has rehearsal plans with the band. They would never bring these concerns to me, and hate themselves for worrying about their own ambitions when so much is going on. But they can't *not* worry. So, increasingly, they are talking to just each other about it. Their bond is separate, and about separate things. Things that have nothing to do with magic.

And I'm grateful for them, and glad for them, but all I can think is: How long can this go on? How long will my problems explode the dreams of my friends?

And what if it takes forever?

"Now," René says. "Manon, can you help me get the party things out of the car?"

"Party things?" Manon repeats, confused. "What party?"

"Oh," he says, raising an eyebrow. "I have never let the end of the world get in the way of a proper New Year's Eve."

34

DESPITE EVERYTHING THAT HAS HAPPENED over the last few days—Roe and I breaking up, my Housekeeper status being confirmed, the revelations at the Lodge—New Year's Eve is more normal than I could have possibly imagined.

This happens with us, sometimes. Sometimes our lives become so insane that we all mutually, silently agree to hide in a pocket of normal for a few hours. Even if we're just pretending. Even if it's just for show. We fake it to ourselves, and if we do it for long enough, we manage to break through to a place where we really are just a bunch of friends who are having a normal New Year's Eve.

Having René there helps. Nuala is always cautious about letting us drink in her house. The lines get blurry because Roe, Manon, and Aaron are all legal. Lily is only a few months off, but Fiona and I aren't eighteen until May and November, respectively. She will allow a few beers or glasses of wine, champagne on a special occasion, but will wordlessly sweep a glass away from me if she sees I'm on my third drink.

René, on the other hand, has brought a bottle of Grey Goose and starts playing drinking games with us using a blackened wine cork. It's a stupid memory game, and everyone ends up with ash all over their faces, and I laugh so much that I feel like I'm going to throw up a lung. No one talks about anything important. Everything is stupid. The New Year countdown comes and goes without anyone realizing.

"It tastes like water." Roe laughs breathlessly.

"That's because it's cold," René replies. "Good cold vodka should taste like nothing."

But it was water, I realize. When I get out of the taxi later I feel strangely sober, as though I've been drinking Evian all evening. This is René's particular trickster magic. To create lightness, levity, silliness, wherever he goes.

God. No wonder Nuala fell in love with him.

When I arrive home, I let myself in quietly. As I take off my shoes by the front door, Tutu scratches at the back door to be let out. I open the kitchen door, and he bolts. He flies through the grass, ears flapping. I turn on the porch lights and squint. We don't get many foxes around here, but maybe he's seen one.

There's a high-pitched little whine coming from the back of the garden, like he's stuck in the neighbors' hedge.

"Come on, Tutes," I yell, and Mum and Dad's bedroom light comes on. Mum cracks the window open.

"Maeve," she calls. "What are you doing?"

"The dog won't come in."

"Well, don't wake the whole street. Go get him."

She goes to close the window again, and then suddenly calls out. "Happy New Year, old beast."

I smile up at her. "Happy New Year, Mum."

We look at each other for a moment, and even though it's dark and I can't see her face, there is a vague, passing, shared hoped that next year will be different. Less dramatic. Fewer disappearing lifelong family friends, sudden deaths, or fires that result in a head-spinning yet dazzling change in fortune. It is a new year and it is also the year I will finish school. It's not just a big deal for me, I realize. It's a big deal for her, too. It will mark the end of this phase of her parenting. She will be fifty-six years old and finally have no children in school.

She closes her window, and I step toward the grass, calling Tutu's name. It's shockingly cold, and rather than just go back into the house and put on my shoes, I take my socks off and start sprinting across the lawn. Calling and calling. Panic rising. Where *is* he?

I do not know the names of the trees at the back of our garden. They're ordinary trees, suburban trees—tall, slim, and spindly. Shivering and naked against the December—no, January!—night sky, skinny girls with no coats on.

I push through and through, and keep expecting to feel the fresh gasp of a green clearing, the emptiness of the McKennas' garden. But I must get turned around, because it's just trees. Trees that get thicker, denser; trees that have not yet lost their leaves, trees that I suddenly know the names of. The red berries on the rowan tree, the clawing arms of the yew, the big oak, high on its own dignity. *The Celts had rules for trees,* I hear her say to me. *There were penalties for cutting them down.*

Is that so? I reply.

They could be severe depending on the tree's importance, the Housekeeper explains. *Oak, hazel, holly, yew—in that order. She was wrong. Ireland was never so wild. It was only wild to people who didn't want to understand it.*

My feet are no longer cold. They are glowing white, their soles covered with a protective callus. I can still feel the earth, but it's a different kind of discomfort. It is the discomfort of living things that dwell beneath you.

I feel the dense warmth of Tutu's body against me, his back flush with my hip. We are on our way. Another full moon, another clearing, another offering of hares. I glance up at the moon and feel a shiver of Maeve run through me.

The transformation is easier now. *The worlds are getting thinner,* she says, and her voice becomes mine completely.

New life is getting closer to me and it's making me cheerful, less lonely, not so tired. The past is never past. People wouldn't behave so stupidly if they knew that. We're all here, all the time, all at once. Two hundred years ago and next week. A little bit of everything, all of the time.

But they never grasp it. It's like asking them to remember an individual leaf on a tree they saw falling thirty years ago. That leaf is still around, baked into the layers of the earth like a lovely cake. But it doesn't comfort them.

This is why I am not in the comforting business.

The dog goes ahead and finds the circle. I hear voices react to him. Voi*ces*. Plural. I stop and listen, irritated. A woman's voice. And a man's voice. The dog gives him a hard time. Growls, wrinkles his face, shows teeth.

"Women only," I say.

They both look up and see me. It's the woman from last time. Una's mother. She's older now, and the boy with her is her son.

"We brought you four," the boy says, and his tone is already argumentative. "Four hares."

I hold his gaze and wonder where he got the idea that overfeeding my dog is the way to get my attention. Or my sympathy.

"Paud," his mother says. *"Shush."*

This, I realize, is the baby she was pregnant with the last time we met. Almost twenty years ago.

"Una," I say, and her name is both a greeting and an inquiry.

"Thriving," she answers. "Thank you."

"They have a girl up at the house," he says, pointing to the building in the distance. The old predator that looms over the village. "She's trapped there."

I raise an eyebrow.

"*Paudie,*" she says again, harsher this time.

"Go on," I say, glad that this is at least *about* a woman, if not coming from a woman. There is no need to ask which house he means. There is only one house around here, and it's where the English live, and they either employ us or they don't.

He goes on. The girl is something like new money. She's local, minor aristocracy, one of those families that can claim a direct line to one of the old castles. Two servants and a horse. Tied-up ancestral documents printed on vellum that prove . . . something, but nobody cares what. A complex web of deaths and some brief blazes of heroism in the Seven Years' War have suddenly rendered this girl an heiress. An unprotected heiress, to a handsome fortune.

"They invited her to stay with them," Paudie says, avoiding my gaze, "and they asked me to put something in the food."

I twitch. So does the dog. "*Something?*"

"I didn't know what it was," he blithers. "I just work in the kitchen. A little silver dish of mushrooms, for the table, cooked in cream and tarragon."

A pause. The moon is briefly clouded over. "But they didn't eat from it," he continues. "Only she did. And the next day she was sick, and delirious, and they said she had better stay, and, well . . ."

"*Well?*"

"She woke up *married,*" he splutters. "And there they all are, talking about her world-wind romance with . . ."

"Whirlwind."

"*Whirlwind* romance. And she's trapped. And they're calling her crazy. And she's *going* crazy. All she does is scream and ask to go home, and no one will let her. They just keep *bleeding* her, telling her it's fever. It's the money, you see. They need it. They need hers."

This is unusual. It's a class of people I'm not used to catering to.

"What's in this for you?" I ask. "Has she struck a deal with you? Promised you some of her money if you get her out?"

He shakes his head.

"It's fine if she *has*," I say peevishly. "But if there are existing bargains in place, I need to know about them. It will influence things."

He looks at me, and then at his mother. "No," he says, and although I detect hesitation, I take the hares, and I tell Paudie and his mother that I will keep her.

"How, I'm not sure," I say. "But I'll do it."

35

"MAEVE," MUM SAYS. "LILY'S HERE."

"Hey," she says, hovering in the door.

"Happy New Year again," I say. "Are you gonna come in?"

She sits on the bed. White boots, Roe's old blazer. A T-shirt she's made herself, of the cat from *Night in the Woods*. Her blue hair a little faded.

She's quiet for a second, staring at her shoes. "Um . . . How are you, you know, feeling?"

"OK," I reply, slightly suspicious. "Kind of weirded out by this whole thing later. The ritual, part two, and all that."

"Well. Part one, for me."

"You were part of it."

"In a way," she sighs. "In a way."

She's preoccupied. I'm used to Lily being the keeper of breezy yet brutal truths. Part of what's magic about her is that she doesn't find things as complicated and grayscale as everyone else. She's direct. Complex, but not complicated. Suddenly, she's hazy.

"What's up, Lil?"

"Are you sure," she says slowly, "that you're doing the right thing?"

"What do you mean?" I ask, even though I know exactly what she means.

"I mean"—she begins to pick at her nails with an artist's scalpel she's drawn from her pocket—"is the Housekeeper a curse you necessarily want to remove?"

"Of course," I say, but I can't make it sound convincing. "Of course I do. She's a murderer."

"Right," Lily says eventually. "Except, that's not my experience of her."

"OK." I feel like we're in a hostage negotiation, a job interview, something where every single word is powerful and could ruin anything. Lily is talking about the Housekeeper. To me. "What is your experience of her, then? You've never quite . . ."

"I know," she says, putting her hands up. "I know. It's just, it's complicated, you know? By the time I came back from the river, everyone had a very fixed idea of who and what the Housekeeper was. Evil revenge demon, you know? But my experience was just . . . this being. This thing. And she didn't seem vengeful, Maeve. She really didn't. She seemed . . . I don't know. Compassionate. Like, ethereal and frightening, but trying to find compassion in the parts of herself that were still human."

"Did she communicate with you?"

"Of course she did." Lily almost sounds shocked by the question. "What do you think happened? I followed her out of my house and to the river?"

"I don't know, I sort of assumed you were in some kind of hypnotic state."

"No," Lily says firmly. "She asked me: 'What do you want?'"

"She said that?"

"She did. And I said, 'For things to go back to what they were.' She said: 'I can't do that.' Or, I don't know. She didn't use words exactly, but that's what she communicated. So I said: 'I don't want to be me anymore.'"

"And then what?"

"And then nothing. She was sort of silent, like she needed more from me. And then . . . I don't know, I think I was listening to Joni Mitchell that night, or drawing, or something—I said, 'I wish I was the river.'"

"Joni Mitchell?"

"You know. She sings 'I wish I was a river.'"

"'I wish I *had* a river.'"

"What? That makes even less sense. You can't *have* a river."

I don't know where to look. My vision doubles, quadruples, multiplies until there are infinite Lilys in a hall of mirrors. Does the defining moment of our lives come down to Lily mishearing a Joni Mitchell lyric?

"Anyway," Lily continues brusquely. "She did it."

"Well, glad to finally have, uh, clarity on that," I reply, trying not to sound too startled. For months, Lily has insisted that she hardly remembered the Housekeeper. She tells us plenty about being the river. But the sliver of time between her bedroom and the riverbank has always been a mystery. Not the point, as far as she was concerned. The point was that she was the river. The method didn't interest her, and we assumed she had forgotten it, the way you forget the duller parts of a dream.

"We should go," she says, and we do.

The ritual that we conducted all those months ago felt very grand to us at the time. I remember the white satin, the candles, the torches.

The darkness. The stuff we had to make do without because Nuala wouldn't sell us the ingredients. But I remember feeling, even though I was frightened, that I was in a Tumblr post about witchcraft. It felt cool and DIY in a way that was instantly photogenic.

But it was nowhere near as beautiful as this.

Manon is still making the salt circle, but it's not the simple ring of table salt that Fiona made. It's a patterned circle, like a maze, with a star in the middle. And she's doing it with a leather sack of salt flakes, squeezed together like a baker's piping bag.

"What's this?"

"Hecate's wheel," Manon says, smiling as she sees me. "She's the guardian of the crossroads."

"Maeve," René says. "Bon passage."

"Isn't it bon voyage?"

"Not today." He smiles. Then looks at me, allowing himself to become serious. Very serious, and very kind. "Are you feeling all right?"

"I feel OK."

Aaron and Nuala are spreading out a huge sheet of white silk. Roe is sharpening an array of blades I have never seen before. "What's going on? Why are there knives?"

"Well, it's a reversal type of spell," René says. "And last time you tied knots, didn't you?"

I agree that we did.

"A genius construction, I have to say," he says, and rubs at his beard. "Well, this will be about breaking knots, cutting ties, unwinding the places where the demon has bound herself to you. Ushering her out, vanquishing her."

"Vanquishing her?"

"Well, yes."

He is confused by my confusion. "I thought we were, you know, releasing her," I say.

He scratches at his beard again, his fingertips disappearing in the dark hair. "To where?"

"I don't know," I say, gesturing to the landscape. "Around?"

"I don't understand how that would work. We have to bring her reign to an end. It's long past time. We have to either end her or transfer her into someone else." He looks down at my feet. "Your dog is here."

"Yeah," I say limply, reeling from the notion of killing the Housekeeper. Not just evicting her from my body, but ending her. "He wanted to come. And he's a part of this, too, I guess. He always comes with me. To, uh, Housekeeper Land."

"I see."

Tutu and Paolo start messing with each other. The bird circling and swooping playfully, the dog yelping and jumping. Tail wagging, delighted by the game. Two enchanted creatures that did not begin their lives this way, but have to deal with it regardless.

Fiona is crushing herbs with a mortar and pestle from Nuala's kitchen. Cross-legged on the ground, focused. Determined.

Darkness eventually settles. The winter solstice has come and gone, and we are waiting slightly longer for the navy light to turn black. I wonder why we never celebrate pagan rituals as a group. Shouldn't that be the kind of thing we do? Why do we never get around to it?

"Lily," René says softly. "Would you mind? The streetlamps?"

"Oh," she says, excited to use her talent. "Sure."

Within moments, the whole riverbank is enveloped in darkness, except for a few pillar candles brought by Manon. She shakes out the

huge sheet of white silk, and we all sit around it, like children awaiting instruction on an arts-and-crafts project.

"Maeve," she says. "Can you please sit in the middle?"

"On the silk?"

"On the silk."

I sit on it, gazing awkwardly at everyone. René stands up, hands
in the pockets of his gray herringbone coat.

"Buona sera, everyone," he begins jovially. "We're here tonight
to perform a ritual that is both ancient and brand-new, simple and
impossible, easy and difficult. A test of character, a test of will, a
purging of a curse, a rebirth and a slaughter. Maeve: Those who came
before you did so with the urge to cross over into godliness, into
enchantment, into immortality. You sit before me with the wish to
cross back. Hold out your hands, please."

I hold out my hands, trying not to be overwhelmed by the
words *rebirth* and *slaughter*. René lets two gold coins drop into my
left palm, and two in my right.

"The two in your right hand are to pay your passage," he says.
"At some point, you will be asked to pay a boatman, or a guardian of
some sort. They may come to you in any form: something from your
subconscious, or something from hers. Listen carefully. Know who
you are speaking to."

I look at the coins. They are old and heavy, and engraved with
some kind of Aztec-looking design. René clocks my expression.
"They're Mayan," he says. "Chichén Itzá, in Mexico. Another powerful Well."

"How . . . How old are these?"

"Eight hundred AD," Manon answers automatically.

"What the *hell*?"

"We need all the help we can get." Manon shrugs. I begin to feel sick. René might be wildly rich, and absurdly confident, but he wouldn't be staking ancient artifacts on this ritual if he wasn't absolutely certain we needed them.

Which means that I, even on my best day, must not be enough.

"Am I metaphorically paying this boatman?" I ask, my voice trembling. "Will I get the coins back, at the end?"

"The other two," René says, ignoring this, "are for the Housekeeper, to place on her eyes after her reign is over."

"After I . . . kill her?"

He blinks. Pauses. "Yes, I suppose so."

I can feel the sweat gathering in my palms, around the precious coins. Can I really do this?

René must sense my hesitation, and puts his hand on my shoulder. "Maeve," he says. "Just follow the path in front of you. Everything will become clear. It will be hard, but you've done much more difficult things before." His eyes flicker over to his daughter, who is nodding sternly. "Your reputation precedes you."

Aaron is watching all this, and has been completely silent since I arrived. "Aaron," I ask, turning to him. "Do you think we can beat the Children without the Housekeeper?"

His eye twitches, and he says nothing.

"You would be a terrible poker player," I say grimly.

"We'll find a way," he blurts. "And if we can't, well . . . I'd rather have the Children on my conscience than you."

"It's Hell either way," I say as I look past his eyes and see the flashes of punishment and decay that live behind them. The most violent moments of the oldest testament, etched on the walls of his brain like cave paintings.

"It's Hell either way," he affirms. I realize that whether Hell is real or isn't, it's real if you believe it is. Just like all forms of magic.

"We need to get a move on," Nuala says softly.

I sit in the middle of the white silk. René takes the blades from Roe.

"All right," he says. "Everyone, pick a knife."

36

"ALWAYS *KNIVES*," FIONA SAYS, WINCING AS she chooses her weapon. "We have become a very knife-y gang."

She picks one. "Damascus folded steel," René says approvingly. "Carved handle from a Lourdes oak. Maeve, you'll need a knife to cut yourself free. Which would you like?"

"I have Sister Assumpta's," I say, and after some brief hesitation I show it to him. "I figured if there was ever a time to use it, it's now."

He lets out a low, impressed whistle. "It's a letter opener," he says. "Lots of power in letter openers."

"How's that?" Roe asks.

"There is never more hope in a human being than in the five seconds before they open a letter." And I don't know if it's true, but it feels true.

They each take a blade and cut upward through the silk in long, fluid motions, like scissors through wrapping paper. Each rope of silk is soaked in a bowl of pungent oil, then rolled in herbs.

René is a big believer in the power of group humming. He tells us that we can gather more intention if we have the same vibrational frequency, that words will just muck things up. Nuala rolls her eyes, as if this—words versus music—is a fight they've had before. But she begins to hum. A simple three-note tune, almost like scales. Roe copies her. Fiona copies Roe.

And soon they are all humming, humming and cutting, humming and soaking, humming and rolling. I hum, too, but I'm not sure if my humming is the point right now. This part of the ritual seems more about them than me. I'm just sitting in the middle, like the center of a flower. Even though René hasn't described the theory of this ritual to me in detail, I can still understand what's happening: they are funneling all their energy, their power, into me, hoping it's good enough and strong enough to fight the Housekeeper and free me from the curse.

A glittering phosphorescence settles around them as they each absorb themselves into the ritual's trance. All of their colors are represented: Fiona's brilliant orange, Lily's cerulean blue, Roe's dazzling white. Aaron, pearl gray. Manon, gold. Nuala is purple—indigo, even. And René, the dappled peach of a sunrise.

I keep my arms folded, the coins in my hands, the letter opener tucked into my waistband, and my friends begin to wrap the ropes of soaked silk around me. I feel like a pharaoh awaiting mummification.

"Tie it tightly," René instructs. "So that when she cuts through, it will mean something."

The strips are like flower petals radiating out from me, each strip lifted from the ground and wrapped tightly, starting from my shoulders and down to my waist. The oil has made the silk heavy, and it feels like iron chains. As each layer of silk is tied to me, I begin to doubt my ability to cut through. Not psychologically. I mean physically. I may be a witch, but I'm not exactly famous for upper-arm strength.

Eventually, when I am tied to the waist, René asks me to lie down. "We're going to drop you in the river now, Maeve," he says softly. "I hope that's all right."

"Can't I just walk?" I ask, as my legs are still free.

"We must all have a part in this," René says solemnly.

I'm carried like that, lying down and covered in white, and I try not to think of how ridiculous it must look: a bunch of people carrying a girl cloaked in white into the filthy Beg River.

The water is excruciating. For some reason, it was the only thing I failed to mentally prepare for: Irish river water in January. Maybe I thought that magic would protect me, or that I would have so many more important things on my mind that I wouldn't even notice how frigid the water is. But I do notice. In fact, it's all I'm able to focus on. I hear myself scream from shock. It feels like knives. I can't think straight, can't remember what I'm here to do.

I look up at the others as the water trickles over my face, and clock their concern, their horror, their doubt that they are doing the right thing to their friend. I feel their hands underneath my body, and then I feel them letting go. Feel the heaviness of my body dropping down into the water, binds getting heavier, the herbs floating off the material and pooling at the river's surface.

I will drown. I will drown and they will watch it.

My hands have gone numb. I try to wake up my fingers, all stiff, my blood turned frozen. I whisper to them from the safety of my own skull.

Wake up, wake up, wake up.

I push the blade toward the silk and eventually feel a snap and release. One rope done. My hands a little freer. The second rope. The third. I can feel each rope unwind and fall to the riverbed.

Finally, both arms are free, but I seem to be much deeper under the water than I initially thought. Which is strange, considering the others were barely up to their knees when they stood around me. Now I feel as though I am leagues under the sea, down where the whales and sharks live.

All there is to do is swim up, up, up, my breath endless, my arms strong. Was this how Lily felt? This kind of power, this kind of infinite strength?

I am beginning to suspect that I will be swimming forever when I suddenly break the surface. The clusters of crushed herbs are still dancing on the water, but everything else has changed.

I am still in Kilbeg. Still on the old riverbank where so many of the major moments of my life have taken place. But the roads are gone, and there are no cars. The only thing that remains is the old shaky bridge, a mile away in the distance, and the peak of the cathedral, barely visible and all the way on the other side of the city.

I am not in my time. I am in hers.

Dawn is breaking. The sky is pink. A reminder of René and what he told me: just follow the path. But what *is* the path? There's nothing to suggest one. Not even a stone slab that might imply a road.

I try to think of what I would do if this were a normal day. I would walk either home or into town. Home is surely the wrong answer. Home is where everything stays the same. The city is where things happen. So should I walk as if I were going to the city, to school? The school, after all, is where the mouth of the Well is.

So I walk on, sticking to the river's edge. If you stick by the river, you end up in the city eventually. My clothes dry quickly. It's quite peaceful, really. The warm early-summer sunlight, the birds chirping. Everything is green here, the trees fully clothed again. Rabbits scurry in different directions as I walk through. I briefly wonder where Tutu is and suddenly I find him beside me, pacing with the long, loping gait of his Housekeeper form.

"Hey, boy," I say, patting his sleek back. "Good to see you."

It's a relaxing way to beat a curse, all told. Just walking and listening to birdsong, the fine company of a large dog beside me. Then, as the shaky bridge comes more into view, I start to panic. The middle of the bridge has blown out, and from the side, it looks like a smile with its front teeth missing.

I initially don't think it's a problem—I'll just cross at the next bridge—and then I remember that there is no other bridge. The two other bridges that connect the suburbs to the city were built in the twentieth century. The fifties, I think. The next really old bridge is miles away. What on earth am I supposed to do? Walk on and on for hours?

I eventually see a person, leaning against the entrance of the ruined bridge. As I get closer, I begin to make out black curls, and start to run.

Roe.

They are wearing a blue satin jacket, white ruffles at the neck and sleeves. Blue shoes, white socks. I don't know why I'm expecting Roe's voice to be different, why I'm shocked when their voice comes out clear and familiar.

"Ladies, meet the Housekeeper card," Roe says, grinning. "Is it downfall, or start?"

"Is it *really* you?"

"Who else would I be?"

"I don't know. Some figment from my subconscious. Some idea of you."

Roe tilts their head slightly and smiles, considering me. "There must be *some* way of finding out."

"How?"

"Kiss me and find out if I'm real."

I draw back and look at their expression. René warned me about this. Nuala did, too. Is this a distraction sent by the Housekeeper, in a last act of self-preservation?

Roe takes my hand and draws me close. Fingers white and cold, the smell of charcoal and roses melting off their skin. Lips so red that there are shades of purple to them, like wild winter berries. Our faces so close that I can feel the warm mist of their breath on the tip of my nose. We stay like that for I don't know how long, but oh, god, how I'm hungry for it: this kind of looking, this kind of touching. Familiar and strange, comfortable and exciting.

Roe smiles again, tilts their head, and places one gentle kiss on the soft skin of my neck. There's a burst of birdsong behind me, the sun melts at my back, and my body feels alive again.

Then I feel the coins in my hand. The hand holding Roe's. I try to withdraw it, and Roe holds tight. I pull away, harder this time, but Roe's hand is like a vise grip. I feel the hard, wet coins rattling in our joined palms. The air turns heavy and humid, the sky darkening to a deep violet.

"Roe," I say softly. "Are you trying to rob me?"

"Kiss me," Roe replies. "Kiss me and find out if I'm trying to rob you."

The violet sky cleaves open, and a warm rain begins to fall in lazy, splashy drops.

"I think you are, Roe. I think you are trying to rob me."

Suddenly Roe's hand clamps down harder and twists my arm behind my back. The pain is instant, searing, a burn that begins in my wrist and roars to my shoulder socket. I scream, cry out, then feel immediate self-hatred that I cannot be stronger and smarter, even here, in this strange world that has been partially invented by me.

The coins fly out of my hands and scatter into the dirt, where a mud puddle is already beginning to form. Both Roe and I lunge for them, and we become tangled at the ankles, falling to the ground. It's only then, when I'm on my belly, that I feel Sister Assumpta's knife tucked into my waistband. The blade pushing against my skin, the hilt bruising my breastbone.

Roe reaches the coin puddle before I do. With them still on their belly, there's nothing for me to do but pull the knife out—and pounce. I try to wrestle the coins away and end up just sitting on Roe, my legs straddling their waist, my knife to their throat.

"Drop them," I say, trying to catch my breath.

Am I really threatening my ex with a knife? Can I even call this Fake Roe—*Foe?*—my ex?

Fake Roe lets the coins fall in the dirt.

"You're supposed to bring me across the bridge, aren't you?"

Fake Roe simply nods. I drive the point of the letter opener closer to their skin.

"And what? You wanted to take the coins and leave me stranded on this side of the river?"

Another nod. Then a spluttered, wet cough. "It doesn't seem so long," Fake Roe says finally, "since I looked at you from down here."

And I almost die, because, yes, of course, if you take away the knife and the rain and the mud and the coins, this is all oppressively, deliciously familiar.

"Take me across the river," I say rigidly, "and I'll give you the coins once I'm across."

"Whatever you say."

We get off the ground, and Fake Roe leads me across. The bridge slowly rebuilds under our feet, stone slabs emerging from the river and rising under Fake Roe's outstretched fingertips. I wonder if Real

Roe could do this, too: If they can talk to machines, then why not the materials that make machines?

I walk behind, my knife at the base of their spine, nudging them forward, Tutu at my heels. Eventually, we get to the other side, and I'm standing barefoot on the warm cobblestones of the old city.

I turn to Fake Roe. "A deal's a deal," I say, handing the two coins over. "Thanks for taking me."

"Thanks for not killing me." Fake Roe smiles. "And sorry about trying to rob you. I didn't really even want to, but. Orders are orders."

"Will the real you know about any of this?"

"Uh . . ." Fake Roe thinks about it carefully, and looks so much like Real Roe that I feel as though my heart might crack. "Probably not. I think this is, you know, a figment thing."

"Oh," I reply, not sure whether to be disappointed or not. "Can I kiss you, then?"

I am braver now. Maybe it's the knife.

They grin. "I don't see why not. Be careful, though, won't you?"

But I am not careful, and neither are they.

37

FAKE ROE DOESN'T FADE INTO THE DIS-
tance so much as they drift apart, particles of them slowly separating
and then floating onto the wind. It's too depressing to consider that
my last kiss from Roe was not even from the real Roe. It was, in a
sense, a form of masturbation. So I walk on, Tutu trotting dutifully
beside me.

The heavy sky is bearing down on me, edging closer like a
watchful god. Is it naive to think that the hardest part is over now?
There was a version of me that wanted to let Fake Roe rob me. To
sink into their arms at the other side of the river. Was that my version
of Heaven trying to tempt Nuala?

There's a gathering power in the center of my chest. I can do
this. I wrestled Roe to the ground. I used a knife as a weapon. I got
across the river. I will do this.

I walk toward the Big House, its shape familiar to me, and I
realize that there is a reason for this. This building will later become
St. Bernadette's, the center of the Well of Kilbeg. In years to come, it
will be owned by Sister Assumpta's family, who must have been rich
but who understood about the old ways nonetheless. They will leave
it to her, a novice still in the convent, and while she will break her
pledge with God she will be called Sister her whole life.

Sister Assumpta. Proof that the wild pagan ways and the steady hand of the Church *can* actually come together. Can not just coexist peacefully, but thrive.

There are people, and there is the smell of people: the curdling aroma of dirt and sweat and boiled food. I know these are the Housekeeper's memories because I feel her revulsion, her tendencies toward cleanliness, toward ruralness, toward solitude.

All at once, I feel the duality of myself: of being both Maeve Chambers, proposed vanquisher of the Housekeeper, and the Housekeeper herself. I know where I am going. I am going to see about the trapped heiress, the final pact I saw the Housekeeper make. I know this is where the visions of the dirty house are leading. I am walking the Housekeeper toward her final moments, leading her to the gallows, to the moment that she stopped being a witch and started to become a demon.

The Big House is hiding the girl. The word was getting out, among the servants and within the village, and while they couldn't do anything as such, there was an idea that should the news get to Dublin Castle, there could be trouble. Forced marriages are common and have a swashbuckling sort of air, the general understanding being that backwater savages who trip into their wealth have no spiritual right to it. But still, you never know. The tides are changing. Not everyone gets away with it. A skeleton staff has been kept on until her assets have been safely transferred and she can be packed off to an asylum.

And so here I am, in the city, here to free her.

And so here I am, in the city, trying to free myself.

I go through the kitchen, the lower street entrance. A housekeeper always uses the service door, after all. I remind myself that I know this building well, that this is just St. Bernadette's, after all, in a different time, in a different costume. The kitchen is just the old sixth-year basement canteen.

There is no staff in the kitchen but there is something steaming in a large pot. It has been there for some time: the lid rattling, the big steel belly quivering with the heat. I take it off the burner and examine the meat, which has been boiling so long that it is virtually unrecognizable. It's hefty, whatever it is. Turkey?

Tutu looks up expectantly. No, I realize. Hares.

It is bad luck to eat hares and worse luck to eat them before the first frost of the year. Why boil hares in summer, when the parasites still living in the flesh could kill you?

I realize that these were supposed to be my hares, the dog's hares, my payment. They have been gutted, quartered, and boiled. My veins stretch out in confusion, needling me to panic.

Someone planned on an offering. Perhaps they left the hares intact on the back step. And someone else took those hares and put them in a pot. Someone stupid. Or, someone trying to send a message.

Remember, Maeve, I tell myself, *you are not here to solve her problems. You're here to solve yours.*

Up the basement stairs. The hallway is empty of people. Fussy, terrible furniture. Chair legs like twigs. Brocade. Dust in the places that servants think masters don't notice, but I see everything, and I notice.

There's noise coming from Sister Assumpta's office. Low and masculine. Laughing. Drunk. There's a weariness, too, the sound of being awake for several days, which happens within these kinds of circles. They invite friends over from England and it's a four-day bender, hunting or cards, everyone soaked and sodden with excess, barely able to move. I don't even bother with them. A loud laugh, then a syncopated mumble. The sound of glasses being refilled.

Upstairs, through the picture gallery, I find the girl. Fading. Failing. Squinting at me as though I am behind a thick blanket of fog.

"Hello," I say. "I'm here."

It's Lily. The Housekeeper's shadowed memories have become colored by my own. My connections, my attachments. I wonder if I will see everyone else here, too, now that I have met both O'Callaghans.

"Maeve," she says. Her voice is clear, the Lily I know. I wonder if she will try to trick me, like Roe did. "Are you here to get me out?"

"Um . . . Well, I'm here to break this curse. I guess I have to repeat every step that *made* the Housekeeper before I *kill* the Housekeeper? Does that sound right?"

She shrugs, seeming quite healthy despite her jaundiced complexion. "I guess."

I look at her suspiciously. "You've not been told to rob me or anything, have you?"

She shrugs again. "I don't think so. I just want to get out of here."

There's a thundering on the stairs, the sound of heavy boots. "Oh, no," Lily says. "Betrayal. Sorry."

"Of course," I say, trying not to be too annoyed. "Existing bargains were already in place."

Suddenly my arms are invisibly bound, and all the weight in my body tilts forward to my chest. I sink to the floor, shoulders first. The clatter of the door.

"All right," comes Aaron's voice. "Get her downstairs."

I am downstairs in the card room, and I am paralyzed. This is how it went down, then: tricked or betrayed into leaving the countryside, where everything is natural, and therefore naturally mine. Did

Paudie betray me? Or did someone whom Paudie trusted betray him? Does it matter, when the unlucky hares are boiling, parasite-rich, and I am facedown under the card table?

Parasite-rich is a word that feels appropriate here, and so I say it, hissing. *Parasite-rich.*

A boot turns my body over, and I am looking at the ceiling.

"Your time is done, witch," Aaron says brightly. "Deepest sympathies. Tie her up."

I feel hands and ropes, and look up to see the familiar faces of Manon and Nuala. I squint and try to make out the other people in the room, and see that Fiona is here, staring at me from under a fan. My brothers sit at cards. The past and present blurring, the worlds finally at their thinnest.

Aaron shuffles a deck of playing cards in his hands and paces the room in a red military jacket, a household antique he's drunkenly donned.

"I don't suppose you play, witch?"

I don't say anything. I am too busy trying to figure out the puzzle here. René did not prepare me for this. Fake Aaron wants to kill the Housekeeper, but so do I. Should I let him?

"I don't know why you're calling *me* witch," the Housekeeper spits angrily, "when you've put your magic on me."

He doesn't answer. Only grins, paces the room, and shuffles.

"You know, the Egyptians are said to have invented the tarot. Stories of the gods, trapped in the cards. They knew the limitations of worship and prayer. Some myths are better off in the form of a game—more accessible to the common people."

I try to summon my magic, to summon my dog, but I can't find either. I'm helpless. A state that Maeve is used to, but the Housekeeper is not.

"The Kings and Queens are all based on real people, did you know that?" He pulls a chair over to where I am lying down. Brings up the King of Hearts. "Charlemagne," he says, then tosses the card. It lands on my chest. Shuffles again. King of Diamonds. "Julius Caesar." He throws the card. It lands on my cheek and slides off.

Shuffles. King of Spades. "King David." It hits my feet.

Shuffles again. King of Clubs. "Alexander."

There's a clattering, heavy footsteps and the sound of metal. The boiled hares have been brought in.

"We can trap their myths into cards, and there they live forever. I wonder if we could do the same to you, witch?"

The sound of blades, and of ripping sinew, of flesh coming apart. A spray of liquid wets my face. They have not been cooked through yet. Hot water and blood.

This is how it ends, and how it begins. How a powerful country sorceress becomes a card, a song, a legend.

There are words spoken: Latin and Greek, Old Norse. The objects around me—the brandy bottle, the milk jug, the picture frames—glow like runes. I will enter the gamblers' cards. I will become an heirloom, a convenience, a weapon they can use against the people I have spent my life protecting. They will use me to evict delinquent tenants and to murder starving poachers. They will distort my humanity until I am nothing but demon, nothing but bloodless hatred.

I can feel my sight leaving me—not an ebbing, but a total withdrawal. A closing of the account. Not just my physical sight, but my mental sight, too. All sensitives have a kind of seeing power. Aaron said that, didn't he?

They took my sight, she whispers. *What is justice without sight? Justice without judgment?*

I can't even answer her.

Justice without sight, she says, *is just mercenary work.*

This is what happens when you take a powerful sensitive, a warden of the Well, a protector of her people, and trap her in a role where she can't use her own judgment, where she has to blindly do what you command. This is how a sensitive becomes a Housekeeper.

You understand, she says. *I never had a choice. They took my sight.*

My eyes flash open, and I can see again. They will hold my strength in a playing card. My magic will be stored in a cardboard piece the length of a human palm.

One of the cards that Aaron threw begins to glow and twitch. He bends down, examines it, turns it over. Smiles.

"You make things too easy for us, witch."

And it's done. The origin story complete. Suddenly, I am not the Housekeeper on the floor, but one of the wordless people watching. She lies there, lifeless, but not dead. Not yet. The card still on her chest. The letter opener twitching in my hand. Tutu, wherever he is, begins to howl.

Fake Aaron turns to me, utterly unsurprised by my appearance.

"Well, go on, then, Charlemagne," he says, pointing toward her body. "Finish her off."

I step forward. The coins for her eyes still with me. Tutu is led in, a rope around his neck. The life has gone out of him, too, although he's still living. His coat entirely gray, his eyes dull.

"Do you want to do her first, or the dog?" Fake Aaron asks politely.

"The dog?!"

He shrugs. "The whole package."

"No one said anything about the dog."

"Do you want this, or don't you?"

Someone hands me the rope, assuming I would prefer to kill an animal first. They want this, I realize: these figments who are simultaneously ghosts from the past, renderings of my imagination, and specters from an ancient magic. Everyone is everything, all at once.

Do you want this, or don't you?

I go to her, the card on her chest. This is what I came for. This is why I brought the knife. Through the card, through her heart. Coins on the eyes. Kill the minor god within me and return to the life of Maeve Chambers. Find a way to end the Children without the Housekeeper's vengeful blood coursing through me.

I sit with my legs astride her, the way I sat on Fake Roe. *It doesn't seem so long since I looked at you from down here.* Her breathing is rattling, rasping, like she's choking on an ocean within her. She looks just like me. I mean, she is me. Dark curls and sallow skin, more girl than witch now. Lift the knife up, Maeve. Stab down, through the card. Through the heart beneath it.

I raise my arms above my head, both hands tight on the hilt. One swift movement. One plunge downward. That's all it would take.

The dog starts to whine.

"We don't have all day," says a sighing Fiona. The first time she has spoken since this whole thing began.

Every person in this world has been trying to throw me off course. Roe, Fiona, Aaron. The only person who hasn't is Lily, still in the bed upstairs. Now everyone is on my side? They want me to do this?

If I do this, the Housekeeper's legacy ends. No one can use her again.

If I do this, no one can benefit from her again. Una, across the ocean. The fur. The way I escaped the Lodge in a cloud of poisonous flame. Lily, wishing she was a river.

"Maeve," Aaron says. "The clock is ticking."

I bring the knife down through the card. Speckles of blood flourish as I break the skin, wetting the paper, and her eyes fly open. She stares at me. Blinks.

"With everything you know about the world," she whispers, "you still think it would be better off without me?"

Do I need to answer her?

I raise the knife up.

"I don't know," I say at last.

38

I WAKE UP AT NUALA'S HOUSE. IN NUALA'S bed. Wearing Nuala's pajamas.

Fiona is walking in backward with a tea tray, shuffling her bum against the door. She puts the tray on the dresser, then jumps when she sees me awake.

"Guys!" she shouts, before saying hello to me. "She's awake!"

"How long was I out for?"

"Two hours?"

"Shit."

She climbs onto the bed. "Did you do it?" Her smile almost cracks her face in half. "Tell me how you did it! Was it scary? René and Nuala are *so* impressed, by the way."

"Um . . ." There's a heavy fog in my brain, and a feeling of deep unreality. A feeling that I have left the real world and am now in the fake one, despite everything I know to the contrary.

The others arrive at the door, all smiles and relief. Lily jumps into bed next to me, and Fiona follows suit, the three of us cozy as cats under the duvet. Roe sits near my left foot, René at my right. Manon takes the chair by the dresser, and Aaron hovers in the doorway.

"Well, Maeve Chambers," René says expansively. "I knew the

rumors were true. The finest young witch of your generation, I'd say. With or without demon blood."

"Who needs demon blood," Fiona says joyfully, "when you're a hard-ass motherfucker like this girl?"

"*Fiona,*" Nuala snaps, walking in with her own mug of tea. "There's no need. How was it, Maeve?"

"We knew you passed the temptation phase when you were under for so long," Manon says. "You were twitching very badly after you climbed out of the water. We gave you a bath and put you in here."

"You gave me a *bath*?"

"Just me and Lily," Fiona says quickly. "Just to warm you up. It wasn't, like, a group activity or anything."

"Tell us," Roe says. "What *happened*?"

"Uh, well, the first person I met was Roe."

"Oh wow." Roe tries not to sound embarrassed. "Cool."

"Are we going all *Wizard of Oz* on this?" Lily laughs. "And *you* were there, and *you* were there, and *you* were there . . ."

"Well, you all were," I say shortly.

My tone is too sharp. The atmosphere shifts in the room. From joy to confusion, then worry.

"Maeve," René says after a brief pause. "Everything did go to plan, didn't it?"

I don't know what to say. Instead, I just open my palm, revealing the two priceless coins I have left over. The coins I was supposed to put on her eyes, after she was dead.

"You didn't have those in the bath," Lily says uncertainly.

The whole room gazes at the coins. Nuala, René, and Manon seem to understand what they mean instantly. It takes the others a minute to register it, the silence doing more work than the coins. The coins that were emphatically not placed on the dead Housekeeper's eyes.

I am so cloaked in shame from having failed everyone that I am speechless, unsure of where or how to begin. So instead, all I say is—

"I hesitated."

René. "You *hesitated*?"

I can feel everyone's disappointment pranging like sheet metal. *How has she messed this up?*

"You don't understand, you don't know what it's like," I say, my voice cracking. "You have to be so sure when you're in there. I had to watch how it all began. She was tricked, and trapped, and used. And I had to kill her, but it wasn't her fault. She was good. She was a *good person.*"

It's here—on *good person*—that I lose it. The tears come quick and fat. No one rushes to comfort me. Nobody quite knows how. They were all united in their quest to rid me of the Housekeeper, and now I'm telling them that I didn't quite want it hard enough.

Or, perhaps, didn't want it at all.

"She was the sensitive of the Kilbeg Well. Right? According to Dorey, it's one of the oldest and most powerful Wells in the Western world. She told me that. And sensitives . . . they see. They're powerful, and they have magic, but they *see* things. Like Aaron's power, and my power, and Assumpta's power all have to do with seeing the invisible: the past, or the future, or inside people's minds. And Heaven, too. Heaven must have had some kind of seeing power, right, Nuala?"

Nuala looks stunned to have been consulted about Heaven. "I don't know," she says after a silence. "She never . . . shared that with me."

"And when they trapped her in this card, they trapped her power, but they took her sight, too. She wasn't able to judge for herself anymore. She just became a contract killer for whoever summoned her. But she herself isn't bad."

They all look at me doubtfully, like I may have lost my mind while under the water.

"What if I . . ." I begin, my voice still shaking. "What if I'm an opportunity for her to become whole again?"

"What?" Fiona says sharply. "What does that even mean?"

"The sight and the power, I mean. It will finally come together. I'm a telepath. I can judge whether someone's intentions are good when they summon the Housekeeper. Maybe I can choose to help them or not help them. My sight. Her power."

"Maeve," René says gently. "She's old, and powerful, and clearly she has anchored herself somewhere in your subconscious. You give yourself over to her, and there's no predicting what she might do. She will devour you, Maeve. That's what demons do."

"She didn't devour Lily," I suddenly say.

"What?" Roe interrupts. "What does Lily have to do with any of this?"

"Lily met the Housekeeper. Right? Lil?"

Lily looks away from me and examines her inner wrist, where another tiny tattoo, of a raindrop, has been administered.

"She offered me the river," Lily says quietly, "and I took it. She just wanted me to be happier. And I was so unhappy, guys. Even before the Maeve stuff, with the tarot reading." She looks to me then. "And not even because of you, either. It didn't help, obviously. But I just hated life. I'm not sure . . ."

She breaks off. Examines her wrist again.

"What, Lil?" Roe says, voice trembling. "You're not sure of what?"

"I'm not sure I would have carried on," she says simply. "But

322

I don't feel that way *now*," she says, stumbling over her words, in a hurry to reassure us. "And I haven't felt that way for ages and ages. I'm happy now, even though things are sometimes awful. I feel like I've figured it out."

Fiona is the only one who doesn't look surprised. I realize that Lily has told her this already, and that this is possibly what made them so close so quickly.

"Lily," Nuala says softly. "Why didn't you tell us about the Housekeeper before? That she was kind to you, I mean."

"I didn't want to tell you all that I was, I don't know, borderline suicidal. It seems like a waste of energy, to tell people after the fact."

"You should have told us," Roe says, mouth tight with restraint. Roe wants to cry, to shout, to smack themself for missing this. "Tell us things that *matter*."

"I *told* you what matters," she says. "I told you I was the river."

"Guys," I say, trying to get everyone back on track. "Look. Think about it. The Housekeeper gave us our power, right? We call them gifts. *We* came up with that. Well, someone has to have *given* a gift, don't they? And what if that someone was her?"

René gets up. "Perhaps I should be going," he says.

Manon looks startled. "Why?"

"You called me for help, Manon, and I've done all I can. Led another poor girl into another failed ritual. Perhaps it's time to hang up my boots."

"Don't go," I plead. "I don't know what I'm supposed to do now."

"Well, neither do I, Maeve," he says, rubbing at his temples. "It looks as though you are determined to become a demon."

A pause. Roe laughs, and we all look over.

"She sort of always has been, though, right?"

We laugh. A tense, exasperated, terrified laugh. But still a laugh.

Here, we laugh when something is funny, and we laugh when something is about to begin.

"Well, then," I say, "we need to figure out how I can be the best demon I can be."

"I didn't sign up for demon training," René answers, sounding peeved.

"No one here signed up for anything." Fiona sighs. "But here we are."

Everyone leaves the room. I get dressed, my fingers quaking as I move from button to button. I've missed my one chance. Fumbled it. Fucked it. I could have ended the Housekeeper's bloody reign, and ultimately chose not to. Am I an idiot?

Nuala has a long, oval mirror in a wooden stand. My hair is matted and smells, too strongly, of shampoo. My guess is that the girls wanted to get the river stench out so they went crazy on the TRE-Semmé. It must have still been damp when they put me to bed and now the back is knotted into big clumps. I sit at the edge of the bed, combing and combing, hoping that undoing the knots in my hair will help me untie the ones in my stomach.

Look at yourself in the mirror too long and you stop looking like yourself. The space between my features seems to drift, like parts of a puzzle flung to either end of a room. I look for so long that I start to think I can see her in there. Her, whom I let live. Her, who gave us the gifts to start with.

I try out a voice. A brave voice.

"I saved you," I say to my reflection. "I could have killed you, and I saved you."

The color changes in my eye, like there's a rain cloud traveling through it. A shadow of gray, the size of an eraser on the tip of a pencil, that passes through the iris of my left eye and into my right. Then it travels back.

"Is that you?" I whisper.

Yes.

"Was I right not to kill you?"

Yes.

"Is there any way I can get out of this alive?"

I don't know.

I lay the comb in my lap and just try to sit with her.

"I'm sorry," I say. "I'm sorry how it ended for you. Or how it started. Both. I'm sorry I didn't understand you. I do now, I think. And, well, thank you. For the gifts."

You are welcome.

The gray circle drifts across my eye line again, and I feel a slow trickle of understanding enter my bloodstream. There is the Housekeeper, the powerful witch who lived in the Kilbeg woods, when there still were Kilbeg woods to live in. And there is the Housekeeper card, the power that they captured and held on to for themselves, the demon they created from the person who once lived. But she still lives on, in glimmers of kindness, in the vividness of humanity. She can access her old self through me.

And this is when I start to think of a plan.

39

"WE'VE GOT TO GIVE ONE BACK."

I say it so loudly that René physically jumps out of Nuala's kitchen chair. I get the sense that everyone was talking about me before I entered the room. Having a big *Well, what on earth do we do with her now?* conversation, the kind that has been happening about me for my entire life.

"Give what back?"

"A gift," I say. "Think about it. Whenever people summon her, it's because they want something. And she gave us all these gifts. So we need to give *her* something."

Roe looks up from cutting vegetables. "Aren't we already giving her something? We're giving her you."

"No, I'm being taken. I'm going no matter what. What if we summon her and we don't ask for anything? What if we give it to her instead?"

"Give her what?" Fiona asks.

"Well, I don't *know*," I answer, exasperated. "But it's the right track, isn't it? Isn't it, Nuala? Manon?"

Manon looks genuinely lost for words.

"Well . . ." Nuala.

"Can we do that?" Fiona.

"*How* would we do that?" Roe.

"I'm not wrong, am I?" I say, excited. "Whenever I'm in the Housekeeper world, people give her offerings, you know? Like treasures, and hares. Dead hares."

"Hair?" Lily asks.

"No, hares. Like the big rabbit."

"Ah." Lily ponders this. "So the idea is that if we give the Housekeeper something, she might go easier on you?"

"Yeah," I answer, nodding slowly. "I mean, maybe we can restore her to being someone who works on behalf of the weak, to someone I can learn to coexist with. And who might help us in taking down the Children. The first time I . . ."

What word to use here. Met her? Experienced her? *Was* her?

"The first time," I start again. "She was helping this young mother get her daughter to safety. There was no pound of flesh or whatever. Except for the hares. She needed an offering, but she didn't need, like, a human death."

Aaron's eye twitches, and I know he's thinking about that bus trip to San Francisco, the morning he woke up to find Matthew dead in the seat next to him. All so they could escape the facility they were locked up in. The bus trip that led to him meeting the Children, that led to him coming here. To Kilbeg.

"I don't want to kill the Housekeeper," I say, trying to gather confidence. "I want to change her. Or, you know. Restore her."

"Maeve," Nuala says, her hand on my shoulder. "This is insane."

"Why is it any more insane than trying to kill her?"

"Because killing something is easier than changing it," Aaron says. "Take it from someone who professionally tried to change people."

The more they argue with me, the more convinced I become that I'm correct. On the right track.

"I didn't say it would be *easy*," I say, and look around. Looking for anyone who might think this idea might have the faintest whiff of sanity about it. Everyone avoids my eye. Everyone thinks that I'm still a little deranged from the ritual, that I've been taken in by the Housekeeper. Then I find Lily. Lily, rubbing her thumb over the water droplet tattoo—or is it a teardrop?—and biting the inside of her lip. But looking at me. Definitely looking at me.

"Lil," I say. "You're the only one who knows her like I do. What do you think?"

She pauses. "I like it," she replies. "Or at least I like this plan better than the other one."

There are two of us now. Two out of eight.

René drums his knuckles on the table. "It is a deranged plan," he says. "But I have seen deranged plans work."

Three out of eight.

Manon looks at her father. A hard, scrutinizing look. "If *you* think it has possibility," she says, "then I think it does, too."

Four. Half the vote.

Fiona looks between me and Manon hesitantly.

"Fi," I tell her softly, "if I have to live with this forever, I'm OK with it. I think it's what I'm supposed to do. Find a way to bring her back in a way that . . . that makes *sense*, and that is fair. I don't think it's college for me. I don't think there's some big job like acting that I want to do. I think it's helping people. I think it's *this*."

I'm talking to Fiona, but I realize that I'm talking to everyone. And most of all, I'm talking to myself.

"What do you mean, Maeve?" Roe asks, and I remember the thousands of conversations we've had. In Bridey's, in my bed, in the back of their car. Talks about how I was going to get through school, how I was going to get into college, what I would do in college, what

I would do after. Roe, always so eager to help. Roe, convinced that everyone has a calling, that everyone is smart in their own way.

"After we broke up," I say hesitantly, "I went out. I went to a club. There was this girl, and some guy was trying to rape her. It was horrible, but I was trying to save her, get her away from him, and I had this realization that even if Dorey and the Children vanished tomorrow, there would still be horrible people in the world, preying on the vulnerable. And I know that's a pretty broad category, and the world is just like that sometimes, but . . . I don't know. I think I could . . ."

"You're an activist," Aaron says. No sarcasm, no edge. Just plainly.

"Yeah," I say. "I think? I don't know. But this is part of it. Me being the Housekeeper, and figuring out how to use her, that's important. For me. For everyone. For helping."

Fiona smiles at me, a sad smile, like she's watching our roads diverge and is frightened they might never meet again. "You found your thing," she says, and she gets it, because she has a thing, too.

Roe nods. "You found your thing."

I laugh a little, because I want to cry. "I found my thing."

Six. Six out of eight.

Aaron and Nuala are leaning by the kitchen sink, both so fair-haired and disapproving that they look like mother and son. I suppose there's more they have in common, too: both of them have lost people to the Housekeeper.

Aaron knows what I'm thinking; or rather, he knows that I know what he's thinking.

"Look," he says, "I saw Matthew, remember? She murdered him and he did nothing wrong. I don't know if you can rehabilitate something that . . . might not have started out evil but has definitely become that way."

"I don't see why not," Roe says. "We did it for you."

"Ha, ha."

"I'm serious, man. You tried to ruin my life. What if you had succeeded, you know? What if I didn't have the girls with me that night? What if I quit the band? What if I quit myself? Went back to being Rory O'Callaghan because people like you proved that the alternative was too unbearable?"

"I'm sorry, Roe," Aaron says. "Really. That period of my life . . . I don't think I'll ever be done atoning for it. But I am sorry. You have to know that. Don't you?"

Roe nods. "I do know that. I'm not going to get *brunch* with you, but I do know that. But maybe you've got to pay that faith forward. Forgive someone else. Forgive some*thing* else."

Aaron crosses his arms. He addresses his next statement to the floor. "Fine. OK. Goddammit. All right."

I look at Roe and realize the depth of the strong, yelping, dog-faithful love that I have. The love that goes on and on, always growing, never quite going away.

And then I realize I don't mean just Roe. I mean both of them.

Both of them understand something about me that no one else does. The silly lightness I can feel with Roe, the goodness and faith that pours out whenever we're alone. The pirouetting giddiness of just being around them. Cava in the bathtub. Conversations in the car. Being good, being bad, being funny, being myself. Roe who sees the world in me. Who thinks I can do anything.

Then there's Aaron, complicated and infuriating, and someone I want to push off a building from time to time. Someone who understands what it's like to live with a curse. I choose to keep him in my life, confide in him, work with him. Do I love him? Yes, I think. But do I love him like I love Lily, Fiona, Nuala? Manon, whom I barely know, really, but would still go to the ends of the earth for? Or do I love him like something else?

I feel all of this, the gray circle of the Housekeeper flickering between my eyes like a lost contact lens. I feel it all, and do nothing. Let it flow and pass. Feelings are not my priority right now. She is.

"So, Maeve," Nuala says, filling the kettle again. "What do you propose we give the Housekeeper?"

Eight. We have all eight, and I know we can do this. I know it can work. I raise both hands up, like a primary-school teacher asking the class a question.

"What do you give a housekeeper, kids?"

Silence.

"You give her the house."

40

"THE HOUSE," AARON SAYS. "*YOUR* HOUSE? The school? Is that what you mean?"

"Yes. That's exactly what I mean."

We've planned rituals before. And what they have always been, really, are requests. Please bring our friend back. Please stop them from draining the Well. Please get out of my body. Please die.

What this is, instead, is: *Here.* Here you go. This is for you.

It immediately feels like a more powerful concept. In primary school, when we learned about prayer, our teacher told us that every day God receives millions of prayers asking for things, but only a few saying thank you. I remember finding that very sad, and at the same time, absolutely inevitable. If you hoard all that power to yourself, then what else do you expect other than requests for help?

"How do we do a thing like this?" Manon asks, and she looks to me for an answer. "Give her a piece of property?"

"I guess we show up there, light her a few candles, and just say, 'Take it. It's yours.'"

"*How* is it hers, though? If she is you and you are her?"

"I think . . ." I close my eyes, feeling the gray circle fall back and forth like a pendulum. "I think if she has the space to make things her own, to make it good, and beautiful, and . . ."

I shake my head, start again.

"Basically, when I go there, I'm going to sit with her. And say, 'What do you want, Housekeeper?'"

"And why would she want that?" René asks. "Presuming that she *wants* things?"

"I think the reason the Corridor appeared is that it was from the original house that she was transformed in. It means something to her, that house. It's the mouth of the Well. It's everything."

"And so, what, you're going to take decorating tips from her?" asks Roe.

"I'm going to let her come out. Let her run wild, if she wants to."

"A shrine," Nuala suggests. "Sort of?"

"A temple, if she wants it. A refuge, if she wants that. I think she wants to protect people. I think if I let her do that, she might be happy."

"And then she might not eat you from the inside out?" Lily asks.

"Yeah, possibly?"

"Worth a go."

We brainstorm, tossing out other ideas. Fiona briefly suggests an exorcism. Then I get a text from my mum, and I realize it's almost midnight.

Where are you

With the gang. Omw home x

A pause. Text bubbles, appearing and disappearing. And then:

You can't keep doing this

"I better go, guys."

When I get home, both my parents are waiting for me at the kitchen table. The dog scampers in, tired, and slumps immediately into his bed by the door.

"It's one a.m., Maeve," Mum says, clearly annoyed. "Do you even care that we are worried sick about you all the time? Does that even register with you, when you go gallivanting around until all hours of the night?"

Oh, god. What to say, what to say, what to say.

"I'm at Nuala's most of the time, Mum. She's a grown-up. It's not like we're unchaperoned."

"Well, why can't you and your friends come here, then?" she asks, sounding like a hostage negotiator.

"Well, Manon is her daughter, and Aaron sort of lives there, and it's right near town, and . . ."

My mother suddenly slams her fist on the kitchen table, rattling the oranges in the fruit bowl.

"Maeve," she says sharply. "Kids are *dying."*

"What?" I know this, but I'm surprised that she knows it, too.

My father wordlessly hands me today's newspaper, and instantly I think it's going to be another "Kilbeg witches" thing. I try not to groan as I take it from him, thinking: *Oh, god, did someone see the ritual at the river tonight? Did they think René and the others were trying to drown me, or something?*

Then I see the headline on the front page.

TEENAGERS' REMAINS FOUND
IN GRAIN SILO

The bodies of two missing teenagers, Sophia Mulready (19) and Lorna McKeon (18), were discovered by a Ballywick farmer this morning. John O'Donovan (61) was examining his silos after detecting a blockage in the spout and found the remains of the young women.

"It was devastating, horrifying," O'Donovan says. "I've

*lived here my whole life, so I know all the young people to
see. There's no question in my mind that they were dumped
here, by someone very sick."*

*While Gardaí cannot confirm this, Mulready and
McKeon were both from Kilbeg city and had recently
become estranged from their families. Estrangement has
quickly become a familiar story in Kilbeg, as more and
more young people have been suddenly leaving home,
with many dropping out of third-level education. The
police have not confirmed whether these estrangements
are linked to the deaths of Mulready and McKeon, but a
spokesperson has said that "parents and families should
be extra vigilant about retaining strong communication
with their children," and also added that "teenage girls, in
particular, need to be extra safe."*

FULL STORY CONT. ON PAGE 2

A grain silo. They are dumping corpses and leaving them to rot.
That's the sum total of the holiness, the clarity, the splendor that the
Children are really offering. They will use your suffering to pump the
Well for magic. They will push your body to its very limit. And if you
die—*when* you die—they will dump you a few miles from the Lodge,
hoping your body decomposes before a sixty-one-year-old farmer
finds you.

Lorna. Lorna Lorna Lorna.

I waited too long. I didn't act quickly enough. And now she's
dead. A girl I went to school with since I was twelve, and never really
spoke to, and now will never know at all.

I put the paper down, hot spit foaming at my jaw. The article, clearly, has more of an effect on me than my parents were hoping. They wanted to scare me into behaving, not give me a mental breakdown. They have no idea where I figure in this, how my life has bumped off of Sophia Mulready's. The learner's permit. The bonfire.

"Oh, god. Maeve. Sit down," Dad says, guiding me into a chair. "I remember Lorna. Or, I remember her father. The other old dad at the gates."

My father's eyes are shining with tears, the same vomiting urge in him. A grain silo. Flesh becoming food for animals.

"I remember her," he says. "Lovely big eyes, like dinner plates. Pretty."

His voice catches on *pretty*. It's the little-girlness to the word, I think. *Don't you look pretty in your party dress.* The idea that she will never ascend to other kinds of beauty, other kinds of personhood. Not elegance, not grandeur, not maturity. The paper falls out of his hands and onto the floor, and my mother puts her forehead on the table.

I pick up the paper. Turn to the full story on page two. Details on how secretive Lorna had become, how cagey, how different. Sophia and her sudden preoccupation with sin.

They all come to me. All find me, somehow, without realizing. I'm the Housekeeper and I was supposed to protect them. So I get these clues, these meetings, these little bits of them. Missing squares on computer screens. Learner's permits. Mixtapes from before I was born. Debris washing up at my feet because I wasn't strong enough to save them.

But I will be strong. I will be.

"I didn't know Lorna very well at all," I say at last. "But I wish I did."

"I don't want you going out anymore," Mum says, and she has to make her voice harsh to keep back the tears. "Not after dark."

Oh, god. Not this.

"Mum, be realistic. It's January, and it gets dark at four p.m."

It is absolutely the wrong thing to say. She explodes.

"When are you going to realize that this is serious, Maeve? It's not a game. I'm sorry that you can't stand to be with us for more than five seconds, but this is about safety. You are not. Going. Out."

"This is the plan, is it?" I say, scanning the double-page spread of the story. "No one's asking why these girls died? The solution is keep your girls inside? What the fuck is that? Why is no one protecting us? Why is no one hunting *them*?"

The gray circle, that Housekeeper lens, starts to settle on my iris, her perspective twinning with mine. *Yes. Why? Why? Why?*

Mum's mouth twitches. "I want you to carry a rape alarm."

It is a suggestion so dazzling, so ridiculous, that I actually laugh. "A rape alarm? Mum? A rape alarm?"

"Why are you laughing?"

"Maeve," Dad says, like a storm warning. "Don't."

But I can't stop because the Housekeeper is laughing, too.

Hahahaha, imagine, imagine, a rape alarm, imagine, imagine, imagine if the only thing between rape and its victims was a sound to let people know it was happening.

"I will wear a rape alarm, Mum," I say at last, wishing I hadn't laughed. "I'll wear two, if it will make you happy."

Then she slaps me across the face. She slaps me so hard that my head turns in the other direction and I can read the clock on the oven.

She seizes the paper again. "This!" she says, her voice rising to a screech. "This was Lily O'Callaghan ten months ago. Do you remember that?"

I hold my face, hot and red. I have never been slapped by a parent before.

"I thought she was dead, Maeve. So did your father. And your siblings. Everyone. This child we watched grow up. Who came in and out of our house—who we took on *holidays with us*—no one thought she was coming back, Maeve. Not really. Not after the first week. You put your head in the sand about it, you nattered on about magic and tarot cards, and I thought, oh, god, she's regressing. She can't deal with the fact that her best friend has been killed, or *worse* than killed, and so she's going back to childhood. Fairies at the bottom of the garden. I was jealous of you. Meanwhile, I was spending every night thinking of Lily rotting. This child that I thought of as family. Your father and I didn't sleep for weeks."

Dad hangs his head, hands over his eyes.

"Nora. She doesn't need to know this."

"Lily came back," I say finally. I feel adrift, in space, a different species. It's too disarming, to see them vulnerable like this.

"Lily came back." Mum nods. "But I don't think I did."

Silence.

And of course, I never thought about it. Lily's disappearance was, after all, a thing that was happening to *me*. Because of me. I would also allow that it was happening to Roe, and by extension the O'Callaghans. But not my own family, who loved Lily.

The ego. God, I hate myself sometimes.

"Mum," I say. "I know you want to protect me, but keeping me inside isn't going to do anything. It just means that some other girl gets found in a grain silo."

She shakes her head slowly, heavily, chewing on her nail.

"I can't look after some other girl, though," she says. "I can only look after you."

I put my arms around her, holding her in the hug until I feel her shoulders relax slightly.

"I want to look after the other girl."

41

THE THOUGHT OF OBEYING MY PARENTS doesn't even enter my head. Not seriously. The next night, I cast my sleeping spell on the house, and I set off to St. Bernadette's.

Without consulting one another, we have all dressed up for the occasion. Our best clothes, our best selves: Aaron in a shirt and tie; Manon wearing an oversize red kimono jacket, a white chemise underneath it, hair in two space buns, devastatingly sexy; Fiona in an emerald-green shift dress. I wonder if they're trying to impress each other.

Nuala is like a different person. It's the first time I've seen her out of drapey, floaty silks. She's in black jeans, tight against her body, and a khaki jacket.

"You're dressed just like when I knew you," René says.

"Like a criminal, you mean?" Nuala responds, taking champagne out of two shopping bags.

"Like a criminal," he repeats, eyes glittering.

"What are *these* for?" I ask, examining the champagne.

"Well," she says, "you're giving her a gift. So it's kind of like a party, isn't it? I thought we'd pour her a glass of champagne."

"A *glass*?" I say, looking at the bags.

"And the rest is for us, in case it doesn't work and we have to get rat-arsed."

"Cool."

Manon smiles at her mother. She unzips her backpack and takes out a bottle of absinthe. "I had the same thought," she says.

"Ha!" Nuala cackles. "So we *are* related."

I walk out to the back, where the destroyed tennis courts are still blackened by the fire. Aaron is pacing, on the phone.

"Hey," he says when he sees me. "I'm on hold."

"With who?"

"The *Kilbeg Star*."

"The paper?"

"Yes."

"Why?"

"Because the *Times*, the *Independent*, the *Examiner*, and the *Sunday Business Post* won't take my calls."

I look at his face, and I realize he hasn't slept.

"The grain silos?"

He nods. "I'm trying to *tell* them," he says tensely, "about Dorey, about the Children. I keep saying, 'I was an insider, I know.' I can tell them everything."

I nod. "You can."

"We know where the Lodge is. But no one will listen. I can hear them, pretending to take notes. Dorey has gotten to them all already."

"I know. It's all this stuff about vigilance. Keeping people safe. She's managed to divert them all."

"A string on every paper," he says. Then pauses, waits. A voice on the other end of the phone. "Aaron Branum," he says. "No, not Brannigan. Branum. You did an interview with me, last year? I was the spokesperson for the youth chapter of the Children of Brigid? I have some informa—"

A click. They're gone.

Aaron does nothing for a second, and then kicks at the court's net post so hard that he screams out loud.

"Aaron! Why the hell did you do that?!"

"Because people are being left to rot and it's my fault, Maeve. Jesus. What are we going to do? No one will listen."

He sinks to the ground, his legs crossed, and holds his feet with both hands.

"Do you want me to get Fiona?"

"No."

"Is it still hurting from the other night?"

"No, will you stop fussing? No."

I try something then. I crouch on the ground behind him, and I hug him. It is the second hug of our friendship.

"Why are you doing that?" he says after a few seconds.

"Because you're sad," I say. "And you hug your friends when they're sad."

I hug him to make a point, but while I'm doing it, I can feel my gift waking up and sparking. Maybe both of our gifts, which are so dependent on touch in order to merge.

I wonder if this is part of the Children's celibacy mission, too. Maybe it's a way to stop their more magical members from finding more power together than they can through the Children.

I can't help wondering, as I hold him, how exactly our gifts would merge. There is no sudden surge, no pop, no fusion. He nudges his gift toward mine, and we each fix our eyes on the same naked tree, stripped bare by the cold. Suddenly the tree bursts into bloom, cherry blossoms the color of a deep blush, cotton candy rioting against the winter sky. We each take a breath, stunned by it. Five seconds of holy wonder.

And then it's gone.

We don't talk about it. I'm not sure why. Our relationship has no language for intimacy and prettiness. We do not know how to bear witness to things like this.

Instead, he just releases himself from the hug. I'm embarrassed for being corny. But we keep sitting there.

Aaron exhales then, and, for a moment, leans his head against my arm. It's a few seconds. A few seconds for that thought again, that feeling, that question. What *are* we to each other? Sensitives, siblings, soul mates? I don't know. I don't even know what he smells like. A few weeks ago he smelled like dirt. Now he smells like Nuala's house: like cooking, and laundry. I don't know what *his* smell is, though.

He straightens, lets go of his trainer, and starts to get up. "Thanks."

We go inside, where Roe and Lily have just arrived. Roe in a houndstooth trench coat, combat boots laced to the knee. And the hair, oh, the hair. Blacker than ever. Glossy as piano keys.

"Everyone looks great," I say, glancing around.

It's weird. With the last ritual, the grand passage, everything was planned. Filled with money, and relics, and stages, and rope. Here, we all seem to be acting on instinct.

"Do you like my dress?" Lily asks, spinning around. And I do. It's absolutely bonkers, but I do. It's a pale pink evening gown, obviously a bridesmaid's dress.

"Is that from the insane store?" Aaron asks. "Basement?"

"The one you tried to protest the existence of?" Fiona says. "Yes."

Aaron just shakes his head. "A *store*. God. You know I really thought I was being a vigilante?"

"Oh, we know."

"Maeve," Roe says. "Can you help me bring the stuff in?"

"Do you guys have booze, too?"

"No." Lily gleams with excitement. "Something better."

I come outside, and Roe opens the trunk of the car to reveal Lily's huge cello case.

"What the hell?" I ask.

"I figured we might as well have music, you know. Party atmosphere."

"I love how we've all decided that party atmosphere is the atmosphere she wants."

Roe shifts the huge case into my arms, then opens the passenger door and takes out a guitar case.

"It's that way you've got about you. You get people thinking. You say a thing like 'The opposite of a request is a gift,' and people start thinking about parties. You set us all off."

I beam, hugging the cello. "Really? I've got a *way*?"

"Yeah." Roe takes out his guitar and straps it on.

"Honestly, I think—if you're serious about this activism stuff, if that's what you want to do—you'll be great at it. You don't patronize people. You're too aware of your own faults to go around trying to teach people about morality. You just get them thinking."

Our eyes meet in the half dark, glimmering with love for each other.

"Roe," I say softly. Knees trembling from the weight of the heavy instrument.

"Well, I did say I'd remember what I like about you."

"Thanks," I say, and pause. "I'm really scared, Roe."

I wasn't, until that moment. Until the moment I realized that the Housekeeper, even if she accepts my gift, will still change me forever. What if she changes me into a version of myself that Roe can't recognize, or that can't be loved? What if the Maeve that Roe loved is gone forever, and if she's gone, how can she be loved again?

"You, scared?"

"Me, scared."

We are so close now. Roe reaches under their clothes and picks out the black jet necklace I gave him for protection, the hard, flat stone as big as a thumbprint.

"Here, this came in handy the first time. Maybe it will come in handy the last." They put the necklace over my head, the stone coming to rest on my heart.

Within the hour, Sister Assumpta's office is the most beautiful it has ever been. White pillar candles—nothing special, Nuala says, four for ten euro at Dunnes—are burning all around us. Champagne in jam jars. Lily, cello between her knees, sawing gently at the strings. It's Bach, I think. It's almost always Bach. I remember when she started playing, and the fight with her mother, who thought—rather reasonably—that a violin would be a better choice for such a little girl. Less lugging around. But Lily hated the sound of the violin, or she did then, because she said it was too high, too like girls chattering. She said she could hear the cello, even when she didn't have her hearing aid in. The vibrations, she said. She could hear them in her stomach.

I can hear them in mine.

Roe accompanies her. Careful finger-picking, delicate strings. It's gorgeous, and they look so good together. Manon joins in on the old fire-damaged upright piano, cocking her ear to pick out the melody. I wonder if this is a party or the occultist equivalent of the quartet who kept playing as the *Titanic* sank.

I go upstairs, ready to kneel in front of the Housekeeper's portrait, ready to give her the house. Only, the Corridor isn't open. 2A is merely 2A, a long, dusty classroom.

345

I call down the stairs. "The Corridor isn't open!"

A pause. Nuala calls back up. "Well, maybe she wants the whole party first."

I descend the stairs. Fiona is standing in the hallway, flicking through a book.

"You seen this before?" she asks, holding up a book so familiar that it knocks the breath out of me. It's the *Schools' Folklore Collection*.

"Yes," I reply, slightly unsteady, gripping the banister. "That's, uh . . . That's the book Heather Banbury gave me, then she lured me to her weird fake house to give it back."

"Wow," Fiona says. She holds it at arm's length, turning it over. "Do you think it's her final Horcrux, or something?"

"You know I didn't watch those movies."

"I know," she says. And then: "So I got it."

"Got it?" It takes me a moment to remember. "The part? *The Coven*?"

She nods stiffly, her eyes wide. "Yep," she says. "Yep yep yep."

"Oh, my god! Congratulations! When does it start?"

"March," she says. "They've decided to wait until the daylight comes back. So I've got a little time."

"And your mum is fine with it? With exams and all that?"

"Here's the thing. Because I'm still underage, I can only work a few hours a day, so the rest of the time I'll be in a hotel room in Belfast, studying," she says. "Once she realized that I won't have *you* around as a distraction, she was quite pro *The Coven*."

I laugh. "Wise. And I guess I won't have you around as a distraction, either."

We suddenly launch into a hug, and we're holding each other tightly, tightly in the way that only girls can do.

"It's only five weeks," Fiona croaks. "It won't be so long."

"Why do you sound so sad?" I say, finally untwining myself from her. "This is your dream. This is perfect. It's what you've been waiting for."

"Kind of a self-centered dream." She shrugs. "And is it really worth the safety of my friends? And not even just my friends—those girls, Maeve. The ones they found in the silo. Lorna. I can't help but just . . . I have this good brain, you know? I have this good, strong brain, and this profound gift . . . I mean, I'm a *healer*! Shouldn't I be in a lab somewhere, working on the cure for cancer? Instead of performing silly stories?"

"Stories are powerful," I say. "Stories can . . ."

"Oh, don't *stories can change the world* me. Chemo can change the world better than stories can. We all know it."

"That's it? Stories or chemo? Those are your options?"

She laughs, rubs at her arms. Her face so complicated that I can't even make it out. I remember the bouncy, happy Fiona of a year ago. Am I responsible for making her this anxious? Or was she anxious then, too?

"And you're doing this noble thing. Staying. Helping. Making the world better. Protecting the Well. I feel like a clown."

"Pal," I say, my heart too full. "You can't worry about what I'm doing. We've all got different stuff going on. Different paths, different destinies."

I say all this thinking, *Wow, this has turned around quickly.* I remember when I resented Fiona for having a destiny while I had none.

"I'm staying here because it's what I'm meant to do, and what I want to do," I explain, putting my arm around her shoulder. "And you're gonna go away, and work all over the world, and come back when you can, and that's what you're supposed to do. And you know what else you're meant to do?"

"What?" she says, sniffing slightly.

"Go on talk shows and gush about this brilliant little city you come from called Kilbeg," I explain. Fiona looks up at me, smiling. "And tell them about how your friend Maeve Chambers is basically the mayor."

She laughs. "Oh, my god, shut up."

"The mayor," I say sweetly, trying not to crack up. "The mayor of Kilbeg."

"You're an arsehole," she says. "Let's get a drink."

Manon appears in the doorway, ushering us in to where Lily and Roe are still playing. She opens her mouth to say something, to deliver a verdict on the ritual, the Housekeeper, or the world in general. Who knows—I don't get to hear it.

There is a scream of a siren, so close and so loud that I can hear it in my teeth.

We look at one another, mystified, as if someone will have the explanation for this. We briefly consider that it is a fluke, something in one of the buildings next door. But no. The siren sounds again, and there's a flash of blue through the windows.

"The police?" we all say at once. And then: *"Here?"*

Then, the sound of a hard shoulder on the door. A door that was supposed to be bolted shut by the property company, but that Roe makes pretty fast work of opening.

"We're coming!" I shout. "Don't break the door."

I open the door, and two policemen in high-vis jackets bustle through. Even in my panic, I can't help thinking about the first day I saw two Gardaí in St. Bernadette's. I remember someone saying there was a Hot Cop in school, and how a "hot" man in a girls' school was basically any man not old enough to be our dad.

I think about all this, and perhaps that is why the Gardaí seem

taken aback by me. They blink, clearly confused, then take in everyone else in the room: the two adults, the smattering of young people,
the champagne, the cello.

"Right," one says finally. "Everybody out."

"Why?" I ask.

"Because this is private property, not to mention deeply unsafe.
There was a fire here not long ago, and the building is structurally
unsound. The place could fall down around us at any moment." He
shakes his head, as if he can't believe he's explaining himself to a
teenager. "And anyway, it's trespassing. We've had a noise complaint."

"Excuse me," I say, as respectfully as I can. "We're really sorry if
there was noise—we were having a sing-along earlier. See, my friends
are musicians?"

I wave my hand across to Roe and Lily, trying to create an idea
of genteel bohemian creativity rather than squalor.

"And actually, it's not trespassing. It is private property, but it's
my private property. I inherited it."

The Garda snorts, but the other one looks perplexed.

"You're the *girl*," he says, as though he has come face-to-face
with an urban legend. Then he looks around, at the crown molding
on the dusty ceiling. "This is the *school*."

"Yes," I say. "I'm Maeve Chambers."

"Maeve Chambers," he repeats, and he sounds like he's heard
the name before. For once, I feel strangely proud of myself. Glad that
someone has heard my name before, growingly conscious that it is a
name people may know for a long time.

"And who are all these people?" the first policeman asks while
the second, who's older, goes back out to the car. He pulls out the
car's radio and begins speaking into it.

"My friends," I say simply.

Nuala steps forward. "Fionnuala Evans," she says. "I'm a business owner in town. We were just having a little birthday party for one of the kids."

A lie with a strange amount of truth in it. It is, in a way, a kind of birthday.

"In a dilapidated building, Mrs. Evans?"

"Miss. And we're so sorry about the noise—we were actually just about to head home."

"And who are these children to you, Miss Evans?"

"That's my daughter," she says, pointing to Manon. Who, incidentally, has changed her face so she is not recognizably Manon at all. I almost jump when I see her blond hair. "And her father, and, well, that's Aaron, who is sort of a foster, and these are all their friends. Sure, I'm very softhearted and said to them, 'If you're going to have a party at Maeve's awful old place, you're bringing me and your dad.' For safety, you know."

She sounds so mumsy, like the woman I met in Divination the first day. It's a kind of disguise she wears, a subtler version of what Manon does. Hiding an iron fist in a velvet glove.

"Anyway, as I say, we're all a bit knackered, so we were going to head home, but we're sorry for the inconvenience."

The second cop comes back to the door and pulls the first away. They have a short, muttered conversation between the two of them.

"I think it's best that you do that, Miss Evans," the first cop says. "We'll need to take Maeve with us, I'm afraid. We need to talk to her about some things. We'll call her parents on the way to the station."

"Talk to me about what?" I ask, feeling real panic for the first time.

"I think it's better if we don't discuss that here. Could you come with us, please?"

350

"Excuse me," Nuala says. "I don't understand what's going on here. Read any newspaper in the country and you'll know this girl is who she says she is. She has every right to be here. She's not breaking the law."

"Oh, we have no doubt. This matter is quite unrelated. And, with respect, Miss Evans, you're not Maeve's guardian."

"Unrelated?" I ask. "Then why . . . ?"

"Miss Chambers," he says shortly. "Did you ever meet a girl called Sophia Mulready?"

Perhaps I should stall for time, or look to any one of my deeply powerful friends for help. We could create a distraction, escape somehow. I can see it all play out in my head: a spark from Lily to keep their eyes off Roe, disabling their squad cars. Some more misdirection from René and Manon, to help confuse matters. But what would it do, really? It would only shine attention on all of us. Aaron and his expired visa. René and his pockets full of ancient treasure. Fiona losing her job on *The Coven*. I think of the headlines that another Maeve Chambers spectacle would create, and what it would really do.

I think of the Housekeeper inside of me and remind myself not to be afraid. I might have to spend the rest of my life working with people like this: with police, with authorities, with government officials. If I want to build something new, I'm going to have to build a reputation for it first. I have to do what Nuala does, and what Aaron did to an extent: build a mask of credibility, a public-facing personality.

"OK," I say. "Let's go talk."

I walk out to the squad car and get quietly into the back seat.

42

I'M LEFT TO WAIT IN AN INTERVIEW ROOM
for almost an hour—a tiny room with no phone reception, which
feels very deliberate. They can't take my phone away, but they look
like they want to. I can't read anyone's mind, because I'm left completely alone.

Eventually, a female officer with a friendly face comes into the
room.

"Maeve," she says. "I just want to know if you have any idea
where your parents are tonight?"

"At home," I answer, confused.

"They're not picking up the phone," she says. "Not any of the
numbers you gave us."

Of course they're not picking up the phone, I realize. I cast a
sleep spell on the house before I left it, so they wouldn't intervene
with my Housekeeper-ing.

"I can give you my sister's phone number," I say. "Or Nuala."

She frowns. "We really need it to be a parent, love. You're under
eighteen, which means we can't take a statement without parental
consent."

"OK, drop me home, then. I'll wake them up."

"We've already called out to your parents; no one's home. Or no one answered the door, anyway."

"I have a key," I say, deeply regretting the sleep spells.

"I'm afraid we can't release you unless it's into parental custody. We'll try your parents again in the morning, pet."

It takes me a moment to put this together. What she's saying, what she's suggesting. "Are you saying that you're keeping me overnight? In prison?"

"Well," she says. "In *jail.* And you won't be sharing a cell or anything, so don't worry. You'll be quite comfortable. We have a little wash-bag sorted for you and everything."

"But I haven't done anything wrong."

"Well," she says again, already sailing out of the room. "There's just a bit of confusion." And she's gone again.

I start pacing the room, worried now. What on earth is going on? A night in *jail*?

Another age passes. I sharpen up my gift like a weapon, ready to read the mind of whoever next walks into the room. One of the original Gardaí who came to St. Bernadette's eventually comes back to see me.

He's holding two steaming mugs of tea, and passes one to me. It's too strong and sugary, the tannins rolling like dirt over my tongue. I take one sip and then ignore it, remembering Heather Banbury. Remembering what happens when strangers make you tea.

"Now, Maeve," he says. "As I'm sure you know, I can't take an official statement from you until the morning. However," he continues, "I can explain a little what the issue is."

"Yes, please explain what the issue is."

He leans back in his chair and takes a long, calculating look at me, like he's trying to decide whether I'm a big enough girl to under-stand the information he needs to tell me. This, I realize fairly quickly, is a trick. He's giving me the dramatic pause, the sizing up, so that when he eventually talks to me like an adult, I will be grateful for any shred of respect. Perhaps this is why he has left me waiting so long.

"Well, Maeve, do you remember where you were on the twenty-sixth of December? Day after Christmas?"

"Yes," I say carefully. "I went to a pub with my sister and brother."

"Which pub?"

"The Silver Crane."

"Now is that Joanne, your next eldest sister? And which brother? You have two, don't you, Maeve?"

There's a glitter of satisfaction in his eyes, like I'm a mob boss he's been keeping tabs on, and not a schoolgirl. Pathetic, really. I try to keep my cool.

"Jo, yes, and my brother Pat. Patrick. We went to the Silver Crane, and then afterward I ran into some friends and we went to a club. Scarlet, it's called."

"And why," he says, that glimmering expression again, "did you go to Scarlet pretending to be Sophia Mulready?"

I nod and take another breath, because I guessed this might be where it was going.

"I ran into Michelle Breen, who was an old friend from school. She was there with Sophia's sister. I forget her name." I have, I real-ize. I have totally forgotten her name. "And the sister gave me an old learner's permit of Sophia's."

"I just find it very strange," he says, "that you would masquerade as a dead girl on the same night that . . . well, you were there, Maeve. Boys reporting strange injuries. Animal remains in a nightclub."

The Night of the Fur.

"I wasn't *masquerading*," I say. "I was using her ID. I didn't know she was dead. I understand it's a strange coincidence, but I'm sure you must have come across teenagers borrowing IDs before. I can't be the first."

It is the wrong tack to take. He is immediately annoyed, all the glimmer gone.

"We have a young man who came in to see us yesterday," he says. "Very upset at the news of Sophia. He said he met her, on Stephen's night."

I don't understand at first, but then it dawns on me. My face starts to go pink. The friendly stranger who caught me on the stairs. I'm distracted by my own pity for him. The poor guy, thinking he was helping some random girl, and then finding out she was dead. Then I realize that Sophia Mulready must have known plenty of people, in small ways and big ones, and they all had woken up to the same news.

"Obviously we rolled back the tapes on the security camera, and there he is, leaving the club with you. He was very relieved, I can tell you, that he hadn't helped out a dead girl."

"I'm sure," I say tightly.

This is the moment I realize that the police officer has a pen and pad out. And has been writing in it for some time.

"I thought I wasn't supposed to give a statement without a parent present," I say.

"Oh, this isn't a statement," he says, smiling. "I'm just taking notes. Now, if you didn't know this girl at all, the sister, I mean, why did she give you the license?"

A flash of an old TV memory. *Anything you say can and will be held against you in a court of law.*

"I have a right to a lawyer," I say, trying to remember the rest of it.

"You're not being arrested."

"I'm being held here against my will. What do you call that?"

"Only because we can't get ahold of your parents."

I'm going to get nowhere with this man, and so I arrange my face as though I'm about to confess something very important. He leans forward, scanning my expression, thinking that we are about to enter a game of silence chicken where the person who breaks loses. This is actually perfect for me, because he's completely quiet while I dig deep into his brain. And behind the logistics, behind the testimonials from random boys I've met, behind the suspicion of Maeve Chambers, there is one single directive.

Keep her inside. Just for the night. Use any reason you can.

I blink, and he seems to think he has won.

Why? Why tonight? What is Dorey doing? Did she know about my plan to give myself over to the Housekeeper, and was she trying to put a stop to it?

There's a certain lightness to this. If Dorey is afraid of me accepting the Housekeeper, of inviting her in, then it must be the right thing to do. It has to be.

Suddenly there is shouting, yelling, the sound of pushing. The Garda ignores it for a bit, trying to preserve the atmosphere of quiet tension between us, but it gets louder. Lots of "Fuck you" and "Fuck this" and "I'll cut you" in a strong city accent.

"Excuse me a moment," he says, getting up from his chair.

I go to the small window at the locked door of my interview room, and there's a rangy guy of about twenty who is being held at the shoulders by two police officers. He's wearing a hoodie over his head, but I catch a glimpse of his face. Long nose, small mouth, tiny protruding teeth. He catches my eye and spits on the floor.

They just have his arms under control when he manages to kick one of his legs up, hitting an officer in the stomach.

"Jesus," I hear my officer say. "Who's this filth?"

"We picked him up carjacking some poor fella in town."

Whoever this guy is, he seems very capable of making as much trouble as is possible for one man to make. I hear them drag him down the hall, the shouting continuing long after he's out of my sightline. I am craning my head to the left, trying to catch a glimpse through the plexiglass, when I feel the door handle move.

I jump back, terrified of being caught, then try to soothe myself that it's not a crime to look at things that are making noise.

Then the door opens, and it's Roe. I'm too relieved to question it. I fling my arms around them, so glad to see someone familiar.

"Come on. Quickly."

"How did you . . . ?" I turn my head down the hall, where the spitting and the struggling are still happening. "That was Manon, wasn't it?"

"Oh yeah. Come on, there's a staff exit to the car park. We won't have to see that poor woman in reception."

Roe grabs my hand and pulls me down the corridor. My nose starts to twitch.

"Do I smell smoke?"

"Lily started a small fire out by the bins. The whole station is either dealing with that or with Manon."

"Wow."

My friends, I think. My friends can really do anything.

A turn, a turn, and then another turn and we're outside. We get into Roe's car, my hands balmy with sweat. I put my forehead on their shoulder, feeling the car jump to life.

"Roe, I . . ."

"HELLO!" Lily jumps up from where she was apparently lying down in the back seat.

"*Jesus*," I splutter, thumping them both on the shoulder out of sheer surprise. "You two!"

"Jailbreak!" Lily says. "Pretty cool, huh?"

"They're going to see the CCTV, and . . ."

Lily smiles.

"You got rid of the CCTV. What about the files they have on me in the computer?"

Roe holds up a USB stick. "All on here."

"They *must* have backup."

"They do. But their system will be down for a day or two, and there will be a lot of admin to sort through."

"Where are we going?"

"For breakfast."

It's almost three in the morning, and there is a big petrol station on the edge of the city where taxi drivers go to refill and eat. It is not a café, not really. It's a mini supermarket with a counter where you can buy dehydrated potato wedges, ham-and-cheese pastries, and the odd sad sausage roll warming under a heating lamp. There are a couple of wipe-clean tables. We drink too-hot coffee from too-thin paper cups, and the windows are so wide and bright that we can see the shadows of fir trees, where the countryside officially begins.

Aaron and Nuala are there, waiting for us. We join them, hug them, collapse into chairs.

"Manon, René, and Fiona are in René's car," Nuala says. "Manon wanted Fiona in case someone got hurt."

"How did I get so lucky?" I say, turning a tired eye on each of them. "To have friends like all of you? This time last year I had no friends."

"Me neither," says Lily.

"Me neither," says Aaron.

"Me neither," finishes Nuala.

A few minutes later, René's car pulls up, and they all traipse in. Exhausted, but triumphant.

"Somebody get me a jambon," Fiona announces. Manon looks confused. "A jambon is a kind of cheese pastry here."

"But it just means 'ham.'"

"We know. No one knows why we call it that."

There, under the strip-lighting of an all-night petrol station, we sit and consider the magnitude of having messed with the police.

"How many of you were seen?" I ask.

"None of us," René says. "Manon and I were the only ones inside, and we didn't use our real faces. And Fiona was in the car."

"Why were they keeping you?" Aaron asks.

I take a long sip of my hot, bad coffee. "They're working with Dorey. Whether they know they're working with Dorey or are just being manipulated, I don't know. But they were instructed to keep me in for the night, for whatever reason they could find."

I close my eyes. Bracing myself for what has to come next.

"I think tonight . . ." I begin. "I think something very bad is happening at the Lodge."

Aaron fixes his eyes on me. Blue and glassy, like ice reflecting off the ocean. Everyone is still talking, wondering, planning, comparing conspiracy theories. But his gaze is steady, quietly interrogating me, noting every reaction and facial twitch.

And then, silently, he lays his hand on top of mine. Between the saltshaker and the paper napkin dispenser, the revenge demon and the former cult leader hold hands. I look at him, puzzled. What is this for? And why?

It is amazing to me how such a small movement can still not escape the notice of everyone at the table. Roe notices first, and then everyone follows their line of sight to our clasped hands. Fiona is about to say something, I think. Something between "What do you guys think you're doing?" and "Is there something you two would like to tell the class?"

"Maeve," Aaron says as if he hasn't noticed the tension shift. "Focus on the Lodge."

His gift is bounding toward mine like a puppy. I let mine unfurl, big jungle cat that it is. I remember the cherry-blossom tree bursting into bloom, how it felt like some kind of romantic nudge from the universe. But as Aaron and I connect again, I realize that it was not a random vision or a mutual delusion.

It was a premonition.

It was spring.

"My gift is that I can delve into people's histories," he says quietly, "and yours is that you can see their present."

I don't say anything. The Lodge is rushing into view, its unfinished walls, its doors without locks.

"And if you know the past and the present"—the whole table is hanging on his words now, and even René is mystified—"you can see the future. You can chart it like an astrophysicist can chart a comet's trajectory."

I see thick, choking smoke.

I see a darkened room, a room under the earth.

And I see bodies hitting the floor.

I feel new power leaving the wasted bodies. I see it entering

Dorey, sorrow having been turned to magic like lead into gold.

Aaron does not break eye contact with me. He can see it, too. He can feel it. He recognizes some of the bodies. He's the reason they joined the Children in the first place.

"She knows you're going to accept the Housekeeper," Aaron says, terror in his voice. "She knows that once you do, the Housekeeper is going to have her sight back. That she'll be whole. She won't be a hired killer anymore. She'll have judgment, and feeling, and she won't be happy about the Lodge. Not one bit."

My body freezes, the magnitude of Dorey's plan coming to me in one horrifying swoop.

"She wants one last miracle," I say. "One big swooping drain of power."

"What does that mean, though?" Roe asks, and I can tell by their voice that they know exactly what it means.

"She's going to kill them," I say at last. "She's going to kill them all, tonight."

43

WE MOVE QUICKLY. RENÉ STEERS ME BY the shoulder into the passenger seat of his rented car. Nuala, Aaron, and Manon in the back.

"Maeve," he says, eyes on the tree-lined country road. "We have not known each other very long, and I feel as though I never have anything pleasant to tell you. Please know that this is very out of character for me, and that I don't enjoy it at all."

A deer trots across his path and René swerves easily around it, not even mentioning its glowing yellow eyes or pretty, nimble body.

"What unpleasant thing do you need to tell me?" I ask. "Other than the fact that two hundred-odd kids could die tonight?"

"Well, it's about who else could die, too," he says. He coughs. Pauses. Collects himself. "You, Maeve. Your death has gone from a matter of being sad yet broadly irrelevant—as all our deaths will someday be—to being a matter of national importance. If you die, the Housekeeper is on the wind. A spirit no longer tied to either a human form or an enchanted object, like a tarot card. She will be loose, a curse on the country. A poison in the air."

"And what would that look like?"

"Like famine. Like drought. Like disease. Impossible to say." The countryside gets deeper and denser as he drives, the streets darkening even as night's curtain starts to lift. "She is in you now. You haven't fully given her 'the house' yet, as you say, but she's in your blood, your bones. Like a virus. What we do not want is the virus to become airborne."

"I guess there's a simple solution," I reply. "And it's to not die."

The plan, insofar as we can make one, is drawn out on a series of napkins using eyeliner. Nuala draws a map from memory.

"As we know," Nuala says, sketching wildly, "the Lodge has no road access. The closest we can get is the deer park about half a mile away, where there's a car park for dog walkers and the like. So we need to get there on foot, and through the deer park."

Aaron reaches forward to me, his hand on my shoulder. Our gifts chatter to each other like birds. We see what's up ahead; we chart the comet's trajectory.

"She's put out some precautions," Aaron says. In the mirror I can see that his eyes are shut, brow furrowed. "She's got people blocking the road."

"Where?" Nuala asks. "Where on the map?"

She marks it off. It's about a quarter mile from the car park.

"D'accord," René says. "Fin and I will drive up ahead and distract the people on the road. We can do a good job of a doddering middle-aged couple, can't we, dearest?" He looks slyly at Nuala in the rearview mirror, as if invoking an old pact. She rolls her eyes at him. "You know, kids, your wise elder here spent the nineties conning tourists on the Riviera with me," he says ruefully. "The best pickpocket I've ever known."

"Shush, René," Nuala snaps. "The six of you will have to go on foot. We will meet you at the Lodge."

"Then what?" Manon asks.

"Then get through to the Lodge from the back entrance, the

same route Aaron and Maeve took last time. Nobody noticed them because they were coming from behind and up the hill. They were in a blind spot, the building blocking their approach," Nuala says, making dotted lines on the napkin to signify our progress. "René and I will meet you at the Lodge, and then we can go from there: confront Dorey, use our combined power to interrupt this . . . this . . ."

"Massacre," Aaron says.

Nuala tests her mouth around the word, as if she can't quite believe it is being used in a practical context. "Yes. Well, we'll interrupt her, disarm her, get her under control."

"With what?" I ask, thinking that I can't rely on handfuls of petals for a second time.

"With these," Nuala says, producing a pack of tarot cards and Sister Assumpta's letter opener.

"How did you get those?" I ask, taking them from her.

"Like I said," René replies, "the best pickpocket I've ever known."

"I kept ahold of them after the last ritual," Nuala says, catching my eye in the mirror. "Tarot is your biggest magical strength, Maeve. Always has been. You need your strength to defeat Dorey."

"She has the harnessed power of her little saints," I say, turning to look at her. "And I have a letter opener, and cards that were made in a board game factory."

"Aaron says she gets her hooks in everyone, doesn't she?" Nuala replies, with a glimmer in her eye. "Well, tarot hooks people, too, doesn't it?"

Aaron's face is white. "The roadblocks are coming up," he says.

Nuala holds her daughter's face and kisses it gently. There's a flicker of something between them. The fact that your mother was not destined to live with you is not an easy thing to hear. But Manon is beginning to believe in the complexity of rituals, I think. Her stubborn, logical brain is beginning to accept that not everything is linear.

"Manon," Nuala says softly. "My goddess baby. You change into Dorey as soon as you can. Send as many kids out of the Lodge and toward us. We'll scoop them up."

"What about me, Nuala?" Aaron says, in what is supposed to sound like a joke but comes out like a very earnest plea for approval.

"You, Aaron," she says to him squarely, "are proof that someone can come back from anything." René looks at her oddly then, as if this might be a promise. "Those kids, once they get out—Aaron, they'll need you more than ever."

"I'll be there," he says urgently. "I promise you. You've taken me in like family, and . . ."

Nuala puts her hand up. "There's no time, pet."

"All right, then," René says. "It's showtime."

44

RENÉ AND NUALA LEAVE US ON THE SIDE OF the road, where the other three join us. The ocean's oily gleam is just barely visible in the distance. We are at the edge of Kilbeg. The edge of the country. The edge of the world.

"You know," Manon says, once her parents have disappeared from view, "nowhere else in the world has light like this."

"What do you mean?" Fiona asks.

"It is because Kilbeg is in the southwest. There is nothing between you and the Atlantic, no country before you reach America. Only a long gap of ocean. It's why you have this kind of blue, melancholy light. I love it. I was not expecting to love it. But I do."

"I've never thought about it, but I suppose you're right. It is beautiful," Fiona replies. "I just thought we had mizzle."

"Mizzle?"

"Mist and drizzle."

Manon laughs. "I didn't know that word," she says. "But it's good."

Fi keeps her eyes on the ground, but I can see a slow smile growing on her face. The gems on Manon's rings glow in Kilbeg's famous blue light, and I wonder if she's changed her mind about Fiona.

I can hear birds. Light, conversational chirping, like two people lying awake in bed and wondering whether they should bother to get up. I see Paolo fluttering overhead. He knows where we are headed. We trudge through farmland, hopping gates, hearing the rustle of sheep frightened by the newcomers. Their eyes light up under our phone flashlights. They bleat at us, telling us to go away.

We trudge, wish for better footwear, better weather, warmer clothes. We are still wearing the stupid formal clothes that we wore to St. Bernadette's. We walk two by two along the fences. Lily and Aaron are in the lead, Fiona and Manon behind, Roe and I bringing up the rear.

"You OK?" I ask them, not knowing what answer I'm looking for. What could possibly be OK about this?

"Yeah. You?"

"Yeah."

The world brightens gradually, with the thin blue light that precedes dawn. As dawn begins to rise, Roe and I watch as Manon's hand silently takes hold of Fiona's. We wonder, briefly, if this is an attempt at gift-merging. But it isn't. It's just hands, ripe for the holding.

We fall back slightly, to give them space.

"René talked to me," I say quietly.

"Oh yeah?"

"Yeah. He said that if I were to die, the Housekeeper would be loose on the wind, and the whole country might go under. Famine, drought, whatever."

"Heavy," Roe says, kicking at a clod of dirt. "Listen, if you're going to die, just . . . don't, OK?"

I laugh. Actually laugh out loud, startling the sheep.

"I'm serious, Maeve. You don't have to be my girlfriend. You don't have to be my friend, even, if you don't want to be. But I need to know you're out in the world like I'm out in the world. You're my compass. You're true north. The magnets would fall dead. The arrow would spin. I would walk in circles forever, and I'd never go in a straight line again."

"And what's a compass," I say, trying to laugh, uncomfortable with grand statements like this, "but another little machine that's trying to impress you?"

They look at me oddly. "It's not done between you and me, is it, Maeve?"

"I don't know," I say. Because I don't. How could it ever be really over? But could I really be brave enough to start it again?

A picture starts to form in my head. Roe trying to make their career work as a touring rock musician while I sweat it out as the Housekeeper at home. Me getting resentful. The phone calls getting further and further apart. Anger settling in. And not just anger, but dislike. Fights. Rage.

"I kissed you, you know," I say quietly. "In the passage."

"Wow. How was it?"

"Hot," I reply, because it was. "You were trying to rob me."

"I don't think it's fair that you got a last kiss and I didn't."

And there, under the tortured glance of a sideways-slanting hawthorn tree, Roe kisses me for perhaps the last time.

·)) ● ((·

We come to the woodland that the pedestrian car park joins on to. There's no going around it. We must go through and lose what little light we have by walking through a bracket of trees.

I can feel our bravery fall away as we journey into the woods. We are not built for this. We are not the folksy teenagers you see in adventure stories. There is no one who's a dab hand at archery, or who can chart our journey by looking at our last few visible stars. I try to channel the Housekeeper's confidence, as she is the only one capable of navigating a darkened forest, but my own human fear clouds my judgment. I can hear our steps. Feel the vast, dense silence of the woods. The dampness of everything, the sharp teeth of nature.

"I hate this," Lily finally says. "It's too dark. And still. But not still enough."

"We're almost out," Aaron says. "Look, there's the Lodge."

There it is, the building perched on a slope that may or may not have been built by fairies. It's too far away to make anything out except the white smoke trailing into the sky.

I feel the weight of Aaron's hand on my sleeve again, and a cacophony of images fall into my head.

"They're burning everything," I say, terror creeping back into my voice. "They're burning furniture. Bedsheets. Clothes."

"No evidence," Aaron says coldly. "No witnesses."

We remain still, bearing witness. Bedsheets, blankets, clothing. Stray hairs, skin cells, period stains. The last of what was human about the Children of Brigid evaporating into the cold morning air.

"There's a fence over there," Lily whispers, motioning her head to the left. "We just need to follow the fence, right, and that will lead to a gate, won't it?"

"That's sort of the rule of fences," Roe murmurs. "There's usually a gate of some kind, somewhere."

The bonfires, huge as they are, have not been burning long. You can still see the shapes of the furniture they were meant to destroy. It feels poorly planned, as if this idea came together quickly. Chairs are not broken down for easy burning, but just tossed on the blaze.

We crouch down by a brick enclosure that was probably meant to house bins, if the road had ever been built, if the bin men ever came.

We watch the Children trail in and out like ants, furniture in their hands. They're young. So young.

"She can't mean to get rid of all of them, can she?" Fiona murmurs.

"She will have gotten her favorites out early," Aaron replies. "They're on the roads, patrolling the area. Hopefully not giving Nuala and René too much trouble."

"Don't worry about those two old showboaters," Manon says. "They can fool anyone."

"Speaking of," Fi says, "what the hell do we do now?"

"I need to get as many of them away from the building as possible," Manon says. "I must become Dorey."

"Manon, you can't," Fiona says. "What if your face slips? What if she catches you?"

"That's why I'm not going inside. Just herding these strays toward the road, like the deer. Fin and René can look after them, help snap them out of it."

"What?" Roe asks. "With magic, or just by being decent people?"

"A little of column A, a little of column B."

"You need to slip inside undetected," Manon says. "So, small groups. Take Fiona, to heal you if you get hurt. And Aaron, so you can see what is happening around every corner. Fuse gifts where you can."

Manon turns to the O'Callaghans. "You need to find weaknesses in the building. Maeve and Aaron's visions: it was choking, smoke. She is planning a bigger fire of some kind. We will need to get out those who are trapped within. You must create escapes, make doorways, cause distractions. You are a demolition crew. Can you do this?"

Lily and Roe look at each other, unsure. "We can try," Lily says haltingly.

"You two will follow me. I will appear as Dorey," Manon says. She commands her little troop like a general. "We will attack from the front. Maeve, Aaron, and Fiona will go around the back. There must be a back entrance. Are we all clear?"

Fiona looks at her worriedly.

"I just don't think . . ."

But we don't hear what Fiona doesn't think, because Manon grabs her and kisses her on the mouth.

"In a few seconds I'm going to look like an old fascist," Manon says. "And then who knows what will happen? If someone has to die, I think it would be better if it were me. Trickster gods are useless things, really. But I can't die and not have kissed you, Fiona. I'm sorry I couldn't say that earlier. Or"—she glances at the rest of us—"in private."

I wonder if this is what it's like during war. Everybody kissing.

We help Manon construct an image of Dorey. All of Aaron's memories of Dorey melt into mine and then pool softly into Manon's demigod body, like liquid clay into a golden mold. My knowledge of Dorey is limited: a handful of meetings, all of them short. But Aaron's feels infinite. Not just the conversations they've had, but the way they have lingered on in his mind, contorting the way he thinks. Her sitting with him, taking his hands in hers. Her saying that she never had a son, but if she'd had one, she would have liked him to be just like Aaron. Dorey as mother, Dorey as boss, Dorey as friend. Dorey asking about Matthew. Dorey telling Aaron that the only hope for his humanity is to save as many people from Hell as is possible, through whatever means necessary.

Manon changes before us. Her skin luminous, her hair between ash blond and steel gray. She is austere, impeccable, terrifying. She is Dorey.

And then, like it's nothing, she strolls into the courtyard of the Lodge and starts directing Children like they're traffic. Roe and

Lily follow her, their faces hopefully unknown to the disoriented Children.

"We need to move," Aaron says. "It's getting light."

I burrow down into my gift, calling on the Housekeeper. *Show me where the real Dorey is,* I say. *Show me where she is so we can end this.*

"Maeve," Fiona says. "We can share gifts, too, remember?"

I smile and reach my hand out to her. And as we stand together, I see the colored lights of the minds around me, but I also see what Fiona must see when she enables her gift. I see wounds that need healing. Rips and sinews. Scar tissue, low red blood cell counts, the papery skin of malnourishment. I see everyone, all at once, in their entirety. Their vulnerability, their confusion.

I gather up Dorey in my mind. *Where is she, where is she?*

She emerges like a pale blue dot. And she is beneath our feet.

"She's beneath us?" Fiona says, confused. "How is she *beneath* us?"

"Basement," Aaron says.

The edges of the property are curiously quiet. We creep around, finding half-completed walls that were supposed to contain gardens but only hold the frozen winter mud.

There is no shortage of emergency exits, staff doors, side entrances. It's picking the right one. I hold on to Aaron, and it's just as Manon says: I can see which corridors are clear, and which are minutes away from being walked down by an errant Child dragging furniture. Finally, we settle on a window. A window in a wing of the hotel that is completely unoccupied, the furniture having already been cleared out.

For all the Wicca and magical study we have between us, we get into the Lodge the old-fashioned way. We smash the window with a construction cinder block. Everything about it feels juvenile, silly, beneath us, but, as Aaron says—while throwing the cinder block—the only thing that is beneath us is Dorey.

The cinder block sails through the window with brutal strength, so straightforward and simple that I feel a huge affection for the big, stupid object.

We're in a reception room, the kind of light, airy space where you might have a wedding if you weren't religious. The floors are hardwood and covered in scratches where furniture has obviously been dragged out. The emptiness is frightening, and we are small animals on a large, empty plain, our vulnerability clear to anyone who might look our way. Fiona is disturbed in a way she is struggling to name. She just looks guilty and confused, wondering why this place upsets her, why she didn't push to do something about it before. I realize then that this is the first time she's seen the Lodge—how could the others really have known how bad it was before now?

"Come on," I say quickly. "We need to look for a staircase going down."

We find it eventually: a narrow staircase that winds downward, becoming wider as we descend under the grounds of the unfinished hotel. We reach a small room with an open elevator shaft, wires and exposed brick glaring at us like an attack dog. The room has white walls, a white desk, and white chairs, making it clinical, eerie, and the empty shaft even more incongruous. There are double doors behind it.

"I suppose this was supposed to be like . . . a health spa or something?" I say, feeling queasy. I remember going on a spa day with Mum and Jo once, all fluffy robes and heated relaxation chairs and sitting in the sauna for as long as you can stand it. The fake light, the strange music. Complimentary things that you didn't want, like lukewarm green tea.

"She's behind there," I say quietly. "Behind those doors."

"Fiona," Aaron says. "Don't listen to anything she has to say about you."

"What do you mean?" Fiona says, looking surprised.

"She gets little ideas into people's brains. It sneaks up on you. Particularly people like you."

"What do you mean, people like me?"

"Confident people, strong people, who might think they can't be touched."

We go through the double doors and find a swimming pool. In an effort to avoid the obvious ugliness of having a spa in a basement with no natural light, the whole room is decorated in an ancient-Roman facade. Alabaster walls. Sculptures of giant vases. Spotlights bedded into the wall to look like soft candlelight. It was almost luxury, once. It was intended to be luxury.

The pool is filled with things, but no water. Tree branches are piled in the center of the oval-shaped hole, which is really what a pool is when there's no water.

Dorey is standing on the other side.

"Hello," she says. Then cocks her head at Fiona. "Oh. You've brought a friend. Fiona—huge congrats on the TV role. You must be so thrilled, to finally get out from under your mother's feet."

I feel Fiona wince beside me. Dorey continues. "It will be a good opportunity to show her who you are, what you can do. You know?"

I can feel this getting into Fiona's brain, pushing on a domino that is connected to many more. She shakes her head, trying to shy away.

Two people emerge behind Dorey. The guy who held me last time, and a pale girl with hair the color of weak tea. They are holding a box of something, flower petals it looks like, and they begin scattering them into the pool.

"Hemlock, Maeve," Dorey says. "It was you who gave me the idea."

The poison flower smoke that I summoned.

I don't want to get into a conversation with her. I don't want her insane rationale. I just walk around the circumference of the pool, come face-to-face with her.

"What are you doing, Dorey? What *is* this?"

Her eyes are sharp, her gaze reptilian. She is wearing her robes again. She pulls out a deck of tarot.

"Can I interest you in a reading, Maeve?"

We lock eyes then. And for a few seconds there is no age gap, no hatred, no judgment. Just two witches, trying to outfox each other.

"I'll go first," she says, and picks one from the middle. It's the Hanged Man. Again.

"People get so frightened when they see him. But it's just as you said last time, Maeve. It doesn't mean hanging. It means discomfort. The struggle before victory," Dorey says.

She examines the card, turning it over. "Of course," she continues, "sometimes it *does* mean hanging."

And with that, Dorey places the card gently on my chest, and a surge of energy so great comes out of her that it casts a luminous white light around the room. It is so beautiful that it takes me a second to realize that my feet are hovering off the ground, and two more to realize that I am choking.

45

I AM HOVERING ABOVE THE GROUND, STRAN-
gled by an invisible rope, and I assume that I will die this way. My
vision begins to blot and blacken, and I feel what René warned me
about. The Housekeeper starts to panic, starts to worry that she is
moments away from losing her host. If I had finished the ritual, the
official acceptance of the Housekeeper, things might be different. But
Dorey interrupted with her brainwashed police to make sure that
very thing didn't happen.

Suddenly I am cut loose and fall feetfirst into the pool.

I hear the crack of bones breaking before I feel them, the xylo-
phone smash of ribs separating.

A voice from above me.

"You're not the only one who has been gathering power, you
know."

The branches around me are juniper. They use it to make gin.
The sap is flammable, I hear from my Housekeeper self. She who
knows everything.

"Maeve, hold on!" Fiona screams.

I'm lying on the tree branches, unable to move my head, and
I can just about swivel my eyes to Fiona. There are people holding
her—more flower throwers, who have emerged from nowhere. I

close my eyes. *She was touched by the same magic you were touched by. You do not need to talk in order to talk. You do not need to touch, to touch.*

I find her, talk to her. *Fiona, calm down.*

They have me, Fiona thinks.

Fi, you can heal me from there. I know you can.

She finds her strength, even though she is out of her mind with fear. My ribs draw back together. Fiona sews me up lovingly, like an old rag doll. I feel the spiky branches underneath me, the tiles underneath that. I push myself up, still feeling the red heat of rope burn around my neck. Still feeling the brief moments when I was the Hanged Man.

I look around for Aaron, who is being held by the magic of another Child. Dorey has not been stingy with her power. I remember what Aaron told me months ago: that the Children store their magic in people, places, and things. They move it around, like money in a bank. The Child—or perhaps, the saint—is standing over Aaron as he twists in agony. He's on his stomach, grabbing at some invisible obstruction in his back.

Of course. The Ten of Swords. One of the most violently unsubtle cards in the deck, and of course a rookie would choose it to inflict the most pain. But nobody ever thinks about the upside of the Ten of Swords: that once you get to ten, things can't get any worse. You either die or you get up. And I know Aaron. He always gets up.

Dorey glares down at me. "You might be the Housekeeper, Maeve. But don't forget: I'm the lady of this particular house. You're a guest, after all."

Aaron and Fiona are thrown into the pool, the crunch of their bodies hitting the branches.

"You see, darling, you might contain the wrath of the House-keeper, but I have the power of the Well. It's been channeling through me for weeks, straight from my *very* committed young saints. You have the power of one card, and, well . . . I have the power of them all."

Despite having just been strangled by an invisible rope, my first thought is: *But how?* The cards are metaphors, symbols, flat draw-ings that originated hundreds of years ago. If the Housekeeper can have her mortal body trapped inside a card, does that mean a card can be used on a mortal body?

"The Devil card," Dorey says, sounding like a schoolteacher. She holds the card high in her hands, showing a man and woman chained to the huge beast that rules over them. "The funny thing about the devil, the thing everyone gets wrong, is that he's not evil in himself. The devil was sent to *test* mankind. How can faith be real if it's not tested? Book of Job, Aaron. You know it all, don't you?"

Aaron says nothing, but I can feel the scripture bouncing in his head as he searches it for clues.

Suddenly I feel my feet bind together, the sensation of iron on bare skin. I look down, feeling the heavy chains pierce at my skin, but not seeing anything.

I look to Fiona next to me, hands invisibly tethered, knees on the floor—like a pilgrim at prayer. At first, I think she is blowing on her hands; then I realize she's composing a very quiet whistle. What on *earth*?

More people begin to file in. The gaunt faces of the half-starved Children, two hundred or so, minus two. Lorna and Sophia. Perhaps more.

Then it hits me.

The entire country is going to wake up to the news of dead teenagers.

"Welcome, everyone," Dorey says. "I hope no one minds a little pagan pageantry this evening. Or this morning. It's dawn now, isn't it?"

They fill the space, lining up alongside the pool, hands together. Their expressions are blank, addled, lacking the depth for even basic confusion.

That's it: that's the frightening thing. There is no *confusion* here. Simply a tacit understanding of what is happening.

"The English language," Dorey begins, "is a dishonest one. Built around verbs, nouns, objects. But what's an object? A chair, a rug, a bed?"

She gestures roundly, as if referring to the bonfires outside.

"But these are just delusions we create for ourselves, things we make in our earthly bodies to distract ourselves from our heavenly ones. They're distractions, really. Things that cloud our vision."

Aaron recoils at this. Is he remembering, like I remember, the speeches he used to give about distractions? About how being gay was . . . what was it again? A bug on a windshield, blurring your vision?

"When we center objects—chairs, phones, technology, our bodies—we let our own clownish self-regard win. We block out our channel to God."

She holds up the pack of cards again. "These," she says, "are an example. Signs and symbols. Perversions of biblical verse. The Hermit, the Emperor, the Sun. The Wheel. And this." She pulls out another card, holds it up. "Judgment."

Judgment. A group of people, standing in coffins, hearing an angel's horn. The last day.

"Judgment refers to the day we leave our bodies behind. Our ego behind. We forget all the objects. We just become essence. Being. Spirit."

Surely not even Dorey is this evil? Not even her?

"Society tries to make us forget that, truly, our lives on earth are a long car journey. And when we are on a very long journey, we forget that the destination is the real thing. Sometimes we forget that there will come a time when we get out of the car. But here I am, talking in objects again."

Power is drawn through the Well by sacrifice. By self-punishment. By martyrdom. And so this, this final great act of martyrdom, will draw it out at its fullest. Dorey cannot drain the Well artificially, so she has to draw it out with blood. By perverting how the Well works. By instructing these people to die.

"But there is one object, one noun that matters. And that's fire."

She pulls out the Ace of Wands. The suit of fire.

And just as I was choked by invisible ropes, and we are bound now by invisible chains, the branches begin to smolder very real smoke with invisible fire. The hemlock catches flame, and a girl in flip-flops starts to cough.

Aaron, Fiona, and I are the only ones in the pool, and the smoke reaches us first. I can feel it, tickling at my nose, daring me to open my mouth. Fiona, refusing to be terrified, pushes her power through me. Healing, molding itself into preservation. She wills our lungs to reject the smoke, pushes it out of our bodies. I can feel her experimenting, feel her using her gift to its very limit. I remember the early days, the tennis court days, when she used to make the skin on an apple grow back. How much stronger we've all become since then, the more we grow together, the more we push one another.

We think in gifts and talents. Specific roles, specific character traits, specific things we can and can't do. But maybe by typecasting ourselves we were also limiting ourselves. Perhaps there are no limits at all.

If Fiona can push the smoke out of our bodies, what can I do?

I center my gift, pull at the deep roots of my telepathy. I can read minds, but how can that help me here, when everyone's mind is so clearly yoked to Dorey? She has ropes on all of them.

Yes, the Housekeeper whispers. *But that also means that they are roped to her.*

And so what can I do?

Oh, I can make them pull back.

I channel myself through Fiona, feeling everyone's hurt, the deep, sickened pain in their bodies, the hunger. Bruises that appear for no reason and do not instantly heal. Can I send that pain back along the string, like sound through two tin cans?

I picture this string, and then I picture yanking on it, like tug-of-war.

And to my immense satisfaction, Dorey stumbles forward. She recovers quickly, her expression flickering in confusion.

Aaron clocks it. Remembers his own gift, his own sensitivity, and I feel his presence behind me, tugging the rope with me. We are making her feel the pain in the room, the weakness.

The smoke rises, collecting in the eaves of the fake Roman baths plonked in the middle of the Irish countryside. There is more coughing. How long will it take for hemlock smoke to fill a room like this?

There is movement now, panic. The room has felt the tug on Dorey's string, felt their own existence once more. A trickle of awareness seems to enter them. *What are we doing?*

They start to cluster nearer to her, like sheep sheltering from the rain.

She puts her hands on the card again. "Three of Swords," she calls out to us, still locked by the Devil's chains in the pool. I feel the card before I see it, feeling each sword scratch at my chest. Hot blades and blood.

"Fiona," I whimper.

She pushes the swords away, imagining a shield for herself. I can feel her struggling against it. But the smoke continues to rise.

There is panic now, raw and from the gut. A room full of people realizing that they do not wish to die. People charging at the locked double doors of the basement wellness center, a location so ironic that it is bound to feature in tomorrow's papers.

This was not her plan. Not remotely.

I look to Dorey, all of her energy focused on tethering her followers, on attacking us with the cards. Fiona, sweating with effort, healing having turned to pure defense. She's a warrior now. Her brow wet, losing hold on her own body as she protects everyone else's. I see her beginning to wheeze, her complexion graying. The hemlock is getting in. She cannot hold like this forever.

And just as I am beginning to think that Fiona will break, Dorey falls. Into the earth, into the pool, into the pit with us.

I look up and see Manon, who has been here all along, and has just pushed her.

46

DOREY FALLS SOFTLY ONTO A STACK OF smoldering tree branches, but her concentration snaps. The heaviness lifts, the spell broken.

Aaron fights his way through the smoke, trying to get to the other side of the pool, his shirt over his mouth. Dorey is a puppet master, and now the tarot itself has become her puppet. But it's not real, or permanent. Aaron can get up after the Ten of Swords has been stuck through his back, just as I can get up after the Hanged Man. These are shadow puppets, dancing on the wall.

But be that as it may, we can't do this much longer. There's already hemlock in our throats.

Then the Roman facade, made of plaster and fiberglass, starts to shift. We can see nothing through the smoke now, but we hear the sound of bricks hitting the floor, of dust tumbling from the ceiling. The Lodge is coming down.

I feel for my cards. I need to trap Dorey, while the chaos of the moment is confusing the Children who might still try to protect her. I need to get close to her, to let the wisdom and the power of the Housekeeper flow. I am relying on intuition, relying on her to steer me, but all I can think of is how my body hurts, how my lungs feel blackened by smoke and my thoughts gripped by terror.

Then, all at once, there's a deafening burst of sound, an explosion, a bomb, and my ears are left ringing. Fresh, clean air tickles my cheek. I look up as the smoke starts to gently dissipate, and I can see two pairs of feet. Battered red Converse, and lace-up combat boots. The O'Callaghan siblings have just blown a hole in the eaves of this false Roman bath. The leisure complex must be wider than the building itself, because they've found a spot near the ceiling that opens onto the grounds outside.

Of course. Roe and Lily together: machinery and electricity. Together that spells knowledge, explosives, demolition. Roe worms their way into a building and Lily fills it with sparks. It feels apt, in a way. Leave it to these two to tear down the world and make it anew.

The smoke isn't dissipating fast enough. I can see Roe and Lily scrabbling at the foundations, trying to widen the hole, creating an escape hatch. Children scurry toward it, their devotion having evaporated within the human instinct for survival.

"Get back," Roe roars at the panicking crowd. "We need to make another explosion, and you need to stand back. You'll get hurt."

Manon tries to control them, tries to shout commands, but her powers are no good here. It doesn't matter who she can transform into, or what subtle trick she can play. They just want out. Now.

"Fall *back*!" she screams. "Fall back, or we will all be killed."

But no one can hear, or at least no one listens. They bottleneck while trying to climb out. The hole is at least two people wide, but it's useless when everyone is cramming toward it, climbing over one another to get out. If Dorey doesn't kill them, they'll kill themselves trying to escape her.

The fresh air from outside is being blocked by the cram of

bodies, and the air quickly becomes thick again. I am trapped by a tangle of charred tree branches, hot under my feet, even though there is no fire visible. Just ghostly smoke.

Dorey is across the pool, upright and rumpled. Her concentration was broken by the fall, but she's regained her control. She's holding out the Ace of Cups. It's a card I've always liked: a goblet overfilling with water, a sign of the regenerative power of love, of friendship, of loyalty. But this is not what it looks like in Dorey's hands. She holds it high, above Aaron, as he chokes on water that I cannot see. He is drowning. Drowning inside his own body, eyes bulging, hands reaching at nothing.

Fiona is still fighting off the poison, protecting all of us from the smoke. She is trying to extend her protection to Manon, too, to make sure the air doesn't invade her body. I wrap my arms around her and try to channel my power into hers. Her skin is slick with sweat, her hair sticking to her scalp. There's nothing left, no fight. Paolo swoops in through the breached ceiling, feeling her exhaustion. He flies to Fiona, wings beating frantically.

Her breath rasps as I hold her to me. I don't know what to do: keep her upright, or leap toward Dorey.

Everywhere there are people, everywhere there is panic and screaming, crying and vomiting. These kids who have spent months fearing Hell are now in the middle of it.

The gap begins to open, and I can see Nuala tearing at the rubble with her hands, René reaching down to pull people out. One. Two. Three. Four Children. Five. The hole widens. I can see more of the dawn light.

But it's not enough. The Children from the road are here now, and whether they knew about Dorey's massacre plan or not, they can tell their queen is in trouble. They are her favorites, her chosen ones, her real Children. They are trying to bark orders at the escapees, shoving and throwing punches as though they were in a bar brawl. They cannot afford to lose this tiny power that Dorey has gifted them.

The Children still trying to escape are skinny and confused, and look around frantically. They are still too damaged to fight back, too used to orders to act beyond them. Who are we, after all? A group of people their own age whom they have been coached to hate.

"Maeve!" I hear Lily scream. I look around, and there she is, jumping into the smoked-out cavern that was once the swimming pool. "I'll hold Fi, you get Aaron."

She grabs hold of Fiona, who's still trying to force the smoke out of everyone's lungs. Fiona falls back into Lily's arms, her body limp, her jaw still set with effort. This is taking everything, everything inside of her. If it doesn't kill them, it might kill her. But Lily's fresh power enters Fiona like an adrenaline shot, and she steels herself.

I try to get to Aaron, who is still drowning on the Ace of Cups, the fire of the branches invisible but still burning hot. I start to retch, climbing through the gray clouds, my skin screaming with the pain of invisible fire. But I get there. I get to Aaron and Dorey, grabbing a smoldering tree branch and striking it across her like a whip.

Dorey jumps, drops the card. Aaron lies motionless, the drowning spell broken.

"Dorey," I scream through the chaos. "Come on. You're done."

Dorey looks around, her expression glazed, almost blissful as she takes in the chaos.

"As long as there's suffering, Maeve," she says, smiling coyly at the people trying to escape, "I'll have strength."

I stand there, my skin white-hot. The air might be letting the smoke escape, but it's also stoking the fire.

"As long as there's suffering," I repeat, "you'll have a use."

Dorey looks confused.

"I have cards, too, Dorey."

I lift my deck up, pluck the top card. I know what it is. I don't even have to look.

"How can you . . . ?" She looks at it, wary of the trick. "You can't draw the Housekeeper card if you *are* the Housekeeper card."

"No," I agree. "But you can make a new card."

And suddenly, I am back in the world of the Housekeeper. How did they do it? Fake Aaron had split a hare over her body, had read texts of Latin and Greek. I have no hares, no texts, no directions. I have only my letter opener, my cards, and the counsel of a demon.

How? I ask her. *How?*

She told you herself, the Housekeeper answers. *It's very hard to make someone unwrite their beliefs. But you can bolt on new beliefs to existing ones quite easily.*

I remember that day in her office. She had been so interested in Aaron's "predicament," and she was right to be. He will spend the rest of his life trying to shake off the belief that he's going to Hell.

But what does Dorey believe?

I hold the card in my hands and tunnel into Dorey's mind. All of the things she promised people: safety, justice, security. A better society, with straightforward values. She really believes all that, in the same way Heather really believed that the Children were the same as any other big, dubious corporation.

What if I held her to that promise?

I am deep in her mind now, dancing on the copper spine that holds her entire worldview together. She is trying to make the world better. Cleaner. Simpler. Safer. It doesn't matter if a few lambs get led to slaughter; we're talking big picture here.

OK, Dorey, I think. The Housekeeper and I are twins now: all of my sight, and all of her power. *I'm going to hold you to that.*

It's like I've flicked a switch inside the Housekeeper. There's a sense of darkness being suddenly shattered by piercing light, and it's so bright that my brain bursts into a flowering migraine. The pain is so strong that I have to cover my right eye with my hand as I lift the card high.

The ink drains from the Housekeeper.

I pick up the knife Sister Assumpta gave me. I open the old scar, the wound I opened to save Lily. The place where the Housekeeper's spirit first nestled within me. I feel my own warmth drip onto the card, and watch the blood turn to ink, and the ink turn to an image. Then I take one step toward Dorey and press the card, still wet, onto her chest.

"Dorey," I whisper.

It begins to dawn on her, her icy blue eyes widening as she takes her fate in.

"Your power is unfathomable, Dorey. And you won't use it to trap people anymore. You'll use it to free them instead. Safety, justice, security. All the things you believe in."

She sinks to her knees, the selfishness leaving her, the greed leaving her, the hatred leaving her. She is only a tool now. A thing that people can call on.

It's working, I realize. It's working.

"You will serve within your own card, Dorey. You said you wanted to create a world where people were safe and untroubled. You will keep that promise. And you will do it through service, and love, and devotion. Not through corruption or isolation."

The smoke covers her, and I look up to see the winter sunlight peeping through the ceiling. The Children are all outside now, thank god. I can only see my people now, gazing down at me in the smoldering pool. My family. My people. René, Manon, Nuala, Roe.

Fiona is on the other side of the pool. She is clutching on to Lily, gasping, her black hair sodden with sweat, Paolo gently pecking at the strands.

Aaron is coughing up water I can't see. But alive.

The wind that bent the hawthorn trees comes rushing over the hill and fills the destroyed basement swimming pool. This all started in a basement, and it looks like it will end in one, too. The wind rustles Dorey's robes, stirs the burnt branches, and creates a cloud of black snow among the ash. The Irish mizzle touches her skin, and she is gone. Dissolved, like the memory of a dream.

And what's left of Isadora Manford is this: a tarot card lying facedown on the blackened tiles.

I bend to turn the card over. I see a woman: white hair, white eyes, standing under a proscenium arch. And written underneath:

THE TRAPPED DORE

"The Trapped Dore," Roe reads aloud. "Oh. Wow. I get it."

THE TRAPPED D ORE

THE HANGED ONE

ACE OF CUPS

47

WE LIMP BACK TO THE CARS LIKE SOLDIERS. We move silently through the countryside, the Lodge smoldering behind us. We can already hear sirens in the distance. The bonfires have gone out of control and begun to spread to the gorse bushes and the farmland that surrounds us.

"This is why," Nuala says quietly, "you do not build a hotel on a fairy ring."

Someone else will have to scoop up the Children. Someone else will have to put out the fires. There's only so much we can do, and we've done it.

Manon holds Fiona's head in her lap on the long car journey home. Fiona's lips bloodless, her body curled up like a baby. Her vocal cords fried. Poor, beautiful Fiona, who never wanted to be a healer, and who almost killed herself protecting people who will never know enough to thank her.

The rest is a blur.

Time passes like the days following a funeral or a natural disaster. Frozen time. The feeling that we are not quite off the hook: that any day now, we will be hauled in for questioning, or appear in the papers. That some ex-Child will rat us out, looking for retribution or revenge. But nothing. We keep close together. We pay attention to the news.

The deaths of Lorna McKeon and Sophia Mulready are eventually linked back to the existence of a religious fundamentalist group that had recently taken up residence in Kilbeg. It's strange. I read about it everywhere, but I never once come across Dorey's name, or the Children of Brigid. Just "a group" or "a cult." It makes me wonder—and maybe fear—how much power the Children might still have, and whether Dorey was just a figurehead in a long line of them.

Perhaps we'll find out.

"My best guess," Aaron says as he sweeps the floor of Sister Assumpta's office, "is that they'll cover this up and move on. They've tried three times now to secure a foothold in Kilbeg: once through me, once through Heather, and once through Dorey. Imagine the money they spent on that Lodge. I think they're going to give it up as a lost cause and go somewhere else."

Manon is on the old couch, reading the paper, looking for mentions of us. "Until the next ambitious person decides they can do what Dorey didn't?"

Aaron shrugs as if this is a possibility.

"And then what?" Fiona says. "We just do it all again?"

"We do it all again," I say, carrying in a crate of champagne that René bought. "But this time, it will be different. Because I'll be full Housekeeper."

We are back at St. Bernadette's to finish what we started. The party where I hand her the keys, and give her the house, my body, and my life. Whatever that means. Whatever she wants it to mean. At minimum, it will mean staying in Kilbeg. To protect the Well, just like she did. To help people who can't be helped elsewhere.

To sign over my youth and my will to this town, this county, these people.

Roe tunes their guitar. "This will be the last time I ask this, Maeve," they say, looking at me from under a mass of curls. "But are you sure?"

"I'm sure." I smile. "It's OK."

Fiona bites her lip. "But . . . it means you'll never leave."

"I never wanted to," I say, and I force my smile to grow wider. It's true that I've never had a dream of leaving Kilbeg, not the way Roe and Fiona have. But I did want to see things. There was a reason that Heather Banbury's promise of a summer in Japan was so tempting. I had envisioned gap years and travel, strange jobs in new places. Now I have only one job, one place. And it's forever.

The seats are all taken, so I set the champagne on the floor and lie on the new rug that René bought because he can't stand to look at ugly things. I stare at the ceiling. The crown molding, the high windows. It's a pretty prison, as prisons go.

Nuala and René come in from the car, carrying candles and fairy lights. They have not told anyone that they are back together, not officially, but body language tells you everything. The way they lean toward each other, watch each other, perform for each other. Even now, Nuala is fussing, telling René he knows nothing about practical things.

"You," she teases, "have never had to untangle a fairy light in your life, have you?"

"That depends," he says. "What is a fairy light?"

Roe and I both look away from them. It's too hard. Too painful. How on earth can we revisit the idea of a relationship when our destinies are so clearly separate? When I have to stay here, and Roe has to conquer the world? I raise my eyes and meet their gaze. Our minds briefly meet, an unspoken conversation. *Yes, we think. But they broke up for fifteen years, didn't they? And now look at them.*

"Maeve, if you're going to doom yourself for eternity," Aaron says, leaning the broom against the wall, "can we at least get drunk first?"

I look up at him. His hair is getting longer, and dull from the lack of sunshine. Tawny brown rather than blond. I pass him a bottle. A lot can happen in fifteen years.

We drink a lot, but we don't seem to get drunk. Or at least, I don't. Maybe everyone else is better at hiding it. Maybe we're too frightened. In any case, we take turns reading from *The Schools' Folklore Collection.*

"'It was said that all hares were witches in disguise,'" I read aloud. "'And they could change at will.'"

"Whoa," Roe says. "Hares had trans rights."

"I really hope that's not true," I say worriedly. "I don't like the idea of the Housekeeper taking dead hares as offerings if they really *are* witches."

"Speaking of folklore," Roe says, fiddling at the guitar. They start to sing.

"She appears in rare readings,
and only to young women,
and only in times of crisis."

Roe sings, and we sing along, most of us dodgy on the words, but all of us knowing the chorus.

"Ladies, meet the Housekeeper card.
Now, she can be your downfall,
or she can be your start.
And she only wants the best for you,
like she never got for herself.

She sees you at the bottom,

and she's coming down to help."

To think, the evidence was there all along. *She only wants the best for you.* We go around and around with the chorus, louder and louder. Lily on her cello, Manon at the piano. René's voice, low and lovely. Aaron not singing at all, but lip-synching. I wonder if singing is hard for him, the way touching is hard for him. It's too much like letting go.

Around and around, singing and singing, afraid to stop. It's like a spell of its own, like a chant for levitation. I feel as though it could lift us off the earth and into the rafters. The house starts to tremble. And just like in my failed ritual, the objects in the room begin to glow.

At first, I think I am the only one who can see them. But as I notice Fiona's eyes slide across the room, and Manon's, and Lily's, I realize that everyone can see the slight lunar glow around us, the pearly outline of enchantment. Everyone keeps singing. No one wants to break the spell, whatever the spell is.

Slowly, without interrupting the song, I begin to leave the room. Holding a lit pillar candle, Sister Assumpta's letter opener, and nothing else.

Ladies, meet the Housekeeper card.

Now, she can be your downfall . . .

I climb the stairs, like I've done a million times, my feet having memorized each dodgy floorboard. The banister glowing like a frosted tree.

Or she can be your start . . .

The door to 2A is ajar, and I see the Corridor behind. I push the door open, trying to glimpse inside without stepping inside.

And she only wants the best for you . . .

The furniture is gone. The carriage clock, gone. The room as old as it should be, maybe a hundred and fifty or two hundred years old. The walls scarred by shadows of where the paintings once were. Every painting gone.

Every painting except one.

I kneel in front of her with my big white candle. I can still hear the singing downstairs. The worlds are thinning once again—her world and mine conjoined, like twins.

"Hello," I begin. I try to be as reverent and as respectful as possible. I've spent enough time as the Housekeeper to know that she commands respect. "It's me. It's Maeve."

Of course she knows it's me. Of course she knows it's Maeve. The building rattles, like it's being buffeted by the sea.

"I want to help people. I want to protect them from the people they need protecting from. I want you to guide me. I want to give you your sight back. And I want to give you this house."

It sounds as though the roof slates are falling off, the noise like plates being flung across the sky.

"As a gift. It's all I have. And, well, myself."

The house seems to groan, the groan of a big dog finally stretching.

"Flourish. Grow. Protect. Don't live in a tarot card, for anyone to use and abuse. Live in this house. Let your spirit flow in here. Live forever, on the Well."

The house moans again, but subtler this time, like it's willing to listen.

"I own this house," I say loudly, standing up. I must make her respect me. "And when I die, I'll make sure there's someone else who understands and can carry on. There are seven people downstairs who understand already. Let me create a legacy. A legacy of protection, and magic, and grace. Not fear, or death, or abuse."

I keep listening, keep talking, trying to decipher the code of the building. I remember the first day I found the tarot cards, all those months ago. I was high on YouTube knowledge and pagan explanations. I told my father that the cards were made of paper and that paper was made from trees and that trees had consciousness. That we were all living and breathing together. I don't know if I really believed that then, but I believe it now.

"Didn't you give me this gift? Didn't you know I was coming?" I burrow down deep into the part of her that is already inside me. "You hoped for this, didn't you? You hoped for someone who would change things."

Silence. The house listens.

"Well, I'm here. I'm not perfect. But I'm trying."

I close my eyes and try to listen back. Listen to her, to the Well, to the ancientness around me. I don't hear anything: no voice in my head, no indication that my promise has been accepted. But there is a communication of sorts happening. A feeling inside, a feeling of padlocks and fine print.

I understand the conditions of the bargain without having it explained to me. I understand that I must protect Kilbeg above anything else. I understand that I will grow more powerful, but in that power, will also become a piece of state-owned property. Something that is never thanked, and only commented on when something goes wrong. Fundamental, like a road or a bridge. Hidden, like a sewer.

"I give you my life," I say out loud. "I'm giving you everything."

I look up, and the Corridor is starting to disappear. The thing that separates my consciousness from the Housekeeper is collapsing in on itself, the walls falling away, the world going dark, dissolving into history.

Soon it's only me, the knife, and the portrait. A spotlight in a dark, dark world. I am knelt before it like a pilgrim before a dead saint, and perhaps it's this notion that makes me want a souvenir. A toe, a finger, a hair. Anything to prove that I have collided with true holiness.

The knife rips through easily. I start with her—my—right hand and tear up through her—my—body, the blade snagging at the heart. There is a dimple in the wall behind, a place where the stone has degraded, and the knife gets caught in the grit. It's dusty, clay turned to powder, and I wriggle the knife around. Cutting her heart out, like the hunter in *Snow White*. Gray dust crumbles from the wall, blinding me briefly. The knife fumbles out of my hands, falling heavily to the floor.

The Housekeeper's heart flaps open like the door of an advent calendar. I push it with my fingers, but it won't settle back into place. The room starts to grow darker, and I'm conscious of being on an island with the portrait as the world falls around me. In a last, frantic act of . . . something, I yank out the heart of the painting and hold it in my fist.

It is the size and shape of a thumbprint.

Is it a coincidence? Can I believe in coincidences anymore?

I yank at the string holding my jet charm, the one I gave to protect Roe, and Roe gave to protect me. It fits in the heart's hollow, and the painting closes up the gap, healing under my fingers.

"I'll protect you," I say, "if you protect me."

It is the last thing I say to her before I am alone at the top of the staircase, and talking to her becomes simply talking to myself.

THE END

For the first few minutes, I cannot breathe.

It's a choking, heaving, undulating sensation of panic. I feel like a dark cloud is trapped between my neck and my guts, an expanding force that threatens to break my ribs if I don't smash them myself. I fall on my knees, hiccuping fear.

The lights. Oh, god, the lights. What was once the speckled light of many existences—people, creatures, friends, strangers, *life*—begins to pulsate like a migraine. All the agonies. There is a woman a quarter of a mile from here who is being mugged. A child in an upstairs bedroom who hasn't eaten dinner for two days. A boy, fourteen, walking and walking and walking because he is afraid to go home.

I don't feel it the way you feel news headlines. There is no distance, no compartmentalization. I feel it in my chest, in my body, I feel it in the notches of my spine, in the fatty lobes of my ears. What have I promised? What have I done?

And more to the point: What did I *think* would happen?

I am on the floor, egg-shaped, crying, helpless. My brain starts to respond, attempts to sort things, tries to do what brains do: filing the various miseries into different categories, trying to sort the urgent from the nonurgent. It's like I can't tell the difference between basic needs and the fact that someone I have never met is being abused by their stepfather.

"Maeve."

I feel a warm hand between my shoulder blades.

"Maeve, it's Lily. Can you hear me?"

I look up from the nest I have made with my hands. "It's done," I whisper. "It happened."

She sits on the floor next to me, pulls me over to the wall. We both rest against the skirting boards, her arm around me, breathing into my hair. Lily smells like baby lotion and toffee and white spirits.

"She took the deal," I say, the waves of the city's sadness rushing through me. I feel like a glass goblet trying to hold the ocean. "I gave her the house."

"You're so brave," she says, rocking me slightly. "You're so, so brave, Maeve."

"Not brave enough," I reply, my voice choked. "I don't know if I'm brave enough for this. It's too hard."

"You can do it," she says weakly. Not sure what else to say. "You can do it," she repeats, squeezing my hand.

We go on, rocking like that, for some time. It occurs to me that the others are downstairs, waiting. Listening.

"What's this?" she asks, feeling the chunk of the portrait in my hand.

"It's her," I answer. "The last of her. The part that isn't inside me, anyway."

"The last of her," she repeats, examining it like a puzzle piece. I cannot see her face, or what shape it is making. But suddenly she calls out. "Fiona."

Fiona comes thumping up the stairs. "Are we OK?"

"Take over for a sec," Lily says, and they exchange places so fluidly that I hardly notice a shift. Fiona is cradling me now. Shushing, humming, soothing. The great sad wash of pain still consuming me. I hold on and on, clinging to my lovely friend. Fiona smells like salt and vanilla and damp flowers.

Then Lily is back, seconds or minutes later. I hear the sound of her backpack hitting the floor. "Keep her talking, Fi," Lily says.

"What's going on up there?" I think it's Roe, but who can be sure?

I hear the sound of clean, slim, metal things. The sound of bottles. The sound of *stuff.*

"What was it like, Maeve?" Fiona asks, her voice low. "Was she grateful?"

"In a way," I reply. Nothing sounds like my voice. Everything sounds like crying. Everything feels like crying. "I don't know."

The sound of scraping, and I briefly think that it's mice, living in the walls. I look up. Lily is holding the heart of the Housekeeper, and she is scraping it with a scalpel.

"What are you *doing*?" I bleat, every noise a screech.

"It's oil," she says as the paint curls on her silver scalpel. "It's oil paint."

"So? Stop it. That's her. That's *hers.*"

But Lily is working too quickly, with too much purpose. There's an open bottle of turpentine next to her, and a saucer next to that. A saucer from Nuala's house that one of the pillar candles had been dripping onto. She scrapes the paint into the saucer, until there's nothing left of the canvas but scratched material.

"What have you *done*?" I try to lunge at her, but my brain is so busy computing its newfound state that my body is oddly limp.

"Fi," Lily says abruptly. "Hold her back. I know what I'm doing."

"How?" I ask.

She takes up the scalpel again and cuts a length from the end of the bridesmaid's gown she's wearing. She soaks it in the turpentine, holding the fabric right up to the bottle, then dabs at the saucer of paint.

Roe rushes up the stairs. "What's going on?"

"Shhh."

And despite my rage, I have never seen Lily more in control of a situation in my life. She reaches into her backpack again, and her little bag of tattoo equipment comes out. Needles. Gloves. Inks. She squirts some black ink into the saucer of oil paint and turpentine.

"Maeve," she says at last. "Hold this."

And suddenly I am holding a needle.

"What?" But then I am holding it, holding it like a pencil between my thumb and pointer.

Then I feel resistance against it, and for a second I think I am piercing an orange with a sewing needle, and then I look up and realize I have tattooed a black freckle to the inner wrist of my oldest friend.

I scream in horror, over what I've done, of what she's forced me to do.

But then there is, bizarrely, relief. The feeling of water that was about to burst a levee suddenly getting diverted.

I look up, meeting Lily's eyes for the first time. The first time today, and maybe the first time ever, in a sense. My funny little friend. Look. Look who she turned out to be.

"Keep going," she says. "I can share this. I know I can."

"Lily," I whisper. "You can't. It's not your responsibility."

"You would do it for me."

I'm about to protest, but she's right, I suppose. We haven't always liked each other, but we've always been willing to save each other's lives.

"Keep going," she urges.

I laugh, the movement shaking the tears from my face.

"I can't draw."

"You can. Anyone can draw."

"What should I draw?" I say desperately. "A fish?"

She thinks for a second. "No. I'm finished with all that." Then she says, "Draw a mouse."

"Why?"

"Because Pikachu is an electric mouse," she says. "And no way can you draw a fucking Pikachu."

Despite everything, I laugh. I laugh as the misery and the weight slowly start to drain away, and I draw the kind of mouse that you might draw in primary school. Big fat body, long stringy tail, ears like crescent moons.

"He's cute!" Lily says as I'm still inking. "I actually low-key love him."

When I'm finished, there is a movement inside me. The grief has shifted long enough to make room for power. For certainty.

"Do you know what this means, Lily?" I ask, clutching her.

She closes her eyes, and I can physically see the Housekeeper register within her. A heaviness settles in her shoulders, her chest expands, and I see terror. Then I see it pass.

She opens her eyes. Looking as though she has had a confrontation.

"Did you talk to her?" I nudge.

"Sort of," she says solemnly. "I think she's OK with it."

I burst out laughing. "She's *OK* with it?!"

"You'll get some years, and I'll get some years," Lily says slowly, to make sure she has it all right. "We're going to share it."

Her words settle over us like a blanket of snow, cool and heavy.

"We'll share it," I repeat.

Fiona sits up, then rolls her sleeve. "Come on."

"Fiona, no," I beg.

"Fiona, yes," she corrects. "Lily. Do mine."

Panic seems to grip Lily. For the first time since she came upstairs, she looks unsure.

"Fiona," I say again. "You can't. You have too much to do. Too many dreams, too many goals. You can't take years of this."

"Don't tell me what I can do," she says forcefully. "Come on, Lily."

Lily still holds back.

"I . . ."

"Look," Fiona says brusquely, all business. "If two makes it easier on Maeve, then three makes it easier on everyone."

"Four," Roe says, stepping onto the landing and pulling up their sleeve.

Lily and I exchange a panicked look. Not Fiona and Roe. Not the talented ones, who have such huge ambitions, and in such tricky fields.

"You two can't be bound to Kilbeg for the rest of your lives," I say.

"What, are we going to leave the fate of the whole country up to you two, then?" Roe says.

"Everyone would be dead in five years," Fi laughs, but I see they are both deadly serious.

"I do want to leave Kilbeg," Fiona says. "But I can't leave knowing you're burdened with this. I can't leave knowing what we've sentenced you to. I can't. I won't."

Fiona looks at me and Lily, eyes full of fire, nostrils flaring. She means this. Really means it.

"So, you either kill my dreams by *not* giving me a tattoo, because I'll just be here, looking after you both, worrying that you're too burdened. Or you give me the tattoo and watch me leave. I can only leave if I know I'm going to come back, to take years off this sentence. Those are my terms."

"I'm afraid I have the same terms," Roe says. But they look at me, and the look says: *I'm not letting you suffer something alone if I can suffer it, too.*

Fiona goes first. A magpie on her inner wrist. "One for sorrow," Lily says warningly.

"Not in China." Fiona winks. "Magpies are just lucky there. No sorrow bullshit."

"We're not *in* China."

"An insignificant detail."

But she breathes in sharply, and it is not just the pain of the tattoo that hits her. I see the waves of grief, of agony, of responsibility. Of realizing that you are now a protector of the vulnerable, and knowing what that means.

"A hare," Roe says when Lily reluctantly gets the ink out again. They look at me. "Well, I'm an offering, aren't I?"

We are running out of ink, running out of paint, running out of raw Housekeeper.

I watch the hare take shape on Roe's wrist, wondering if I can ever forgive myself. Roe shivers, coughs, looks briefly sick. A great look of burden passes through them. Yet, somehow, they adjust.

It's hard to describe the feeling that comes over us then. Or rather, the combination of feelings that layer and clash like bad clothing choices. We are sad and sullen, yet we are together, and young, and full of hope. Our youth occurs to me for the first time. I picture us as children, which wasn't really so long ago, and our lives like wide expanses of white snow—every footstep rupturing us, creating dents of pure experience.

I feel a slight burning in my wrist, and look down. A black line begins to appear, and I hold out my wrist to the others. We all watch in silence as the hound tattoo appears. I'm suddenly conscious of Manon and Aaron, who have been quietly observing us from the bottom of the stairs.

The line begins to curve, and we actually start to laugh as the image takes shape, like a Magic Eye painting.

"I guess this means she agrees," Lily says, breaking the spell.

"And that Maeve's the first witch to be a dog person," Fiona says, smiling. "RIP, cats."

"Pardon me," Aaron says. "But can one of you please explain what the hell is going on?"

The four of us descend the stairs, returning to our friends as something brand-new.

"Ladies," Lily says. "Meet the Housekeeper cards."

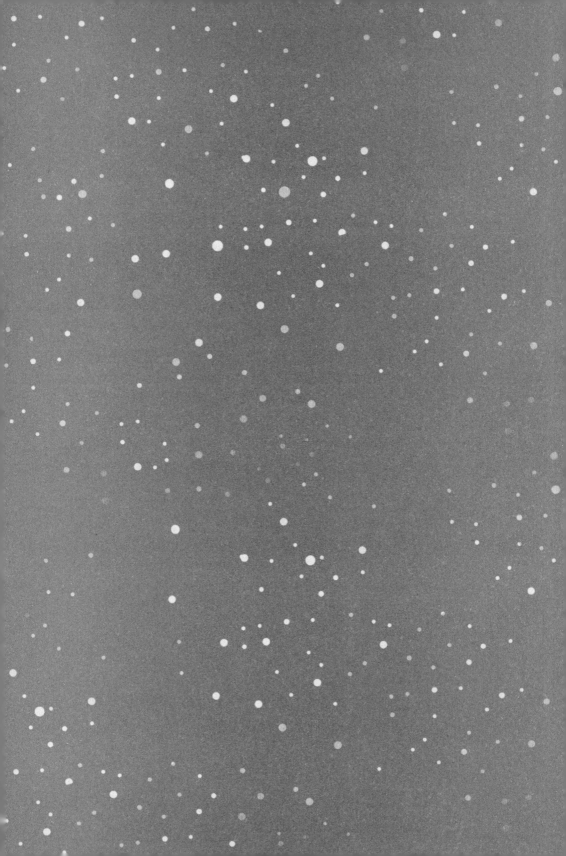

ACKNOWLEDGMENTS

I began writing the Gifts series in early 2019, almost four years before I sat down to write these acknowledgments today. Three books in four years is a hell of a lot of book, and in that time I think I've spent more time with Maeve, Roe, Lily, and Fiona than I have with my own friends and family. In fact, sometimes I forget that they aren't my friends and family. They are figments of my imagination, and my real friends, family, and colleagues ought to be thanked properly.

Here is a whistle-stop tour of the people whom I couldn't have completed this series without. I will try to do it chronologically. Thank you to Harry Harris, who first created the Housekeeper legend with me. Thank you to my agent, Bryony Woods, for suggesting that the time was now finally right for me to try YA. Thank you to my family and those strange two weeks in my childhood bedroom that brought all my most Maeve memories back. Thank you to Susan Van Metre and Denise Johnstone-Burt for buying the series, and championing it at every turn. Thank you to Frances Taffinder for her early edits, and to Grainne Clear for her continued ones. Thank you to Rebecca Oram, Lizz Skelly, and Rosi Crawley for getting these books in front of booksellers, teachers, and students. Thank you to my copy editors,

Susan Van Hecke and Maggie Deslaurier. Thank you to Darran Stevens for the authenticity read. Thank you to Stefanie Caponi, Lisa Sterle, and Helen Crawford-White for creating such a distinctive look for these books. Inevitably I will be tagged in "look how pretty this book is!" posts from now until my death.

Thank you to Ella Risbridger for—I want to say being my "first reader" here, but it's much more than that, and we both know it. Thank you for the advice-giving, the problem-solving, the game-playing, the graph-drawing, the nervous-breakdown-calming. Thank you for all of it.

Thank you to the man who is going to be my husband soon! I'm going to have a husband, can you believe it? Thank you to Gavin Day. I'm very excited to be your wife.

Thank you to the friends who always lent an ear whenever I needed one. Thank you to tarot geniuses Sarah Maria Griffin and Jennifer Cownie. Thank you to the president of the Aaron Fan Club, Tom McInnes. Thank you to Natasha Hodgson: I hope they ask you to audition for *The Coven*.

Thanks to Christophe Rosson for his help with Manon's Frenchness.

The following resources were incredibly helpful in *Every Gift a Curse*, and thank you to their creators for making them:

Heiresses by Laura Thompson

Cultish: The Language of Fanaticism by Amanda Montell

The Gateway and *Revelations*, which are both podcast documentaries by Jennings Brown

ABOUT THE AUTHOR

CAROLINE O'DONOGHUE is the author of the *New York Times* bestseller *All Our Hidden Gifts* and *The Gifts That Bind Us* as well as fiction for adults. She hosts the acclaimed podcast *Sentimental Garbage* and has contributed to *Grazia*, the *Irish Times*, the *Irish Examiner*, *BuzzFeed*, *Vice*, and the *Times* (London). Caroline O'Donoghue was born in Cork, Ireland, and lives in London.